"American troops go to hell and back to save the free world. Push comes to shove, then fire-away! And Carrumph!"

—*Kirkus Reviews*

"Editor Coonts has gathered an impressive group of technothriller authors for this testosterone laden anthology. These John and Jane Wayne meet *Star Wars* tales offers a chilling glimpse into warfare in the 21st Century. The most successful focus is not on weird military technology, but on the men and women who must actually fight."

—*Publishers Weekly*

"War is as inevitable in this new century as it was in the past. A thought-provoking, pausible, and exciting look at the "interesting times" the proverbial ancient Chinese curse says that we are condemned to live through."

—*Library Journal*

"This anthology reads quickly. It has the kind of pages that keep you turning them long into the night, your sleepless eyes glued like a terrified double-agent on the run from the bad guys . . . can be considered a mission success."

—*Readers and Writers Magazine*

"*Combat* [is] a look at the future through the eyes of ten acknowledged masters of the techno military thriller. As the Bush administration undertakes a review of the who, what, when and where of military spending, *Combat*—through the eyes of 10 well-respected experts—offers a realistic look at what American men and women may face on the battlefields of the not-so-distant future."

—*The Ocala Star-Banner*

EDITED WITH AN INTRODUCTION BY

STEPHEN COONTS

COMBAT

Volume 1

LARRY BOND

DALE BROWN

DAVID HAGBERG

A TOM DOHERTY ASSOCIATES BOOK
NEW YORK

To the memory of the seventeen sailors who
lost their lives on the USS *Cole*

COMBAT, Volume 1

A Forge Book
Published by Tom Doherty Associates, LLC
175 Fifth Avenue
New York, NY 10010

www.tor.com

Forge ® is a registered trademark of Tom Doherty Associates, LLC.

ISBN: 0-812-57615-2
Library of Congress Catalog Card Number: 00-048451

First edition: January 2001
First mass market edition: January 2001

Printed in the United States of America

0 9 8 7 6 5 4 3 2 1

Contents

Introduction

The milieu of armed conflict has been a fertile setting for storytellers since the dawn of the written word, and probably before. The *Iliad* by Homer was a thousand years old before someone finally wrote down that oral epic of the Trojan War, freezing its form forever.

Since then war stories have been one of the main themes of fiction in Western cultures: *War and Peace* by Leo Tolstoi was set during the Napoleonic Wars, Stephen Crane's *The Red Badge of Courage* was set during the American Civil War, *All Quiet on the Western Front* by Erich Maria Remarque was perhaps the great classic of World War I. Arguably the premier war novel of the twentieth century, Ernest Hemingway's *For Whom the Bell Tolls*, was set in the Spanish Civil War.

World War II caused an explosion of great war

novels. Some of my favorites are *The Naked and the Dead, The Thin Red Line, War and Remembrance, From Here to Eternity, The War Lover,* and *Das Boot.*

The Korean conflict also produced a bunch, including my favorite, *The Bridges at Toko-Ri* by James Michener, but Vietnam changed the literary landscape. According to conventional wisdom in the publishing industry, after that war the reading public lost interest in war stories. Without a doubt the publishers did.

In 1984 the world changed. The U.S. Naval Institute Press, the Naval Academy's academic publisher, broke with its ninety-plus years of tradition and published a novel, *The Hunt for Red October,* by Tom Clancy.

This book by an independent insurance agent who had never served in the armed forces sold slowly at first, then became a huge best-seller when the reading public found it and began selling it to each other by word of mouth. It didn't hurt that President Ronald Reagan was photographed with a copy.

As it happened, in 1985 I was looking for a publisher for a Vietnam flying story I had written. After the novel was rejected by every publisher in New York, I saw *Hunt* in a bookstore, so I sent my novel to the Naval Institute Press. To my delight the house accepted it and published it in 1986 as *Flight of the Intruder.* Like *Hunt,* it too became a big best-seller.

Success ruined the Naval Institute. Wracked by internal politics, the staff refused to publish Clancy's and my subsequent novels. (We had no trouble selling these books in New York, thank you!) The house did not publish another novel for years, and when they did, best-seller sales eluded them.

Literary critics had an explanation for the interest of the post-Vietnam public in war stories. These novels, they said, were something new. I don't know who coined the term "techno-thriller" (back then newspapers always used quotes and hyphenated it) but the term stuck.

Trying to define the new term, the critics concluded that these war stories used modern technology in ways that no one ever had. How wrong they were.

Clancy's inspiration for *The Hunt for Red October* was an attempted defection of a crew of a Soviet surface warship in the Baltic. The crew mutinied and attempted to sail their ship to Finland. The attempt went awry and the ringleaders were summarily executed by the communists, who always took offense when anyone tried to leave the workers' paradises.

What if, Clancy asked himself, the crew of a nuclear-powered submarine tried to defect? The game would be more interesting then. Clancy's model for the type of story he wanted to write was Edward L. Beach's *Run Silent, Run Deep*, a World War II submarine story salted with authentic technical detail that was critical to the development of the characters and plot of the story.

With that scenario in mind, Clancy set out to write a submarine adventure that would be accurate in every detail. Never mind that he had never set foot on a nuclear submarine or spent a day in uniform—his inquiring mind and thirst for knowledge made him an extraordinary researcher. His fascination with war games and active, fertile imagination made him a first-class storyteller.

Unlike Clancy, I did no research whatsoever when writing *Flight of the Intruder.* I had flown A-6 Intruder bombers in Vietnam from the deck of the USS *Enterprise* and wrote from memory. I had been trying to write a flying novel since 1973 and had worn out two typewriters in the process. By 1984 I had figured out a plot for my flying tale, so after a divorce I got serious about writing and completed a first draft of the novel in five months.

My inspiration for the type of story I wanted to write was two books by Ernest K. Gann. *Fate Is the Hunter* was a true collection of flying stories from the late 1930s and 1940s, and was, I thought, extraordinary in its inclusion of a wealth of detail about the craft of flying an airplane. Gann also used this device for his novels, the best of which is probably *The High and the Mighty*, a story about a piston-engined airliner that has an emergency while flying between Hawaii and San Francisco.

Gann used technical details to create the setting and as plot devices that moved the stories along. By educating the reader about what it is a pilot does, he gave his stories an emotional impact that conventional storytellers could not achieve. In essence, he put you in the cockpit and took you flying. That, I thought, was an extraordinary achievement and one I wanted to emulate.

Fortunately, the technology that Clancy and I were writing about was state-of-the-art—nuclear-powered submarines and precision all-weather attack jets—and this played to the reading public's long-standing love affair with scientific discoveries and new technology. In the nineteenth century Jules Verne, Edgar Allan Poe, Wilkie Collins, and H. G. Wells gave birth to science fiction. The technology at the heart of their stories played on the public's fascination with the man-made wonders of that age—the submarine, the flying machines that were the object of intense research and experimentation, though they had yet to get off the ground, and the myriad of uses that inventors were finding for electricity, to name just a few.

Today's public is still enchanted by the promise of scientific research and technology. Computers, rockets, missiles, precision munitions, lasers, fiber optics, wireless networks, reconnaissance satellites, winged airplanes that take off and land vertically, network-centric warfare—advances in every technical field are constantly re-creating the world in which we live.

The marriage of high tech and war stories is a natural.

The line between the modern military action-adventure and science fiction is blurry, indistinct, and becoming more so with every passing day. Storytellers often set technothrillers in the near future and dress up the technology accordingly, toss in little inventions of their own here and there, and in general, try subtly to wow their readers by use of a little of that science fiction "what might be" magic. When it's properly done, only a technically expert reader will be able to tell when the writer has crossed the line from the real to the unreal; and that's the fun of it. On the other hand, stories set in space or on other planets or thousands of years in the future are clearly science fiction, even though armed conflict is involved.

In this volume of *Combat* you will find novellas by Larry Bond, David Hagberg and Dale Brown.

Larry Bond is the designer of *Harpoon*, the premier war game of all time. He collaborated with Tom Clancy on *Red Storm Rising*, then went on to write bestsellers under his own name. The novella that he wrote for this collection, *Lash-Up*, showcases Bond's huge talents.

The author of thirteen *New York Times* bestsellers, Dale Brown gets my nomination as the premier military aviation fiction writer doing it today. His research is impeccable, his plots terrific, and his flying so realistic he will make you wish you had strapped yourself to your chair. His novella, *Leadership Material*, explores the very real tension between technocrats and warfighters that all branches of the military wrestle with today.

David Hagberg is a professional writer's professional. He has been in the business for twenty-five years, writing solid action-adventure and suspense. In the novella he wrote for this collection, *Breaking Point*, Hagberg explores the real-world tension between Taiwan and the People's Republic of China that could explode into a shooting war at any time.

Two more mass-market volumes of *Combat* follow this one. Look for them in your favorite bookstore.

STEPHEN COONTS

LASH-UP

BY LARRY BOND

One

Unexpected Losses

San Diego, California
September 16, 2010

Ray McConnell was watching the front door for new arrivals, but he would have noticed her anyway. Long straight black hair, in her late twenties, casually dressed but making jeans and a knit top look very good. He didn't know her, and was putting a question together when he saw Jim Naguchi follow her in. Oh, that's how she knew.

Ray stood up, still keeping one eye on the screens, and greeted the couple. The woman was staring at the wall behind Ray, and he caught the tail end of her comment. ". . . why you're never at home when I call."

Jim Naguchi answered her, "Third time this week," then took Ray's offered hand. "Hi, Ray, this is Jennifer Oh. We met at that communications conference two weeks ago—the one in San Francisco."

As Ray took Jennifer's hand, she said, "Just Jenny, please," smiling warmly.

"Jenny's in the Navy, Ray. She's a computer specialist . . ."

"Which means almost anything these days," McConnell completed. "Later we'll try to trick you into telling us what you really do."

Jenny looked a little uncomfortable, even as she continued to stare. Changing his tone a little, Ray announced, "Welcome to the McConnell Media Center, the largest concentration of guy stuff in captivity."

"I believe it," she answered. "Those are Sony Image Walls, aren't they? I've got a twenty-four-incher at home."

McConnell half turned to face the Wall. "These are the same, still just an inch thick. But larger," he said modestly.

"And four of them?" she said.

Every new guest had to stop and stare. The living room of Ray's ranch house was filled with electronic equipment, but the focus of the room was the four four-by-eight flat-screen video panels. He'd removed the frames and placed them edge to edge, covering one entire wall of his living room with an eight-foot-by-sixteen-foot video screen—"the Wall."

Just then it was alive with flickering color images. Ray pointed to different areas on the huge surface. "We've set up the center with a map of the China-Vietnam border. We've got subwindows," Ray said, pointing them out, "for five of the major TV networks. That larger text subwindow has the orders of battle for the Vietnamese and Chinese and U.S. forces in the region."

He pointed to a horseshoe-shaped couch in the center of the room, filled with people. "The controls are at that end of the couch, and I've got two dedicated processors controlling the displays."

"So is this how the media keeps track of an international crisis?" Jennifer asked.

"Maybe." Ray shrugged, and looked at Jim Naguchi, who also shrugged. "I dunno. We're engineers, not reporters."

"With a strong interest in foreign affairs," she responded.

"True," he added, "like everyone else here." He swept his arm wide to include the other guests. Half a dozen other people watched the screens, talked, or argued.

"There's people from the military, like you, and professionals from a lot of fields. We get together at times like this to share information and viewpoints."

"And watch the game," she added. Her tone was friendly, but a little critical as well.

"That window's got the pool on the kickoff times," Ray answered, smiling and indicating another area filled with text and numbers. "Most of the money is on local dawn, in"—he glanced at his watch—"an hour or so."

"And I brought munchies," Naguchi added, holding up a grocery bag.

"On the counter, Jim, like always," Ray responded. One side of the living room was a waist-high counter, covered with a litter of drinks and snacks.

"It's my way of feeling like I have some control over my life, Jenny. If we know what's going on, we don't feel so helpless." He shrugged at his inadequate explanation. "Knowledge is Power. Come on, I'll introduce you around. This is a great place to network."

Raising his voice just a little, he announced, "People, this is Jenny Oh. Navy. She's here with Jim." Everyone waved or nodded to her, but most kept their attention on the Wall.

McConnell pointed to a fortyish man in a suit. "That's Jim Garber. He's with McDonnell Douglas. The guy next to him is Marty Duvall, a C coder at a software house. Bob Reeves is a Marine." Ray smiled. "He's also the founding member of the 'Why isn't it Taiwan?' Foundation."

"I'm still looking for new members," the Marine answered. Lean, and tall even sitting down, with close-cropped black hair, he explained, "I keep thinking this is some sort of elaborate deception, and while we're looking at China's southern border, she's going to suddenly zig east, leap across the straits, and grab Taiwan."

"But there's no sign of any naval activity west of Hong Kong," Jenny countered, pointing to the map. "The action's all been inland, close to the border. I'm not in intelligence," she warned, "but everything I've heard say it's all pointed at Vietnam . . ."

"Over ten divisions and a hundred aircraft," Garber added. "That's INN's count this morning, using their own imaging satellites."

"But why Vietnam at all?" countered Reeves. "They're certainly not a military threat."

"But they are an economic one," replied Jenny. "They're another country that's trading communism for capitalism, and succeeding. The increased U.S. financial investment makes Beijing even more nervous."

Ray McConnell smiled, pleased as any host. The new arrival was fitting in nicely, and she certainly improved the scenery. He walked behind to the counter into the kitchen and started neatening up, trashing empty bags of chips and soda bottles. Naguchi was still laying his snacks on the counter.

"She's a real find, Jim," McConnell offered. "Not the same one as last week, though?"

"Well, things didn't work out." Naguchi admitted. "Laura wanted me to have more space. Like Mars." He grinned.

"Where's she stationed?"

"All she'll tell me is NAVAIR," Naguchi replied. "She knows the technology, and she's interested in defense and the military."

"Well, of course, she's in the business," McConnell replied. "She's certainly involved in the discussion." Ray pointed to Jenny, now using the controls to expand part of the map.

"That's how we met," Naguchi explained. "The Vietnam crisis was starting to heat up, and everyone at the conference was talking about it between sessions, of course. She was always in the thick of it, and somewhere in there I mentioned your sessions here."

"So *this* is your first date?" Ray grinned.

"I hope so," Naguchi answered hopefully. "I'm trying to use color and motion to attract the female."

"Ray! You've got a call." A tall African-American man was waving to Ray. McConnell hurried into the living room, picked up the handset from its cradle, and hit the VIEW button. Part of the Wall suddenly became an image of an older man, overweight and balding, in front of a mass of books. Glasses perched on his nose, seemingly defying gravity. "Good . . . evening, Ray."

"Dave Douglas. Good to see you, sir. You're up early in the morning." The United Kingdom was eight hours ahead of California. It was five in the morning in Portsmouth.

"Up very late, you mean. I see you've one of your

gatherings. I thought you'd like to know we've lost the signals for two of your GPS satellites."

Naguchi, who'd moved next to Jennifer, explained. "Mr. Douglas is head of the Space Observer Group. They're hobbyists, mostly in Britain, who track satellites visually and electronically. Think high-tech bird-watchers."

"I've heard of them," she answered, nodding, "and of Douglas. Your friend knows *him*?" She sounded impressed.

Naguchi replied, "Ray's got contacts all over."

Jennifer nodded again, trying to pick up the conversation at the same time.

". . . verified Horace's report about an hour ago. It was number seventeen, a relatively new bird, but anything mechanical can fail. I normally wouldn't think it worth more than a note, but then Horace called back and said another one's gone down as well, and quite soon after the first one."

"Why was Horace looking at the GPS satellite signals?" McConnell asked.

"Horace collects electronic signals. He's writing a piece on the GPS signal structure for the next issue of our magazine."

Ray looked uncertain, even a little worried. "Two failures is a little unusual, isn't it?" It was a rhetorical question.

Douglas sniffed. "GPS satellites don't fail, Raymond. You've only had two go down since the system was established twenty-five years ago. By the way, both satellites are due over southern China in less than an hour."

Ray could only manage a "What?" but Douglas seemed to understand his query. "I'm sending you a file with the orbital data for the constellation in it. I've marked numbers seventeen and twenty-two.

They're the one's who've failed." He paused for a moment, typing. "There . . . you have it now."

"Thank you, Dave. I'll get back to you if we can add anything to what you've found." Ray broke the connection, then grabbed his data tablet.

While McConnell worked with the system, speculation filled the conversation. ". . . so we turned off two of the birds ourselves. Deny them to the Chinese," Reeves suggested.

"If so, why only two?" countered Jenny.

"And the most accurate signal's encrypted anyway," added Garber. "The Chinese can only use civilian GPS."

"Which still gives them an asset they wouldn't otherwise have," reminded Reeves.

"Unless the Chinese have broken the encryption," countered Duvall.

"But we need GPS even more," said Garber. "It's not just navigation, it's weapons guidance and command and control."

Jennifer added, "All of our aircraft mission planning uses GPS now. If we had to go back, it would be a lot harder to run a coordinated attack. We could never get the split-second timing we can now."

"Here's the orbital data," McConnell announced.

The smaller windows on the Wall all vanished, leaving the map showing southern China and Vietnam. A small bundle of curved lines appeared in the center, then expanded out to fill the map, covering the area with orbital tracks. As Ray moved the cursor on his data pad, the cursor moved on the map. When it rested on a track, a tag appeared, naming the satellite and providing orbital and other data. Two of the tracks were red, not white, and were marked with small boxes with a time in them.

"Where are the satellites right now?" someone asked.

Ray tapped the tablet and small diamonds appeared on all the tracks, showing their current positions.

"Can you move them to where they'd be at local dawn for Hanoi?" suggested Garber.

"And what's the horizon for those satellites at Mengzi?" Jennifer prompted, pointing to a town just north of the Chinese-Vietnamese border. "That's one of the places the Chinese are supposed to be massing."

"Stand by," answered Ray. "That's not built in. I'll have to do the math and draw it." He worked quickly, and in absolute silence. After about two minutes, an oval drawn in red appeared on the map, centered on the location. Everyone counted, but Ray spoke first. "I count three."

". . . and you need four for a fix," finished Naguchi.

National Military Command Center, The Pentagon
September 17

". . . and without the GPS, General Hyde had to issue a recall." The assistant J-3 looked uncomfortable, as only a colonel can look when giving bad news to a room full of four-star generals.

The meeting had originally been scheduled to review results of the first day's strikes in Operation CERTAIN FORCE. A total of eighty-three targets in China had been programmed to be hit by 150 combat aircraft and almost two hundred cruise missiles. It hadn't happened.

"The gap in coverage was only twenty minutes,"

Admiral Kramer complained. "Are we so inflexible that we couldn't delay the operation until we had full coverage?"

"It would have meant issuing orders to hundreds of units through two levels of command," answered General Michael Warner. Chief of Staff of the Air Force, it was one of his men, General Tim Hyde, who was Joint Task Force Commander for CERTAIN FORCE. Warner, a slim, handsome man whose hair was still jet-black at sixty, looked more than a little defensive.

"Sounds like 'set-piece-itis' to me," muttered the Army Chief of Staff.

The Chairman, also an Army general, shot his subordinate a "this isn't helping" look and turned back to Warner. The Air Force, through the Fiftieth Space Operations Wing, operated the GPS satellites.

"Mike, have your people found out anything else since this morning?"

"Only that both birds were functioning within norms. Number seventeen was the older bird. They'd recently fired up the third of her four clocks, but she was in good shape. Number twenty-two was still on her first atomic clock. All attempts to restart them, or even communicate with them, have failed. Imaging from our telescopes shows that they're still there, but they're in a slow tumble, which they shouldn't be doing . . ."

"And the chance of both of them suffering catastrophic failure is nil," concluded the Chairman.

"Yes sir. The final straw is that we started warm-up procedures on the two reserve birds twenty-eight and twenty-nine. Or rather, we tried to warm them up. They don't answer either."

General Sam Kastner, Chairman of the Joint Chiefs, was a thinker, more a listener than a speaker, but he knew he had to take firm charge of the meeting. He sighed, knowing the answer before he started, "What about Intelligence?"

The J-2, or Joint Intelligence officer, was a boyish-looking rear admiral. His normal staff was two or three assistants, but this time he had a small mob of officers and civilians behind him. The admiral moved to the podium.

"Sir, the short answer is that we don't know who did this or how. If we knew who, we could start to guess how they did it. Similarly, knowing how would immediately narrow the list of suspects.

"We know that the DSP infrared satellites detected no launches, and we believe that they also would have detected a laser powerful enough to knock out a GPS bird—although that's not a certainty," he added quickly, nodding to an Army officer with a stern expression on his face.

"The Chinese are the most likely actors, of course, but others can't be ruled out. CIA believes the attack was made by agents on the ground or in cyberspace, but we've detected no signs of this at any of the monitoring stations. The Navy believes they've adapted their space-launch vehicles for the purpose. Although it's a logical proposition, we've seen no sign of the launch, or the considerable effort it would require. And we track their space program quite closely."

The frustration in his voice underlined every word. "It's possible that the Russians or someone else is doing it to assist the Chinese, but there aren't that many candidates, and we've simply seen no sign of activity by any nation, friendly or hostile." He almost threw up his hands.

"Thank you, Admiral," replied Kastner. "Set up a Joint Intelligence Task Force immediately. Until we can at least find out what's being done, we can do nothing, and that includes reliably carry out military operations. Spread your net wide."

He didn't have to say that the media were also spreading their net. Television and the Internet were already full of rumors—the attack had been scheduled but called off for political reasons, that the entire exercise was just a bluff, that the U.S. had backed down because of the risk of excessive casualties, and others more fanciful. U.S. "resolve" had been shattered.

Gongga Shan Mountain Launch Complex, Xichuan Province, Southern China
September 23

General Shen Xuesen stood quietly, calmly, watching the bank of monitors, but wishing to be on the surface. He had a better view of the operation from here, but it did not seem as real.

It was their fifth time, and he could see the staff settling down, nowhere as nervous as the first launch, but China was committed now, and her future hung on their success.

Everyone saw the short, solidly built general standing quietly in the gallery. In his early fifties, he'd spent a lot of time in the weather, and it showed. An engineer, he looked capable of reshaping a mountain, and he had Gongga Shan as proof. It was a commander's role to appear calm, even when he knew exactly how many things could go wrong, and how much was at stake, both for him and for China.

Shen had already given his permission to fire. The staff was counting down, waiting until they were in the exact center of the intercept window. The

"Dragon's egg" sat in the breech, inert but vital, waiting for just a few more seconds.

The moment came as the master clock stepped down to zero. The launch controller turned a key, and for a moment, the only sign of activity was on the computer displays. Shen's eyes glanced to the breech seals, but the indicators all showed green. He watched the video screen that showed the muzzle, a black oval three meters across.

Even with a muzzle velocity of four thousand meters per second, it took time for the egg to build up to full speed. Almost a full second elapsed between ignition and . . .

A puff of smoke and flame appeared on the display, followed by a black streak, briefly visible. Only its size, almost three meters in diameter, allowed it to be seen at all. Shen relaxed, his inward calm now matching his outward demeanor. His gun had worked again.

"Hatching," reported the launch controller. Everyone had so loved the egg metaphor that they used the term to report when the sabots separated from the meter-sized projectile. Designed to hold the small vehicle inside the larger bore, they split and fell away almost instantly. Effectively, the projectile got the boost of three-meter barrel but the drag of a one-meter body.

Speed, always more speed, mused Shen as he watched the monitors. The crews were already boarding buses for their ride up the mountain to inspect the gun. Other screens showed helicopters lifting off to search for the sabots. Although they could not be used again, they were marvels of engineering in their own right and would reveal much about the gun's design.

The goal was eight kilometers a second, orbital velocity. First, take a barrel a kilometer long and three meters across. To make it laser-straight, gouge out the slope of a mountain and anchor it on the bedrock. Cover it up, armor and camouflage it, too. Put the muzzle near the top, seventy-nine hundred meters above sea level. That reduces air resistance and buys you some speed. Then use sabots to get more speed. You're halfway there. Then . . .

"Ignition," announced one of the controllers. Put a solid rocket booster on the projectile to give it the final push it needed. "She's flying! Guidance is online, sir. It's in the center of the basket. Intercept in twenty minutes."

General Shen had seen the concept described in a summary the Iraqis had provided of Supergun technology after the American Persian Gulf War. American technological superiority had been more than a shock to the People's Liberation Army. It had triggered an upheaval.

The Chinese military had always chosen numbers over quality, because numbers were cheap, and the Politburo was trying to feed one and a half billion people. They'd always believed that numbers could overwhelm a smaller high-tech force, making them reluctant even to try. Everyone knew how sensitive the Americans were to casualties, and to risk.

But if the difference in quality is big enough, numbers don't matter anymore. Imagine using machine guns in the Civil War, or a nuclear sub in WWII. Shen and his colleagues had watched the Americans run rings around the Iraqis, suffering trivial casualties while they hammered the opposition.

So the Chinese army had started the long, expensive process of becoming a modern military. They'd bought high-tech weapons from the Russians, fortunately willing to sell at bargain-basement prices.

They'd stolen what they couldn't buy from Western nations. They'd gotten all kinds of exotic technologies: rocket-driven torpedoes for their subs, exotic aircraft designs.

It wasn't enough. Running and working as hard as they could, they'd cut the technology lag from twenty to fifteen years. They were following the same path as the West, and it would just take time to catch up.

General Shen had seen the answer. He'd seen a vulnerability, then planned, convinced, plotted, and argued until the Politburo had listened and backed his plan. If your opponent strikes at you from above, take away his perch. Take away that technological edge.

Build a prison camp deep in the mountains, in a remote spot in southern China. Send the hard cases and malcontents there. The State has useful work for them. Watch the prisoners dig away the side of a mountain. You need a rail line to the nearest city, Kangding, 250 kilometers southwest. That had been a job in itself. Then add army barracks, the launch-control center, and SAM and AAA defenses. It had taken years before it looked like anything more than a mistake.

Meanwhile, design the "T'ien Lung," or Celestial Dragon, to fly in space. And design a gun, the biggest gun in the history of the world, the Dragon's Mother, to fire it. Such designs were well within the grasp of the West, but they were barely possible for China's limited means. Her civilian space program had provided a lot of the talent, as well as a convenient excuse for foreign study and purchases.

"Control has been passed to Xichuan," the senior controller announced. "Intercept in ten minutes." A look of relief passed over his face. If a screwup occurred after this, it was their fault, not his.

Shen longed to be in two places at once, but the gun was his, and Dong Zhi, the scientist who had actually designed the Dragons, was at the space complex. Xichuan handled China's civilian space program, and they had the antennas to watch the intercept.

Everyone in the room watched the central display, even though it was only a computer representation. Two small dots sat on curved lines, slowly moving to an intersection point. Then the screen changed, becoming completely black, with the characters for "Terminal Phase," displayed in one corner.

General Shen Xuesen smiled. He had insisted on the television camera for terminal-phase guidance. Not only was it hard to jam, it made the result understandable. Seeing the target grow from a speck to a shape to a recognizable satellite had made it real, not only for the leadership who had watched the tests, but for the people who had to do the work, who fought the war from so far away.

The image was a little grainy, because of the lens size, but it also had the clarity of space. He could see the boxy, cluttered body of the American GPS satellite, and the outspread solar panels, each divided into four sections.

The controller started counting down as the image slowly expanded. "Five seconds, four, three, two, one, now." He uttered the last word softly, but triumphantly, as the image suddenly vanished. A few people clapped, but they'd all seen this before, and most didn't feel the need now.

All that work, all that money, to put a ten-pound warhead in orbit. More like a shotgun shell, the explosive fired a cone of fragments at the unarmored satellite. Filled with atomic clocks and delicate electronics, it didn't have a hope of surviving the explosion. The carcass would remain in its orbit, intact, but pocked with dozens of small holes.

In fact, the kill was almost an anticlimax. After all the work of getting the vehicle up there, it was over far too quickly.

Skyhook One Seven, Over the South China Sea
September 23

"We just lost GPS," reported the navigator. "Switching to inertial tracker." The navigator, an Air Force major, sounded concerned but not alarmed.

"Is it the receiver?" asked the mission commander. A full colonel, it was his job to manage the information gathered by the ELINT, or Electronic Intelligence, aircraft. Running racetracks off the China coast, it listened for radar and radio signals, analyzing their contents and fixing their location. The digested information was datalinked directly back to Joint Task Force Headquarters.

"Self-test is good, sir, and the receiver is still picking up satellites, but we just lost one of the signals, and now we're outside our error budget." Each satellite over the minimum required narrowed the area of uncertainty around a transmitter's location. GPS was accurate enough to target some missiles directly, or give pilots a good idea of where to search for their objective.

"So we've lost another one," muttered the colonel.

USS *Nebraska* (SSBN—739), On Patrol
September 24

The sub's Operations Officer knocked on the captain's open door. "Sir, they've lost another one." He handed the priority message to the skipper. It detailed the loss and showed how coverage was affected for their patrol area.

The captain looked over the printout. "Have you compared this with our navigation plan?"

"Yes, sir. We have to change one of our planned fix times. It falls in one of the new 'dark windows.' We can move it ahead two hours or back six."

The captain scowled, more than one might think appropriate for a minor inconvenience. But ballistic missile subs had to come up to periscope depth periodically to check their navigation systems' accuracy. A few meters of error at the launch point could be hundreds of times that at the target.

When the full GPS constellation had been operational, the captain could take a fix anytime he chose. Now there were times he couldn't. That made him less flexible, more predictable, and thus easier to find. He really didn't like that.

"Move it up," ordered the captain. "Let's take a fix before they lose any more birds. And draw up a new schedule reducing the interval between fixes."

INN News
September 24

"With the loss of another satellite, emotions at the Fiftieth Space Operations Wing have changed from grim or angry to fatalistic." Mark Markin, INN's defense correspondent, stood in front of the gate to Cheyenne Mountain. The Fiftieth's operations center was actually located at Schriver Air Force Base nearby, but the drama of the mountain's tunnel entrance was preferable to Schriver's nondescript government buildings.

Markin wore a weather-beaten parka, zipped up against the chill Colorado wind. His carefully shaped hair was beginning to show the effects of the wind as well, and he seemed to rush through his report in an effort to get out of the weather.

"Although it is widely acknowledged that loss of the GPS satellites is no fault of the people here at the Fiftieth, they are still suffering a deep sense of helplessness.

"Since the GPS network became active in 1989, it has become almost a public utility. The men and women here took pride in providing a service that not only gave the U.S. armed forces a tremendous military advantage, but benefited the civilian community in countless ways.

"Now, someone, possibly the Chinese, but certainly an enemy of the United States, has destroyed at least three and possibly as many as five satellites. Yesterday's loss shows that last week's attack was not an isolated act.

"And the United States can do nothing to stop it."

San Diego, California
September 24

Jim Avrell had gone to only a few of Ray's gatherings. His "discussion groups" were famous throughout SPAWAR, and were always worthwhile. Although Arvell would have liked to go, two preschoolers and another on the way limited his free time.

Tonight, though, he'd made the time. In fact, his wife Carol had urged him to go. After he'd described Ray's sudden leave of absence and the rumors from the other coworkers, she'd urged him to go and get the straight story.

Avrell was an antenna design specialist in Ray's working group. He knew and liked the outgoing engineer, even if McConnell could be a little fierce in technical "discussions." He was worried about their project, which was suffering in Ray's absence, and about Ray himself. With the brass so upset about GPS, it was no time for Ray to play "missing person."

The car's nav console prompted, "Turn left here," and he signaled for the turn onto Panorama Drive. It had been over a year since he had visited Ray's place, that time with Carol at a reception for a visiting astronaut. That had been an occasion.

But nothing like this. As he made the turn, Avrell saw the street almost completely lined with cars. This was definitely not typical for a quiet residential community. Avrell ended up parking a block away.

As he hurried up the path, he heard the expected hubbub, but Ray didn't meet him at the door, and everyone wasn't in the living room. A group of four men huddled around a coffee table there, and he could see another clustered in the kitchen. McConnell appeared out of the one of the bedroom doors, hurrying. He looked tired.

"Jim Avrell! It's great to see you." Genuine pleasure lit up Ray's face, but there was a distracted air to it. And surprise.

Avrell saw no point in dissembling. "Ray, what's going on over here? You haven't been at work . . ."

"I've got bigger fish to fry, Jim. Promise you won't tell anyone what's going on here? Unless I OK it?"

"Well, of course."

Ray looked at him intently. "No, Jim, I mean it. You can't tell anyone. Treat this as classified."

Avrell studied McConnell carefully, then agreed. "I promise not to tell anyone what I see here." He fought the urge to raise his right hand.

McConnell seemed to relax a little, and smiled again. "You'll understand in a minute, Jim." He called over to the group at the coffee table. "I'll be right there."

One of them, whom Avrell recognized as Avrim Takir, a mathematician from the work group, answered. "Fine, Ray. We need another ten minutes, anyway." Takir spotted Avrell and waved, but quickly returned his attention to the laptop in front of him.

McConnell led his coworker down the hall into his home office. Ray's desk was piled high with books and disk cases and printouts. The center display, another Image Wall mounted above the desk, showed an isometric design for an aircraft—no, a spacecraft, Avrell realized.

Used to polished CAD-CAM designs where they worked, he was surprised. This one was crude. Some of it was fully rendered in 3-D space, but parts of it were just wireframes. At least one section was a two-dimensional image altered to appear three-dimensional.

"*Defender* isn't pretty, but we're a little pressed for time," McConnell declared. He had the air of a proud parent.

Avrell, surprised and puzzled, studied the diagram, which filled the four-by-eight display. Data tables hovered in parts of the screen not covered by the vehicle. He started tracing out systems: propulsion; communications; weapons? He shot a questioning look at McConnell.

Ray met his look with one of his own. "Question, Jim. What's the best way to protect a satellite? If someone's shooting them down, how can you stop them?"

"They haven't even confirmed it's the Chinese . . ."

"Doesn't matter who's doing it!" McConnell countered. "Someone is." He paused and rephrased the question. "Can you effectively protect a satellite from the ground?"

Avrell answered quickly. "Of course not. You're on the wrong end of the gravity well, even if you're near the launcher site, and you might be on the wrong side of the planet."

"Which we probably are," McConnell agreed. "Here on the surface, even with perfect information, we can't defend a satellite until something is launched to attack it, so we're always in a tail chase. If we're above the launcher, with the satellite we're trying to defend, Isaac Newton joins our team."

"And this is going to do the job?" Avrell asked, motioning toward the diagram. He tried to sound objective, but skepticism crept into his voice in spite of his efforts.

McConnell seemed used to it. "It can, Jim. There's nothing startling in here. The technology is all there: an orbital vehicle, sensors, and weapons."

"And you've been tasked by . . ."

"It's my own hook, Jim. This is all on my own," Ray admitted. Then he saw his friend's question and answered it without waiting.

"Because I can't wait for the government to think of it, that's why. The answer is obvious, but by the time they hold all the meetings and write all the Requirements we won't have any satellites left."

McConnell sat down heavily, fatigue and strain showing on his face. "This isn't about just GPS or the Chinese, Jim. Someone's developed the capability to attack satellites in space. That means they could attack manned spacecraft. They can probably launch orbital nuclear weapons at us, or anyone else they don't like. And we certainly know they don't like us."

Avrell leaned back against the edge of a table and

looked carefully at Ray. "So you're going to design the answer to our problems." He phrased it as a statement, but it was still a question.

"Me and all the other people here," Ray corrected. "Why not, Jim? I've got a good idea, and I'm running with it. I might not be in the right bureau in the right branch, but I believe in this. Ideas are too precious to waste."

Inside, Avrell agreed with his friend, but practicality pushed that aside. "You can't build it," he stated quietly.

"Well, that's the rub," McConnell said, actually rubbing the back of his neck in emphasis. "I've made a lot of friends over the years. I'm going to shotgun it out—only within the system," he hurriedly added, referring to the procedures for handling classified material. "I won't go public with this. It's a serious design proposal."

"Which needs a Requirement, a contractor, and research and development . . ."

"And congressional hearings and hundreds of man-hours deciding what color to paint it," continued McConnell. "A small group can always move faster and think faster than a large one. I want to present the defense community with a finished design, something so complete they'll be able to leapfrog the first dozen steps of the acquisition process." He grinned. "We can skip one step already. The other side's writing the Requirement for us."

Ray stood and turned to face Avrell directly. "I know I'm breaking rules, but they're not rules of physics, just the way DoD does business. I'm willing to push this because it needs to be done, and nobody else is doing it."

Avrell sighed. "So who's working on your comm system?"

McConnell grinned. "The guys in the kitchen, but they've got almost all the electronics. There's lots to do. Come on, I'll introduce you . . ."

"Wait a minute, Ray." Avrell held up his hand. "Let me make a call first."

"Carol?"

"No. Sue Langston. She's in graphics."

Ray laughed and pointed to the phone. Heading out of the office and down the hall, his intention was to check with the propulsion group in the living room, but then he heard the doorbell again. Fighting impatience, he hoped for another volunteer, or the Chinese takeout he'd ordered.

Jennifer Oh stood on the doorstep, and Ray blinked twice in surprise. Another unexpected caller.

"Can I come in?" she finally asked.

"Oh, certainly, please come in, Jenny," trying to sound as hospitable as he could. His distraction increased. She'd obviously come straight from work, and her naval uniform, with lieutenant commander's stripes, jarred after the casual outfit he'd seen her in last week. Her long black hair was tied up in an ornate bun.

She didn't wait for him to speak. "Jim Naguchi told me a little about what you're doing here. I think it's an incredible idea." She held up three square flat boxes. "And I brought pizza."

"Thank you on both counts, Jenny. Jim's not here tonight, though."

"I came to help you, Ray. I can see what you're doing. I've got a lot of experience in command and control systems," she offered.

Ray suddenly felt that *Defender* was going to work.

Two

Suggestions

National Military Command Center, The Pentagon
September 25

The Joint Chiefs of Staff didn't normally meet at two in the morning, but Rear Admiral Overton's call was worth getting out of bed for.

Most of the Chiefs had been in the Pentagon anyway, trying to manage the crisis, the troops, and the media. Although only three active GPS satellites had been lost out of a constellation of twenty-four, it had still created periods when there was no coverage in some parts of the world at some times, and there was no indication that they'd be able to fill the gaps soon. Everyone was assuming it would get much worse before it got better.

There was also the continuing problem of the Vietnam Crisis. U.S. forces could not execute a coordinated, precision attack without complete GPS coverage, but they could not maintain such high readiness levels forever. And what if China had started attacking American satellites? Had a war already started?

As they hurried into the Command Center, the J-2, Frank Overton, compared the generals' normal polished appearance with the tired, overworked men in front of him. He was glad he had good news.

The Chief of Staff of the Air Force and the Chief of Naval Operations were both last, coming in together and breaking off some sort of disagreement as they walked through the door. Overton didn't even wait for them to sit down.

"We have proof it's the Chinese. We figured out where, and that led to how," he announced.

Overton's data pad and the screen at the head of the table showed a black-and-white satellite photo. A date in the corner read "Jun 2006."

"This is the Gongga Shan prison camp in southern China—at least, we had identified it as a prison camp. We named it after the mountain." Using his pointer, he showed areas marked as "Prisoners' Barracks, Guard Barracks," and so on. "As far as we know, it was built about five years ago, and can accommodate several thousand prisoners."

He pressed the remote again, and the first image slid to one side, and a second, of the same area, appeared alongside it. "This was taken about six hours ago. This construction work"—he indicated a long scar on the side of the mountain in the first photo—"has been finished or just stopped. We think finished, because if they'd just abandoned it, the excavation would still be there. In fact, if you look in the second photo, the mountain's been restored to its original state. The original analysis four years ago speculated that the prisoners might be mining, or building an observatory, or an antenna. The site goes right up to the top of the mountain, and it's one of the tallest around."

Admiral Overton paused, looking at the group. A hint of embarrassment appeared on his face. "That analysis was never followed up." He shrugged.

General Kastner spoke for the group. "And the real answer is?"

Overton pressed the remote again. A gray-green infrared image appeared, superimposed over the second photo. "We wanted to see what they'd been working on. This is a satellite infrared picture taken about an hour ago. We were lucky," he explained. "There was one already tasked to cover the region because of the crisis."

Most of the shapes in the image duplicated the buildings and other structures, but one shape was unique: a long, thick, straight line, laid east–west along the spine of the mountain.

"It's one kilometer long, and based on careful measurements, we know it's angled along the western face of the mountain at about forty degrees elevation. At the base you'll see a series of buried structures, including what we think are several bunkers for the launch crew. The buildings at the base are warm, and the entire structure is slightly warmer than the surrounding rock. We think it's made of metal."

"A buried rocket launcher?" wondered the Army Chief of Staff.

"No, sir. A buried gun barrel. See these shapes?" He used the cursor to indicate two round structures. "We believe these are tanks for the liquid-propellant fuel. Here where the barrel widens is the breech and combustion chamber."

"The barrel looks to be about ten feet in diameter. We're still working on the numbers, but I believe it's capable of launching a boosted projectile into earth orbit."

Even while the generals and their staffs took in the news, Kastner replied, "Great job, Frank. We're pressed for time, but I've got to know how you found this."

"We're putting together a complete report right now, sirs; you'll all have it in a few hours." He paused for a moment, then said, "Elimination and luck. Two of our satellites were killed in the same area just east of Okinawa. We assumed a west-to-east trajectory, back-calculated the origin, and tried to find a launching site in the region. We got lucky because we figured they'd start with an established installation, and the Gongga Shan Prison Camp was on the list. It probably never was anything but a construction site for the gun. That still took us over a week." He didn't sound proud.

Kastner was complimentary but grim. "Well, Frank, your work is just beginning. We need to know a lot more about this weapon. First, is this the only one? It probably is, but I've got to know absolutely. How many more satellites can they kill with it? And what would it take to stop it?"

Overton nodded silently, as grim as the general. He and his staff quickly left.

Kastner turned to the others. "Immediate impressions, gentlemen? After we finish here, I'll wake the President."

INN News,
September 25

Mark Markin stood in front of a map of China and Vietnam, a familiar image after weeks of confrontation. He read carefully from a data pad.

"Xinhua, the official Chinese News Service, today released a statement claiming a victory over 'an American plan to seize control of Southeast Asia.' "

Markin's image was replaced by Chinese Premier Li Zhang, speaking to a crowd of cheering citizens. Thin, almost scrawny, the elderly leader spoke with energy in Chinese. English subtitles appeared at the bottom of the image.

"In response to preparations for a massive attack on Chinese territory, the forces of the People's Liberation Army have hamstrung the Imperialist aggressor by shooting down his military satellites.

"Deprived of his superiority and given pause by our new technological strength, the Americans have canceled their attack plan. This shows that America is not all-powerful, that any bully can be stopped if one faces him directly and exposes his inner weakness.

"We call on all the nations of the world, oppressed and suffering under American world hegemony, to topple the corrupt giant."

Markin reappeared, looking concerned. "U.S. defense officials have refused to comment officially, but it has been a working assumption that the Chinese were responsible for the missing spacecraft. They also were unable to say how or when U.S. military forces would react to this news.

"Sources at the State Department were slightly

more forthcoming, but only about the reasons for the Chinese announcement. They believe that the Chinese are openly challenging the U.S. in a field the Americans consider theirs exclusively: their technical edge. They hope to leverage their victory into an alliance of nations opposed to American policy.

"There was no comment from the White House, except that the President and his advisors are considering all options to protect American interests in this widening crisis."

China Lake Naval Weapons Center, California
September 26

Tom Wilcox worked in the Test and Evaluation shop at China Lake. The entire base's mission was to evaluate new weapons systems for the Navy, but his shop was the one that did the dirty work. He spent a lot of time in the desert and would be out there at dawn, half an hour from now.

Wilcox looked like someone who's spent a lot of time on the desert. Lean, tanned, his face showed a lot of wear, although he would joke that was just from dealing with the budget. He'd been in his current job for twenty-five years, and claimed he was good for that many more.

This morning, he had to inspect the foundations for a new test stand. Before too long they'd be mounting rocket motors on it, and he didn't want a motor, with stand still attached, careening across the landscape.

First, though, he always checked his e-mail. Working on his dan-ish, and placing his coffee carefully out of the way, he said, "New messages."

The computer displayed them on his wall screen,

a mix of personal and professional subjects listed out according to his own priority system. The higher the rank of the sender, the less urgent the message had to be. Anything from an admiral went straight to the bottom of the pile.

He noted one unusual item. Ray McConnell had sent a message, with a medium-sized attachment. He'd known Ray for quite a while as a colleague, but he hadn't seen him since Wilcox had been to SPAWAR for that conference last spring, about six months ago. They'd exchanged some notes since then.

Wilcox noted that it had a long list of other addressees, and it had been sent out at four this morning. He recognized a few of the addressees. They were all at official DoD installations.

The cover letter was brief: "I think you'll know what to do with this. It's completely unclassified, but please only show it to people inside the security system. Thanks."

Well, that was mysterious enough to be worth a few minutes. He downloaded the attached file, waited for the virus and security check sums to finish, then had a look.

It was a hundred-page document. The cover page had a gorgeous 3-D-rendered image of a wedge-shaped airfoil. It had to be a spacecraft, and the title above it read, *"Defender."*

Wilcox's first reaction was one of surprise and disappointment. He almost groaned. Engineers in the defense community receive a constant stream of crackpot designs from wanna-be inventors. The unofficial ones were ignored or returned with a polite letter. The official ones, that came though a congressman or some other patron, could be a real pain in the ass. Why was Ray passing this on to him?

Then he saw the name on the front. It was Ray's own design! *What is this? It's not an official Navy project. McConnell must have put some real time into this, and he's no flake,* thought Wilcox. *Or at least, not until now.*

He opened the cover and glanced at the introduction. "The Chinese attack on our satellites is the beginning of a new stage of warfare, one that we are completely unprepared for. Even if the source of the attacks is found and destroyed, the technology now has been demonstrated. Others, hostile to U.S. interests, will follow the Chinese example.

"*Defender* is a vehicle designed to protect spacecraft in orbit from attack. It uses proven technology. Please consider this concept as an option to protect our vital space assets."

Below that was a long list of names, presumably people who either endorsed the idea or who had helped him with the design. Wilcox scanned the list. They were helpers. He didn't recognize any of the names, and there were none with a rank attached.

He skimmed the document, watching the clock but increasingly absorbed in the design. Ray had done his homework, although his haste was obvious. At least the art was good. Diagrams were important for the higher-ups. They had problems with numbers and large words.

The phone rang, and Wilcox picked it up. "We need you in five," his assistant reminded him.

"I'll be there," Wilcox replied, and hung up.

He sat for another ten seconds, thinking and staring at the screen. *All right, Ray's got a hot idea, and he wants to share it. In fact,* Wilcox realized, *he wants me to share it, to send it up the line. He's trying to jump-start the design process.*

Wilcox knew, and so did anyone else who worked for the DoD, that it took millions of dollars and years of effort to produce a design like this, and that only happened after an elaborately crafted Requirement for such a design was issued by the Pentagon. The U.S. didn't have time for that kind of deliberate care.

Wilcox knew it was a good idea. The U.S. had no way of protecting their satellites.

Taking the few minutes it needed, he had the computer call up his address book and flagged ten names. Most were senior engineers, like him, but a few were military officers of senior rank. He wanted to see if they were still capable of recognizing an original idea when they saw it.

That morning, Ray had sent his document out to over thirty friends and colleagues. All had clearances, and all worked in some area of defense. By lunchtime, eight hours after its transmission, over 150 copies existed. By close of business, it was over five hundred and growing.

Crystal Square 3, Arlington, Virginia
September 27

Captain "Biff" Barnes was more than ready to leave for the day. His skills as a pilot were supposed to be essential for this project, but he spent most of the day wrestling with the Pentagon bureaucracy.

"Biff's" name was Clarence, but he'd acquired the nickname, any nickname, as quickly as he could. He hated "Clarence." Barnes was a little short, only five-eight, but average for a pilot. He kept in very good shape, counting the months and weeks until his desk tour was finished. His thin, almost angular face showed how little fat he carried. His hair was cut as short as regulations would allow. The Air Force didn't like bald pilots, but he'd have shaved his head if he could.

He'd flown F-15s before being assigned to the Airborne Laser project. He understood the work was important, but doing anything other than flying was a comedown. He'd been promised a billet in an F-22 squadron once this tour was complete.

His job was interesting, when he actually got to do it. He had to determine, as accurately as possible, how vulnerable aircraft were to laser attack. He'd gotten to look at a lot of foreign hardware up close, and his degree in aeronautical engineering was proving quite useful.

But most of the time he futzed with the system. Some congressman wanted to be briefed on the status of the project. That was easy. Some other agency didn't want to provide information he needed. That took some doing. The General Accounting Office wanted to review their phone records. Or some reporter on a fishing expedition filed a Freedom of Information Act request. That had to be dealt with immediately.

Because the project was classified, and only a limited number of people could be cleared into the program, everyone involved had to do double or triple duty. The junior troops, like Barnes, drew most of the nasty ones.

He couldn't have dodged the latest flap, anyway. A government office concerned with equal opportunity needed to know if Barnes, who was African American, felt his "capabilities were being fully utilized," and had included a five-page form to fill out. He'd used all of the comments section to share his feelings about "utilization."

He sat at his desk, closing up files and locking his safe, but still reluctant to go without something productive to show for his day. He checked his mail, at that point even willing to read Internet humor.

The page opened, and the first thing he noticed was another two copies of the *Defender* document, from separate friends at Maxwell and Wright-Pat. He'd gotten the first one yesterday morning from a pilot buddy at March Air Force Base in California, and another copy later in the day. He'd tabled it then, busy with paperwork, but his mind was ready for distraction now.

He opened the file and almost laughed when he saw the cover. Someone had taken the new VentureStar, a single-stage-to-orbit space vehicle, and tried to arm it, using "his" laser. The introduction had touted it as a way of defending the GPS satellites.

A worthy goal, although Barnes had no expectation that this lash-up was anything more than a time-wasting fantasy. Still he was motivated by curiosity to see what this McConnell had said about the Airborne Laser.

Carried by a modified Boeing 747, the Airborne Laser could engage ballistic or cruise missiles, or even aircraft, at long range. Just what range was one of the problems Barnes was trying to solve. The prototype aircraft, which had been flying for several years, was still in test, proving not just the laser but the basic concept of engaging aircraft with a beam of light. How much did weather affect it? What if some country developed a cheap antilaser paint?

McConnell had taken the laser out of the 747 and mounted it in the cargo bay of the spacecraft. Barnes flipped to the section labeled "Laser Weapon," and started to read. Whoever this McConnell was, thought Barnes, he didn't write science fiction. He hadn't made any obvious mistakes, but he didn't have detailed information, which of course was classified. There certainly wasn't any weather in space. The laser would be much more effective in a vacuum.

But what about targeting? He started working through the document, answering questions and become increasingly impressed with McConnell's idea.

He knew about spacecraft, not only because of his degree but because he'd actually been selected for the Astronaut Corps after his first squadron tour. He'd flown one mission, but then left the program. He hated the constant training, the public relations. And what he really hated was the lack of flight time.

Barnes's stomach growled, and he looked up from the screen to see it was seven-forty-five. He'd missed the rush hour, anyway. Biff said, "Print file," and pages started to fill the hopper. He wanted to show this to his buddies.

Barnes pulled himself up short. His friends would be interested, but they didn't have security clearances, and the cover message had explicitly asked that it not be shown to anyone who wasn't cleared. Respect for the design made him want to respect the author's wishes, and treat it seriously.

The Vietnam Crisis, another Desert Storm/Balkans exercise in U.S. diplomacy, had suddenly transformed itself into a much wider challenge. McConnell proposed this *Defender* as an answer—maybe the only answer, since he hadn't heard of any others.

He looked at the proposal. Did he buy into it? He did, Biff realized. McConnell had gotten the laser right. He knew what he was doing.

Biff sat back down at the keyboard. He had some friends in high places.

U.S. Navy Space Warfare Command, San Diego, California
September 27

Ray McConnell came back to his office and shut the door quickly. He was shaken, almost physically trembling, after his meeting with Admiral Carson.

Rear Admiral Eugene Carson was not just the head of Communications, which was Ray's division, but of the entire Space and Naval Warfare Systems Command. It had taken Ray two days to work his way up the chain, first with Rudy White, his own division head, then Dr. Krauss, the technical director, and Admiral Gaston. With increasing force, he'd made his case for *Defender*. His unsolicited, unrequired, unwanted proposal had been shown dozens of times.

Rudy White had been concerned with the lost time from Ray's assigned projects. "Why haven't you put some of that creative energy into the new communications system?" he'd demanded.

"Because someone's shooting down GPS satellites right now," Ray had responded. He'd worked with White for years, and knew he could press his point. "I thought of this, but I can't build it, and it needs to be built, and soon."

White had agreed to let McConnell see the technical director, with the strict understanding that the *Defender* proposal was Ray's own idea. White was relaxed enough about his career to take the risk.

Dr. Krauss had been even less helpful, wondering aloud if *Defender* was SPAWAR property, since a SPAWAR employee had created it. Ray had been nonplussed, unsure whether Krauss was greedy or simply trying to cover his bureaucratic ass.

He'd decided to play the doctor's game. Krauss

had been shocked when he heard about the several hundred copies of the proposal already circulating through the defense community.

"I'd be delighted to have official SPAWAR endorsement of *Defender.* I'm sure that would be all the help she needed." Ray fought hard to keep a straight face when he saw the look of horror. Krauss hadn't been able to get him out of his office quickly enough.

The vice commander had been the final hurdle, Ray thought. He'd been more than aware of *Defender*'s popularity. "You realize that you have no credibility as a spacecraft design engineer," Gaston explained coolly. He'd been polite, but a little condescending.

"I didn't think I had to be qualified to have a good idea, sir."

Gaston shook his head. "I disagree. Without credentials, why should anyone waste their time looking at this design? As far as the Navy is concerned, you're no different that anyone off the street, bringing it some design it didn't ask for. And to the wrong agency," he added.

"I know that this isn't SPAWAR's area, sir, but I'm SPAWAR's employee. I didn't want to go outside our own chain of command."

Gaston nodded, smiling approvingly. "Quite right. Your actions have been correct, although"—he glanced at his data pad—"your supervisor's concerned with the amount of leave you've taken lately."

"All of this work had been on my own time, sir. I didn't want to do it on Navy time."

Gaston scowled. "We're on Navy time now." He sat silently for a moment, pretending to consider the issue, while Ray fretted.

To be truthful, Gaston had made up his mind before McConnell ever walked in the room. He'd just wanted to interview the engineer himself before letting him go on to Carson.

Defender was too widely known, at least at the lower levels. It was a miracle the media hadn't picked it up already. It was popular, the kind of grassroots concept reporters loved. No matter that it would never be built. If he said no, then he'd be blamed as one of the people who kept it from happening. Better to let McConnell hang himself. Gaston didn't have to support it, just pass it on.

"All right, I'll forward it 'without endorsement.' "

Ray had begun to hope.

The meeting with Admiral Carson had begun poorly. The admiral had granted him fifteen minutes between other appointments, and appeared distracted. Ray had started his pitch, but Carson had cut him off after only a few words, chopping with one hand as if to cut off the stream.

"I'm familiar with the design, Mr. McConnell," Carson had said with irritation. "I've received three copies in the past two days, besides this one. I'm also familiar with the problem. I've spent most of the last week in Washington, answering questions about our own vulnerability and what SPAWAR could do to counter it.

"I've also been fully briefed about Chinese antisatellite threat," he said finally. "The current estimation is that the Chinese can't possibly have many more of the kill vehicles."

He walked over to where McConnell sat, almost leaning over him. "I've also looked over your personnel file. I was looking for your academic credentials. They're bad enough: No doctorate, a master's in electrical engineering and an undergraduate degree in physics. What made you think we'd take a spacecraft designed by you seriously?"

Carson picked up a data pad and checked something on the display. "And then I found this: After your master's degree, you applied for the astronaut program. Correct?"

Ray nodded. "Yes."

"And were turned down. And then you joined the Air Force. You served six years as a junior officer, and during that time applied three more times to become an astronaut. Also correct?" His tone was more than hostile.

"Yes sir. Each time I missed by just a few percentage points. I hoped . . ."

"You hoped to get into space with this half-baked fantasy!" shouted Carson, pointing to *Defender*. "Did you plan on scoring the theme music for your little adventure, too?"

"Admiral, I've always been interested in space, but that doesn't have anything to do with this. I just want to get this idea to where it will do the most good."

Carson had sat, glowering, listening while Ray protested.

"Your idea is worthless, Mr. McConnell. At best, it's a distraction at a very difficult time. At worst, it's a personal attempt at empire building, but a very crude one.

"Although you've broken no rules I'm aware of, I am directing the Inspector General's office to review your activities and your work logs to see if any of your fantasizing has been done on government time. If that is the case, docking your pay will be the weakest punishment you will suffer. Now get back to work and hope I never hear about *Defender* again!"

* * *

Sitting in his office, Ray struggled with his feelings. He'd created *Defender* because he'd seen the need for it. Why didn't the chain see that need as well? Was he wrong? Maybe he didn't know enough to do it. But he'd had lots of help in designing *Defender*. And he'd gotten lots of mail back, some critical, but more supportive, some even offering help.

Was it time to sit down and shut up? He liked his job and the people he worked with. He didn't want to lose it over *Defender*.

He hadn't expected the command to be hostile. Indifferent, yes, but once he'd shown them the logic of the design, he'd hoped for some support.

He picked up the phone then, remembering, put it down, and pulled out his personal cell phone. No personal calls on a Navy line. He looked up a number and punched it in.

"Jennifer Oh."

"Hi, Jenny. It's Ray McConnell." He tried to sound cheerful, but even he could tell it didn't work.

"Ray, you don't sound too good. What's wrong? Problems with *Defender*?"

"Only if I want to keep my job." He sighed. "Let's just say that the Space and Naval Warfare Systems Command won't be giving me its endorsement. Admiral Carson almost had me thrown in the brig."

She laughed, half at his joke and also to cheer him up. "You're joking." He could hear the smile in her voice.

"He's siccing the IG on me, to see if I've wasted any Navy time on this quote half-baked fantasy unquote."

"That's not good." She paused, then asked, "So, you've gone all the way up your chain of command with no success?"

"I'd call that an understatement," he replied.

"Well, then it's time to try another chain," she said forcefully. "Let me make some calls."

"What?" McConnell was horrified. "Jenny! I'm poison. Please, just ditch anything you have with my name on it. *Defender*'s all over the Web. We'll just have to hope someone picks it up and uses it."

"No, Ray. We're not going to just sit. *Defender*'s a good idea, and I'm going to do everything I can for it." She paused again, and her tone softened, almost calming. "Let me call some of my friends on the NAVAIR staff. Admiral Schultz is a pilot and an 'operator,' not some bureaucrat. I've met him, and I think he'll give you a chance."

Ray didn't know what to say except, "Thanks, Jenny. I hope this doesn't backfire on you."

"Anything worthwhile is worth a risk, Ray. I'll call you this evening and tell you what I find out."

Office of the Chief of Naval Operations, The Pentagon, September 28

"I am not going to go into the Joint Chiefs of Staff and propose that we adopt some crackpot design that came off the Internet!" Admiral John Kramer was so agitated he was pacing, quickly marching back and forth as he protested.

Admiral William Schultz, Commander in Chief, Naval Aviation, sat quietly in his chair. He'd expected this reaction, and waited for Kramer to calm down a little. Schultz was calm, sure of himself and his mission.

"I've checked out this design, John, and the engineer. Both are OK. There are some technical questions, but nothing he's done here is science fiction. The man who designed it, Ray McConnell, had a lot of help. It may be unofficial"—Schultz leaned forward for emphasis—"but it's good work."

He sat back, straightening his spine. "It's also the only decent idea I've heard in almost two weeks."

Kramer and Schultz were both pilots, and had served together several times in their Navy careers, but where Kramer was tall, and almost recruiting-poster handsome, Schultz was only of middle height, and stockier. And his looks would never get him any movie deals. His thinning sandy hair was mussed whenever he put his navy cap on, while he was sure Kramer kept his in place with mousse. Kramer was a good pilot, but he'd also been the staff type, the "people person." Or so he thought.

Used to the convoluted, time-consuming methods of the Pentagon, the CNO continued to object. "Even if we did propose it, and even if it was accepted, where would we get the money?"

"Somewhere, John, just like we've done before. The money's there. We just have to decide what's the most important thing to spend it on."

Schultz continued, mentally assigning himself three Our Fathers and three Hail Marys. "Look, I've heard the Air Force is buying into *Defender* in a big way. They think it can work, and as far as they're concerned, if it's got wings, it belongs to them."

Kramer looked grim. The Air Force was shameless when they talked about "aerospace power." He nodded agreement.

"Let them get their hands on any armed spacecraft, and the next thing you know, we'll lose SPAWAR. Remember the time they tried to convince Congress that we should scrap our carriers and buy bombers with our money?" Kramer frowned, listening.

Schultz pressed his point. "Do we have any viable

alternative for stopping the Chinese, sir?"

Kramer shook his head. "The launch site is out of Tomahawk range, and the President has already said that he won't authorize the use of a ballistic missile, even with a conventional warhead. And you'd need lots of missiles. The way that site is hardened, I'm not certain a nuke would do it."

"Air Force B-2s could reach it," Schultz said quietly.

"But they can't be sure they'd get out alive. The defenses are incredibly thick, and they're expecting us to use bombers. And it would take several aircraft to destroy the gun. We might have to commit as many as ten and expect to lose half."

"This is better, John. Look, McConnell's flying in here tomorrow. You can meet him yourself. I've listened to him, and I'm convinced."

"Then that's what we'll try to sell," Kramer decided.

Three

Indecision

Office of the Chief of Staff of the Air Force
September 30

General Michael Warner was an unusual Chief of Staff. He flew bombers, not fighters. In an Air Force that gave fighter pilots most of the stars, it was a sign of his ability, not only as an officer, but as a politician. Looking more like a banker than a bomber pilot, he had an almost legendary memory, which he used for details: of budgets, people, and events.

Pilots lived and died because of details. They won and lost battles because of them. And the general kept looking for some small detail that his deputy, General Clifton Ames, had missed. The three-star general had put the target analysis together personally.

Ames had nothing but bad news. An overhead image of the Gongga Shan launch site filled the wall screen. "I've confirmed there's no way the Navy can stretch the range of their Tomahawk missiles. They've got smaller warheads than our air-launched cruise missiles anyway. And even if we could adapt a ballistic missile with a conventional warhead, they aren't accurate enough for this target."

His data pad linked to the screen, Ames indicated various features of the site as he talked. "The Chinese built this installation expecting it to be attacked by cruise missiles. It has heavy SAM and AAA defenses. They've mounted radar on elevated towers to give them additional warning time of an attack. They've even constructed tall open framework barriers across the approach routes a cruise missile might use." He pointed to the large girder structures, easily visible in the photograph.

"The barrel and all vital facilities are hardened, and there's the matter of the gun itself. Given its three-meter bore, intelligence says the barrel thickness is at least a foot. Damaging that will require precision at a distance—precisely the capability we're now lacking."

"To get an eighty percent chance of success would take twelve B-2s, each carrying eight weapons." Ames knew he was talking to a bomber pilot, and watched for Warner's reaction. The chief just nodded glumly, and Ames continued.

"And the worst part is that the Chinese would have the gun back in operation again within a few months, possibly a few weeks. We're certain the barrel is constructed in sections, like the Iraqi gun. If a section is damaged, you remove it and replace it with a spare section. We've even identified in the imagery where they probably keep the spares.

"We estimate follow-up strikes would be needed every two weeks—indefinitely."

Even as he said it, Ames knew that wasn't an option. Airpower provided shock and speed, but it had to be followed up by something besides more air strikes.

"What about losses?" Warner asked.

"Using the standard loss rates," Ames replied, "there's a good chance we'll lose several bombers in the first few raids. And part of the flight path is over Chinese territory." The implications for search and rescue were not good.

"All right, Cliff. Send this on to the Chairman's office with my respects. And my apologies," Warner muttered.

"Sir, I've been looking at *Defender*," Ames offered. "One of my friends in the ABL Program Office passed it to me with his analysis. I think we should consider it."

Warner had heard about *Defender*, of course, but hadn't had time to do more than dismiss it as a distraction. "Are we that desperate?" the chief asked.

Gongga Shan Mountain, Xichuan Province, China
September 30

General Shen Xuesen stood nervously in the launch center. It was hard to maintain the unruffled demeanor his troops needed to see. He needed all of his experience to look calm and relaxed.

Visitors at such a time would make anyone nervous, and worse, distract the launch team. A television crew was unthinkable, but there they were. It was a State-run crew, of course, and they were being carefully supervised, but they brought lights and confusion and, worst of all, exposure.

Now they were filming an actual launch. Beijing had even asked if they could film the intercept, but Shen had refused absolutely, on security grounds. He understood the propaganda value of the Dragon launch, and offered to supply tapes of previous shots. They all looked alike. Who would know?

But the piece needed shots of activity in the launch center, and the reporter would add his narration. At least the general had been able to avoid an interview, again citing security reasons.

INN News
September 30

The oval opening erupted in flame, and a dark blur shot upward. Mark Markin's voice accompanied the video. "Released less than two hours ago, this dramatic footage from Gongga Shan Mountain in China shows the launch of a *T'ien Lung*, or Celestial Dragon." Markin's voice continued as the scene shifted to a more distant shot. The mountaintop, a rugged texture of browns, was capped by a small white cloud of smoke that lingered in the still morning air.

"That is their name for the spacecraft, or 'ASAT vehicle,' as U.S. officials describe the weapon. They also confirmed the destruction of another GPS satellite just a short time ago, the time of loss consistent with the launch shown here.

"This footage was released through Xinhua, the Chinese official news agency. The narrator claimed that China had now demonstrated military superiority over the United States, and that their superiority had halted American aggression in the region."

The mountaintop and its fading smoke were replaced by a computer-drawn representation of the gun, angled upward inside a transparent mountain.

"Intelligence officials here believe that the gun is based on the work of Dr. Gerald Bull, who designed a smaller weapon for Iraq. That weapon had a barrel of almost a hundred feet and a bore of nearly a meter. It was capable of launching a projectile several hundred kilometers, and although it was fired successfully in tests, it was never put into service. The Chinese would have no problem obtaining this technical knowledge from the Iraqis, probably in exchange for weapons."

Computer animation showed the process of loading the projectile, the launch, and sabots falling away from the projectile before a rocket booster fired.

"Before he was killed, possibly by foreign agents, Bull wrote of using such guns to launch spacecraft. Sources have hinted that a smaller gun, believed capable of firing across the straits of Taiwan, was built and tested. They now speculate that gun may never have been made fully operational, and have just served as a test bed for this much larger weapon."

The animation disappeared, replaced with Markin, with an image of a GPS satellite behind him. "This brings to four the number of GPS satellites known to have been destroyed by China. While American officials have wondered publicly about how many *T'ien Lung* vehicles the Chinese can build, China threatened during the broadcast to destroy the entire GPS constellation unless 'America abandoned its plans for Pacific hegemony.' "

United Flight 1191, En Route to Washington, D.C.
September 30

Ray McConnell turned off the screen and put his head back against the seat. He hated being right, and he knew those "American officials" were indulging in wishful thinking. China's space program had a good base of design experience. The kill vehicle, the *T'ien Lung*, was not trivial, but it was well within their capabilities. The GPS satellites were unarmored and had only the most limited ability to maneuver. Technically, it wasn't a problem.

And logically, if they'd committed themselves to this premeditated confrontation, would they only have four or five bullets for their gun? *I'd have two dozen stockpiled, and a factory making more,* Ray mused.

It was bad news, although it helped strengthen his case.

He said it again. His case. Schultz had called him from Washington last night, telling him to come out ASAP, on Navy orders.

Sitting in his apartment, still depressed about his meeting with Carson, Schultz's call had struck like lightning. McConnell hadn't known what to think or hope.

He'd called Jenny to thank her, then frantically packed. He'd spent most of the night trying to organize the jumble of material that had supported the *Defender* design effort. McConnell hadn't even phoned work, just sending an e-mail asking for leave.

Ray glanced at his watch, still on California time. By rights, Rudy only got the e-mail at seven, about the same time the plane had taken off. Ray would be on the ground in another few hours, and hopefully by the time the brass heard anything, he'd know one way or the other.

McConnell decided he did feel hopeful, but he couldn't tell whether it was for *Defender* or his own personal success. Ray hadn't even realized that he personally had anything at stake until his meeting with Carson yesterday. He'd thought of *Defender* as just an engineering project. His personal stake in it was greater than he'd realized, but that was all right. Other people, like Jenny, were committed to it as well, and that spurred him on.

He hooked his data pad up to the screen built into the chair back and started opening files. *Defender* still needed a lot of work. He'd seen enough Pentagon briefings to know what was expected. He couldn't make her perfect, but he could at least hit the high points.

"Ladies and gentlemen, this is the pilot. We've just received word that Air Traffic Control has rescheduled our arrival into Dulles to four-fifteen instead of three-ten this afternoon. There's no problem with the weather, but because of the recent problems with the GPS system, they've just announced they'll be spacing aircraft farther apart near the airports, as a precaution.

"United apologizes for the delay. Passengers with connecting flights . . ."

McConnell smiled. For once, he was glad for the extra time in the air.

Office of the Chief of Staff of the Air Force, The Pentagon
September 30

Captain "Biff" Barnes tapped his data pad and the file collapsed down into a small spaceship icon. His presentation had condensed McConnell's hundred-page design document down to fifteen minutes. It had been a long fifteen minutes, with Warner, his deputy, General Ames, and a flock of colonels watching intently. They'd all asked a lot of questions. Barnes had been able to answer many of them, especially about the laser installation, but not all. *Defender* was definitely a work in progress.

General Warner opened the discussion. "Captain, you've told General Ames that you think *Defender* will fly."

Well, thought Barnes, *actually I passed the file to Ed Reynolds in the ABL Program Office and Eddie gave it to the general. Also, I only told Eddie that* Defender *was better than anything else I'd heard of. The next thing I know, I've got two hours to prep a brief for the Chief of Staff of the Air Force.*

But Barnes didn't feel like correcting either general. "It's the best shot we have, sir," trying to sound positive, "unless there's something in the 'black' world." The armed forces ran a lot of "black" programs, secret projects with advanced technology. The F-117 had been one of the most famous. Was there one to deal with this threat?

"Nothing that will help us, I'm afraid." The general shook his head, half-musing to himself. "The X-40's operational, but she was never supposed to be more than a test bed. She doesn't have the payload for this in any case."

Looking at Barnes directly, Warner continued, "Yes, Captain, there is technology in the classified world that would help us—in anywhere from five to twenty years. The Chinese have jumped the gun on us." He sounded angry.

"We should own this crisis, and we just don't have the tools to deal with it! And now some SPAWAR employee and his buddies in their free time have come up with this, and we're all taking it seriously?"

Barnes waited for the general to continue. When it appeared he'd run down, the captain said, "Well, sir, at least he's former Air Force."

Warner laughed, a little grimly, then looked at the wall clock. "All right, then, Captain. Let's go see if the Joint Chiefs have a sense of humor."

National Military Command Center, The Pentagon
September 30

Ray McConnell looked around the fabled War Room. Every available chair was filled, usually by someone in uniform, and often by a uniform with stars on it.

The Joint Chiefs themselves sat on both sides of a long table, with the Chairman at the head on the left. A briefer's podium stood empty at the head, and behind the podium, the entire wall was an active video display. Ray almost felt at home.

He also felt rushed and a little unorganized. His plane had landed just a short time before. The Metro had taken him straight from Dulles to the Pentagon, and Admiral Schultz himself had met Ray. The outgoing admiral had quickly filled him in and shared some of his enthusiasm with the hurried engineer. They'd dropped his bags in the CNO's office, of all places, and made the meeting with only minutes to spare.

Several rows of chairs to one side of the main table were filled with a gaggle of aides, experts, and assorted hangers-on, including Ray. Nervously, he typed on his data pad, working on the design that was never finished.

The Vice Chairman, a Navy admiral, stepped up to the podium, and the buzz in the room quickly died. "Gentlemen, the Chairman."

Everyone rose, and Ray saw General Kastner, the Chairman of the Joint Chiefs of Staff, enter and take his seat. McConnell wasn't normally awed by rank, but he realized that this collection of stars could really make things happen. They literally were responsible for defending the country, and that's what they'd met to do.

The Vice Chairman, Admiral Blair, tapped the data pad built into the podium. A bullet chart appeared on the screen. It was titled "Protection of Space Assets."

"Gentlemen, our task today is find a course of action that will protect our satellites from Chinese attack. Any solution we consider"—and he started to tick off items on the list—"must include the cost, the technological risk, the time it would take to implement, and the political repercussions." He glanced over at Kastner, who nodded approvingly.

Blair continued. "Above all," he said, scanning the entire room, "it must work, and work soon. The material costs alone have been severe, and the potential effects on American security and the economy are incalculable.

"For purposes of this discussion, while cost should be considered, it is not a limitation. Also, the President considers these attacks by China an attack on American vital interests, although he has not made that decision public."

Nor will he, Ray thought, *until we can do something about them.* So cost wasn't a problem, just shut down the Chinese, and do it quickly.

Blair put a new page up on the display, listing some conventional methods of attack. "You've all sent analyses indicating that these are not viable options. Our purpose is to see what other means you've developed since those initial reports."

Kastner stood up, taking Blair's place at the podium. Blair sat down at his left. The Chairman looked around the room. "To save time, let me ask a few questions. The President has asked me if we can arm a shuttle and use it to defend the satellites." His tone was formal, as if he already knew the answer.

Kastner looked at General Warner, who glanced around the table before replying. "The Air Force would recommend against that. Not only would it take too long to prepare, it's too vulnerable during launch. Certainly if they can shoot down a GPS satellite, they can shoot down a shuttle."

The Chairman nodded, then looked at the Chief of Naval Operations. "Can we use a missile to shoot down the kill vehicle?"

Admiral Kramer answered quickly. "We'd hoped that would work, sir, but we're sure now that we can't. We had two Aegis ships in a position to track the last ASAT shot seven days ago. We've been analyzing the data since."

"The *T'ien Lung*," Kramer pronounced the Chinese name carefully, "is too fast. Our Standard Block IVs can shoot down a ballistic missile, but as hard as a ballistic intercept is, it's easier than this. At least a ballistic missile is a closing target, but the ASAT is outbound. It's a tail chase from the start. Even if we launched at the same moment, the intercept basket is nonexistent."

"Does the Army concur?" Kastner looked at the Army's Chief of Staff. The Army also had an active antiballistic-missile system.

"Yes, sir. It has to be from above." General Forest didn't look pleased.

Ray realized the general had just told the Chairman that the Army didn't have a role in solving the crisis. Of course, the Commandant of the Marine Corps looked even unhappier. This was one beach his men couldn't hope to storm.

General Kastner announced, "I'm also allowed to tell you that there are no special assets that might be able to destroy the launch site using unconventional methods."

In other words, Ray thought, *they can't get an agent into the area.* McConnell didn't even want to think about how he'd destroy the launcher. Talk about the Guns of Navarone . . .

Which meant they were getting desperate. McConnell saw what Kastner was doing, eliminating options one by one. He knew about *Defender.* He had to know. Ray didn't know what to feel. Was this actually going to happen? Fear started to replace hope.

General Warner finally broke the silence. "Sir, the Air Force thinks we can make the *Defender* concept work."

Admiral Kramer shot a look at Schultz, sitting next to Ray. Then both looked at McConnell, who shrugged helplessly. Warner's aide was loading a file into the display, and Ray saw *Defender*'s image appear on the wall. This was becoming a little surreal.

"Captain Barnes from our ABL Program Office has put together a presentation on the design." Ray saw a black Air Force captain with astronaut's wings step up to the podium. As he started to describe the spacecraft, McConnell felt irritation, an almost proprietary protectiveness about the ship. His ship. Ray wanted to speak up, to protest that he could describe it better than anyone, but Kramer wasn't saying anything, and Ray could only remain silent.

It seemed to take forever for Barnes to work his way through the different sections: space frame, weapons, sensors, flight control. The final slide was a list of unsolved design issues.

Ray spoke softly to Schultz beside him. "He's got an old copy of the file. I've solved two of those questions and added a new one."

Schultz nodded, then pulled out his data pad and typed quickly. Kramer, watching the presentation, looked down at his pad, and tapped something, then turned to look at Schultz, nodding.

General Forrest had started to ask about one of the issues when Admiral Kramer spoke up. "Excuse me, General, but that list may be a little old. Mr. McConnell, the engineer who designed *Defender*, is here, and has solved some of those problems."

Schultz nudged Ray, and the engineer stood up and moved toward the podium. As he passed Admiral Kramer, the naval officer muttered, "Go get 'em, Ray." The engineer never felt less like getting anyone in his life.

As he approached the podium, Captain Barnes shot him a hard look, seemingly reluctant to leave. Ray said, "Hello," conscious of the captain's sudden obsolescence, and tried to smile pleasantly. Barnes nodded politely, if silently, picked up his notes and data pad, and returned to his chair.

Ray was acutely aware of the many eyes on him. He linked his pad into the screen and transferred the most recent version of the file to the display. He used the moment's fiddling to gather his wits. He'd given dozens of briefs. This was just a little more impromptu than most. And much more important.

"I'm Ray McConnell, and I designed *Defender* to protect assets in space from ground-based attacks. It uses the Lockheed VentureStar prototype with equipment currently available to detect launches, maneuver to an intercept position, and kill the attacking vehicle. It also has the capability to destroy the launch site from orbit."

Barnes had said that much, Ray knew, but he'd felt a need to also make that declaration, to say to these men himself what *Defender* was and what it could do.

He opened the file, and rapidly flipped through the large document. McConnell realized that the pilot had done a pretty good job of summarizing *Defender*, so he concentrated instead on the work that had gone into selecting and integrating the different systems. That was his specialty, anyway, and it improved the credibility of his high-tech offspring.

A message appeared on his data pad from Admiral Schultz as he talked. "Are there any Army or Marine systems in the design?" Ray understood immediately what Schultz was driving at, and spent a little time on the kinetic weapons, adapted from Army antitank rounds. There wasn't a piece of Marine gear anywhere on the ship, and McConnell mentally kicked himself for not understanding the importance of Pentagon diplomacy.

Ray made it to the last slide as quickly as he could, and felt positive as he assured the assembled generals that all the questions listed there could be answered.

"Thank you, Mr. McConnell." Kastner rose again and Ray quickly returned to his seat, barely remembering to grab his data pad. "I'm much more confident about *Defender*'s ability, and probability, than I was at the start of this meeting. It is my intention to recommend to the President that *Defender* be built, and soon."

McConnell felt a little numb. Schultz gave him a small nudge and smiled.

"We haven't really discussed the political implications of arming spacecraft." General Forest's tone was carefully neutral, but his expression was hard, almost hostile. Would he fight *Defender*?

Kastner was nodding, though. "A good point, Ted, and part of our task." He looked around the table. "Admiral Kramer?"

"I believe the Chinese have solved that issue for us, sir. They've fired the first shot, and said so proudly and publicly." He smiled. "I think *Defender*'s name was well chosen."

General Warner added quickly, "I concur. GPS is dual-use. The gaps are already starting to affect civilian applications, and that will only get worse. And those civilian applications are worldwide, not just here in the U.S."

"All of our public statements will emphasize that we are taking these steps only as a result of Chinese attacks," Kastner stated.

Admiral Kramer quickly asked, "Should *Defender* even be made public? With enough warning, the Chinese might be able to take some sort of countermeasure."

Kastner considered only a moment before answering. "All right, my recommendation will be that *Defender* remain secret until after its first use."

General Warner announced, "I'll have my people look for a suitable development site immediately. With all the Air Force bases we've closed . . ."

"Your people aren't the only ones with runways, General. This is a Navy program. Mr. McConnell is a Navy employee."

"And that's why he put his design on the Internet, because of the tremendous Navy support he was receiving." Warner fixed his gaze on Kramer, almost challenging him to interrupt. "It was my understanding that he offered this design to the DoD as a private citizen. Certainly the Air Force is the best service to manage an aerospace-warfare design. We'll welcome Navy participation, of course."

"The Navy has just as much technological expertise as the Air Force. And more in some of the most critical areas . . ."

Ray understood what was going on even as it horrified him. *Defender* would mean a new mission, and if it worked, a lot of publicity. That mattered in these lean times, for money, for recruiting, maybe for the future in ways they couldn't guess. But now they were arguing over the prize like children.

"The Army's experience with ballistic-missile defense means we should be able to contribute as well." General Forest's tone wasn't pleading, but his argument almost was.

Kastner spoke forcefully. "We will meet again at 0800 hours tomorrow morning. Every service will prepare a summary of the assets it can contribute, and any justification it might feel for wanting to manage the project."

Oh, boy, thought McConnell. *It's going to be a long night.*

INN Early News, London
October 1

Trevor West stood outside Whitehall while morning traffic crept past him. His overcoat and umbrella protected him against a rainy London day, but the wind fought his words. He spoke up, and held the microphone close.

"After an emergency meeting of Parliament this morning, in which the Prime Minister spoke on the Chinese antisatellite attacks, the British government has officially condemned the Chinese and demanded that they stop. The Official Note, which was given to the Chinese ambassador here approximately half an hour ago, protests not only the attacks themselves but the 'militarization of space.'

"The Chinese ambassador received the Note without comment.

"The American ambassador, provided with a copy of the Note, welcomed the British support and stated that the United States was doing everything in its power to defend its property.

"Ministry of Defense sources are unsure what the Americans plan to do about the Chinese attacks. They believe a direct attack on the launcher in southern China would be difficult, and the GPS satellites themselves are defenseless.

"One source speculated that the Americans may try to threaten Chinese interests elsewhere in Asia, pressuring them into stopping their attacks. They say they've even seen some signs that this may already be occurring. Of course, military pressure risks a wider conflict—a general war between the United States and China.

"MoD officials refused to speculate what Britain's position would be in such a case."

Office of the Chief of Staff of the Air Force, The Pentagon, October 1

Biff Barnes sat in a conference room with half a dozen other officers. Printouts and data pads covered the table, mixed with a litter of coffee cups,

Chinese food from last night, and doughnut boxes from this morning.

The past twenty-four hours had been a blur to the captain. First the flurry of preparing to brief the Chief of Staff, then the JCS meeting. Barnes considered himself a good pilot, but a minor cog in a much greater machine. Suddenly he'd been asked to do new and challenging things, all at breakneck speed. And those things might change the Air Force. A corner of his mind also asked if this was going to help or hurt his chances for major.

As they had left the meeting yesterday, General Ames had said, "You did a good job on your presentation, Clarence."

Barnes, already in a foul mood, interrupted. "Please, sir, just 'Biff.' " Why was the general getting on a first-name basis?

Ames smiled. "Fine, Biff. Who knew they would back *Defender* as well? You did fine."

"Thank you, sir." Biff was unsure where this was going, but the back of his neck was starting to tingle.

"I need someone to put that presentation together, Biff. I'll give you as many of the staff as you need, and you can set up in my conference room. We've got until 0800 to come up with the arguments that will sell General Kastner on the Air Force owning *Defender*."

"Maybe you should get a lawyer," Biff suggested. He was half-serious.

"No, I want a pilot, and you're the only one in sight who's been an astronaut."

By now they'd reached Ames's office, but Biff didn't respond immediately. Finally, the general asked him flatly, "Do you want it?"

Biff knew he could say no if he wanted to. He believed Ames was a fair enough officer not to hold it against him. But Barnes was still mad at the Navy, and McConnell in particular. "Yes, sir. It's in the bag." He grinned, a fighter-pilot grin.

Now, the summary was almost ready, deceptively small for all the effort that had gone into it. Barnes was staring at the file's icon, wondering what he'd missed, when General Ames hurried into the room. He'd checked on their progress several times during the night, and Biff started to report when Ames cut him off.

"Turn on the news," Ames ordered a lieutenant at the far end of the room. The officer looked for the remote and grabbed it, then fumbled for the power control. ". . . no response to the Chinese demands yet. The spokesman only repeated demands by U.S. government that the Chinese stop their attacks."

The INN defense reporter, Mark Markin, stood in front of a sign that read, U.S. DEPARTMENT OF STATE.

"To repeat, the Chinese have now stated what their price is for stopping their attacks on the NAVSTAR GPS satellites. The U.S. must reduce its forces in the region below precrisis levels, especially in Korea and Japan. According to the statement this is 'to permanently remove the threat of U.S. aggression against China.' If the U.S. does so, the Chinese promise to cease their attacks. The ambassador also hinted that they might restart the stalled talks on human rights, piracy, and other long-standing disputes."

Ames said, "That's enough," and the lieutenant turned it off.

The general looked at Barnes. "The answer's '-*Hell*, no,' of course, but you've gotta love the way they're taking it to the media. And some of the reporters aren't helping the situation. 'Think about all those poor commuters without their GPS.' " Ames sounded disgusted.

Biff announced, "We're ready. Let's clean up and go get us a program."

National Military Command Center, The Pentagon
October 1

Ray McConnell had gotten about three hours of jet-lagged sleep last night, and that only because his eyes wouldn't focus on the screen any longer. He'd worked like a fiend, trying to finish *Defender* in one night while the CNO and his staff tried to figure out a way to keep her a Navy project.

He realized he should be on cloud nine right now. Not only was *Defender* going to be built, but the services were fighting over who would run it! Maybe it was fatigue, or the idea of the Air Force taking it away from him, but he wasn't even feeling optimistic.

Schultz had gotten no sleep, and looked it, but they'd all been energized in the morning by the Chinese ultimatum. Anger could substitute for sleep, for a little while anyway.

A group only slightly smaller than yesterday's waited for the Chairman's arrival. He arrived within seconds of eight o'clock, but followed by the Secretary of Defense. Both were hurrying, and the Secretary reached the podium before everyone had even finished standing.

Secretary of Defense Everett Peck was a political appointee, with little experience in the government. The balding, professorial lawyer had served as campaign manager for the President's election two years ago. He'd stayed out of trouble by letting the DoD alone while he dealt with Congress.

He motioned everyone back down, saying, "Seats, please, everyone," and then waited for half a moment while General Kastner took his chair.

The Secretary spoke, sounding rushed. "The Chairman and I have just come from a meeting with the President. This follows another meeting last night when General Kastner briefed us on *Defender.*"

He paused, and tried to look sympathetic. "I understand the purpose of this meeting was to choose a service to run the *Defender* program, but that decision has been taken out of the Chairman's hands."

What? McConnell looked at the admirals, who looked as puzzled as he felt. In fact, everyone was exchanging glances. Secretary Peck was carefully reading from his data pad.

"The President has decided to create a new service to manage this new military resource. It will be structured similarly to the Special Operations Force, with assets and personnel seconded to it from the other services on an as-needed basis."

Peck didn't wait for that to sink in, but continued reading. "This service will be known as the Space Force and will be headed by Admiral Schultz." McConnell looked at Admiral Schultz, who looked thunderstruck.

The Secretary looked at Admiral Schultz, who was slowly recovering from the surprise announcement. "Your title would be 'Head of U.S. Space Forces.' You would retain your current rank. Do you accept?"

Just like that. Sitting next to Schultz, Ray heard the admiral mutter, "Ho boy," then stand. "I accept, sir."

"Good. Admiral, you will notify your deputy at NAVAIR to take over your duties immediately. You will no longer report to the CNO, but to the Chairman on administrative matters. You will report to me regarding operational matters. You can establish your headquarters wherever you wish, but I assume you will want to be colocated with the construction effort, wherever that is based."

Kramer, suddenly Schultz's former boss, still looked confused, as did most of the officers in the room. Kastner was smiling, and didn't seem like someone who'd had a decision taken out of his hands.

"I won't congratulate you, Admiral. You'll come to regret it, I'm sure, but I'm also sure you'll give it your best effort. And we are desperately in need of that. You have Presidential authority to call on any resources of the Department of Defense to get *Defender* built and stop the Chinese."

Peck glanced at his pad again, but didn't read verbatim. "Now for the bad news. Most of you know that the two spare satellites in orbit are also nonfunctional and presumed destroyed."

Ray's heart sank. He hadn't known that, and had assumed the spares were being kept in reserve.

"I will also tell you that although contracts have been let for replacement satellites, the President has decided that none be launched until the threat is contained."

Reasonable, Ray thought. *No sense giving the Chinese another three-hundred million-dollar target to shoot down. It'll take a long time for those replacements to be built, though.*

Peck continued. "The Chinese appear to be able to launch one vehicle a week. Given the number of satellites destroyed, at that rate the system will be fifty percent destroyed in seventy days. That is how much time we have to build *Defender.*"

Suddenly, that three hours of sleep seemed like a lot.

Four

Skunk Works

Andrews Air Force Base, Washington, D.C.
October 1

One of Admiral Schultz's first requisitions had been an Air Force C-20F transport plane. The militarized Gulfstream executive jet was equipped for "special missions," which meant transporting high-ranking officers and government officials. It was loaded with communications equipment.

As the plane taxied for takeoff, Ray McConnell listened to Admiral Schultz as he argued with the Office of Personnel Management. Technically, as a civil servant, Ray worked for them.

"Of course I understand that you'd want to verify such an unusual order," he said calmly, almost pleasantly. "It's now been verified. And I need you to process it immediately. I know you've spoken to your director." His voice hardened a little. "I'm sure I won't have to speak to the director as well."

Schultz smiled, listening. "Certainly. There will be other personnel requests coming though this same channel, possibly quite a few. I'm certain you'll be able to deal with them all as swiftly as this one."

He turned off the handset and turned to Ray. "Congratulations. Say good-bye to Ray McConnell, SPAWAR engineer, and hello to Ray McConnell, Technical Director, U.S. Space Force."

Automatically, Ray protested. "I'm not senior enough . . ."

The admiral cut him off. "You're as senior as you need to be. You're now an SES Step 3, according to OPM." Schultz saw Ray's stunned look and smiled. "It's not about the money. You're going to be doing the work of a technical director, and you'll need the horsepower. If there was ever a test of the Peter Principle, this will be it."

Schultz leaned forward, and spoke softly and intently. "Listen, Ray, you're going to have to grow quickly. I gave you this job not because *Defender* was your idea, but because you had an original idea and put the pieces together to make it happen. Now you're going to have to do a lot more original thinking. You're going to build *Defender*, and set speed records doing it. Don't worry about bureaucratic limitations. Those are man-made. Our only barrier is the laws of physics, and I want you to bend those if you need to."

Schultz leaned even closer. "I'm also going to give you this to think about. This isn't just an engineering problem. You're going to deal with people—a lot of them, and you can't expect them all to automatically commit to *Defender* the way you have. There's a transition everyone in charge goes through as they increase in rank, from foot soldier to leader. Foot soldiers only have to know their craft, but leaders have to know their people as well."

He straightened up in his chair. "End of lecture. We're due to land in San Diego in five hours. By then, I've got to find us a headquarters and a place to build *Defender*. Your first job is to set up your construction team. Use names if you can, or describe the skills you need and let the database find them. After that—" He paused. "Well, I'll let you figure out what to do next."

Ray thought of plenty of things to do next. During the flight, Ray found himself searching thousands of personnel records, balancing the time it took to review the information with the need to fill dozens of billets. Taking a page from Admiral Schultz, he was careful to take people from all the military services, and to look for key phrases like "team player" as well as professional qualifications. He also included people from NASA, the National Weather Service, and even the FCC.

Then he went outside the government, requesting people from private industry. The government couldn't order them to participate, but if he had to, he'd hire them out from under their employers.

Remembering the JCS meeting and Captain Barnes, he called up the officer's service record. Eyes widening slightly, he'd added the pilot to his list. He could find a use for a man with his qualifications.

He added Jenny as well, without looking at her record. Somehow it seemed improper. He knew he needed comm specialists, and that he'd never have to wonder about her commitment to the project.

He also took five minutes to call Jim Naguchi at home. Ray had decided not to include Jim on the list. Although he was a good friend, he was very much involved with his own work, designing a new naval communications system. Naguchi had never shown up for any of the design sessions, either, although he knew all about *Defender.* Ray had been a little disappointed, but not everyone was as crazy as he was.

It was just before seven in California, and McConnell knew the engineer was still getting ready for work. "Naguchi here."

"Jim, I need you to clean out my office for me, and keep the stuff for a day or two. I'll send someone around to collect it."

"What?" Naguchi sounded surprised and worried at the same time. "I knew Carson was pissed. Did he bar you from the building?"

"No, it's nothing like that, Jim." Ray almost laughed. "I can't tell you everything, but I'm going to be very busy for a while. Remember *Defender*?"

"Sure."

"Has Jenny been keeping you briefed?" Ray asked.

"No, I haven't seen her for a while," he replied. "We only saw each other a few times. I was too laid-back for her. She's really competitive, Ray. We weren't good together."

"She's been over at the house a few times, with the design group," Ray remarked.

"Good for you, Ray. Brains and looks. But watch out. She's a hard charger."

Ray grinned. "I will. But get all my stuff from my office, would you please?"

"Sure, if someone doesn't think I'm ripping you off."

"No, I sent an e-mail to Rudy. He'll know. And don't tell anyone about this."

"Okay, and later you can explain where you are."

"I promise." McConnell hung up and sat, holding

the phone. He had a hundred things to think about, but Jenny kept on moving to the top of the pile. Deal with it, Ray.

He used the phone to send her some flowers, with the message, "You've saved *Defender.*"

Miramar Marine Corps Air Station, Near San Diego
October 2

Miramar was a big base, over twenty-three thousand acres of desert west of San Diego. During the Cold War it had been a Naval Air Station, home to the famous "Top Gun" fighter school. During the defense build-downs of the 1990s the Navy had moved out and the Marine Corps had moved in. They hadn't needed the whole base, though, and that made it attractive to the new U.S. Space Force.

Miramar had several airstrips, and the newly formed Defense Systems Integration Facility took over the most remote, along with a complex of unused buildings nearby. Authorization for the transfer had come in within an hour of Schultz's request, and they'd diverted the Gulfstream from their intended destination, North Island Naval Air Station, to land at Miramar.

They'd spent yesterday afternoon, after their arrival, speeding around the base with the commandant, a Marine general, in tow. General Norman had made it clear he'd been told to ask no questions, believe anything Schultz told him, and give them all the help he could.

By the time they'd finished the tour, transport aircraft had already started arriving. Schultz, as part of the security program, had ordered that as much of the supplies and as many people as possible be brought in by air.

General Norman had been more than true to his orders. Squads of Marines had appeared to unload transports. Armed patrols suddenly beefed up the perimeter. Teams of engineers had helped Public Works open and ready the buildings for use. A Marine Corps air-control unit had been flown in to handle the extra traffic, and a field kitchen had turned out their first dinner in their new home.

Besides the Marines, a gaggle of Navy officers had met the plane. During the flight to Miramar, Ray had heard the admiral dickering with his newly promoted replacement over how many of his staff could come with him and who had to stay. NAVAIR was located in nearby Coronado, so they'd all been able to get to Miramar in time to meet the plane. They would form the nucleus of the Space Forces administrative staff.

Ray had gone to sleep in a bare barracks room feeling almost optimistic.

October 3

The next morning, their first full day at Space HQ, had taught Ray more about engineering, and people, than he'd thought there was to learn.

Breakfast at 0530 had been a good start, but quickly interrupted. He and Schultz had been planning out the day when a civilian in an expensive suit and tie had hurried into the conference room being used as a mess hall. Escorted by an armed Marine, the middle-aged man had spotted the admiral and almost rushed to the table. Schultz saw him coming and stood.

The civilian had been looking for him. "Admiral Schultz? I'm Hugh Dawson, head of VentureStar Development." Dawson was tall, in his mid-fifties, and well built. Ray wondered if he'd played football in college.

Schultz smiled broadly and extended his hand. "Mr. Dawson. Please sit down and join us. We'll be working closely . . ."

Dawson did not sit down. "I don't know what we'll be working on," he replied, a little impatiently. "Yesterday afternoon my security director suddenly calls me in and briefs me into a new secret program. Then I get orders from the head of Lockheed Martin, Mr. Peter Markwith himself, to prepare VentureStar for immediate shipment here. Trash the rest of the test program, never mind the next set of modifications, just trundle her on up here for God knows what."

Schultz looked concerned, and asked, "Didn't you get the file on *Defender*?"

The executive was still standing. "I spent most of last night reading it. That has to be the worst cover story I've ever seen. Arming VentureStar? In two months? I came up here this morning to find out what's really going on."

Schultz said calmly, "That's not a cover story."

Dawson sat down.

The admiral motioned to one of the mess cooks. "Bring Mr. Dawson some coffee." He sat down facing the civilian. "I'd like you to meet Mr. Ray McConnell, Technical Director for the project, and for the U.S. Space Forces. He designed *Defender*."

Dawson automatically took McConnell's hand, but was still reacting to Schultz's words. "There's a U.S. Space Force?"

Schultz smiled proudly. "As of yesterday morning

there was, and you and VentureStar are going to be a big part of it. Did you start the preparations to move her?"

Dawson nodded, replying automatically. "Yes, we've started. You don't argue with Peter Markwith. They're finishing up some work on the flight-control systems, but that will be done by the time the carrier plane arrives. Figure two days to make her safe and preflight the carrier, and a day to mate the two." He paused, suddenly.

"Markwith said you paid four billion for the VentureStar program. The whole thing. All of a sudden, we're a DoD program."

Ray looked over at Schultz, waiting for him to respond, but the admiral said nothing. In fact, he was looking sideways at McConnell. All right, then.

"Mr. Dawson, the design is sound," Ray ventured. "The Joint Chiefs, even the President have signed off on this. I know it can work."

Dawson sat, impassive. He wasn't convinced.

Damn it. McConnell realized he knew nothing about this man. *What does he care about? There has to be one thing.*

He tried again. "The Chinese are shooting down our GPS satellites, Mr. Dawson. VentureStar can stop that. She's the only platform with the space and payload to carry all the equipment we need. In seventy days we'll have her flying, doing things nobody ever imagined her able to do, and you'll be the one making the changes. She'll still be your project."

Dawson responded, "But the time! We can't possibly do it."

"We can if we decide we can, Hugh." McConnell was getting motivated himself. "No papers, no bureaucracy, no congressional briefings. Just results."

"Some of that paper is necessary," Dawson reminded him. "They laid out the P-51 on the floor of a barn, but that doesn't work anymore."

"We'll keep some, of course, but how much of that paper is needed to do the work? A lot just fills the government in on how you're doing, or tells the boss what he needs to know. A lot of it takes the place of good supervision. I'm not here to document a failure."

Ray pressed his point. "The rules will be different here. We're going to keep this group small. And I'm the government, as far as *Defender* goes. You won't have to write a memo to me because I'll be there on the floor with you."

Dawson sat, considering for a moment. "Marilyn's going to think I've taken up with another woman," he observed, smiling. "What about security?" Dawson asked. "Our PR people will want to know . . ."

Ray smiled. One down.

By late afternoon, enough people had arrived and been settled in so that they could start preparations to receive the vehicle. Or rather, preparing to prepare.

One of the hangars was big enough, but only with extensive modifications. A launchpad would have to be built next to it. A new computer hub, independent from the net, needed to be established, and some of the buildings were so old they weren't even wired for a network. They had to decide where to put launch control. Housing needed to be expanded. And the galley arrangements. And what about recreation?

Ray's to do list made him wish for a larger data pad. He had one idea and ran it past Schultz. "I love it," the admiral said. "I'll have one of my staff get right on it."

At Ray's suggestion, the evening meal was held outside. Even in the fall, San Diego's weather was excellent, and the Marine Corps cooks fixed an impromptu barbecue.

It was an important occasion. Almost everyone was a stranger to each other, and combined with the uncertainty of the times and the mission, he'd felt the stress level ramp up all day. McConnell realized he needed to get these people together, make them one team, with one mission. Schultz had approved of this idea as well.

Ray waited just long enough for everyone to be served. It was nothing special, just burgers and fried potatoes and greens and soft drinks. Ray was too nervous to eat himself. He'd tried to eat something, at Schultz's urging, but the first two bites started circling each other in his stomach, like angry roosters squaring off.

The time had finally come, though, and Ray had climbed up on an improvised stage. The portable amplifier gave its customary squeal as he adjusted the volume, and suddenly everyone's eyes were on him.

"Welcome to Space Force HQ." He paused for a moment, and heard a few snickers, mostly from the civilians. He smiled broadly, so he could be seen in the back, "I like the sound of it. The good news is, you are all founding members of America's newest and most modern military service."

He made the smile go away. "The bad news is, we're at war. The Chinese are killing our satellites, denying us the use of space, for both military and civilian use. *Defender* is going to regain control of space for us, for our use.

"You all understand the danger we face. They

aren't on our shores, or bombing our cities, but they are overhead. And we know about the high ground.

"I'm expecting each of you, once you're settled, to take your job and run with it. More than that, though, if you see something that needs doing, don't wait for someone else to notice.

"There are going to be a lot more people coming in over the next few weeks. By the time the last of them arrives, you'll be the old hands, and I want you to tell them what I'm telling you now.

"You'll also wish we were twice as many. It's not for lack of resources. We've got a blank check from the President himself for anything or anyone we need. You're here because you're some of the best. I could have asked for more, but I didn't. A small organization thinks fast and can change fast.

"Some of you may think that this is an impossible task, or that even if it's possible, we don't have enough time to do it. It's just a matter of adjusting your thinking. The question to ask is not, 'Can this be done in time?' but 'What needs to be done to finish it in time?' "

Ray got down quickly, to gratifying applause. Schultz nodded approvingly, and Ray noticed someone standing next to him, still holding an overnight bag. Suddenly recognizing him as Barnes, Ray hurried over.

The captain took his hand, and was complimentary, although he didn't smile. "Good speech." He motioned to the crowd of perhaps fifty, eating and talking. "Did they buy it?"

Ray pointed out a small group of men and women. They sat around a circular table, talking as they ate. Their attention was on a sheet of paper in the center. One would point, or draw, and then someone else would take a turn.

"They'll never stop working on it," McConnell replied. "We should probably have a curfew so that we'll know they're getting enough sleep."

"So what do you have for me?" Barnes asked.

"We need someone to survey all the "black" DoD programs to see if there's any technology that we can use." Ray said it simply, like he wanted a list of names out of the phone book.

Barnes felt like telling him he was crazy, but only for a second. The Department of Defense ran dozens, possibly scores of "black" programs, not only classified, but also "compartmented." In other words, you didn't even know they existed unless you needed to know they existed. Each had its own security program, and it normally took a week or longer to get "briefed" into a program. Biff didn't think he had that much time.

McConnell was watching him closely. Was this some sort of test? He didn't think they had time to waste on such things. How to do it quickly?

"We'll have to go through the head of DoD security," Barnes suggested. "He's the only one who can grant me blanket access, and tell everyone to honor it."

"I'll call him tomorrow morning," said Schultz. "You'll have that clearance by lunchtime, along with Ray and me."

"We'll need a secure facility," Barnes added. High-security information was supposed to be kept in special rooms, electronically shielded, with carefully controlled access.

"We'll get you a shielded laptop tomorrow as well. That will be our secure facility until Public Works gets a real one set up."

Coronado Hotel, San Diego, California
October 4

The outside line rang, and Geoffrey picked up the phone. "Good morning, Coronado Hotel Concierge Desk. Geoffrey Lewis speaking."

"Mr. Lewis? This is Captain Munson, U.S. Navy. I'm sorry to call you at work, but we couldn't reach you before you left your home."

"The Navy?" Geoffrey was a little confused. He'd served in the Navy ten years ago, as a storekeeper. That was before he'd gotten his hotel management degree, before he started work here.

"I'll be brief, Mr. Lewis. I need someone to take care of a large group of people. They're very busy. You and a small staff will see to their needs while they work on other matters."

"Captain Munson, I'm not sure I understand. I'm quite happy . . ."

Munson named a figure over twice what Geoffrey made as a junior concierge. Lewis wasn't sure the senior concierge made that much.

"The job will last at least three months. You'll work hard for that money, and you'll have to live on site."

"And where is that site, exactly?" Geoffrey asked. The mystery of it was intriguing.

"Not too far," answered Munson carefully. "Your quarters will be quite comfortable. What's your decision?"

"Just like that?"

"Just like that," replied Munson. "We're a little pressed for time."

"The money's good," Lewis admitted. "But you don't know enough about me."

"We know quite a bit about you, Mr. Lewis. Please, if you don't want the job, I have other calls to make."

Geoffrey looked at the first thing on his list. Theater tickets for a couple from Kansas. Whoopie.

Space Forces Headquarters
October 5

Ray woke up thinking about housing. He'd gone to bed worrying about it, and was still thinking about it this morning. He was supposed to be building *Defender,* and instead he had to find places for people to live. But the first contingent of the Lockheed Skunk Works people would arrive from Palmdale this afternoon.

He hurried from the barracks past the office complex to the mess hall. None of the buildings he passed had originally served that purpose, but those were their present functions. The compound was already bustling, with people hurrying about on different errands. He could hear the sound of power tools from inside one empty building.

Coffee and a bagel were all he usually had for breakfast, and he could have had that at his desk, but people were already expecting him to put in an appearance in the morning, to be available. It was a tradition he'd decided to encourage.

He was taking his first bite when Biff Barnes walked in the door. Ray still felt uneasy about Barnes, guilty about embarrassing him at the JCS meeting. Was that why he'd picked him to work on *Defender*? But his qualifications made him a natural.

Barnes walked over to the table, and Ray motioned for the officer to join him. Ray's eyes were automatically drawn to Biff's astronaut wings.

"When were you in the astronaut program?" Ray asked. He tried not to sound like some autograph seeker.

"From '05 to '08," Barnes replied casually. "I flew one mission, then missed another because of mission change. I'd only missed one tour with the regular Air Force, so I decided to get back to real flying." His voice hardened a little. "And now this. I was supposed to get major and an Ops Officer billet after my tour in the program office. God knows what's happened to that."

Ray hadn't expected to hear that Barnes had voluntarily left the astronaut program. McConnell had worked as hard as he could for as long as he could remember to become an astronaut. And Barnes had walked away from it?

Almost without thinking, McConnell asked, "It wasn't medical?" His tone was incredulous.

"No," replied Barnes with a little irritation. "People do leave the program voluntarily. Proficiency time on T-38s is not the same as helping run a squadron or flying a fighter."

It was clear Barnes didn't think of his time as an astronaut fondly. And he was not happy with his assignment here. He liked to fly.

Ray offered, "I'm sorry I disrupted your tour, but I need pilots to help build *Defender*. In addition to all your other skills, you're a reality check on what's going on around here."

Barnes smiled, the first time Ray had seen the pilot pleased. "I think you'll need a bigger dose of reality than I can provide."

McConnell automatically smiled back. "Look, I'm sorry I upstaged you at that meeting. We had no idea the Air Force was going to back *Defender*."

"Yeah. I was the guy who suggested it to the brass."

Biff looked like he was regretting the idea.

"And thanks for that support. I'm sorry I can't promise to make it up to you."

"Stop apologizing," Biff ordered. "I'm here, and I'll help you build her."

Ray nodded silently. It wasn't a ringing commitment, but he felt the air was clear.

Biff looked around, making sure there were no eavesdroppers, then turned on his data pad and passed it to McConnell. "Here's the review of those classified programs you asked for. It took me most of the night, but it was so interesting I didn't want to stop."

McConnell took the pad, handling it carefully. As he studied the long list, his eyes widened. "I had no idea . . ."

"Neither did I. After this is all over, we'll both have to burn our brains. The point is, there are some programs here that we might be able to use. I need a secure facility to work in, to store stuff."

Ray grimaced. "The engineers are working on beefing up the handling crane. Without that, we can't lift the VentureStar off her carrier. And after that they have to start work on the pad."

"Can we get more engineers?"

McConnell shook his head. "Not quickly. We're already using all the ones available on the West Coast. We'll have more in a week." He paused, considering. "Where are the programs you're interested in located?"

Biff saw where he was going. "They're spread all over the map, but they all have offices in D.C." He paused. "I leave right away, right?"

"You can take the C-20," Ray told him. "Hell, you can *fly* the C-20. We'll have something with metal walls set up by the time you get back."

Barnes face suddenly brightened. "Ray, the C-20 has metal walls."

McConnell smiled, nodding. "We'll need to post a guard, but Marines like guarding things. It lets them carry guns. Go get it set up."

Biff nodded and left quickly, almost running. Someone else was waiting.

Space Forces Headquarters
October 5
0430

They'd scheduled the arrival carefully. You couldn't count on overcast, especially in the California desert, so they'd chosen a satellite-free window after dark.

They all got up early to see it. Ray, standing by the end of the runway with a cup of coffee, saw them start to stream out of the buildings, walking slowly over to the tarmac. The handling crews were ready, and General Norman had arranged for a "nighttime base security exercise" that filled the area with patrols. The base fire department had also sent their equipment. Ray approved, but the thought made a small knot in his stomach.

Ray waited, impatient. They'd heard nothing, so everything should be fine. But nothing would be fine, not until it was all over.

Admiral Schultz walked up with a civilian in tow. "Ray, meet Mr. Geoffrey Lewis, our new morale officer." Seeing McConnell's distracted look, he reminded Ray, "Your idea? The concierge?"

Suddenly remembering, Ray shook the man's outstretched hand. "Welcome to the Space Force, Mr. Lewis." Lewis was a sandy-haired man, in his mid-thirties. Large glasses on his round face made his head seem large for the rest of his spare frame. While most of the civilians wore jeans and polo shirts, Lewis was dressed in khakis and a sport coat.

"Thank you, Mr. McConnell. The admiral's explained what you want done. I'm to take care of the people here. Run their errands, reduce their distractions. I've never had to sign a security form to be a concierge before."

McConnell grinned. "And you've never had Army quartermasters as your staff. But these people have all had their lives and jobs interrupted to work here. Do as much as you can to take care of their personal needs."

Lewis smiled. "I've already got a few ideas."

"Here she comes," said Schultz softly.

Ray turned as Schultz spoke, his attention drawn by the plane's landing lights as they came alive. The 747's white underside reflected the lights, but everything above the wing was in shadow.

Instinctively, Ray stepped back, awed by the size of the four-engined monster. It looked a lot bigger from the ground than it did from an airport jetway. The noise of the jet engines also grew until it was almost unbearable.

Ray began to fear that some terrible mistake had been made, that the jet had come in alone, but as it descended, the light finally caught the broad white wedge on top of the 747's fuselage.

The VentureStar was just half the length of the jumbo jet, and as wide as it was long. A smooth, blended shape, two short wings jutted out from the back, angling up and back. He knew it was huge, but it looked so fragile perched on top of the big jet.

He was suddenly afraid, and his insides tightened as he watched the plane come down and touch the runway. The engines crescendoed and the noise washed over him as the pilot cut in the thrust reversers. He could smell jet exhaust and burnt rubber as the plane's wake shook his clothing. He didn't relax until the plane came to a stop, then turned to taxi over to the hangar.

VentureStar was the prototype for a fleet of commercial single-stage-to-orbit space vehicles. In development since the early 1990s, an experimental small-scale version, the X-33, had successfully completed testing just after the turn of the century.

Like the space shuttle, VentureStar carried its payload in a big cargo bay, fifteen feet wide by fifty feet long. It used the same fuel, as well, liquid hydrogen and liquid oxygen. But the shuttle took months to prepare for a launch, and used expendable boosters that had to be reconditioned after each launch. VentureStar launched using her own aerospike engines, and landed conventionally like the shuttle. She could take fifty tons to low-earth orbit after two weeks' preparation.

The engineers were already preparing to lift VentureStar off the carrier aircraft. They had barely enough time before the satellite window closed. Teams also stood by to unload the 747, which carried instruments and spare parts. Some of them had strange looks on their faces, and Ray made a note on his pad to check with the security director. There was . . .

"Thanks for the flowers, Ray." A voice startled him, breaking his concentration. He turned to see Jenny smiling at him. She explained, "I came out to watch the landing and saw you over here."

"You're welcome," he replied automatically. Gathering his wits, he asked, "Are you okay with your job?"

"Setting up communications for an entire space

program?" She laughed. "I could have waited ten years for that big a job, if I ever got it at all." She knew what he wanted to ask, and told him before he could. "I can do it. I've had to expand my consciousness a little, but I'll get it done."

She looked up at the huge spacecraft, perched on the even larger carrier plane. "This makes it real, doesn't it?" Her tone was half pride, half pleasure.

Ray caught himself about to say something stupid, about to brag about it all being his idea. But it only took one man to have an idea. It had taken a lot more to get it going, and would take that many more to bring it to life.

"It's starting to be real, Jenny." He wanted to stay, and talk, and he could see she would if he wanted to, but that wasn't why they were there.

Wishing each other good luck, they went to work.

Space Force Headquarters
October 7

His phone rang while Ray was inspecting the hangar. He'd been waiting all day. It was Schultz's voice, sounding resigned. "They've done it again. Check your pad."

McConnell activated his data pad. ". . . have confirmed the latest Chinese claim, made less than fifteen minutes ago. Another 'American targeting satellite' has been destroyed, and the Chinese renewed their promise to do the same to every American satellite unless they 'acknowledge Asian territorial rights.' "

The correspondent's face was replaced by a press conference, while his voice added, "In response to growing pressure to act, U.S. defense officials today announced a new program."

Ray's heart sank to the floor. Has some fool decided to take them public? Automatically, he started walking, while still watching the pad.

The official at the podium spoke. "To deal with this new threat to American commerce and security, an Aerospace Defense Organization has been established under the direct command of General David Warner, Chief of Staff of the Air Force. The other services will also take part. Its mission will be to defend American space assets against any aggression. Here is General Warner, who will take a few questions."

By now Ray was walking quickly, still watching the pad. He made it to Schultz's office just as the general was assuring the press that he had no intention of taking over NASA.

Ray's data pad was echoed by Schultz's wall screen. The admiral saw Ray and waved him in, with one eye on the screen. The rest of the admiral's attention was on the phone. "I appreciate the need for security, Mr. Secretary, but the effects on staff morale should have been considered. A little warning would have let us brief them. And I must have your assurance this will not affect our resources. Thank you. I'll call tonight, as always, sir. Good day."

Schultz hung up, almost breaking the little handset as he slammed it into its cradle. "Peck assures me this new organization is a blind, designed to distract attention away from us."

"And get rid of some of the heat DoD's been taking," Ray added.

"For about one week, I'll bet," Schultz agreed. "As soon as the Chinese shoot down another satellite, they'll be all over the general, asking him why he hasn't done something."

"And what about resources?" Ray asked, concerned.

"Well, he's going to need people, and money, and I have a hunch Warner's going to take his charge seriously. I'd have to agree with him, too. I'm a belt-and-suspenders kind of a guy. So he might get people or gear we need."

Ray suggested, "Well, can we draw on his program? Use it as a resource?"

Schultz sharply disagreed. "No way. We don't want any links with them. Any contacts might get traced back. And if we start poaching, we'll make enemies. We have the highest possible priority, but we can't throw our weight around. There are people in every branch of the government who would love to see us fail, if they knew we existed."

Ray sighed. "I'll put a notice on the local net, and I'll speak personally to every department head, especially Security."

Schultz's attention was drawn to the wall display. A new piece, labeled REACTION, was on. A congressman was speaking on the Capitol steps to a cluster of reporters. Schultz turned up the volume. ". . . done the math, this new Aerospace Defense Organization will have to act quickly or we'll have nothing left to defend."

Space Force Headquarters
October 13

Barnes knocked on McConnell's open door, then stepped in almost without pausing. Everything was done quickly, Barnes thought, with the formalities honored, but only barely.

McConnell, in the middle of a phone call, waved him into a folding chair, the only other seat in the office, then said into the phone, "I'll call you back." He hung up and turned to face Barnes.

Expecting to be questioned about the technology survey, Barnes started to offer his data pad to McConnell, but Ray waved it back.

"You're close to done, aren't you?"

"Yes," agreed Biff. "We've already started to receive some material. But there's a lot of follow-up to be done."

"That's old business, Biff. I need you to turn it over to someone else as soon as you can." McConnell paused, but kept looking at him. "We need you to be mission commander for the flight."

Biff didn't say anything. He absorbed the information slowly. Although he'd wondered in his few spare moments who would get to fly the mission, he'd assumed NASA would supply rated astronauts.

Did he want the job? Well, hell yes. Biff suddenly realized how much he wanted to fly in space again, and on what would be a combat mission. He knew he could do it. He was a fighter pilot, after all.

McConnell pressed a key on his data pad. "Here's a list of the prospective flight-crew candidates." Biff heard his pad chirp and saw the file appear. He opened it and scanned the list as Ray explained.

"Most are already here, a few are not, but all met the criteria Admiral Schultz and I came up with. You'll need six: A mission commander, a pilot, a copilot and navigator, a weapons officer, a sensor officer, and an engineer. We listed all our requirements. If you disagree with any . . ."

"Your name isn't here," Biff interrupted.

"What? Of course not. It's not the whole team, just the . . ."

"No," Barnes insisted. "You're flight crew. You should be the engineer. You're putting her together. You know her best."

McConnell was as surprised as Barnes had been. "What?"

"Articulate answer, Ray." Barnes grinned. "Look at it this way. It's the ultimate vote of confidence. You build it, you fly it."

McConnell couldn't say no. "This only fulfills one of my lifelong ambitions," he answered, a little light-headed.

"One of mine, too. I get to boss you around."

Five

Exposure

INN News
October 26

Mark Markin's backdrop for his scoop was an artist's animation of the Chinese ASAT weapon, the Dragon Gun as it had been dubbed in the Western press. The artist had added a hundred-foot-long tongue of flame emerging from the barrel as a projectile left the muzzle. Markin didn't know if it was accurate, but it looked dramatic.

"With the crisis now into its second month, and seven GPS satellites destroyed, continued inaction by the United States has been taken as proof of their helplessness. Their refusal to act to protect these vital assets has been puzzling.

"But the situation may not be as it seems. Presuming that the administration would not stand idle, I was able to find hints that they may be acting after all. Residents surrounding the Miramar air base east of San Diego have reported heavy traffic at the front gate and cargo aircraft arriving at all hours."

The image shifted to a picture of Miramar's front gate. "On a visit to the base yesterday, we noticed increased security, and we were not allowed to take photographs on the base. There are also portions of the base we were not allowed to visit at all. All these provisions were blamed on an increased terrorist threat, but the Marine spokesman could not tell me the source of that threat.

"There have also been stories of hurried requests at defense contractors for personnel and equipment, but these could not be verified.

"All this could be attributed to activities of the Air Force's new Aerospace Defense Organization, but why at a U.S. Marine base? And why did this activity start weeks before the ADO was announced?"

Gongga Shan Mountain
October 28

The smoke was still swirling out of the muzzle when they left the command bunker. The group was small, just the general, Secretary Pan, and their aides.

Pan Yunfeng was First Party Secretary, and General Shen continually reminded himself of that as he answered the same questions he'd answered dozens of times now.

It was impossible to speed up the firing rate. The ablative lining inside the barrel had to be replaced after each launch. In tests, two-thirds of the projectiles had been damaged when the lining was reused, and there had been one near burn-though. Better lining would be more durable, but required exotic materials that were unavailable in sufficient quantity.

No, more men would not get the tubes relined more quickly. Although a kilometer long, it was just three meters in diameter, so only a limited number of men could work inside. All the old lining had to be removed, then each section of new lining had to be anchored and tested before the next section could be added.

Unlike many of China's leaders, Pan was relatively young, in his late fifties. His hair was black, and there was an energy about him that was missing from some of the other men Shen had dealt with. His impatience personified the feeling of the entire Chinese leadership. Why was it taking so long?

Now Pan stood on the side of the mountain, nudging one of the used liners with the toe. The ten-meter section was one quarter of a circle, and several inches thick. The outside was smooth, marked with attachment points and dimples, which Shen explained allowed for some flexing as the projectile passed.

The inside curve of the liner told the real story. The concave metal surface showed hints of the former mirror polish, but the heat and gun gases had pitted the lining, some of the pits deep enough to fit a fingertip. The different layers that made up the lining were visible, a mix of metal and ceramic and advanced fibers.

"Dr. Bull came up with this solution," Shen had explained. "The best steel in the world can't withstand the forces inside that barrel when it fires. Instead we just replace the liner after each launch."

"Which takes a week," the Secretary remarked with a sour face.

"It's not wasted, First Secretary. We use the time

to upgrade the control system, test the breech, even improve the antiaircraft defenses." He pointed to a nearby hilltop, a new excavation on the side holding a massive billboard radar antenna.

"That radar is part of a new bistatic system designed to detect stealthy aircraft. We've also increased the depth of the antiaircraft belt and added more standing fighter patrols."

Later, in the general's office, Pan had questioned Shen even more, looking for ways of shaving a few days, even a few hours, off the interval between launches.

"We're concerned about the time it's taking, General. In any campaign of several months, we have to assume the enemy will take some action to counter our plans."

Shen listened respectfully. "I've seen the intelligence reports. I'm expecting, of course, that the Americans will do something eventually, but by then we will have won the first battle. And in a few months, we will have our advanced version of the T'ien Lung ready. And when you approve the construction of the second launcher, we will be even less vulnerable."

"But what measures have you taken in the meantime?"

"You know about the Long March booster modifications. You know our intelligence services are blanketing America and her allies."

Shen tried to reassure the official. "All we have to do is deny them the use of space. It's easier to shoot spacecraft down than it is to put them up. Have the Americans tried to replace any of the lost satellites? Have they launched any satellites at all since we started our campaign?"

The Secretary didn't answer, but Shen knew they both saw the same data.

Shen wanted to make his point, but was careful to keep his tone neutral. It didn't pay to argue Party officials into a corner. "The Americans have no choice. They'll either lose their valuable satellites, or publicly acknowledge our rights in the Pacific region. I think they'll wait until the last minute, refusing to accept the inevitable for as long as possible. When they do see they're backed into a corner, they'll give in. Either way, America is weaker, and we are the new champion of the countries opposing imperialism."

Space Force Headquarters, Miramar
November 5

They all looked at the wall display in Schultz's office. It showed a spiderweb of lines linking boxes. One box at the left was labeled "Begin Construction," and a dozen lines angled out of it. All the lines eventually led to a single box at the end that said "Launch." A dotted line with that day's date ran vertically across the diagram. Colors indicated the status of a task, ranging from deep red to grass green. Over half the chart was red, and a lot of the red was on the wrong side of the line.

Ray McConnell had called the meeting, officially to "brief" Schultz, unofficially to ask him to make a decision Ray couldn't.

"We've made tremendous progress." Ray hated the words as soon as he'd said them. *Trite, Ray. Be specific.* Using his data pad, he started to highlight boxes on the chart.

"The kinetic weapon rack will be installed this

week, and the mounts for the laser are being installed right now. Sensor integration is time-consuming, but we've got good people on it."

He came to one box, labeled FABRICATE LASER PROPELLANT TANKS. "It's the one thing we couldn't plan for. Palmdale only had two fabrication units, and one has gone down. The parts to fix it will take two weeks to obtain and install."

McConnell nodded in the direction of Hugh Dawson, who had become a de facto department head at Space Forces HQ. "Lockheed Martin has moved heaven and earth, but we've only got one fabricator and two tanks to make. This is what happens to the plan."

He tapped the data pad and the boxes on the wall shifted. Lines stretched. One line, darker and thicker than the others, the critical path, changed to run through the Propellant box.

"At least the heat's off the software," someone muttered.

The new schedule added three weeks to the construction schedule. Luckily, Ray didn't have to say anything, because he couldn't think of anything to say. They'd struggled to cut corners, blown through bureaucratic roadblocks, invented new procedures. They'd carried positive attitudes around like armor against the difficulty of their task. Suddenly, he didn't feel very positive.

Schultz stared at the diagram, then used his own data pad to select the Propellant Tank task. It opened up, filling the screen with tables of data and a three-dimensional rendering of the two tanks in the cargo bay of *Defender*.

Defender's laser needed fuel to fire, hypergolic chemicals stored as liquids and mixed to "pump" the weapon. The ABL-1 aircraft carried fuel for fifty shots, an extended battle. *Defender* would carry thirty, enough for three or four engagements.

While the laser and its mirror could be taken out of its 747 carrier aircraft and used almost as it was, the laser's fuel tanks had been built into the aircraft's structure. They were also the wrong size and shape for the bay. New ones had to be made.

Schultz grunted and selected the 3-D diagram. It was replaced by a schematic of the cylindrical tank, not as neat and showing signs of being hurriedly drawn. The date on the drawing showed it was a month old. The multilayered tanks were built up in sections, then the end caps were attached.

"Reduce the number of sections in each tank," remarked the admiral. "That reduces the number of welds to be made."

"We can't make the sections larger," answered Dawson. "They come prefabricated from the subcontractor, and they're limited by the size of the jig."

"Then we reduce the number of shots," Schultz replied. "What if we cut the number of shots in half, six sections per tank instead of three?"

Ray heard an inrush of breath in the room. The laser was *Defender*'s main battery. Halving its firepower was a drastic step.

Schultz said, "Better any laser on time than a laser too late. We can replace the small tanks with larger as soon as they've been built."

McConnell nodded and started working. He ticked off points as he worked. "We'll save weight by carrying less laser fuel, but we'll need more structure surrounding the tanks. It's less weight overall, but it throws off all the center-of-gravity calculations." He paused. "And we only get enough ammunition for two engagements."

While Ray worked on the design, he saw Dawson

recalculating the fabrication times. The executive finished first, and Ray watched him send the figures to the main display.

The chart shifted again, shrinking, but not enough. They were still a week late.

Ray spoke up this time. "We need more time. If we can't raise the dam, let's lower the water. Launch another satellite. That gets us a week." That was the decision he couldn't make. Would Admiral Schultz?

"At $300 million a bird, that's a pretty expensive week," Biff Barnes remarked.

Schultz nodded, agreeing with Barnes. "There are political costs as well. The public won't know why. Even the people launching the satellite won't know they're buying time for us."

Ray persisted. "There aren't any more corners to cut."

The admiral sat silently for a minute. Ray prayed for everyone to be silent. Schultz knew the situation as well as anyone in the room. He didn't look pleased, but it wasn't a pleasant situation.

"This is where I start earning my pay, I guess," Schultz announced. "All right. I'll pass this up the line." He looked over the assembled group. "And I'll make it happen. But you should all understand the political capital that will be spent here. We can't do this twice.

"You've got another week. Don't waste it."

INN News
November 11

"The addition of a name, one word, has caused the security dam around *Defender* to burst."

Holly Moore, INN's White House correspondent,

reported this piece, rather than Markin, since it covered the political implications more than the military ones. She stood on the wind-whipped U.S. Capitol steps. The image lasted only seconds, though, before being replaced by the cover of the *Defender* design document.

"INN has obtained a copy of this detailed design for an armed spacecraft designed to attack targets in space and on the ground. According to our source, it was widely distributed in classified defense circles.

"Based on the civilian VentureStar spacecraft, soon to be entering commercial service, the design equips it with radar and laser sensors, guided ground-attack weapons, and a laser from the Air Force's Airborne Laser program.

"No one in the Defense Department would comment on the document, and everyone referred us to the Aerospace Defense Organization. We also tried to contact Mr. Ray McConnell, listed on the cover as the designer, but attempts to locate him have failed. There is another list of names on the inside, all described as contributors to the document. The few INN have located have either denied knowledge of *Defender* or refused to comment.

"Sources have linked *Defender* with the mysterious activity at Miramar. Since the initial reports about this Marine air base, security has been tightened to extraordinary lengths, with a recent notice banning all flights within ten miles of the base.

"Opposition to *Defender* has appeared just since reports of its existence were aired earlier today. Some are opposed to the militarization of space. Others don't believe the spaceship can be built in time to do any good, and are asking for an accounting of the cost. Links to websites opposing *Defender*, as well as the original document, are available on our website.

"Tom Rutledge, Democratic Senator from Kentucky, spoke on the Capitol steps moments ago."

The image changed to show a tall, photogenic man with a cloud of salt-and-pepper hair fluttering in the fall wind. "As a member of the Senate Armed Services Committee, I intend to find out why we were not consulted on this wasteful and extremely risky project. The investigation will also deal with the administration's continued inability to cope with this crisis. In less than three weeks, our expensive and valuable GPS satellites will be unable to provide even a basic fix."

Moore reappeared. "Here, with a related piece, is INN's defense correspondent, Mark Markin."

Markin appeared in front of the animated Dragon Gun again. "I interviewed Mr. Michael Baldwin, a well-known expert on the NAVSTAR GPS system. I asked him how long the system would be able to function under continued Chinese attacks."

Baldwin was a slim, long-faced man in his fifties with a short gray haircut. He sat against a backdrop of jumbled electronic equipment and computer screens. He spoke with ease, secure in his knowledge. "The constellation's been severely affected. There are few places on earth now where the military can get the kind of accurate fix it needs for missile guidance or precision navigation. There are a lot of places worldwide where civilian users can't get a basic fix. This has affected not only airline travel, but also more basic functions like rail and truck shipping. We've come to expect that GPS will always be there, like the telephone or electricity."

"How long before it ceases to be any use at all?"

"If the Chinese continue shooting down satellites

at the rate of one a week, on November 25 it will be completely unusable."

The reporter asked, "Some people are saying that if we can't destroy the gun with Tomahawk missiles or air strikes, we should use nuclear weapons. What do you think of that?"

Baldwin seemed surprised by the question, but answered it quickly. "Nobody's died yet, but they're hurting the economy, and the military's ability to fight. It's too deep inside Chinese territory for anything but a ballistic missile, but I don't want us to use nuclear weapons. I don't know anyone who does." He grinned. "I'm hoping this *Defender* is real."

Markin asked, "Can we do anything to repair the constellation?"

Baldwin shook his head. "Not until they can protect the satellites somehow."

"So we shouldn't launch any replacement satellites right now?"

The expert shook his head. "That would be lunacy."

Space Force Headquarters, Miramar
November 15

"Be glad you're such a bad typist." The Security director's face was grim, but his tone was triumphant. He stood before McConnell's wall display, which held a diagram. It repeated the same symbol, an icon-sized image of the *Defender* document file. Starting at the left, it was labeled McCONNELL. Line segments connected it to other nodes, each labeled with a name and sometimes a date.

"INN took off the version number, trying to hide the source, but each version of your design had different typographical errors. We were able to determine the version number and its creation date in a half a day."

"Checking the e-mail records you gave us, we found out who received this version of the design. We also could make a good guess as to when INN got their hooks on it. We got a lot of cooperation from some of the addresses, and not much from others, which in itself helped us focus our search."

Ray had listened to the presentation with both anger and fear. INN's scoop had devastated morale. Secrecy had been part of their strength. It allowed them to move quickly, unhindered. Now friend and enemy alike could interfere with a timetable that had no room for delay.

He knew *Defender* was a long shot. The Chinese now knew where they were. Could they take some sort of counteraction? Even well-meaning friends could derail the project.

The Army colonel handed Ray his data pad. "Here's the report. I've found two individuals, one at SPAWAR and the other at NASA. Both received copies of this version, third- or fourth- or fifth-hand, and according to investigators I sent out, both have openly criticized *Defender*. One, at NASA, was quoted saying that, '*Defender* had to be stopped. It could interfere with NASA's plans for developing spacecraft technology.' "

Ray nodded, acknowledging the information, but not responding immediately. The colonel respected his silence, but obviously waited for a reply. McConnell wanted to strike out at these people, but there was little he could do.

Ray stated flatly, "The *Defender* document was never classified, so it's not a crime to release it."

"The ones who gave it to the press certainly

weren't our friends," countered the colonel. "And by exposing us, they've hurt our chances of stopping the Chinese. I'd say that's acting against the interests of national security."

"By the time we indicted them, it would be moot. Our best revenge will be to succeed." Part of Ray didn't agree with what he was saying, but he was trying to think with his head, not his emotions.

"I could give it to the press. Fight one leak with another," suggested the colonel.

McConnell shook his head slowly. "Tempting, but that would open the door to more accusations and counteraccusations. I need you for other things, now. All our energy has to go toward finishing *Defender*. We don't have to provide a cover story anymore, but we have to assume they'll try to attack us at this location. Increase our defenses accordingly. If we need to bring in a Patriot battery or a division of paratroopers, that's what we'll do."

"Meanwhile, I'll report to Schultz." Ray knew Schulz wouldn't enjoy his decision, but he knew it was the right one.

The colonel left, and Ray started to get up, to go report to his boss. But Schultz would want to know what they were doing about the exposure, and Ray knew that just increasing security wasn't the full answer.

Opposition to *Defender* was forming fast. Ray had assumed that there would be opposition, but he'd been so behind the idea he couldn't look at it objectively. Web pages already? Congressmen could order the program stopped or delayed for review.

The war in space had turned into an information war. Anyone who'd seen the news knew the media would pick up and report anything that was fed to them. Well, it was time for him to do some of the feeding.

He opened the address book on his data pad. He had contacts all over the defense and space and computer industries. They'd helped him get *Defender* started. Now he needed them again.

He started typing. "*Defender* needs your help . . ."

Six

Assembly

Gongga Shan Launch Site
November 17

Shen had insisted on having the meeting here, in the shadow of the mountain. Ignoring the recall order to Beijing had seemed suicidal, but the general knew that once away from the mountain, any flaw or error here could be blamed on his neglect. So far, the gun had worked perfectly, but that had just made him a more important target.

Friends in Beijing kept him informed. There were those who resented his success, even if it helped China against the U.S. There were those who wanted to weaken him, then take over the gun for their own political empires. Some simply thought he had too much power.

He'd been able to fabricate some sort of excuse

for remaining on the mountain, and to his relief Dong Zhi had backed him up. He'd expected the scientist to do so, but the first rule of Chinese politics was that trust was like smoke. When it was there, it blocked your vision. And it would disappear with the first puff of wind.

Instead, Dong and what seemed like half the Politburo now sat in the observation gallery, while an intelligence officer briefed them on the new American warcraft.

The Army colonel had passed out edited copies of the original design, annotated in Chinese with an engineering analysis attached. He'd reviewed the systems—the laser, the projectiles, the radar and laser sensors. The general, Dong, and the other technical people present had been fascinated. It was a dangerous craft. Shen noticed that the politicians had spent more time gazing out the window. Had they already heard it? Or were the exact details unimportant? Maybe they'd already decided.

The colonel finished his briefing, but the Politburo members wanted definite answers. When would it be ready? Would it interfere with the Dragon campaign? How could it be countered?

The colonel refused to make any conclusions. "We're still gathering information, Comrade Secretary. We have no information on how much they've actually accomplished. We're moving agents into place, but it takes time to infiltrate even with normal security, and the safeguards around the Miramar base are extremely tight."

Shen spoke up for him. There was no risk in stating the obvious. "If their design works as shown, it can interfere with our satellite attacks."

"And the chance of that happening?" Pan Yunfeng

demanded. The First Secretary had headed the delegation himself.

"Impossible to say, Comrade Secretary. However, this is not something they can build in just a few months. While the VentureStar space vehicle is complete, it had not yet been fully certified for service. It will have to be adapted to the new role, and many of the systems he describes do not exist."

"Is it possible that this is a disinformation campaign?" Pan asked the briefer.

The colonel looked at Shen, who nodded. "Unlikely, sir," the intelligence officer assured them. "The American administration is suffering intense criticism because of this now-exposed secret project. They've gained nothing from the revelation."

"Then what is its purpose?" Pan asked.

Shen replied again, his tone carefully chosen, almost casual. "Oh, they're building it, all right, but there will be very little to defend once it is operational. By that time, the new T'ien Lung II will also be ready. It has stealth features, more energy, armor, and it's semiautonomous. And we have designs for our own armed spacecraft." Shen smiled, imagining Chinese ships orbiting the earth, shattering America's military hegemony.

"We'll use the Dragon's Mother to keep them on the ground. We can destroy anything they launch."

Kunming Air Base, Xichuan Province
November 18

The aging Il-76 transport lumbered off the taxiway and stopped. A cluster of uniformed Chinese and Russian military personnel waited on the tarmac. The instant the rear ramp touched the surface, they ran aboard, and only a few minutes later, the huge GAZ missile launcher rolled out of the aircraft.

The forty-five-foot wheeled eight-by-eight truck inched out of the transport and down the ramp. Four canisters took up two-thirds the length of the vehicle, overhanging the end of the chassis.

The command and radar vehicles were already on the ground and had moved off to a clear area to one side of the hangars. Technicians swarmed over the two vehicles, checking them quickly before letting them proceed. Rail cars and loading equipment stood ready.

The first battery, consisting of the command and radar vehicle and eight launcher vehicles, was already emplaced around the base. It would protect the airfield while the rest of the equipment arrived.

National Military Command Center, The Pentagon
November 19

"At least three batteries of S-400s have arrived so far. One was used to cover the airfield, while one was sent by rail to the Gongga Shan launch site. We believe the other will be used to cover the Xichuan control center."

None of this was good news, but Admiral Overton had more to tell. He displayed a list of Russian military units, along with their strength and their location.

"Additional Russian forces, including aircraft and more SAM units, are heading for the Chinese border. These are not weapons sold to China, but active Russian units stationed in the Far Eastern Theatre. I believe that these units are going to deploy to Chinese bases.

"Although they're deployed defensively, they will free up Chinese units to move south. More disturbing are the close military ties these represent. Russian official statements have always supported the Chinese in the Vietnam crisis, but they've been quiet about their attacks on our GPS satellites. These movements may indicate that they've decided to take sides."

Overton saw their reaction, and mentally throwing the rest of his presentation over his shoulder, just summarized the rest. "A North Korean MiG-29 squadron has moved across the border, while other North Korean units are mobilizing."

He put a new list on the display. "Indian and Indonesian forces are mobilizing, for reasons not clear right now. There are even signs of activity in Iraq."

"We've only seen the early signs of mobilization, but if they continue, other powers like Japan, South Korea, and Malaysia, will have to follow suit."

General Kastner looked thinner after almost two months of crisis. He listened to Overton's brief quietly, then asked, "And the Chinese are still completely ready?"

"All the deployed units are still in place, sir, and they've begun mobilizing other units throughout the country. Half their fleet is at sea or ready for immediate steaming. Stockpiles at staging areas near the Vietnamese border have actually increased, and thanks to the Russians, the Chinese will probably be able to protect them better. They could attack the Vietnamese with less than twenty-four hours' notice."

"They certainly know about the congressional resolution," fumed Kastner. Opposition members in the House had started a resolution cutting funding for troops in Japan and Korea. "With Russia and North

Korea holding her coat, the Chinese may now feel free to act."

Kastner looked at the assembled service chiefs. "Are there any other comments?" Only the Marine general spoke. "The Chinese know they have a free hand—against Vietnam, Taiwan, wherever they want."

The Chairman said, "We all know the status of *Defender*, and their request for more time. Do we recommend for or against the replacement satellite launch? General Warner?"

The Air Force Chief of Staff controlled the GPS constellation, although it was used by all the services. "I'd hate to waste the last replacement satellite, sir. We've contracted for new birds, but it will be a long time before they're ready. I say hold it until after *Defender* proves herself."

"If we go to war, we'll need any GPS capability we can get." General Forest, the Army Chief of Staff, wasn't shy. "Even if we can't get full coverage, more partial coverage is better than less partial coverage."

"And when that coverage is lost? We only have the one spare GPS bird," Kastner reminded him. "Once we lose that satellite, we're helpless."

"The Chinese will shoot down one GPS satellite a week whether we launch a new bird or not. This buys us a week. Putting it in my terms, we're fighting a rearguard action, trading casualties for time." The soldier looked grim, but determined.

"And we hope for the cavalry," Kastner concluded. "I'll make the recommendation."

Space Force Headquarters, Miramar
November 21

Biff Barnes resisted the urge to shout, give orders, or any kind of direction. These people were supposed to do their jobs on their own. He'd be too busy to give orders when the time came.

Jim Scarelli, the designated pilot, was off working on the flight-control systems with the techs. The Lockheed Martin test pilot for VentureStar, there was no question of his ability to fly *Defender.* That part was easy.

The rest of them struggled to train on half-built systems in a jury-rigged simulator. Six metal chairs mimicked ejection seats, and plywood and plastic boxes pretended to be control consoles. A plywood arch covered them, because many of the controls were positioned on the overhead. Network and power cables were tightly bundled, but still required attention to avoid a misstep.

Steve Skeldon, the navigator and copilot, sat in the right front seat. A Marine captain, his time flying fighters was less useful than his master's degree in physics. That morning, he had taken over Scarelli's flight duties as well, which made him a very busy man.

Behind the pilot, Sue Tillman, the sensor officer, pretended to scan the earth and space. An impressive array of infrared, visible light, and radar equipment was being installed in *Defender.* Hopefully it would act like the mocked-up control panels. She also took care of the voice and data links that would tie *Defender* in to the ground-based sensors she needed.

The weapons officer on the right was Andre Baker, a captain in the U.S. Army. Although he had no flight experience, he did know lasers, and he was a ballistics expert as well.

Biff sat in the rearmost row. As mission commander, he didn't need to look out the window. The displays on his console gave him the big picture. From the back, he could also watch his crew.

Ray McConnell's chair, for the flight engineer, was on Biff's right, also in the rear. It was empty, as well. Ray was able to train only occasionally, but that was the least of Biff's worries.

Barnes worked the master console at his station. In addition to simulating his own controls, he could inject targets and create artificial casualties for the team to deal with. Right now, he was just trying to get the simulator's newest feature to behave.

"Sue, tell me what your board sees."

"Bingo! I've got an IR target, below us bearing two seven zero elevation four five. Shifting radar to classification mode. I'll use the laser ranger to back up the radar data." She sounded triumphant, and somewhere behind Biff, a few technicians clapped.

"Velocity data is firming up. It should be showing up on your board."

Biff checked his own console, and said "Yes, it is." He'd dialed in a T'ien Lung target for Sue to find, and she had. Considering they'd just installed the infrared detection feature at four that morning, it was a significant achievement.

In spite of the frustration and lost time, Biff smiled, pleased with the results. More than procedural skills, simulators taught the crew to work together through shared experience. These experiences weren't what he'd planned on, but the result was the same.

"It's good to see you smiling, Biff." McConnell's voice would have startled him a few moments earlier, but Barnes felt himself relaxing a little.

McConnell sat down in his designated chair, then clapped his hands. "Attention please! We're short of time, so we can't arrange a ceremony, but I believe these are yours."

Everyone's eyes followed McConnell as he handed a small box over to Barnes. As Biff's hand touched it, a photoflash went off, and he turned in his seat to see a photographer behind him, smiling, his camera still ready.

He opened the small dark box to see a pair of golden oak leaves.

"We thought *Defender*'s mission commander should be at least a major." Admiral Schultz stepped into Barnes's view, reaching out to shake his hand.

Barnes, surprised and pleased, automatically tried to stand, but was blocked by the console.

"At ease, Major," smiled Schultz. "I'm glad to be the first one to say that." As Biff took the admiral's hand, both automatically turned their faces to the cameraman, and the stroke flashed again.

"Thank you, sir."

"Don't thank me, thank Ray. He's the one who insisted you should wear oak leaves. A full year ahead of zone, isn't it?

"And by the way," Schultz said, raising his voice so the flight crew could all hear him clearly, "you're all going to get astronaut flight pay, backdated to the day you reported here for duty."

It was Ray's turn to look surprised. Schultz just smiled. "You had a good idea. I had a good idea."

INN News,
November 23

"Preparations to launch the only available replacement GPS satellite have brought a storm of criticism down on the administration. With only two days until the generally agreed-on deadline date, some observers have interpreted this as a desperate attempt to buy time. Others have suggested that this satellite will be used as part of a U.S. offensive, or that the satellite is being wasted in some American act of defiance."

Senator Rutledge's image, at the podium of the Senate floor, thundered with indignation. "Has our leadership lost all sense of reality? Having lost billions of dollars' worth of hardware, we're about to throw away another few hundred million. This is more than insanity."

Markin's image reappeared. "Congressional support is growing for some sort of accommodation with the Chinese. Few here believe the not-so-secret *Defender* project will ever get off the ground. The latest buzzword around the halls of Congress is 'the new reality.' "

Seven

Deadline

Xichuan Space Center, China
November 23

General Shen watched Markin's report with pleasure. American political will was beginning to weaken. Pan Yufeng, however, did not see it as clearly.

The Party Secretary, along with his aides, had watched the piece, with Chinese subtitles added. He'd only seen the problems.

"Why are they launching another navigation satellite? And how real is *Defender*?" He turned to face Shen, his tone accusing. "Your entire plan was based on the premise that the Americans could do nothing before we gained control of orbital space."

The man's frightened, Shen realized. *He's betting his political life on something he doesn't really understand.*

He's used to controlling everything, and he can't control this. He's already trying to set me up, digging my grave if this fails.

"We do control space, Comrade Pan." Shen controlled his voice carefully. He had to be respectful, but the Party Secretary needed a dose of backbone. "Right now, we can kill anything in low or mid-level orbit. Soon, we'll be able to attack even geosynchronous satellites.

"This conflict, any conflict, is about wills. We want to impose our will on the Americans. We've shown them how vulnerable they are in space, and how that vulnerability affects them down here. They are starting to realize that. Their will is starting to break.

"*Defender* is their last hope. We're ready for it. We know enough about the VentureStar design to guess at her performance, and we know they'll be launching from California. Within minutes of her launch, we'll be able to take action."

Space Force Headquarters
November 25

Ray McConnell tried to stay focused on the tour as Jenny Oh explained the Battle Center's status. He hadn't seen much of her in the past two months, although they were on the same base, working toward the same goal. He'd wanted to see her, of course, but he didn't need distractions.

Originally, she'd been assigned to set up the communications network that would support the mission. It was an immense job. She had to integrate links between Air Force's Space Command, Navy tracking stations, NASA, and even some civilian facilities. It had to be done quickly and with the real purpose secret.

All that data would be fed to a single point, the Battle Management Center, and her task had such an impact on the Center that she ended up taking over that, too. She'd done both jobs well, almost elegantly.

They'd set up the Battle Center in an empty service school. The classrooms and offices were taken over by the support staff, and the large central bay, which had housed a simulator, now held the command display. The building itself looked weathered, worn, and misused by its new occupants. The few windows had been covered, and other modifications were left raw and unpainted.

She'd met him at the door, standing proudly under a sign that said "Battle Management Center." He'd been glad to see her, of course, and had felt a little of the tension leave. He'd smiled, but it might have been a little larger than he'd intended. She smiled back, but it was a tired smile.

She seemed different, and he realized she looked harder, a little thinner, and wondered if the strain showed on him as well.

Jenny led him down the central hallway, past security, past rooms crammed with electronic equipment or people hunched over workstations. There was more security at the door to the Display Center, and a vestibule that served as a light lock.

They entered the darkened two-story room in one corner. An elevated scaffold had been erected that ran around three sides of the room. It was about fifteen feet wide, with a waist-high rail on the inside edge. The fourth wall was lined with gray equipment cabinets, and Ray could see more boxy shapes tucked under the scaffolding.

Jenny trotted up the steps to the scaffolding, putting them one story up, then led Ray along the walkway. Desks lined it, facing the center, with an aisle behind them. "This section's communications, that's electronic warfare, that's intelligence." They turned the corner. "This wall is spacecraft systems. We don't get a tenth of the telemetry that NASA gets, but we still monitor critical systems."

They turned the last corner, and she pointed to the last group, on the third side. "Admiral Schultz and his staff will sit here. I've got communications rigged to the White House, the NMCC, and to all the major commands."

He looked around the space. Everything was neatly arranged. The cabinets were fully installed. They'd even taken the time to paint safety warnings near the stairways. "It looks great, Jenny. You've done a wonderful job."

"Don't praise me yet," Jenny replied. "It's looked like this for almost a week. The real test is what's inside."

She walked over to one of the desks, labeled "Staff," and picked up a virtual-reality headset. It was an older model, and still had a cranial framework to hold the eyepieces. Slipping it on easily, she pulled on the gloves and touched a switch on the headset. He heard her say "Begin test three bravo."

The center bay, until then dark and empty, suddenly filled with a bright white sphere, easily ten feet across. It floated in the air halfway between the floor and the ceiling. Ray barely had time to see it before it changed color, becoming a deep blue. Patches of blue lightened to a medium shade, then lightened more, shifting to brown and green. He realized he was watching the world being built, starting with the deepest part of the ocean. Then higher elevations were added, one level at a time.

As Jenny tapped the air with her data gloves, points of light appeared on the surface, and Ray recognized one as Miramar. Lines appeared circling the earth, and he knew they were orbits.

Visually, it was stunning. The implications for command were even more impressive. It was the situational awareness a commander needed to fight a worldwide battle.

"Here's the hard part," Jenny announced. A flashing symbol appeared in southern China, becoming a short red line segment. A transparent red trumpet appeared around the symbol as it quickly climbed toward orbit. "This is a recording of their last intercept," she told him, taking off the helmet and watching the large display. "Here's what we added."

A new point of light flashed, at Miramar. It started to rise, and the display went dark.

The sudden blackness left Ray momentarily blind, and he heard a loud, "Damn! I wanted that to work." He could hear the frustration in her voice.

"The gear was a piece of cake. This display duplicates the one at Space Command, and I could get off-the-shelf components for nine-tenths of what we needed. Hooking it up was straightforward.

"But programming in the new systems has been difficult. We have to be able to track *Defender* in real time. The display was originally designed to show a friendly unit's location based on GPS data. We can't depend on that, so we're using radar and optical sensors all over the world to track your position. That information has to be collected and fused, then sent to the display. That software is all brand-new." She smiled a lopsided smile. "I hear they're having a lot of problems at Space Command as well."

Ray waited for a moment, then asked quietly, "Is there anything we can get that will help you finish on time?"

She shook her head. "I wish I knew what to ask for."

Her tone shook McConnell. He heard someone near the end of her rope. She'd accomplished miracles, but in a week this gear had to be rock-solid. *Defender* needed guidance from the Battle Center. They didn't have the onboard sensors to run the entire engagement from the ship.

He couldn't bring in more people. At this late date, they'd have to be brought up to speed. They wouldn't be ready in time. She certainly didn't need any more gear. If she had the resources, then it was all about leadership.

"You can do this," Ray said carefully. "I can't give you a sunshine speech. Nobody's more committed to *Defender* than you, but I think you're afraid of failing. You care so much about the project that the fear of not making it is tying you up in knots."

She almost shook as she nodded. "I don't like to fail. I never have, more so than most. And this is especially important." Jenny's fatigue was more evident now, as she leaned heavily on the rail.

Gently taking her arm, Ray led her over to a chair and sat her in it. He sat on the edge of the desk. He looked at her steadily.

"You've been a rock for me since the day this began. But also since that day, there hasn't been the time I'd like for us. I've had to say focused, and that's meant putting my feelings for you in deep freeze, until this is over. Your belief has kept me going. I hope my belief in you can do the same."

She smiled and looked up at him. "I want it to."

"Then it will." He stood. Ray tried to sound positive without being too enthusiastic. "We will make it, Jenny, and I'm glad you'll be here in the Center when I'm up."

Ray's phone beeped, and, reluctantly, Ray answered it. It was Admiral Schultz. "They're moving," he said without waiting for Ray to speak.

Ray didn't have to ask who. "Where? What are they doing?"

"Imaging satellites have been watching along the southern border. They're leaving their staging areas. They'll be in position to invade at first light tomorrow."

National Military Command Center
November 26

"There has been no communication from the Chinese government, either to us or to the Vietnamese." Secretary Peck sat next to General Kastner. He'd listened to Admiral Overton's briefing on the movement of Chinese and Vietnamese forces. Now he added a few more details, things the Joint Chiefs weren't normally privy to.

"The Chinese have purchased Russian and North Korean assistance with promises of economic concessions in Vietnam and the Spratlys."

General Forest, the Army Chief of Staff, started to laugh, out of surprise, but stopped himself.

Peck nodded. "I agree. Normally I'd say Moscow and Pyongyang would be fools for agreeing to such an arrangement. Talk about a pig in a poke."

"But the source is reliable," insisted Peck, "and we believe it shows what they all think of our chances. We've been top dog for a long time, gentlemen, but some of the dogs don't think we're that tough anymore."

"It's still a bargain made in hell," Kastner remarked.

Peck nodded. "The President publicly committed us to defend Vietnam from Chinese aggression. Now it's time to put up or shut up."

"The reasons for defending Vietnam haven't gone away," Forest reminded them.

"But the job's gotten a lot harder," said General Warner. Air Force and Navy aircraft would have been the weapons used to stop Chinese forces. Now, their power was reduced, and their vulnerability increased.

"That was the entire purpose of the Chinese plan. They knew we would commit ourselves publicly if our risk was low, and once we committed, they changed the game. It was a setup from the start, and we're trapped."

"It would still be bad if they overran Vietnam," Admiral Kramer observed. "There'd be an economic cost, and domestic and foreign political cost."

"The damage to our reputation abroad could be severe," agreed Peck.

" 'There go the Americans again, not keeping their promises,' " chimed in General Forest. "Let's use a Chinese term. It's about face. They've already gained some by giving us a black eye, and it's paying off. Does anyone want to guess how many new friends they'll have if they actually take over Vietnam?"

General Kastner shook his head. "We can't trade lives for pride."

"I have to disagree, sir," countered Forest. His tone was respectful, but firm as well. "That isn't the tradeoff. It's fight here," he paused looking around the room, "and lose some people, or fight later in a lot of different places, and against a stronger enemy. Does anyone think the Chinese will stop here? They've already promised their allies a piece of the Spratlys!"

Peck said, "What if we change the rules? Can we increase their cost?"

"Widen the war," said Kramer. "Threaten them anywhere and everywhere. We can't hit the gun, but there are a lot of targets that are in Tomahawk range, or in range of carrier aircraft. We can sink every naval unit and shoot down every aircraft we can find. And we know about the Spratlys," he said, nodding toward Peck.

"Wide-scale warfare," Kastner wondered out loud, but then his voice changed. "Hit them where they can't hit us back. I agree."

Peck nodded. "It's an option. I'll convey your recommendations to the President."

USS *Ronald Reagan* (CVN-76) in the South China Sea
November 27

On the flight deck, everything was normal, if a maelstrom of noise, metal, and hot exhaust can ever be called normal. Rows of strike aircraft sat armed and ready, while fighters and radar-warning aircraft took off and landed at regular intervals, protecting the task force.

The pilots' orders were clear. Push right up to the Chinese coast. Shoot down any aircraft in Chinese markings you find, sink any ship flying the Chinese flag. But don't cross the coast. Not until we're ready.

Below in plot, they were still trying to get ready, hours after targets had been assigned and authorization received. Squadron commanders waited impatiently while the planners struggled and argued.

The target list was ambitious, with primary, secondary, and tertiary targets assigned to each aircraft. Defense-suppression missions were supposed to arrive moments, just seconds before the strikers made their runs. Enemy defenses were supposed to be located by reconnaissance UAVs that would data-link the position back to command aircraft. Those planes would in turn task in-flight aircraft to attack those targets.

But every step in that process involved a position—a GPS position. The heavily automated precision-targeting systems had to be adapted to other, less precise navigation systems. Those systems had errors, much more error then the planners were used to. In many cases, the errors were too great for the precisely timed tactics of the manuals.

The strikes would launch, late, and the planners could not guarantee that all the strikers would come back.

Space Force Headquarters, Miramar
November 29

Ray heard the klaxon in his office. He ran outside, expecting to see fire engines racing by. His first thought, of the hydrogen and oxygen tanks at the pad, was so frightening that his mind raced, searching for some other emergency. A toxic spill? Did someone fall? Terrible things to hope for, but better than a fire in the fuel area.

He rounded the corner of his office building, which gave him a clear line of sight to the launch compound. It was over a mile away, but seemed normal. Then he heard machine-gun fire. He ran faster.

An open-topped Humvee loaded with armed Marines roared past and he waved frantically, and yelled, still running. He heard someone recognize him. "It's McConnell, hold up," and it skidded to a stop.

They made room for him in front and he jumped in, the driver flooring the accelerator. Someone behind yelled into his ear over the noise of the diesel engine.

"It's a full alert. Radar's detected a slow-moving aircraft headed for the base. He's already inside the prohibited zone, and he won't answer on the radio."

The street ended, and the open area surrounding the launchpad replaced the buildings on either side. McConnell heard the machine gun again, and located the firer from the sound. It was another Humvee with a pintle-mounted machine gun. They were stopped, and the gunner was pointing his weapon up. Ray followed the line of tracers, and saw a small speck. It looked like a light plane still a few miles away.

"He can't hit anything at that range," Ray shouted.

"He's trying to warn him off," the driver shouted back. Ray noticed the driver was an officer, a Marine lieutenant. The Marine picked up the vehicle's radio microphone. "This is Hall. I can see him. It's a light plane, a Cessna or something like it. He's at low altitude, and he's headed straight for the pad complex."

"What's he going to do?" asked McConnell.

Lieutenant Hall shrugged. "You tell me. It could be a suicide crash, or loaded with commandos. Or he could drop leaflets that say 'Save the Whales.' "

Hall continued at breakneck speed, arriving at the hangar after the longest sixty seconds of Ray's life. As the vehicle braked, Marines jumped to the ground and ran to take up positions covering the hangar and its precious resident.

Ray could see other squads racing into position, and more weapons opened up on the approaching plane. It was closer, and he could hear the plane's small engine snarl as the pilot opened up the throttle. Its speed increased slightly, and he lowered the nose. Was he going to crash the hangar?

Tracers surrounded the plane. Ray knew intellectually how hard it was to hit even a slow aircraft with a machine gun, but right then he was infuriated with the gunners who couldn't hit something that large, that slow, flying in a straight line.

It was even closer, and he could see it was a high-winged civilian plane, a four-seater. He'd flown them himself. It was nose-on, headed straight for him. The drone of the engine increased quickly, both in pitch and volume.

Although he couldn't see any weapons, he suddenly felt the urge to run for cover, but they hadn't planned for an air raid. The hangar was poor protection. Besides, wasn't that what they were aiming for?

Something fluttered away from the side of the aircraft, and for a moment Ray thought the machine gunners had actually hit. Then he recognized the shape as one of the side doors. A parachute jump? But they were too low, no more than five hundred feet.

They were almost at the hangar, and the Marines nearby had raised their weapons, tracking the plane but not firing without an order.

"Hold fire!" Hall shouted, then repeated the order into the radio. He turned to Ray. "If we hit it now, it could crash into the hangar."

"Assuming that isn't their plan," Ray muttered.

McConnell watched its path, wishing it would vanish. It didn't, but at the last moment it did veer a little to the left, and in a few seconds Ray was sure it was not headed for hangar. He couldn't feel relief.

The plane was headed for the launchpad, about a hundred yards away. He saw a man-sized object leave the plane and drop toward the ground. It had fins on one end and a point on the other. It looked like nothing so much as a giant dart.

Ray stood and watched the object fall, looking even more dartlike as it fell nose-first. Out of the corner of his eye, he saw that the Marines, with better reflexes, were all hugging the ground.

It struck almost exactly in the center of the pad, exploding with a roar. The concussion was enough to stagger him a hundred yards away, and misshapen fragments cartwheeled out from the ugly brown smoke cloud.

Ray was still standing, dazed and unsure of what to do next, when a pair of Marine SuperHornets zoomed overhead in pursuit of the intruder. His eye followed the jets as they quickly caught up with the Cessna, still in sight, but headed away at low altitude.

One of the Hornets broke off to the right, then cut left across prop plane's path. McConnell heard a sound like an angry chain saw, and a stream of tracers leapt from its nose in front of the trespasser. The other jet was circling left, and had lowered its flaps and landing gear in an attempt to stay behind the Cessna.

Lieutenant Hall's radio beeped, and he listened for a minute before turning to Ray. "They've ordered him to land, and he's cooperating." Glancing at the lethal Hornets circling the "slow mover," he said, "I sure would."

Remembering the bomb, Ray ran over to the still-smoking pad. Acrid fumes choked him, but he ignored them, then almost stumbled on the debris littering the once-smooth surface. Slowing down, he picked his way over metal fragments and chunks of concrete.

His heart sank when he saw the crater though the clearing smoke. Easily three meters across, it was at least that deep. Torn steel rods jutted out from the sides at crazy angles.

Admiral Schultz came up though the smoke, standing beside Ray and gazing at the crater. Ray saw Schultz look him up and down, then ask, "You look fine. Is everyone OK?"

Ray stared at him for a minute, then replied, "I don't know."

Schultz shook him by the shoulder, not roughly, but as if to wake him. "Ray, snap out of it. We've got to check for casualties, and see what the damage to the pad is. We can't let this slow us down."

Ray nodded, and started to check the area. He spotted people he knew, and set them to work. He saw Marines working as well, moving from person to person, making sure everyone was all right, helping some who were hurt.

Lieutenant Hall trotted up to Schultz and saluted. "Sir, they've got the intruder lined up for landing."

"Right, let's go, then." He called to McConnell. "Ray! Can you come?" McConnell had overheard the lieutenant and was already heading for the Humvee.

The lieutenant drove almost as fast to the runway as he had to the launchpad. It was located on the part of the base still being used by the Marines, and at speed, it took five minutes to cover.

Ray saw armed patrols all over the base and signs of heavier weapons being deployed. Wheeled vehicles with SAM launchers on top rumbled by, and he saw a column of tracked fighting vehicles being loaded and fueled.

A sentry at the end of the airfield spotted the Humvee's flashing light and waved them onto a taxiway, pointing to the far end. A cluster of vehicles surrounded the Cessna, and the two Hornets whoostled overhead, as if they were daring it to take off.

Ray recognized General Norman, standing to one side, as armed Marines secured the plane. Its two occupants were being half-dragged out of the plane and efficiently searched. A man and a woman, both were in their early twenties, dressed in fashionably mismatched pastel colors, their hair short on top, long on the side. To Ray's eyes, they looked like a couple of college students, straight off the campus.

"Don't put weapons in space!" one of them shouted as he was searched.

"Down with *Defender*!" the girl shouted. "We won't let you turn space into a battlefield."

Ray was in shock. He wanted to grab the two of them, show them the damaged pad, the injured being taken to the hospital. Or show them the Battle Center, and what was at stake.

General Norman's face was made of hard stone, and Schultz looked ready to order two executions on the spot. But they weren't moving or saying a word. Maybe they couldn't. But Ray didn't either. He watched the MPs cuff the two civilians and lead them away.

Later in the day, Ray reported to the admiral. Schultz's office was filled with people. General Norman occupied the only other chair, but a Marine JAG officer, the base's Public Relations officer, and *Defender*'s Security officer took up most of the remaining floor space. They'd all been waiting for Ray.

He didn't bother with introductory remarks. "The engineers say they can fix the pad by tomorrow evening. They'll use the same stuff they use to repair bombed-out runways. It won't be worth much after *Defender* uses it, but it will be fine for the launch. Some of the handling equipment was damaged, but again, it can be repaired quickly." He half smiled. "One of the advantages of jury-rigging all this gear is that it's pretty easy to fix."

Schultz just said, "Thanks, Ray," and turned to the Security officer.

"They're not Chinese agents, of if they are, the Chinese are making some bad personnel choices. Their names are Frank and Wendy Beaumont, and they're siblings, students at UCSD. They're well-known activists at the school, and belong to several political organizations. The plane's their dad's, and both have been taking flying lessons."

"We think they had help with the bomb, but only from other students. It was an improvised shaped charge. The boy, who's a sophomore, described it in detail, and claims he did it all himself, but I doubt it."

Schultz nodded, then looked at the Public Relations officer, a Marine major, who reported, "The press is having a field day with this. Half the headlines read, 'Marines Fire on College Students,' and the other half read 'Marines Fail to Protect Secret Spacecraft.' Either way we can't win. Some of them are even speculating that the *Defender* actually was damaged, and of course we can't show them that it isn't."

Schultz replied, "Let them say it is. If the Chinese think we're hurt, that's fine. Also, show them the people who were hurt in the blast.

"I just got off the phone with the hospital," he

continued. "The total is five hurt, one seriously enough to need surgery to remove a bomb fragment. All of them will recover fully."

"I'm glad nobody was killed," General Norman rumbled. "But we can't assume that there won't be another attack. I personally want to apologize for letting that plane get through. It won't happen again. The Commandant has told me I can have anything I need to protect you and this base."

"For as long as you need it, we will stay at full alert. We're keeping fighter patrols and helicopter gunships overhead twenty-four hours a day. There will be no further interruptions."

Space Force Headquarters, Miramar
December 1

Biff Barnes knocked twice on the door to Ray McConnell's BOQ room, then tried the knob. It was unlocked, and as Biff opened it, he heard someone typing. Ray sat hunched over the keyboard, in his pajamas.

"Ray, this is supposed to be a wake-up call. Remember? I told you about something called 'Crew Rest'?"

"I remembered something early this morning that I had to deal with," McConnell answered, his attention still on the screen.

"After dealing with stuff last night until one o'clock." Barnes dropped onto the edge of the bed. "I need you alert and at peak for tomorrow, Ray. When did you wake up this morning?" His question had a slight edge to it.

"Four."

"So you think three hours is enough?"

"Okay, I'll take a nap after lunch."

"That's when we're supposed to review the new sensor handoffs."

"Oh."

"Join us halfway through," Biff told him. "Now I'll see you at crew breakfast in fifteen minutes."

Barnes left and Ray quickly showered and dressed. In spite of his fatigue, it didn't take any effort to hurry, and Ray wondered what percentage of his blood was composed of adrenaline. He'd been running on nerves for way too long.

Feeling like a fool, he put on the blue coveralls Barnes had given him. The left shoulder had a patch that said U.S. SPACE FORCES, and the left breast had one that said DEFENDER, along with his name stenciled below it. Although they were attractive, if flashy, Ray didn't remember approving either design. When asked, Barnes had told him that some things were better left in the hands of fighter pilots.

Barnes had insisted on Ray wearing the coveralls at all times this week. "Of course it makes you stand out. You're flight crew, and that makes you different. Let everyone see it. You not only built *Defender*, you've got the balls to fly in her as well. That's the ultimate vote of confidence, and your people will appreciate it."

The mess hall looked better and better. Geoffrey had changed the décor again, this time from Southwest to Space. Posters of starfields and spaceships filled the walls, and the classical music was appropriately grand.

Ray hurried over to the crew table, and was gratified to see he was not late. Steve Skeldon and Sue Tillman were also just sitting down. Both of them wore military insignia with their coveralls, and made them look natural. Ray thought he probably looked all right, as long as he stood close to one of them. He still felt like a pretender.

Instead of going through the cafeteria line, Ray checked off what he wanted on a menu data pad. The theory was that the crew should be doing useful work instead of standing in line, but it was just another perk, a way of making them feel special. Ray had allowed it reluctantly.

They did work, Barnes drilling them relentlessly on safety procedures, equipment locations, technical characteristics, and each other's duties. His favorite trick was to ask one question, then ask another in the middle of the answer. The victim had to answer both correctly, in order, within seconds.

At first Ray thought Barnes was picking on him, grilling him repeatedly on engine-out procedures. Then after watching him work over the others, McConnell thought Barnes might have been cutting him some slack.

The recital continued throughout breakfast, and Barnes prepared to take the crew to the simulator. Ray found that he wanted to stay with them, but knew that there were too many last-minute problems to fix.

Part of him couldn't wait for tomorrow morning. The rest of him wanted the day to go on forever. He needed the time.

INN News
December 1
2200

Mark Markin stood as close to Miramar's front gate as he could, which meant across Miramar Way, off

Highway I-15. At night, there was still a lot of traffic on the arterial, but most of it passed by. The camera followed one heavy truck that did turn in, centering on the armed sentries that surrounded it and checked it carefully before allowing it to move on. It lingered on a dog held by one of the guards.

"Following the attack two days ago, the Marines here have increased security to extraordinary heights. Civilian traffic on and off the base has been severely restricted, and most of the traffic into the base has been official.

"All our attempts to contact the military regarding the damage inflicted by the attack have been fruitless. The Coalition against Military Space, which claims responsibility for the action, says that the launchpad was destroyed and a nearby hangar damaged. Major Dolan, the base Public Relations officer, still denies the existence of *Defender*, and is therefore 'unable to discuss damage to something that doesn't exist.' "

A grainy black-and-white image replaced Markin. It showed a squarish building with rails leaving one side. They led to a rectangular flat area, with a girder structure in the center. The framework was undercut with a sloped trench. It could only be a spacecraft launchpad.

The image was skewed, as if the camera had been tilted well off the vertical. "This photo was taken from an INN plane flying just beyond the prohibited area over the air station. Using a special lens and computer enhancement, we were able to get this image of the 'nonexistent' hangar and launchpad. While there is little that can be seen at this distance, the hangar and pad appear intact. Presumably, *Defender* is undamaged.

"INN news will monitor developments at the base

closely and let you know the instant that there are any developments."

Space Force Headquarters, Miramar
December 1
2215

Admiral Schultz turned off the wall display angrily. There was little pleasure in pushing a button. What he wanted to do was push in Markin's face. "War in a fishbowl," he grumbled.

Colonel Evans, *Defender*'s Security officer, could only agree. "Radar's tracked civilian planes flying just outside the prohibited area. There's a good chance at least one of them is an INN plane with a TV camera aboard, waiting for us to launch."

Schultz grinned. "Then let's give them something to look at. I need to talk to General Norman, and Jenny Oh. You might have to wake them, but tell them it's urgent."

Evans asked, "How about McConnell?"

Schultz shook his head. "No, let him sleep. He can't help with this, and he's got a busy day coming." He stifled a yawn. "And once he launches, I'm taking a nap."

Battle Center, Space Force Headquarters
December 2
0200

Schultz had found Jenny Oh at work, testing and refining the tracking software so critical to the mission. She also planned on sleeping after the launch.

Now she sat at the chief controller's desk, considering Schultz's idea. She was tired and worried, but it was an intriguing plan, even if it complicated these last few precious hours.

"We've run similar drills," she replied carefully. She couldn't give Schultz a resounding yes, much as she wanted to. She needed to think it through herself. "And my programmers could continue running their tests separately."

"I don't want to do anything that interferes with readiness for the launch tomorrow," the admiral assured her.

"It would mean transmitting on the launch frequencies."

"We have more than one set, don't we?" he asked.

"Yes, but only a limited number. Once they're used, we have to assume the Chinese or anyone else will be able to monitor them."

"But they're encrypted," Schultz replied.

"I don't assume anything," Jenny answered firmly.

"You're right, of course, but it's worth it." He looked at his watch. "I want it nice and dark, so you'll need to be ready by 0500 hours."

"We'll be ready."

Eight

Arrival

Gongga Shan
December 2

General Shen paced a path in the launch center. The staff, familiar with their duties, gave him a wide berth and paid attention to the upcoming launch. He left them to it. Events were taking their own course. He was no longer in complete control of the situation, and he hated it.

The launch base, always on alert for attack, was on a war footing. Every man of the garrison had been turned out, and patrols went out twice as far as usual. Flanker fighters ran racetrack patterns overhead.

They had cause to be concerned. American strikes up and down the coast had hurt the People's Liberation Army badly. Vital bases were damaged, ships had been sunk, and dozens of aircraft destroyed in the air. The Politburo had forbidden the services to discuss casualty figures, even among themselves.

Still, the American attacks had been carefully chosen to strike weak points. Heavily defended areas had been spared, so far. It was as if the Americans had lost confidence. They no longer believed in their invincibility. He hoped that feeling was right, because it meant they were weakening.

Shen knew it would be difficult for the Americans to strike so far inland, but he had to be prudent. Especially since this was where the real battle lay.

Li Zhang, the Premier, had asked the Politburo if they should seek some compromise with the Americans. Both sides stop shooting, in return for security guarantees. Pan Yunfeng, at Shen's urging, had finally convinced them to continue the launch program without interruption. Shen's reasoning had been irrefutable: Even if *Defender* really existed, there was no way to know when it would be ready to launch. A week? A month?

It was frustrating, but really irrelevant, since *Defender* would be destroyed soon after it took off. Shen was almost eager for the Americans to launch. Its appearance would resolve so much of the uncertainty he had to deal with. Its failure would break their will.

Miramar Marine Corps Air Station
0400

Admiral Schultz watched the pilot preflighting his SuperHornet. It was dark on the flight line, illumination coming from spotlights nearby. The drab gray camouflage scheme didn't reflect the lights, and the plane appeared to be built from angular shadows.

The fighter was unarmed, but carried three of the big 480-gallon drop tanks. The pilot paid a lot of attention to them.

General Norman had joined Schultz on the flight line. "It seems so simple," the general said, looking at the plane's payload.

"It'll work just fine," Schultz reassured him. "We used to have this as a problem with A-6s and F-14s. In fact, once the pilots found out how to do it, we had to explicitly forbid the practice. There are some risks."

"Which Major O'Hara understands," Norman reassured him. "But I'm taking all this on faith. I'm just a dumb grunt."

"And I'm just an old pilot." Schultz grinned at him. "I'm needed elsewhere. Would you care to join me, Carl?"

"I'd love to, Bill," replied the general.

Space Force Headquarters, Miramar
0400

Suiting up for the flight was still a novelty for Ray. He'd practiced the procedure twice before, also a fitting for the suit and other systems. Like the shuttle crew, they would work in a shirtsleeve environment, but for the launch they would wear the full rig.

McConnell moved through the morning in a haze. It didn't feel real. It had happened too fast. He felt adrift. His role in building *Defender* and preparing her for flight was over. He was so used to the pressure of the deadline that he still felt it there. Like taking finals, it took a while to realize they were over.

Add to that the fulfillment of a dream. He would fly in space. He'd flown before, of course, in light planes that he piloted and joyrides in high-performance jets. This would be much different. He'd see and feel things he'd never seen or felt before.

He knew he was afraid. There were risks, of course. Mechanical failure or human error could bring them to grief, but it was the uncertainty of the mission that really frightened him. Did they have the right tools? Ray was so closely tied with *Defender*, he felt part of her, and the thought of her failing almost paralyzed him. He remembered his talk with Jenny, and tried to say to himself the words he'd said to her.

Space Forces Battle Center, Miramar, California
0415

The visit was as important as fueling *Defender* or loading her software. Led by Biff Barnes, *Defender*'s crew filed up onto the scaffolding surrounding the slowly rotating globe of the earth. They were dressed for the mission, wearing their flight suits and, purely for photo purposes, carrying their helmets.

Although nobody announced their arrival, someone, then several people, and finally the entire center clapped and cheered as they made their way to Admiral Schultz's position.

Ray felt embarrassed and proud at the same time. He would depend on these people while he was up. In fact, without them he was helpless. But he and the rest of the crew were the ones taking the risks.

Biff Barnes understood it better. There'd always been a special bond between the people who maintained the planes and those who flew them. *Defender*'s crew was here to acknowledge that bond, and to let the support staff have one more look at the crew before launch. They were the stars of the show, but stars had to let themselves be seen.

Admiral Schultz also wanted to say good-bye and wish them luck as well. After this they would start the final launch preparations, and there'd be no time for ceremony.

Schultz shook everyone's hands, and had a few words for each member of the crew. When Ray took his hand, the normally outgoing admiral was silent for a moment, and finally just said, "Good luck."

Space Forces Launch Center, Miramar, California
0430

The crew left the ready room together and walked outside. Only a few people saw them, but they clapped and waved at the six as they approached *Defender.*

Ray had visited Cape Canaveral several times, and loved the huge Vertical Assembly Building and the massive tracked transporter that carried the assembled shuttle on its six-mile-per-hour crawl to the launchpad. They were tremendous technical achievements, needed because of the shuttle's boosters and fuel tanks. They were also tremendously expensive.

That morning, before dawn, they'd brought *Defender* out of her hangar. Two rails helped them guide her onto the pad, where she was elevated to the vertical for launching. Fueling began as soon as she was locked in place. With an 0300 rollout, she'd be ready for launch at 0600. The sheer simplicity of the preparations amazed him.

She was still an overall white, a broad snowy wedge that reflected the work lights. The swept-back wings on either side only made her look wider and taller.

The ship sat on a short framework, the beam used to elevate her now lowered again.

They'd left the American flag, but painted out the Lockheed Martin logo and the VENTURESTAR lettering. Star-and-bar insignia had been added on the wings and the center of the fuselage, top and bottom. Below the insignia, in black capital letters, was her name. To Ray, she was more than beautiful.

The crew access elevator took them two-thirds of the way up, where the square black of the open access hatch led them inside. The moment the last of them was in, technicians closed the hatch and removed the elevator.

Ray became wrapped up in the checklist. The six of them each had their own tasks, and had to work as a team to do it correctly . . .

Runway 15, Miramar Marine Corps Air Station
0530

Major Tim O'Hara smoothly lined up the jet on the runway. Night takeoffs required caution. The lights of the town in the background could confuse a pilot looking for a runway marker or a signal light. He set his brakes and watched the tower. As he waited, he checked his radio again. The transmit switch was off, and would stay off until he was ready to land.

The runway was dry and clear, the weather perfect. He fought the urge to double-check his armament panel. He did double-check that his nav lights were off. He wasn't supposed to attract any attention, and the tower would keep all other traffic clear. He heard them vectoring the standing fighter patrol to the far end of the base.

A green light flashed from the tower, and he

pushed the throttle forward to full military. The runway lights slid past him on either side, quickly becoming streaks. With long practice, he pulled back on the stick, feeling the ship almost leap off the runway. He cleaned her up, bringing up the flaps and gear.

Throttling back, he stayed low, and started his first turn quickly. Buildings rushed by frighteningly close below him, but the route had been carefully planned to avoid any obstructions. He had to stay low to avoid the civilian air traffic control radars. You could never tell who had tapped into their signal.

At jet speeds, he crossed the base almost instantly, and spotted the IP ahead. They'd decided to use the motor pool. After his turn there, it would be a straight shot to *Defender*'s launchpad.

He banked precisely over the motor pool's parking lot, then pushed the throttle to full military again. Even at low altitude, he could see the pad ahead of him, and he pointed the nose straight at it.

The jet built up speed again, quickly passing four hundred knots, and passed over a small service building he'd noted on the map. It marked the spot where he had to begin his zoom.

O'Hara pulled the nose up sharply. By the time he'd reached the vertical, he was directly over the launchpad. He hit the afterburner, and an instant later, the DUMP switch on his drop tanks. Fuel sprayed out vents on the back of the tanks and was immediately ignited by the jet's exhaust.

Accelerating, he concentrated on keeping the nose straight up, and hoped someone was getting a picture.

INN News
0532

"FLASH. This is Mark Markin, INN News, outside Miramar. We've just seen a flame rising to the east." Turning to someone off-camera, he asked, "Is it still there? Get it linked!"

Markin's face was replaced by a bright red streak moving against a black background. Jerky camera motion gave the impression of great distance. The end of the streak flickered and wavered. It seemed to be going very fast.

"Less than a minute ago, a red flash appeared in a part of the base used by the *Defender* program. The flash shot up into the sky at terrific speed, and is now fading at high altitude.

"Without any announcement, and presumably to protect the American GPS constellation, *Defender* has launched.

"I say again . . ."

Space Forces Battle Center, Miramar, California
0532

General Norman watched INN's transmission, grinning. "That's what you get for peeping over fences," he joked at Markin's image. The INN reporter was rehashing the recent event yet again.

Schultz was listening on his headset, and watching Jenny move among the launch controllers. Instead of watching their screens, they read from a paper script. Normally used for training, it drilled the controllers in what they were supposed to say at each point as they guided *Defender* during its launch. They'd practiced the procedure dozens of times, but this time their transmissions were being broadcast. Nobody was sure who would be listening in, but if anyone did, they would hear what sounded like the real thing.

Gongga Shan, December 1
0540

From the look on the controller's face, Shen knew it was an urgent call. He took the headset and heard Dong Zhi's voice. "They've launched. It's all over INN."

"What did they show?" he asked, motioning to one of the technicians. Although they had access to the Internet, they were not allowed to link INN except in "special circumstances." Shen thought this would qualify. Along with the launch staff, he watched the launch and heard Markin's commentary.

"Time of launch was 5:30 local, about ten minutes ago," reported Dong. "We've picked up increased radio traffic from Miramar, as well. We're calculating the intercept basket now."

"We're still seventeen minutes from launch here," said Shen, checking the time. He could feel a pre-battle excitement build in him. The Americans had moved.

"I recommend holding your launch until we finish the intercept," the scientist replied. "I don't want my staff having to deal with two vehicles at once. Without worldwide tracking, we'll have to move fast once the American appears."

"All right." Shen was reluctant to hold the launch,

but agreed with Dong. He knew the staff's capabilities. "I'll wait for word from you."

Dong reassured him, "Preparations for the booster have started and are on schedule. It should launch in ten minutes."

Shen broke the connection and turned to find his launch crew suddenly busy at their posts. He should be worried about the American spacecraft, but felt relieved instead. He really hadn't expected them to launch so soon. It would have a short life.

Space Force Battle Center, Miramar
0552

Wrapped up in the launch sequence, Ray was almost irritated when Schultz's voice came over the comm circuit. "SITREP, people," Schultz announced. Conversation stopped immediately, and the admiral continued, speaking quickly. "We've got a launch."

The crew all looked at their displays, expecting to see a line over Gongga Shan. Ray cursed his luck. Intel had firmly assured him that they would be able to launch before the Chinese sent up another ASAT vehicle—maybe by less than an hour, but they needed that time to get into position.

Then Ray saw it was from Jinan, farther to the north. The thin red line grew slowly, angling east and steadily climbing in a graceful curve. He heard a controller announce, "It's faster than a T'ien Lung."

"A bigger gun?" wondered Ray amazedly.

"No, that's their manned space center," replied Barnes. "It has to be a standard booster. But what's on top?"

"We can't wait to figure that out," Schultz said.

"We'll continue with launch preparations while Intelligence tries to sort it out."

It was less than five minutes later when Schultz interrupted their preparations again. With only a few minutes until ignition, Ray knew it would be important news.

"The launch was from their Jinan space complex, and the telemetry is consistent with a Long March 2F booster. That's the vehicle they use for manned launches, but it's moving too fast for a manned spacecraft. We think it has a much smaller payload."

"Aimed at us, no doubt," Barnes remarked. "An orbital SAM."

"Aimed at what they thought was us," Schultz replied. "That fireworks display was more useful than we thought."

"With that much energy, they may still be able to engage us," Ray countered.

"And with what?" asked Barnes.

"Probably another T'ien Lung," guessed Ray. "But it could be modified."

"Nukes?" Barnes didn't look worried, but some of the other crew did.

"Anything's possible."

Schultz asked, "Are we go or no-go? We can hold on the pad."

"With that thing waiting in orbit for us? No way," Ray responded. Suddenly he remembered he was out of line. Barnes should be the one answering. He looked at the major. "I recommend we go, sir."

Biff nodded, then looked at the rest of the crew. All were silent, but they all nodded yes.

"They're still aiming at something that isn't there. Let's go now, before they get a chance to regroup. We're go," Biff answered firmly.

Gongga Shan
0605

General Shen had left the INN webcast on, in the hopes that some additional information might be added, but after running out of ways to repeat themselves, they'd just started speculating. While amusing, it wasn't very useful.

He was in an unusual, in fact unique, situation. The projectile was ready, it had been for almost ten minutes, but they were not firing. Technicians sat idle, the gun crews crouched in their launch bunkers, and they waited. Xichuan was still waiting for *Defender* to appear on their tracking radars, while the interceptor raced to their best guess of its future position.

Shen found himself drawn to the INN show. Much of the material shown was coverage of the war. Most was propaganda, but the coverage was extensive. He learned a few things Beijing would certainly forbid them to discuss . . .

"FLASH. This is Mark Markin, in Miramar, California." Markin's familiar image replaced the physics professor who had been explaining *Defender*'s engines.

"We are receiving many, many reports of a spacecraft launch from inside the Miramar Marine Corps Air Station." Markin looked and acted rattled and confused.

"Our reporters at the scene and numerous civilian sources have reported another launch just a few minutes ago. They described the noise as 'shattering,' much, much louder than the event earlier this morning. What?"

Markin looked off to the side, then answered, "Good, put it up."

"Here is an image of the launch taken by a local resident who grabbed his camera when he heard the noise." The picture showed a blue sky with an angled white pillar, almost a cone, across two-thirds of the frame. A small arrowhead sat on top of the pillar.

Markin's voice said, "We're going to enhance the picture." A box appeared around the arrowhead, and Shen watched as it expanded, then rippled, and finally sharpened. Individual pixels gave it a jagged look, but he could see swept-back wings, and make out clusters of flame at the base.

"Get me Dong!" he shouted to the communications chief, then stared at the image on the screen. "Somebody print that out," he ordered, as the chief handed him a headset.

"Are you watching it, too? I don't know what we saw earlier. This one looks real enough."

Defender
0605

The experience of the launch filled Ray's senses. Every part of him inside and out was affected by the sound, which had faded, and by the acceleration that continued seemingly forever.

One far corner of Ray's mind said something about "time dilation," but the acceleration pushing him down was much more immediate. He found himself struggling to take a deep breath, although he'd been taught to take shallow breaths. The mask gave him all the oxygen he needed. There was nothing for him to do during the ascent, and he forced himself to relax, to accept the weight.

* * *

Biff watched the crew and hated the acceleration. The physical sensation was familiar to him, but his mind was filled with the responsibility he held. Mission commander. He tried to take comfort in his training as a combat pilot, but the rules were different. All the rules. Not just movement, but sensors, and weapons as well. He'd drilled himself mercilessly in the simulators, never sure if it was enough. Now he'd find out. At least he didn't have to pull lead.

Ray focused on the board, letting his body do unconsciously what he couldn't tell it to. All the systems were working well, although they'd have to deploy the sensors to really check them out. They'd traded payload for time and overengineered the shock mountings. He had a feeling that would pay off.

Risking a small movement, he touched a switch on his jury-rigged hand controller and checked the tactical display. Two screens simultaneously displayed a side and overhead view of the situation. The Chinese intercept vehicle, marked TL1 on the display, was above them, but eastbound. They had launched to the north, into a polar orbit. Its high velocity would make it difficult, no, almost impossible, to attack *Defender.*

Gongga Shan
0610

General Shen knew that as well. And there were other problems. He pressed his point over the link to Xichuan. "If we try to intercept *Defender* on the next orbit, the T'ien Lung will be out of our view for over an hour. We can't tell what the Americans will do to it during that time.

"Instead, we should use it to kill another GPS satellite. Their orbits are fixed, and it's got plenty of energy for the intercept. I'll attack *Defender* with my weapon instead."

"It's our last shot," Dong countered. "Shouldn't we use it to kill a GPS satellite? Two kills in one day, both while *Defender* is supposed to be protecting them, will be even a bigger embarrassment."

Shen disagreed. "Better to destroy *Defender*. We may have missed with the Long March, but that doesn't change the value of the target."

It was Shen's decision to make, but he wanted Dong to agree. His people would now have to handle the two vehicles, although only for a short time. Although he knew they could, the general asked, "Can you do it?"

"Yes," Dong admitted.

"Then tell them to prepare. We'll be firing in less than five minutes." He raised his voice for the last sentence, and the staff in the center hurried to obey.

"One more thing," General Shen added. "Tell Beijing we need to initiate the special attack." Shen lowered his voice without trying to sound conspiratorial. Security was so tight even his launch staff didn't know about it.

"Good," Dong answered, sounding relieved. "Liang has been after me to use it since the first launch this morning."

Battle Center
0615

Jenny noticed it first. She ran the whole Center, but without communications, there was no Center. Consequently, she dedicated one of her displays to continuously monitoring the data links from dozens of other sites. These included command centers like NORAD and the NMCC, radar-tracking stations, and intelligence aircraft orbiting off the China coast. The Battle Center had no sensors of its own, but took the data from all these sources and created the global situation display.

The audio beep and the flashing red icon had her immediate attention. She called one of the controllers on her headset. "Carol, check on the link to Kwajalein. We've lost the signal."

No sooner had the controller acknowledged her order than another link went red, this time the one to Pearl Harbor. Used to looking for patterns, she instantly compared the two, but could see no similarity. Pearl was a command site.

She started to detail another of her small staff to check out the link to Hawaii when a third one went red, this time in Ascension, and then others, coming so rapidly it was hard to count.

"Admiral, we're losing all our sensors!" Jenny tried to control the panic in her voice. She started to listen to Schultz's reply when Carol cut in with a report on the Kwajalein tracking station.

"I'm in voice comms, Jenny. They say the gear's fine, but they're under electronic attack. Someone's hacking their controller."

"That's impossible," Jenny exclaimed before realizing how silly that sounded. She paused, examining the situation, then suggested, "Their filters must be down. They're supposed to reject anything that's not encrypted."

"They say this stuff is encrypted," Carol explained, "at least well enough to get through the filters."

"We've got another launch," a different controller

reported. "This time from Gongga Shan."

Jenny saw the track appear on the globe and checked the sensor log. The detection had been made by an Air Force surveillance aircraft, one of several off the coast. So far they hadn't been . . .

The globe, smoothly rotating in the center of the room, suddenly stopped, then moved jerkily before freezing again. What now?

Even as she switched her headset to the computer staff's channel, Chris Brown, the head of the computer section, reported. "We're being flooded. Someone's sending bogus tracking data over the links."

"The filter's aren't stopping it?" Jenny asked.

"Not all of it."

Jenny walked over to Brown's console and watched him analyze the false information being sent from supposedly secure sites. "Here's the header data on one that got through. It's good."

"They're not all getting through the filters?"

"No, about one in ten makes it." He tapped his console, bringing up another stream of data. "This one has a similar header, but the encryption isn't quite right, and it was rejected."

"But the ones that do get through are enough," he continued. "They force our system to chew on each for a while before rejecting it, and for every real packet, we're getting dozens of these fakes."

"Jenny, I need to know what's happening." Admiral Schultz's voice in her headset was soft, but insistent. She looked across the open space at the admiral, who met her gaze expectantly.

"We're under electronic attack, sir, through our tracking stations. It's sophisticated. They not only deny us sensor information, but they're piggybacking bad data on the links to bog us down."

"How do we block it?"

She sighed. "I'll have to get back to you, sir."

Chris Brown had been listening to her conversation with the admiral, and spoke as soon as she signed off. "It's completely down now. We just lost sensor processing."

Defender
0620

They were still setting up when Jenny called. The pilots, Scarelli and Skeldon, had opened the bay doors, then Andre Baker, the weapons officer, extended the laser turret above the bay. While the specialists readied their gear, Ray watched power levels and the health of the data link.

He'd noticed the problems a few minutes earlier, but had concentrated on the systems at his end. The thought of the Battle Center going down left him feeling very alone.

Her message clarified the situation but didn't help solve it. "Ray, we've lost sensors. We're under attack down here." Her words chilled him, but he forced himself to be silent, to listen. She explained the problem, but its effects were obvious. They were on their own. She could not say when they'd be back on-line.

Suddenly Ray felt vulnerable. Somewhere below, another T'ien Lung was climbing toward them.

Biff Barnes looked at the display screens. They were flat and two-dimensional, nothing like the Battle Center's fancy displays. He selected different modes, looking at projected paths and engagement envelopes.

He ignored the new threat, somewhere below

them. They could do nothing about it, so he'd decided to work on the one target they did have.

Ray looked over at Barnes studying the display. "They've missed their chance at us. They'll have to go for a satellite."

"I agree," Biff responded. "Look at this." He sent the plot to Ray's console. It showed the remaining GPS satellite tracks and the area covered by the Chinese tracking radars.

"The easiest one to reach is number eighteen, here." He highlighted one of the satellites. "If they make a course change anytime in the next half hour, they can nail it. They'll be able to watch the intercept, as well."

Barnes waited half a moment while McConnell studied the screen. Ray nodded slowly. "All right," the engineer replied. It was almost a question.

"We're taking it out," Biff stated. "Right now. Before it gets any farther away. Before TL2 shows up to ruin our morning. Pilot, align us on TL1. Crew, engage TL1."

Ray watched the stars and the earth spin slowly as Scarelli oriented the open bay so it faced toward the Chinese spacecraft. The distance was a problem, but at least they didn't have to maneuver to keep the target in *Defender*'s limited sensor arc.

Sue Tillman, the sensor officer, went from busy to extremely busy. She fiddled with the radar settings, then chose one of a number of search patterns for the radar to follow. Everything had to be done manually, and that took time.

The lieutenant finally reported, "I've got a hit with the radar, 151 miles, 330 relative, 80 degrees elevation. Changing to track mode." A few moments later, she said, "Track established."

Checking another display, she reported, "IR confirms."

Ray suppressed the urge to comment on the gear actually working.

By rights, the detection should have been automatically tracked and evaluated. But systems integration takes valuable design time. Instead, it was all done manually, and with each second the target moved farther away.

Captain Baker, the weapons officer, didn't miss a beat. He'd slaved the laser to the data sent by the Tillman's radar. "Ready," he reported, as calmly as if he reporting the weather.

Ray had seen the seven-ton laser turret tested on the ground. The motors made an unholy whine. Now, there was no sound, just a slight vibration felt through the ship's structure, as it tracked the target.

"It's at the edge of our envelope," Ray reminded the major.

"And I figured out what that envelope was. Shoot six shots."

Ray felt more thuds and vibrations as pumps pushed chemicals into a combustion chamber. The intense flash of their ignition "pumped" the chemical laser and a two-megawatt beam angled out and away.

Inside *Defender*, Ray watched five seconds come and go. Sue Tillman, looking disappointed, turned to look over Captain Baker.

The weapons officer watched a spectrograph slaved to the laser mirror.

"Nothing," he reported.

Set for five shots, the laser automatically fired again. McConnell watched a TV camera set to cover the bay. Puffs of vapor left the combustion chamber, and he could see the turret slowly moving, but it was a silent combat.

Both Baker and Tillman spoke this time. The army officer announced triumphantly, "I've got an aluminum line." The laser had caused part of the target to glow. Baker's spectrograph had seen that light, and told him what that part was made of.

Tillman confirmed, "IR's up now. It's a lot hotter than before."

"But it's still there on radar?" Barnes asked.

She nodded. "Trajectory's unchanged."

"Continue firing."

The third shot, five seconds of intense energy, also struck the Chinese vehicle, but with no better result than before. Ray fought the urge to fiddle with the systems display, or remind Barnes that the target was growing more distant with every shot.

They'd spent a lot of time trying to decide how they would know when they'd actually "killed" a target. You couldn't shoot down something in space, and at these distances they couldn't see the effects of their attacks.

During the fourth shot, Biff asked, "Sue, can you measure the temperature rise?"

"No, sir. The equipment's resolution isn't that fine. Physics says it can't radiate heat away as fast as we're adding it, but we're also adding less heat with each shot, because of the increasing distance."

By the time she answered Barnes's question, the fifth shot of the salvo had been fired as well. They'd used up almost half the magazine, but the mission commander didn't wait a moment. "Keep firing. Another five."

Well, we're here to shoot down satellites, Ray thought. He tried to stay focused on his monitors, watching for signs of trouble. It would be hell if a mechanical failure interfered at this point.

Tillman saw it first, on the second shot of the new salvo. "IR's showing a big heat increase!"

"Spectrograph's full of lines!" Baker reported triumphantly. "I've got silicon, nitrogen. . . ."

"Kill the laser!" Biff ordered. "Silicon means the electronics, and nitrogen's either solid propellant or the explosive warhead."

"There's also hydrogen and plutonium," she added, her voice a little unsteady.

Barnes nodded as if he'd expected it. "They were gunning for us."

"Multiple contacts. Radar shows debris as well," Tillman confirmed. *Defender*'s millimeter-wave radar would have no trouble distinguishing individual pieces of wreckage.

"It's a kill," she said with satisfaction. Sue Tillman also handled voice comms with Miramar, and said "They're cheering in the Battle Center!"

Ray noted the time. They'd been up half an hour.

Gongga Shan
0635

"It's gone, sir!" The communications tech handed him the headset. Shen listened to Dong's report quietly. The Americans had destroyed the special T'ien Lung. They'd made the kill at long range, on an opening target. *Defender* was more than capable.

Shen worked to control his surprise and disappointment, making his face a mask. *Defender* had proved itself. Now more than before, it was vital that the second vehicle destroy the American spacecraft. Unfortunately, there was nothing more he could do to ensure its success. Like countless commanders before him, Shen could only wait for the dice to stop rolling.

Battle Center
0635

"It's a brute force attack, Jenny." Chris Brown sat surrounded by display screens. Some showed packets of invading data. Others listed tables of statistical data—numbers of packets sent from each site, numbers rejected by the filter, amount of processor time lost, and many other values.

"They don't have our encryption completely broken, but they've learned enough to get through occasionally. See," he said, pointing to two invading data packets. "The body of the message is the same. And most of the header data is valid. All they have to do is vary the part they don't know.

"And they're getting better at it. Look at this curve." It showed the percentage of successful penetrations since the attack began, and the number steadily increased.

Jenny forced herself to think clearly, to ignore the rest of the center and the craft in space above her. This was a battle of minds.

"The encryption key is time-based," Jenny said. "To mimic it at all, they'd have to be monitoring our communications in real time."

"Then that's what they're doing," replied the computer analyst. "All of the communications are hardened land lines." Jenny had insisted on that, for obvious reasons.

"Except the signal to *Defender*," countered Brown.

"Which we have to leave up," finished Jenny. That link was the reason for the Battle Center's existence. She visualized the flow, out from the Center, picked up by intercept antenna somewhere, then fed back into the system though pirated computers. The Chinese were using their own codes against them.

"Chris, we have to change the encryption schemes."

"That won't help, they'll only . . ."

"Only for the link to *Defender*," she continued. "Right now we all use the same coding scheme. Change the time-based key for *Defender*'s link, and the filters will reject it automatically."

Brown's face lit up. "Yeah, I can even optimize the coding to make it easier for the filters to spot. I can use a modifier . . ."

The analyst trailed off into thought, but quickly resurfaced. "I'll have to upload a patch to *Defender*, but the Chinese haven't interfered with the link. I can have us up in five minutes."

Jenny hurried back to her own console, keying her handset as she went. "Good news, Admiral."

Defender
0645

Brown's patch had an immediate effect. Cut off from the ground, the computer had been displaying the estimated position of the second T'ien Lung. It had been close, but the uncertainty of the estimate had prevented them from taking any action.

Now, within moments, the display flashed with the real position of TL2. A red arc showed its track history, a red dot its present location, and a red cone its possible future position. *Defender*'s orbit lay square in the center of that cone, and another flashing symbol showed the intercept point.

Intercept was only five minutes away. They couldn't hope to set up and kill it before it reached them. Barnes ordered "Countermeasures!" and then told the pilots, "Take this vector. Pull in the turret, close the doors."

Ray saw the stars swing again, then felt pressure against his back as *Defender*'s engines came to life. They quickly increased to full power. The rest of the crew quickly carried out Barnes's orders, bringing the laser turret inside.

The doors might protect the turret against small fragments from the T'ien Lung if it did detonate. Of course, with the doors closed, they were blind as well as defenseless. More than ever, Ray felt grateful for the data link.

Scarelli had oriented the craft so that its top side faced the T'ien Lung. They'd argued about it during one of the many strategy sessions, and decided they'd rather have fragments in the doors and upper fuselage than in the heat shield. They could live without weapons and sensors, but they couldn't reenter without the heat shield.

The acceleration wasn't as bad as takeoff, but it was still intense, and mixed with uncertainly.

His board showed the same tracks as Barnes's, as well as other ship's systems. He watched the radar decoys leave the ship, a cluster of simple radar corners, based on their best guesses about the design of the kill vehicle's sensors.

McConnell also watched as the line of *Defender*'s orbit slowly curved. The engines stopped, and Ray saw that they were just outside the Chinese intercept cone.

The arc carrying the T'ien Lung did not change

for two long minutes. It finally started to shift, back toward an intercept on their new course. "Look at that," Barnes said, pointing to the display. "Their reaction times are very slow."

He waited for a moment, then announced, "They're not buying the decoys. All right, pilot, now take this vector. Stand by for a long burn, people."

This time Ray was ready for the acceleration, and better still, welcomed it. The Chinese lag in controlling the T'ien Lung would be their undoing.

Barnes's new course zigged *Defender* away from the T'ien Lung, exactly opposite to the course correction the Chinese vehicle was making. *Defender*'s engines were more powerful than the T'ien Lung's thrusters. The Chinese vehicle had been designed to engage satellites, not maneuverable spacecraft.

"Past closest point of approach!" the copilot reported. Skeldon didn't sound relieved. The Chinese could always command-detonate the warhead if they felt there was a chance of damaging them.

They did, after another thirty extra seconds of distance. There was no sound of explosion, but two sharp bangs, like rifle shots, sounded over their heads, and part of Ray's board went from green to red and yellow. One corner of his eye noted that the symbol for the second T'ien Lung was now gone from the screen.

Ray reported, "We're losing hydrogen pressure. One of the tanks has been holed!"

"Continue the burn," Barnes ordered. "Move as much hydrogen out of the tank as you can before it escapes."

"Doing it," Ray responded. "It'll screw up our center of gravity," he warned.

"Compensating," responded Scarelli. "What about that other strike?" the pilot asked.

"That'll take a little sorting out," Ray replied.

Part of the electrical system flashed red, but what was the problem? Was it a component, or the wiring? They'd installed redundant lines on the critical systems. It was time to see if it was working. He started isolating components. His mind focused on the technical problem, he hardly noticed the acceleration.

There. "Primary actuators for the ailerons are offline. Backups seem all right." But something else aft still glowed red. He closed a few more systems, but the news wasn't good. "We've lost number three hydrogen pump."

"Which means no number three engine," Scarelli continued.

"We can cope," Barnes reassured him. "We don't have another burn until we reenter."

The burn finished, and Ray was surprised by the sudden weightlessness. His stomach complained a little, but he mastered it.

Barnes asked. "Jim, how long until we're over Xichuan?"

Scarelli checked his plot, then answered, "Twenty-three minutes. That last burn brought our orbit right over them!" He looked at Barnes with a "How'd you do that?" expression.

The major grinned. "I picked the first burn vector directly away from where I wanted us to end up. That way I could make the long burn in the right direction. Set up for ground attack. Here are the targets."

Ray watched as he designated two points on the map display. Scarelli had to make one small burn to refine the course, then he and Skeldon turned *Defender* so her bay faced the globe of earth below.

After that, they waited. Baker and Tillman checked out their equipment, and pilots monitored their course. For the first time since they had taken off,

Ray had a moment to realize he was in space.

His stomach was still under control, and they were all strapped in anyway. No floating during General Quarters, he mused. He looked at the monitors, one of which showed the earth "above" them. They were over the North Pole, coming down on the other side of the world from California. It seemed different, somehow. Smaller, and more vulnerable.

"Five minutes," Scarelli warned, and Baker and Tillman both acknowledged. Ray and Barnes both watched silently as the specialists worked. Tillman reported "Imaging first target," and activated her radar. The millimeter-wave signal easily found the Xichuan space center, a cluster of large buildings. Ray selected the radar display, and studied the buildings. They'd seen it before in satellite photographs, and he quickly picked out the administration buildings, the control center, the powerhouse, and the other structures. The image was clear enough to show the chain-link fence that surrounded the compound.

Baker designated his rods, and Ray saw three small symbols appear over the control center, and two more on the antennas. "Ready for drop," he reported.

"Drop on the mark," Barnes ordered calmly.

"Roger, in ten," the weapons officer replied, and then counted the seconds down. "Dropping now."

Ray saw his board change but felt nothing.

The rods were not as noisy or complex as the laser. Each simply consisted of a long, pointed tungsten cylinder weighing fifty kilograms, with a small motor and finned guidance unit on the back. Springs ejected them in quick sequence from their rack in *Defender*'s bay, and McConnell watched the stream drift clear of the ship.

As fast as the rods had been ejected, their individual motors fired, driving them down toward the earth and reentry. The tungsten projectile would easily withstand the heat, and was aerodynamically shaped. The guidance unit would burn up, but by then they'd be aligned on their target, and with so much speed that nothing would deflect them.

Xichuan was still several hundred miles ahead of them, but of course the rods needed that time to cover the distance to the ground. It also made it difficult for the Chinese to predict where the attack would strike. If they could even see *Defender*. The ship was approaching from the north, where Chinese radar coverage was limited.

"Five minutes to next target," Baker announced.

Gongga Shan
0720

The call came over a standard phone line, not the command net. General Shen Xuesen took the receiver from the communications chief.

"General, this is Wu Lixin." Shen knew the man. He was one of Dong's assistants at the control center. He sounded absolutely shattered.

"Wu, what's happened?"

"They bombed us, sir. Dong is dead, and so are most of the staff. The center's gone, ripped apart."

"Bombs. Was it an air attack?"

"No, no airplane, nothing was seen. No planes, no missiles."

The general felt his heart turn to ice. It had to be *Defender*. So the detonation hadn't hurt them at all. They were still capable.

Shen looked at their predicted orbit. She was moving from north to south, and . . .

"Out! Everybody outside right now! Head for the shelters!" he turned to the comm chief. "Get the gun crews out as well." Theoretically, the gun and the control bunkers were hardened, but Xichuan's control center had been hardened as well.

There was no way to tell when, or even if, an attack would happen, but Shen wasn't risking his people's lives. The instant he saw everyone in the center moving, he headed for the door himself.

He sprinted outside, intending to head for one of the slit trenches that had been dug nearby, but he had made it no more than a dozen steps before the explosions started.

It wasn't from behind him, but from the mountain, to his right. He turned just a little and saw a series of bright yellow explosions ripple over the gun's location. Earth spouted into the air hundreds of feet, and he could feel the concussions from over a kilometer away.

At least three deadly flowers blossomed at the base of the gun, right over the breech. Another four or five landed in a neat line on top of the barrel, and another three clustered closely around the muzzle. In the darkness, the mountain was outlined for several seconds by the flash from the explosions.

One of the first group must have found the liquid-propellant piping, because the entire building suddenly disintegrated in a ball of orange flame. Pieces of debris arced high into the air, and Shen suddenly found himself running again, diving headfirst into the trench as pieces of cement, steel, and rock began raining down on him.

The deadly rain stopped, and Shen untangled himself from the others who had sought shelter with him in the trench. Reluctantly, he knelt, and then stood, a little unsteadily. Knowing and hating what he would see, he nonetheless had to find out what they'd done to his gun.

The breech building was gone, replaced by a crater filled with flaming debris. Most of the installation had been below ground, and the crater had carved a massive gouge out of the mountain's roots.

The slope of the mountain looked almost untouched, but a line of craters neatly followed the path of the gun barrel, and the mouth was hidden in a mound of loose rock.

Five years of work. Ten years of convincing. Twenty years of dreaming, all lost. His friend Dong was dead, with many of China's brightest dead with him. How many bodies would they find just in the ruins below?

Shen realized others were trying to help him out of the trench. Passively, he let them lift him out and steady him on the grass. He turned automatically to head for the center, and saw it was in ruins, flames outlining the ruined walls. He hadn't even heard the explosions.

It was finished. Shen was suddenly very sorry he'd lived.

Defender

With most of their fuel used up, they'd made one small burn to line up for reentry after two more orbits. With nothing to do but wait, Ray felt his sensation of unreality return. His mind and emotions sought to understand this new experience.

They'd fought and won a battle in space. He'd played a role, a major one, in making it happen, but he knew he wasn't the only one. More importantly, others would follow after him. Not all would be Americans, maybe not all of them would be friends, but warfare had changed, as it always does.

Biff Barnes checked the displays over and over again, looking for the smallest fault, but the ship was performing well. Reentry was now only a few minutes away. Scarelli and Skeldon were handling the preparations perfectly.

For some reason Barnes was having problems trying to determine how he would fill out his personal flight log. Would the T'ien Lungs count as "kills"? Three more to become an "orbital ace"? He suspected there would be more missions after this one.

That thought led to another, and he started to make a mental list of improvements *Defender* would need before she flew again.

Battle Center

Jenny Oh fought hard to keep her emotions under control. Her first cheer, when *Defender* had destroyed the first T'ien Lung, had been followed by another when they'd escaped the second kill vehicle. Her heart had leapt to her throat when she saw the symbols for *Defender* and the kill vehicle merge, and then soared when they'd said all were safe.

And that had been followed by the destruction of the Dragon Gun at Gongga Shan. They'd watched it all on *Defender*'s imaging radar, data-linked down to the Center. The sudden transformation of the neat structural shapes to rubble had been unmistakable, and she'd yelled as loud as any of them. It was the success of everything they'd worked so hard for. *Defender* had proven herself.

Jenny had looked over at Admiral Schultz, who sat quietly, his head in his hands. He stayed that way, aware but silent, for some time. After the celebration stopped, he'd left, then come back later, in time to watch the reentry. He slowly walked over to Jenny's station, checking his watch as he approached.

"Check INN," the admiral suggested, smiling. It was just 1600.

Jenny selected to broadcast, and saw Markin's now-familiar face. Behind him was a commercial satellite image of the destroyed gun. Markin was excited, almost frantic.

"Flash! Only a short time ago sources revealed the destruction of the Gongga Shan Dragon Gun by *Defender*, and also the destruction of two orbital kill vehicles. The Chinese attempted to use these to shoot down the American spacecraft and a GPS satellite, but according to my source, both weapons were destroyed after an extended battle."

"Extended battle?" Jenny wondered aloud.

"Well, it was extended in orbital terms." The Admiral's smile widened.

"*You're* his source?" Jenny asked, almost shouting, and then controlling her voice.

"This time, yes. I felt bad about bamboozling him earlier this morning. There's no more need for secrecy, and I figured the best way for the media to get it straight was to get it straight from me."

They watched Markin's piece together for a few more minutes, as he detailed the engagements in space and the damage to the Chinese. Finally, he started to repeat himself, and Jenny checked the status board. *Defender* was now blacked out, and would be until she finished reentry.

The admiral watched her for a moment, then said, "Congratulations, Jenny. You made it happen."

"Congratulations to all of us, Admiral. We all did it."

"We all believed we could make it work, Jenny, and worked our tails off to prove it to the rest of the world. But you and Chris Brown saved the mission. Chris is a civilian, and he'll get a commendation for his civil service file. I'm recommending you for the Navy Cross. Nobody fired a shot in your direction, but you were in the fight as much as anyone. Your quick thinking saved lives, and won a battle."

Jenny felt herself flush, and she automatically came to attention. "Thank you, sir!" Then she wavered. "But what about *Defender* . . ."

Schultz waved a hand, cutting off her protests. "Oh, yes, there'll be medals and parades and all the glory a grateful nation can provide. They've earned all of it."

"Do you think Ray will be able to get a little free time?" she asked quietly.

LARRY BOND is forty-nine and lives with his wife, Jeanne, and daughters, Katie and Julia, in Virginia outside Washington, D.C. After coauthoring *Red Storm Rising* with Tom Clancy, he has written five novels under his own name: *Red Phoenix, Vortex, Cauldron,* and *The Enemy Within.* The latest is *Day of Wrath,* which was published by Warner Books in June 1998. His writing career started by collaborating with Tom Clancy on *Red Storm Rising,* a runaway *New York Times* best-seller that was one of the best-selling books of the 1980s. It has been used as a text at the Naval War College and similar institutions. Since then, his books have depicted military and political crises, emphasizing accuracy and fast-paced action. *Red Phoenix, Vortex,* and *Cauldron* were all *New York Times* best-sellers.

He has also codesigned the *Admiralty Trilogy* series of games, which includes *Harpoon, Command at Sea,* and *Fear God & Dreadnought.* The first two have both won industry awards, while the third will be published in late 2000.

Now in its fourth edition, *Harpoon* won the H. G. Wells Award, a trade association honor, in 1981, 1987, and 1997 as the best miniatures game of the year. It is the only game to win the award more than once. The computer version of the game first appeared in 1990, and won the 1990 Wargame of the Year award from *Computer Gaming World,* an industry journal.

LEADERSHIP MATERIAL

BY DALE BROWN

ACKNOWLEDGMENTS

Thanks to Don Aldridge, Lt. General, USAF (ret.), former vice commander of the Strategic Air Command, for his help and insights on the inner workings of an Air Force promotion board, and to author and former B-52 radar nav Jim Clonts for his help on living and working on Diego Garcia.

Special thanks to my friends Larry and Maryanne Ingemanson for their generosity.

March 1991

The alarm goes off at 6 A.M., the clock radio set to a soothing easy-listening music station. Air Force Colonel Norman Weir dresses in a new Nike warm-up suit and runs a couple of miles through the base, returns to his room, then listens to the news on the radio while he shaves, showers, and dresses in a fresh uniform. He walks to the Officers' Club four blocks away and has breakfast—eggs, sausage, wheat toast, orange juice, and coffee—while he reads the morning paper. Ever since his divorce three years earlier, Norman starts every workday exactly the same way.

Air Force Major Patrick S. McLanahan's wake-up call was the clatter of the SATCOM satellite communications transceiver's printer chugging to life as it spit out a long stream of messages onto a strip of thermal printer paper, like a grocery-store checkout receipt gone haywire. He was sitting at the navigator-bombardier's station with his head down on the console, taking a catnap. After ten years flying long-range bombers, Patrick had developed the ability to ignore the demands of his body for the sake of the mission: to stay awake for very long periods of time; sit for long hours without relief; and fall asleep quickly and deeply enough to feel rested, even if the nap only lasted a few minutes. It was part of the survival techniques most combat aircrew members developed in the face of operational necessity.

As the printer spewed instructions, Patrick had his breakfast—a cup of protein milk shake from a stainless-steel Thermos bottle and a couple pieces of leathery beef jerky. All his meals on this long overwater flight were high-protein and low residue—no sandwiches, no veggies, and no fruit. The reason was simple: no matter how high-tech his bomber was, the toilet was still the toilet. Using it meant unfastening all his survival gear, dropping his flight suit, and sitting downstairs nearly naked in a dark, cold, noisy, smelly, drafty compartment. He would rather eat bland food and risk constipation than suffer through the indignity. He felt thankful that he served in a weapon system that *allowed* its crew members to use a toilet—all of his fighter brethren had to use "piddle packs," wear adult diapers—or just hold it. *That* was the ultimate indignity.

When the printer finally stopped, he tore off the message strip and read it over. It was a status report request—the second one in the last hour. Patrick composed, encoded, and transmitted a new reply message, then decided he'd better talk to the aircraft commander about all these requests. He safetied his ejection seat, unstrapped, and got to his feet for the first time in what felt like days.

His partner, defensive systems officer Wendy Tork, Ph.D. was sound asleep in the right seat. She had her arms tucked inside her shoulder straps so she wouldn't accidentally trigger her ejection handles—there had been many cases of sleeping crew members dreaming about a crash and punching themselves out of a perfectly good aircraft—her flying gloves on, her dark helmet visor down, and her oxygen mask on in case they had an emergency and she had to eject with short notice. She had her summer-weight flight jacket on over her flight suit, with the flotation-device harness on over that, the bulges of the inflatable pouches under her armpits making her arms rise and fall with each deep sleepy breath.

Patrick scanned Wendy's defensive-systems console before moving forward—but he had to force himself to admit that he paused there to look at Wendy, not the instruments. There was something about her that intrigued him—and then he stopped himself again. *Face it, Muck,* Patrick told himself: *You're not intrigued—you're hot for her. Underneath that baggy flight suit and survival gear is a nice, tight, luscious body, and it feels weird, naughty, almost* wrong *to be thinking about stuff like this while slicing along forty-one thousand feet across the Gulf of Oman in a high-tech warbird. Weird, but exciting.*

At that moment, Wendy raised the helmet's dark visor, dropped her oxygen mask, and smiled at him. Damn, Patrick thought as he quickly turned his attention to the defensive-systems console, those eyes could melt titanium.

"Hi," she said. Even though she had to raise her voice to talk cross-cockpit, it was still a friendly, pleasant, disarming sound. Wendy Tork, Ph.D., was one of the world's most renowned experts in electromagnetic engineering and systems development, a pioneer in the use of computers to analyze energy waves and execute a particular response. They had been working together for nearly two years at their home base, the High Technology Aerospace Weapons Center (HAWC) at Groom Lake Air Station, Nevada, known as Dreamland.

"Hi," he said back. "I was just . . . checking your systems. We're going over the Bandar Abbass horizon in a few minutes, and I wanted to see if you were picking up anything."

"The system would've alerted me if it detected any signals within fifteen percent of detection threshold," Wendy pointed out. She spoke in her usual hypertechnical voice, female but not feminine, the way she usually did. It allowed Patrick to relax and stop thinking thoughts that were so out of place to be thinking in a warplane. Then, she leaned forward in her seat, closer to him, and asked, "You were looking at me, weren't you?"

The sudden change in her voice made his heart skip a beat and his mouth grow dry as arctic air. "You're nutty," he heard himself blurt out. Boy, did *that* sound nutty!

"I saw you though the visor, Major Hot Shot," she said. "I could see you looking at me." She sat back, still looking at him. "Why were you looking at me?"

"Wendy, I wasn't . . ."

"Are you sure you weren't?"

"I . . . I wasn't . . ." *What is going on?* Patrick thought. *Why am I so damned tongue-tied? I feel like a school kid who just got caught drawing pictures of the girl he had a crush on in his notebook.*

Well, he did have a crush on her. They'd first met about three years ago when they were both recruited for the team that was developing the Megafortress flying battleship. They had a brief, intense sexual encounter, but events, circumstances, duties, and responsibilities always prevented anything more from happening. This was the *last* place and time he would've guessed their relationship might take a new, exciting step forward.

"It's all right, Major," Wendy said. She wouldn't take her eyes off him, and he felt as if he wanted to duck back behind the weapons bay bulkhead and stay there until they landed. "You're allowed."

Patrick found himself able to breathe again. He relaxed, trying to look cool and casual even though he could feel sweat oozing from every pore. He held up the SATCOM printer tape. "I've got . . . we've got a message . . . orders . . . instructions," he stammered, and she smiled both to chide him and to enjoy him at the same time. "From Eighth Air Force. I was going to talk to the general, then everybody else. On interphone. Before we go over the horizon. The Iranian horizon."

"You do that, Major," Wendy said, a laugh in her eyes. Patrick nodded, glad that was over with, and started to head for the cockpit. She stopped him with, "Oh, Major?"

Patrick turned back to her. "Yes, Doctor?"

"You never told me."

"Told you what?"

"Do all my systems look OK to you?"

Thank God she smiled after that, Patrick thought—maybe she doesn't think I'm some sort of pervert. Regaining a bit of his lost composure, but still afraid to let his eyes roam over her "systems," he replied, "They look great to me, Doc."

"Good," she said. "Thank you." She smiled a bit more warmly, let her eyes look him up and down, and added, "I'll be sure to keep an eye on your systems too."

Patrick never felt more relieved, and yet more naked, as he bent to crawl through that connecting tunnel and make his way to the cockpit. But just before he announced he was moving forward and unplugged his intercom cord, he heard the slow-paced electronic "DEEDLE . . . DEEDLE . . . DEEDLE . . ." warning tone of the ship's threat-detection system. They had just been highlighted by enemy radar.

Patrick virtually flew back into his ejection seat, strapped in, and unsafed his ejection seat. He was in the aft crew compartment of an EB-52C Megafortress bomber, the next generation of "flying battleships" Patrick's classified research unit was hoping to produce for the Air Force. It was once a "stock" B-52H Stratofortress bomber, the workhorse of America's long-range heavy-bombardment fleet, built for long range and heavy nuclear and nonnuclear payloads.

The original B-52 was designed in the 1950s; the last rolled off the assembly line twenty years ago. But this plane was different. The original airframe had been rebuilt from the ground up with state-of-the-art technology not just to modernize it, but to make it the most advanced warplane . . . that no one had ever heard of.

"Wendy?" he radioed on interphone. "What do we got?"

"This is weird," Wendy responded. "I've got a variable PRF X-band target out there. Switching between antiship and antiaircraft search profiles. Estimated range . . . damn, range thirty-five miles, twelve o'clock. He's right on top of us. Well within radar-guided missile range."

"Any idea what it is?"

"Could be an AWACS plane," Wendy replied. "He looks like he's scanning both surface and air targets. No fast PRFs—just scanning. Faster than an APY scan, like on an E-2 Hawkeye or E-3 Sentry, but same profile."

"An Iranian AWACS?" Patrick asked. The EB-52 Megafortress was flying in international airspace over the Gulf of Oman, just west of the Iranian coastline and just south of the Strait of Hormuz, outside the Persian Gulf. The director of the High Technology Aerospace Weapons Center, Lieutenant General Brad Elliott, had ordered three of his experimental Megafortress bombers to start patrolling the skies near the Persian Gulf to provide a secret, stealthy punch in case one of the supposedly neutral countries in the region decided to jump into the conflict raging between the Coalition forces and the Republic of Iraq.

"Could be a 'Mainstay' or 'Candid,' " Patrick offered. "One of the aircraft Iraq supposedly surrendered to Iran was an Ilyushin-76MD airborne early-warning aircraft. Maybe the Iranians are trying out their new toy. Can he see us?"

"I think he can," Wendy said. "He's not locking on to us, just scanning around—but he's close, and we're approaching detection threshold." The B-52 Stratofortress was not designed or ever considered a "stealth" aircraft, but the EB-52 Megafortress was much different. It retained most of the new anti-radar technology it had been fitted with as an experimental test-bed aircraft—nonmetallic "fibersteel" skin, stronger and lighter than steel but nonradar-reflective; swept-back control surfaces instead of straight edges; no external antennas; radar-absorbent material used in the engine inlets and windows; and a unique radar-absorbing energy system that retransmitted radar energy along the airframe and discharged it back along the wing trailing edges, reducing the amount of radar energy reflected back to the enemy. It also carried a wide variety of weapons and could provide as much firepower as a flight of Air Force or Navy tactical fighters.

"Looks like he's 'guarding' the Strait of Hormuz, looking for inbound aircraft," Patrick offered. "Heading two-three-zero to go around him. If he spots us, it might get the Iranians excited."

But he had spoken too late: "He can see us," Wendy cut in. "He's at thirty-five miles, one o'clock, high, making a beeline for us. Speed increasing to five hundred knots."

"That's not an AWACS plane," Patrick said. "Looks like we picked up some kind of fast-moving patrol plane."

"Crap," the aircraft commander, Lieutenant General Brad Elliott, swore on intercom. Elliott was the commander of the High Technology Aerospace

Weapons Center, also known as Dreamland, and the developer of the EB-52 Megafortress flying battleship. "Shut his radar down, Wendy, and let's hope he thinks he has a bent radar and decides to call it a night."

"Let's get out of here, Brad," Patrick chimed in. "No sense in risking a dogfight up here."

"We're in international airspace," Elliott retorted indignantly. "We have as much right to be up here as this turkey."

"Sir, this is a combat area," Patrick emphasized. "Crew, let's get ready to get the hell out of here."

With one touch, Wendy ordered the Megafortress's powerful jammers to shut down the Iranian fighter's search radar. "Trackbreakers active," Wendy announced. "Give me ninety left." Brad Elliott put the Megafortress in a tight right turn and rolled out perpendicular to the fighter's flight path. The plane's pulse-Doppler radar might not detect a target with a zero relative closure rate. "Bandit at three o'clock, thirty-five miles and steady, high. Moving to four o'clock. I think he lost us."

"Not so fast," the crew mission commander and copilot, Colonel John Ormack, interjected. Ormack was HAWC's deputy commander and chief engineering wizard, a commander pilot with several thousand hours in various tactical aircraft. But his first love was computers, avionics, and gadgets. Brad Elliott had the ideas, but he relied on Ormack to turn those ideas into reality. If they gave badges or wings for technogeeks, John Ormack would wear them proudly. "He might be going passive. We've got to put some distance between us and him. He might not need a radar to intercept us."

"I copy that," Wendy said. "But I think his IRSTS is out of range. He . . ."

At that moment, they all heard a loud, faster-paced "DEEDLE DEEDLE DEEDLE!" warning on the intercom. "Airborne interceptor locked on, range thirty miles and closing fast! His radar is huge—he's burning right through my jammers. Solid radar lock, closure rate . . . closure rate moving to *six hundred knots*!"

"Well," John Ormack said, "at least that water down there is warm even this time of year."

Making jokes was the only thing any of them could think about right then—because being highlighted by a supersonic interceptor alone over the Gulf of Oman was just about the most fatal thing a bomber crew could ever face.

This morning was a little different for Norman Weir. Today and for the next two weeks Weir and several dozen of his fellow Air Force full colonels were at Randolph Air Force Base near San Antonio, Texas, for a lieutenant colonel's promotion board. Their task: pick the best, the brightest, and the most highly qualified from a field of about three thousand Air Force majors to be promoted to lieutenant colonel.

Colonel Norman Weir knew a lot about making choices using complex objective criteria—a promotion board was right up his alley. Norman was commander of the Air Force Budget Analysis Agency at the Pentagon. His job was to do exactly what he was now being asked to do: sift through mountains of information on weapon and information systems and decide the future life-cycle costs and benefits of each. In effect, he and his staff of sixty-five military and civilian analysts, accountants, and technical experts decided the future of the United States Air Force every day. Every aircraft, missile, satellite, computer, "black box," and bomb, along with every man and woman in the Air Force, came under his scrutiny. Every item on every unit's budget had to pass his team's rigorous examination. If it didn't, by the end of the fiscal year it would cease to exist with a single memo to someone in the Secretary of the Air Force's office. He had power and responsibility over billions of dollars every week, and he wielded that power with skill and enthusiasm.

Thanks to his father, Norman decided on a military career in high school. Norman's father was drafted in the mid-sixties but thought it might be safer serving offshore in the Navy, so he enlisted and served as a jet power-plant technician on board various aircraft carriers. He returned from long Pacific and Indian Ocean cruises with incredible stories of aviation heroism and triumph, and Norman was hooked. Norman's father also came home minus half his left arm, the result of a deck munition explosion on the aircraft carrier USS *Enterprise*, and a Purple Heart. That became Norman's ticket to an appointment to the United States Naval Academy at Annapolis.

But Academy life was hard. To say Norman was merely introverted was putting it mildly. Norman lived inside his own head, existing in a sterile, protected world of knowledge and reflection. Solving problems was an academic exercise, not a physical or even a leadership one. The more they made him run and do push-ups and march and drill, the more he hated it. He failed a physical-conditioning test, was dismissed with prejudice, and returned to Iowa.

His father's almost constant niggling about wasting his appointment and dropping out of the Naval Academy—as if his father had chosen to sacrifice his arm so his son could go to Annapolis—weighed heavily on his mind. His father practically disowned his son, announcing there was no money for college and urging his son to get out and find a job. Desperate to make his father happy, Norman applied and was accepted to Air Force Reserve Officer Training Corps, receiving a degree in finance and an Air Force commission, becoming an accounting and finance specialist and earning his CPA certification a few months later.

Norman loved the Air Force. It was the best of all worlds: He got respect from the folks who respected and admired accountants, and he could demand respect from most of the others because he outranked and outsmarted them. He pinned on a major's gold oak leaves right on time, and took command of his own base accounting service center shortly thereafter.

Even his wife seemed to enjoy the life, after her initial uncertainty. Most women adopted their husband's rank, and Norman's wife spit-shined and paraded that invisible but tangible rank every chance she got. She was "volunteered" by the higher-ranking officers' wives for committeeships, which at first she resented. But she soon learned that she had the power to "volunteer" lower-ranking officers' wives to serve on her committee, so only the wives of lower-ranking officers and noncommissioned officers had to do the heavy work. It was a very neat and uncomplicated system.

For Norman, the work was rewarding but not challenging. Except for manning a few mobility lines during unit deployments and a few late nights preparing for no-notice and annual base inspections, he had a forty-hour workweek and very little stress. He accepted a few unusual assignments: conducting an audit at a radar outpost on Greenland; serving on advisory staffs for some congressional staffers doing research for a bill. High-visibility, low-risk, busywork assignments. Norman loved them.

But that's when the conflicts began closer to home. Both he and his wife were born and raised in Iowa, but Iowa had no Air Force bases, so it was guaranteed they weren't going home except to visit. Norman's one unaccompanied overseas PCS assignment to Korea gave her time to go home, but that was small comfort without her husband. The frequent uprooting hurt the couple unequally. Norman promised his wife they'd start a family when the cycle of assignment changes slowed down, but after fifteen years it was apparent that Norman had no real intention of starting a family.

The last straw was Norman's latest assignment to the Pentagon to become the first director of a brand new Air Force budget oversight agency. They said it was a guaranteed four-year assignment—no more moving around. He could even retire from that assignment if he chose. His wife's biological clock, which had been ringing loudly for the past five years, was deafening by then. But Norman said wait. It was a new shop. Lots of late nights, lots of weekends. What kind of life would that be for a family? Besides, he hinted one morning after yet another discussion about kids, wasn't she getting a little old to be trying to raise a newborn?

She was gone by the time he returned home the next evening. That was over three years ago, and Norman hadn't seen or spoken to her since. Her signature on the divorce papers was the last thing he ever saw that belonged to her.

Well, he told himself often, he was better off without her. He could accept better, more exotic assignments; travel the world without having to worry about always going either to Iowa in the summer or to Florida in the winter, where the in-laws stayed; and he didn't have to listen to his ex-wife harping about how two intelligent persons should be having a better, more fulfilling—meaning "civilian"—life. Besides, as the old saying went: "If the Air Force wanted you to have a wife, they'd have issued you one." Norman began to believe that was true.

The first day at the promotion board at the Selection Board Secretariat at the Air Force Military Personnel Center at Randolph was filled with organizational minutiae and several briefings on how the board worked, the criteria to use during the selection process, how to use the checklists and grading sheets, and an overview of the standard candidate's personnel file. The briefings were given by Colonel Ted Fellows, chief of the Air Force Selection Board Secretariat. Fellows gave a briefing on the profile of the candidates—average length of service, geographical distribution, specialty distribution, and other tidbits of information designed to explain how these candidates were selected.

Then, the promotion board president, Major General Larry Dean Ingemanson, the commander of Tenth Air Division, stepped up before the board members and distributed the panel assignments for each board member, along with the Secretary of the Air Force's Memorandum of Instruction, or MOI. The MOI was the set of orders handed down by the Secretary of the Air Force to the board members, informing them of who was going to receive promotions and the quotas for each, along with general guidelines on how to choose the candidates eligible for promotion.

There were three general categories of officers eligible for promotion: in-, above-, and below-the-primary zone candidates. Within each category were the specialties being considered: line officers, including flying, or rated, officers, nonrated operations officers such as security police and maintenance officers, and mission-support officers such as finance, administration, and base services; along with critical mission-support subspecialties such as Chaplain Corps, Medical Service Corps, Nurse Corps, Biomedical Sciences Corps, Dental Corps, and Judge Advocate General Corps. General Ingemanson also announced that panels could be convened for any other personnel matters that might be required by the Secretary of the Air Force.

The board members were randomly divided up into eight panels of seven members each, adjusted by the president so each panel was not overly weighted by one specialty or command. Every Air Force major command, direct reporting unit, field operating agency, and specialty seemed to be represented here: logistics, maintenance, personnel, finance, information technology, chaplains, security police, and dozens of others, including the flying specialties. Norman noticed right away that the flying or "rated" specialties were especially well represented here. At least half of all the board members were rated officers, mostly unit commanders or staff officers assigned to high-level posts at the Pentagon or major command headquarters.

That was the biggest problem Norman saw in the Air Force, the one factor that dominated the service to the exclusion of all else, the one specialty that screwed it up for everyone else—the flyers.

Sure, this was the U.S. *Air* Force, not the U.S. Accountant Force—the service existed to conduct battles in the national defense by taking control of the sky and near space, and flyers were obviously going to play a big part. But they had the biggest egos and the biggest mouths too. The service bent over backward for their aviators, far more than they supported any other specialty no matter how vital. Flyers got all the breaks. They were treated like firstborns by unit commanders—in fact, most unit commanders were flyers, even if the unit had no direct flying commitment.

Norman didn't entirely know where his dislike for those who wore wings came from. Most likely, it was from his father. Naval aircraft mechanics were treated like indentured servants by flyers, even if the mechanic was a seasoned veteran while the flyer was a know-nothing newbie on his first cruise. Norman's dad complained loud and long about officers in general and aviators in particular. He always wanted his son to be an officer, but he was determined to teach him how to be an officer that enlisted and noncommissioned officers would admire and respect—and that meant putting flyers in their place at every opportunity.

Of course, it was an officer, a flyer, who ignored safety precautions and his plane captain's suggestions and fired a Zuni rocket into a line of jets waited to be fueled and created one of the biggest noncombat disasters at sea the Navy had ever experienced, which resulted in over two hundred deaths and several hundred injuries, including Norman's father. A cocky, arrogant, know-it-all flyer had disregarded the rules. That officer was quickly, quietly dismissed from service. Norman's unit commanders had several times thrown the book at nonrated officers and enlisted personnel for the tiniest infractions, but flyers were usually given two, three, or even four chances before finally being offered the opportunity to resign rather than face a court-martial. They always got all the breaks.

Well, this was going to be different. *If I get a flyer's promotion jacket,* Norman thought, *he's going to have to prove to me that he's worthy of promotion.* And he vowed that wasn't going to be easy.

"Let's hit the deck," Patrick said.

"Damn fine idea," Brad said. He yanked the Megafortress's throttles to idle, rolled the plane up onto its left wing, and nosed the big bomber over into a relatively gentle six-thousand-foot-per-minute dive. "Wendy, jam the piss out of them. Full spectrum. No radio transmissions. We don't want the whole Iranian air force after us."

"Copy," Wendy said weakly. She scrambled to catch flying pencils and checklists as the negative Gs sent anything unsecure floating around the cabin. Switching her oxygen regulator to "100%" helped when her stomach and most of its contents threatened to start floating around the cabin too. "I'm jamming. He's . . ." Suddenly, they all heard a fast-pitched "DEEDLEDEEDLEDEEDLE!" warning, and red alert lights flashed in every compartment. "*Radar missile launch, seven o'clock, twenty-five miles!*" Wendy shouted. "*Break right!*"

Elliott slammed the Megafortress bomber into a hard right turn and pulled the throttles to idle, keeping the nose down to complicate the missile's intercept and to screen the bomber's engine exhaust from the attacker as much as possible. As the bomber slowed it turned faster. Patrick felt as if he were upside down and backwards—the sudden deceleration, steep dive, and steep turn only served to tumble his and everyone's senses.

"*Chaff! Chaff!*" Wendy shouted as she ejected chaff from the left ejectors. The chaff, packets of tinsel-like strips of metal, formed large blobs of radar-reflective clouds that made inviting spoof targets for enemy missiles.

"Missiles still inbound!" Wendy shouted. "Arming Stingers!" As the enemy missiles closed in, Wendy fired small radar- and heat-seeking rockets out of a steerable cannon on the Megafortress's tail. The Stinger airmine rockets flew head to head with the incoming missiles, then exploded several dozen feet in the missile's path, shredding its fuselage and guidance system. It worked. The last enemy missile exploded less than five thousand feet away.

It took them only four minutes to get down to just two hundred feet above the Gulf of Oman, guided by the navigation computer's terrain database, by the satellite navigation system, and by a pencil-thin beam of energy that measured the distance between the bomber's belly and the water. They headed southwest at full military power, as far away from the Iranian coastline as possible. Brad Elliott knew what fighter pilots feared—low-altitude flight, darkness, and heading out over water away from friendly shores. Every engine cough was amplified, every dip of the fuel gauge needles seemed critical—even the slightest crackle in the headset or a shudder in the flight controls seemed to signal disaster. Having a potential enemy out there, one that was jamming radar and radio transmissions, made the tension even worse. Few fighter pilots had the stomach for night overwater chases.

But as Wendy studied her threat displays, it soon became obvious that the MiG or whatever it was out there wasn't going to go away so easily. "No luck, guys—we didn't lose him. He's closed inside twenty miles and he's right on our tail, staying high but still got a pretty good radar lock on us."

"Relaying messages to headquarters too, I'll bet," Elliott said.

"Six o'clock, high, fifteen miles. Coming within heater range." With the enemy attacker's radar jammed, he couldn't use a radar-guided missile—but with IRSTS, he could easily close in and make a heat-seeking missile shot.

"Wendy, get ready to launch Scorpions," Brad said.

"Roger." Wendy already had her fingers on the keyboard, and she typed in instructions to warm up the Megafortress's surprise weapon—the AIM-120 Scorpion AMRAAM, or Advanced Medium-Range Air-to-Air Missile. The EB-52 carried six Scorpion missiles on each wing pylon. The Scorpions were radar-guided missiles that were command-guided by the Megafortress's attack radar or by an onboard radar in the missile's nose—the missiles could even attack targets in the bomber's rear quadrant by guidance from a tail-mounted radar, allowing for an "over-the-shoulder" launch on a pursuing enemy. Only a few aircraft in the entire world carried AMRAAMs—but the EB-52 Megafortress had been carrying one for three years, including one combat mission. The enemy aircraft was well within the Scorpion's maximum twenty-mile range.

"Twelve miles."

"When he breaks eight miles, lock him up and hit 'em," Brad said. "We gotta be the one who shoots first."

"Brad, we need to knock this off," Patrick said urgently.

Wendy looked at him in complete surprise, but it was Brad Elliott who exclaimed, "What was that, Patrick?"

"I said, we should stop this," Patrick repeated. "Listen, we're in international airspace. We just dropped down to low altitude, we're jamming his radar. He knows we're a bad guy. Forcing a fight won't solve anything."

"He jumped us first, Patrick."

"Listen, we're acting like hostiles, and he's doing his job—kicking us out of his zone and away from his airspace," Patrick argued. "We tried to sneak in, and we got caught. No one wants a fight here."

"Well, what the hell do you suggest, nav?" Brad asked acidly.

Patrick hesitated, then leaned over to Wendy, and said, "Cut jamming on UHF GUARD."

Wendy looked at him with concern. "Are you sure, Patrick?"

"Yes. Do it." Wendy reluctantly entered instructions into her ECM computer, stopping the jamming signals from interfering with the 243.0 megahertz frequency, the universal UHF emergency channel. Patrick flipped his intercom panel wafer switch to COM 2, which he knew was set to the universal UHF emergency channel. "Attention, Iranian aircraft at our six o'clock position, one hundred and seventy-six kilometers southeast of Bandar Abbas. This is the American aircraft you are pursuing. Can you hear me?"

"Patrick, what in *hell* are you doing?" Elliott shouted on interphone. "Defense, did you stop jamming UHF? What in hell's going on back there?"

"That's not a good idea, Patrick," John offered, sternly but not as forcefully as Elliott. "You just told him we're Americans. He's going to want to take a look now."

"He'd be crazy to answer," Brad said. "Now stay off the radio and . . ."

But just then, they heard on the radio, "*Shto etah? Nemalvali pazhaloosta.*"

"What the hell was that?" Wendy asked.

"Sounded like Russian to me," Patrick said.

Just then, in broken English, they heard, "American aircraft at my twelve of the clock position from my nose, this is Khaneh One-Four-One of the Islamic Republic of Iran Air Force. I read you. You are in violation of Iranian sovereign airspace. I command you now to climb to three thousand meters of altitude and prepare for intercept. Reduce speed now and lower your landing-gear wheels. Do you understand?"

"One-Four-One, this is the American aircraft. We have locked defensive weapons on to your aircraft. Do not fly closer than twelve kilometers from us or you will be attacked. Do you understand?"

"Range ten miles."

"You are at sixteen kilometers," Patrick radioed. "Do not come any closer."

"Patrick, this is *nuts*," Brad said. "You're going to try to convince him to turn around? He'll never go for it."

"Nine miles. Closure speed five hundred knots."

"One-Four-One, you are at fourteen-point-five kilometers, closing at thirteen kilometers per minute. Do not, I repeat, do not fly closer than twelve kilometers to us, or you will be attacked. We are not in Iranian airspace, and we are withdrawing from the area. This is my final warning. Do you understand?"

"Eight miles . . ."

"One-Four-One, we have you at twelve kilometers! Break off now!"

"Stand by to shoot, Wendy! Damn you, McLanahan . . . !"

"Here he comes!" Wendy shouted. "Closure rate . . . wait, his closure rate dropped," Wendy announced. "He's holding at eight miles . . . no, he's slowing.

He's climbing. He's up to five thousand feet, range ten miles, decelerating."

"Cease jamming, Wendy," Patrick said.

"What?"

"Stop jamming them," Patrick said. "They broke off their attack. Now we need to do the same."

"Brad?"

"You're taking a big damned chance, Muck," Brad Elliott said. He paused, but only for a moment; then: "Cease jamming. Fire 'em up again if they come within eight miles."

"Trackbreakers and comm jammers to standby," Wendy said, punching instructions into the computer. "Range nine miles. He's climbing faster, passing ten thousand feet."

"You Americans, do not try to approach our Iran, or we will show you our anger," the Iranian MiG pilot said in halting English. "Your threats mean nothing to us. Stay away or be damned."

"He's turning north," Wendy said. "He's . . . oh no! He's diving on us! Range ten miles, closure rate seven hundred knots!"

"Jammers!" Brad shouted. "*Lock on and shoot!*"

"No! Withhold!" Patrick shouted. He keyed the UHF radio mike button again: "One-Four-One, don't come any closer!"

"I said *shoot* . . . !"

"Wait! He's turning and climbing!" Wendy reported with relief. "He's climbing and turning, heading northeast."

"Prick," John Ormack said with a loud sigh of relief. "Just a macho stunt."

"Scope's clear," Wendy said. "Bandit at twenty miles and extending. No other signals."

"Pilot's clearing off," Brad said. He didn't wait for John's acknowledgment, but safetied his ejection seat, whipped off his straps, and stormed out of his seat and back to the systems officer's compartment.

"He doesn't look happy, guys," John warned Patrick and Wendy on interphone.

The instrument console was right behind the hatch leading to the lower deck, so Brad couldn't go all the way back. He plugged into a free interphone cord, so everyone on board could hear his tirade, stood over the console with eyes blazing, pointed a gloved finger at Patrick, and thundered, "Don't you *ever* countermand my orders again, Major! He could've blown us away—twice! You're not the aircraft commander, I am!" He turned to Wendy Tork and shouted, "If I say 'shoot,' Tork, you obey my orders instantly or I will kick your ass, then kick your ass into prison for twenty years! And don't you dare cease jamming an enemy aircraft unless I give the order to stop! You copy me?"

"I hear you, General," Wendy shot back, "but you can go straight to hell." Elliott's eyes bulged in rage. Wendy hurried on: "Who gave us the order to shoot? Who even gave us permission to jam a foreign power's radar and radios?" Elliott remained silent.

"Brad?" John Ormack asked. "This mission is supposed to be a contingency mission, in case Iran opens a second front against the Coalition. We're not supposed to be flying so close to disputed territory—I don't think we were supposed to engage anyone."

"In fact, I don't ever recall being given an order to fly *at all*, sir," Patrick said. "I read the warning order, and it says we were supposed to stand by for possible action against Iran or any other nation that declares neutrality that might be a threat to the U.S. I never saw the execution order or the rules of engagement. We never received any satellite photos or tactical printouts. Nothing to help us in mission planning."

"What about that, General?" Wendy asked. "I never saw the execution order for our mission either. I never got the order of battle or any intelligence reports. Is this an authorized mission or not?"

"Of course it is," Brad said indignantly. His angry grimace was melting away fast, and Patrick knew that Wendy had guessed right. "We were ordered to stand by for action. We're . . . standing by. This is tactically the best place to be standing by anyway."

"So if we fired on an Iranian fighter, it would be unauthorized."

"We're authorized to defend ourselves . . ."

"If we were on an authorized mission, we'd be authorized to defend ourselves—but this isn't authorized, is it?" Patrick asked. When Brad did not answer right away, Patrick added, "You mean, *none* of the Megafortresses we have in-theater is specifically authorized to be up here? We've got three experimental stealth warplanes loaded with weapons flying ten thousand miles from home and just a few miles from a war zone, and no one knows we're up here? Jesus, General . . ."

"That will be all, Major," Elliott interjected. "The sorties were authorized—by me. Our orders were to stand by and prepare for combat operations in support of Desert Storm. That is what we're doing."

Patrick unstrapped, unplugged his interphone cord, got to his feet, leaned close to Brad Elliott, and said cross-cockpit, so no one else could hear, "Sir, we can't be doing this. You're risking our lives . . . for what? If we got intercepted by Iranians or Iraqis or whoever, we'd have to fight our way out—but we'd be doing it without sanction, without orders. If we got shot down, no one would even know we were missing. *Why?* What the hell is all this for?"

Brad and Patrick looked into each other's eyes for a very long moment. Brad's eyes were still blazing with indignation and anger, but now they were shadowed by a touch of . . . what? Patrick hoped it would be understanding or maybe contrition, but that's not what he saw. Instead, he saw disappointment. Patrick had called his mentor and commanding officer on a glaring moral and leadership error, and all he could communicate in return was that he was disappointed that his protégé didn't back him up.

"Is it because you didn't participate in Desert Storm?" Patrick asked. The Persian Gulf War—some called it "World War III"—had just ended, and the majority of troops had already gone home. They were enjoying celebrations and congratulations from a proud and appreciative nation, something unseen in the United States since World War II. "Is it because you know you had something that could help the war effort, but you weren't allowed to use it?"

"Go to hell, McLanahan," Elliott said bitterly. "Don't try any of that amateur psychoanalyst crap with me. I'm given discretion on how to employ my forces, and I'm doing it as I see fit."

Patrick looked at his commanding officer, the man he thought of as a friend and even as a surrogate father. His father had died before Patrick went off to college, and he and his younger brother had been raised in a household with a strong-willed, domineering mother and two older sisters. Brad was the first real father figure in Patrick's life in many years, and he did all he could to be a strong, supportive friend to Elliott, who was without a doubt a lone-wolf character, both in his personal and professional life.

Although Bradley James Elliott was a three-star general and was once the number four man in charge of Strategic Air Command, the major command in charge of America's long-range bombers and land-based ballistic nuclear missiles, he was far too outspoken and too "gung ho" for politically sensitive headquarters duty. To Brad, bombers were the key to American military power projection, and he felt it was his job, his duty, to push for increased funding, research, and development of new long-range attack technologies. That didn't sit well with the Pentagon. The services had been howling mad for years about the apparent favoritism toward the Air Force. The Pentagon was pushing "joint operations," but Brad Elliott wasn't buying it. When he continued to squawk about reduced funding and priority for new Air Force bomber programs, Brad lost his fourth star. When he still wouldn't shut up, he was banished to the high Nevada desert either to retire or simply disappear into obscurity.

Brad did neither. Even though he was an aging three-star general occupying a billet designated for a colonel or one-star general, he used his remaining stars and HAWC's shroud of ultrasecrecy and security to develop an experimental twenty-first-century long-range attack force, comprised of highly modified B-52 and B-1 bombers, "superbrilliant" stealth cruise missiles, unmanned attack vehicles, and precision-guided weapons. He procured funding that most commanders could only wish for, money borrowed—many said "stolen"—from other weapons programs or buried under multiple layers of security classification.

While the rest of the Air Force thought Brad Elliott was merely sitting around waiting to retire, he was building a secret attack force—and he was using it. He had launched his first mission in a modified B-52 bomber three years earlier, dodging almost the entire Soviet Far East Air Army and attacking a Soviet ground-based laser installation that was being used to blind American reconnaissance satellites. That mission had cost the lives of three men, and had cost Brad his right leg. But it proved that the "flying battleship" concept worked and that a properly modified B-52 bomber could be used against highly defended targets in a nonnuclear attack mission. Brad Elliott and his team of scientists, engineers, test pilots, and technogeeks became America's newest secret strike force.

"It's not your job or place to second-guess or criticize me," Elliott went on, "and it sure as hell isn't your place to countermand my orders or give orders contrary to mine. You do it again, and I'll see to it that you're military career is terminated. Understand?"

Patrick thought he had noted just a touch of sadness in Brad's eyes, but that was long gone now. He straightened his back and caged his eyes, not daring to look his friend in the eye. "Yes, sir," he replied tonelessly.

"General?" John Ormack radioed back on interphone. "Patrick? What's going on?"

Brad scowled one last time at Patrick. Patrick just sat down without meeting Brad's eyes and strapped into his ejection seat again. Elliott said, "Patrick's going to contact Diego Garcia and get our bombers some secure hangar space. We're going to put down until we get clarification on our mission. Plot a course back to the refueling track, get in contact with our tankers and our wingmen, and let's head back to the barn."

When Brad turned and headed back to the cockpit, Wendy reached across the cabin and touched Patrick's arm in a quiet show of gratitude. But Patrick didn't feel much like accepting any congratulations.

"I want to go over the highlights of the Secretary's MOI with you before we get started," Major General Larry Ingemanson, the president of the promotion board, said. He was addressing the entire group of board members just before they started their first day of deliberations. "The MOI defines the quotas set for each promotion category, but you as voting members aren't required to meet those quotas. We're looking for quality, not quantity. Keep that in mind. The only quotas we must fill for this board are for joint-service assignments, which are set by law, and the Secretariat will take care of that. The law also states that extra consideration be given to women and minorities. Bear in mind that your scores are not adjusted by the Secretariat if the candidate happens to be female or a member of a minority—no one can adjust your score but you. You are simply asked to be aware that these two groups have been unfairly treated in the past.

"You are also asked to keep in mind that since the start of hostilities in the southwest Asian theater, some candidates may not have had the opportunity to complete advanced degrees or professional military education courses. Eventually I believe this will become more and more of a concern as deployment tempos pick up, but so far the law has not been changed. You're just asked to keep this fact in mind: If a candidate hasn't completed PME or advanced degrees, check to see if he or she is serving in some specialty that requires frequent or short-notice deployments, and take that into consideration."

General Ingemanson paused for a moment, closed his notes, and went on: "Now, this isn't in the MOI—

it's from your nonvoting board president. This is my first time presiding over a board but my fourth time here in the box, and I have some thoughts about what you are about to undertake:

"As you slug through all the three thousand-plus files over the next several days, you may get a little cross-eyed and slack-jawed. I will endeavor to remind you of this as the days go on, but I'll remind you now, of the extreme importance of what you're doing here: If you have ever thought about what it would be like to shape the future, this, my friends, is it.

"We find ourselves in a very special and unique position of responsibility," Ingemanson went on solemnly. "We are serving on the Air Force's first field grade officers' promotion board just days after the end of Operation Desert Storm, which many are calling the reawakening of America and the reunification of American society with its armed forces. We are seeing the beginning of a new era for the American military, especially for the U.S. Air Force. We are tasked with the awesome responsibility of choosing the men and women who will lead that new military into the future."

Norman Weir rolled his eyes and snorted to himself. What drivel. It was a promotion board, for Christ's sake. Why did he have to try to attach some special, almost mystical significance to it? Maybe it was just the standard "pep talk," but it was proceeding beyond the sublime toward the ridiculous.

"I'm sure we've all heard the jokes about lieutenant colonels—the 'throwaway' officer, the ultimate wanna-bes," Ingemanson went on. "The ones that stand on the cusp of greatness or on the verge of obscurity. Well, let me tell you from the bottom of my soul: I believe they are the bedrock of the Air Force officer corps.

"I've commanded four squadrons, two wings, and one air division, and the O-5s were always the heart and soul of all of my units. They did the grunt work of a line crewdog but had as much responsibility as a wing commander. They pulled lines of alert, led missions and deployments, and then had to push paper to make the bosses happy. They had the most practical hands-on experience in the unit—they usually were the evaluators, chief instructors, and most certainly the mentors. They had to be the best of the best. Us headquarters weenies could get away with letting the staff handle details—the 0-5s pushing squadrons never got that break. They had to study and train just as hard as the newest nugget, but then they had to dress nice and look sharp and do the political face time. The ones that do all that are worth their weight in gold."

Norman didn't understand everything Ingemanson was talking about, and so he assumed he was talking flyer-speak. Naturally, Ingemanson himself was a command pilot and also wore paratrooper's wings, meaning he probably graduated from the Air Force Academy. It was going to be a challenge, Norman thought, to break the aviator's stranglehold on this promotion board.

"But most importantly, the men and women you'll choose in the next two weeks will be the future leaders of our Air Force, our armed forces, and perhaps our country," Ingemanson went on. "Most of the candidates have completed one or more command and staff education programs; they might have a master's degree, and many even work on doctorates. They've maxed out on flying time, traveled to perhaps five or six different PCS assignments plus a few specialty and service schools. They're probably serving in the Sandbox now, and perhaps even served in other conflicts or actions. They are beginning the transition from senior line troop, instructor, or shop chief to fledgling unit commander. Find the best ones, and let's set them on track to their destinies.

"One more thing to remember: Not only can you pick the candidates best eligible for promotion, but you are also charged with the task of recommending that candidates be *removed* from extended active duty. What's the criterion for removal? That, my friends, is up to you. Be prepared to fully justify your reasons to me, but don't be afraid to give them either. Again, it's part of the awesome responsibility you have here.

"One last reminder: it is still *our* Air Force. We built it. I'd guess that most of the candidates you'll look at didn't serve in Vietnam, so they don't have the same perspective as we do. Many of our buddies died in Vietnam, but we survived and stayed and fought on. We served when it was socially and politically unpopular to wear a uniform in our own hometowns. We played Russian roulette with nuclear weapons, the most deadly weapons ever devised, just so we could prove to the world that we were crazy enough to blow the entire planet into atoms to protect our freedom. We see the tides turning in our favor—but it is up to us to see that our gains are not erased. We do that by picking the next generation of leaders.

"It is our Air Force. Our country. Our world. Now it's our opportunity to pick those who we want to take our place. In my mind, it is equally important a task as the one we did in creating this world we live in. That's our task. Let's get to it. Please stand, raise your right hand, and prepare to take the oath of office to convene this promotion board." General Ingemanson then administered the service oath to the board members, and the job was under way.

Norman and the other board members departed the small theater and headed toward the individual panel meeting rooms. There was a circular table with comfortable-looking chairs arrayed around it, a dry-marker board with an overhead slide projector screen, a bank of telephones, and the ever-present coffeepot and rack of ceramic mugs.

Norman's seven-member panel had five rated officers—four pilots and one navigator, including one officer who looked as if he had every possible specialty badge one person could have: He wore command pilot and senior paratrooper wings, plus a senior missile-launch officer badge on his pocket. The flyers all seemed to know each other—two were even from the same Air Force Academy class. To them, it was a small, chummy Air Force. None of the flyers wore any ribbons on their uniform blouses, only their specialty badges on one side, name tags on the other, and rank on their collar; Norman almost felt self-conscious wearing all of his three rows of ribbons before deciding that the flyers were probably out of uniform.

Introductions were quick, informal, and impersonal—unless you were wearing wings. Along with the flyers and Norman, there was a logistics planning staff officer from the Pentagon. Norman thought he recognized the fellow Pentagon officer, but with almost five thousand Air Force personnel working at the "five-sided puzzle palace," it was pretty unlikely anyone knew anyone else outside their corridor. None of the panel members were women—there were only a couple women on the entire board, a fact that Norman found upsetting. The Air Force was supposed to be the most progressive and socially conscious branch of the American armed services, but it was as if they were right back in the Middle Ages with how the Air Force treated women sometimes.

Of course, the five flyers sat together, across the table from the nonflyers. The flyers were relaxed, loud, and animated. One of them, the supercolonel with all the badges, pulled out a cigar, and Norman resolved to tell him not to light up if he tried, but he never made any move to do so. He simply chewed on it and used it to punctuate his stories and jokes, shared mostly with the other flyers. He sat at the head of the semicircle of flyers at the table as if presiding over the panel. He looked as if he was very accustomed to taking charge of such groups, although each panel didn't have and didn't need a leader.

The supercolonel must've noticed the angry anticipation in Norman's eyes over his cigar, because he looked at him for several long moments during one of the few moments he wasn't telling a story or a crude joke. Finally, a glimmer of recognition brightened his blue eyes. "Norman Weir," he said, jabbing his cigar. "You were the AFO chief at Eglin four years ago. Am I right?"

"Yes; I was."

"Thought so. I'm Harry Ponce. I was the commander of 'Combat Hammer,' the Eighty-sixth Fighter Squadron. Call me 'Slammer.' You took pretty good care of my guys."

"Thank you."

"So. Where are you now?"

"The Pentagon. Chief of the Budget Analysis Agency."

A few of the other flyers looked in his direction when he mentioned the Budget Analysis Agency.

One of them curled his lip in a sneer. "The BAA, huh? You guys killed an ejection-seat modification program my staff was trying to get approved. That seat would've saved two guys deploying to the Sandbox."

"I can't discuss it, Colonel," Norman said awkwardly.

"The first ejection seat mod for the B-52 in twenty years, and you guys kill it. I'll never figure that one out."

"It's a complicated screening process," Norman offered disinterestedly. "We analyze cost versus life cycle versus benefit. We get all the numbers on what the Pentagon wants to do with the fleet, then try to justify the cost of a modification with its corresponding . . ."

"It was a simple replacement—a few feet of old worn-out pyrotechnic actuators, replacing thirty-year-old components that were predicted to fail in tropical conditions. A few thousand bucks per seat. Instead, the budget weenies cut the upgrade program. Lo and behold, the first time a couple of our guys try to punch out near Diego Garcia—actuator failure, two seats. Two dead crewdogs."

"Like I said, Colonel, I can't discuss particulars of any file or investigation," Norman insisted. "In any case, every weapon system from the oldest to the newest has a cost-reward break-even point. We use purely objective criteria in making our decision . . ."

"Tell that to the widows of the guys that died," the colonel said. He shook his head disgustedly and turned away from Norman.

What an idiot, Norman thought. *Trying to blame me or my office for the deaths of two flyers because of a cost-analysis report.* There were thousands, maybe tens of thousands of factors involved in every accident—it couldn't all be attributed to budget cuts. He was considering telling the guy off, but he saw the staff wheeling carts of personnel folders down the hallway, and he kept silent as they took seats and got ready to work.

In a nutshell, Norman observed, careers were made or destroyed by a simple numbers game. The Selection Board Secretariat's staff members wheeled in a locked lateral file cabinet on wheels with almost four hundred Officer Selection Reports, or OSRs, in them. Although there was supposedly no time limit on how long each panel member considered each OSR, the board members were asked to finish up the first round of scoring in the first week. That meant they had no more than about five minutes to score each candidate.

Five minutes to decide a career, Norman thought as he opened the first file. Five minutes to decide whether this person deserved to be promoted, or should stay where he was, or even if he or she should even be in the Air Force to begin with.

Well, maybe it won't be that hard, Norman thought as he scanned the OSR. The first thing he saw on the right side of the folder was the candidate's photo, and this guy was a mess. Hair too long, touching the ears. A definite five o'clock shadow. Cockeyed uniform devices. Norman had a chart available that showed the proper order ribbons should be displayed on the uniform, but he didn't need to refer to it to know that the Air Force Training Ribbon was not placed over the Air Force Achievement Medal.

Each board member had a checklist of things to look for in a personnel jacket, along with a sheet for notes or questions and a scoring summary block. Each jacket was given a score between 6.0 and 10.0

in half-point increments. The average score was 7.5. Norman decided he would start at the maximum score and deduct half points for every glitch. So this guy was starting out with a 9.5, and he hadn't even gotten to the job performance and effectiveness reports and ratings yet. Below the photo was a list of the officer's decorations and awards and an officer selection brief, outlining the candidate's duty history. This guy was not wearing a ribbon he had been awarded, so Norman deducted another half point. How inept could one officer be?

And yes, Norm noted that he was a flyer.

On the left side of the OSR were the candidate's OERs, or Officer Effectiveness Reports, starting with the most recent. Norman scanned through the files, paying close attention to the three rater's blocks on the back page. Each OER was endorsed by the officer's three sequential superior officers in his chain of command. He received either a "Below Average," "Average," "Above Average," or "Outstanding" rating, plus a block below for personal comments. An OER with all "Outstanding" ratings was called a "firewalled" OER, and all officers seeking promotion aspired to it.

After filling out hundreds of OERs in his career, Norman knew that anything short of an "Outstanding" rating was cause for concern, and he dinged a candidate for any "Above Average" or lower ratings. But since some commanders always "firewalled" OERs, Norman had to take a quick glance at the rater's comments, even on "firewalled" OERs. He looked for examples of deficiencies or nuances in the wording to suggest what the rater really thought of the candidate. Most all raters used the word "Promote" in his comments, so if the word was missing, that was a big ding—the rater obviously did not think the candidate was worthy of promotion, so why should Norman? If the candidate was really good, the rater might put "Promote ASAP" or "Promote without fail;" if the candidate was exceptionally good, he might say "Promote immediately" or "Promote ahead of contemporaries." Some were more creative: They sometimes wrote "Promote when possible," which was not a strong endorsement and earned a ding, or "Promote below the zone immediately without fail" for a really outstanding candidate. Sometimes they just said "Promote," which Norman considered a big ding too.

By the first lunch break, Norman was slipping right into the groove, and he realized this was not going to be a really difficult exercise. Patterns began to emerge right away, and it soon becomes clear who the really great officers were and who were not. Out of thirty or so OSRs, Norman had only marked a few above 8.0. Most of his scores drifted below the 7.5 average. No one was ranked over 8.5—not one. Norman had to adjust his own scoring system several times because he started to read better and better OERs and realized that what he thought were good comments were actually average comments. Occasionally, he had to ask the flyers what this school or that course was. Norman disliked acronyms on OERs and dinged a candidate for them if he couldn't understand what it meant—especially if he or she was a flyer.

So far, Norman was not too impressed. Some of the candidates they were reviewing were above-the-primary-zone candidates, meaning they had not been promoted when they should have been, and they seemed worse than the others. It was as if they had already given up on the Air Force, and it showed—missing or outdated records, snotty or whining letters to the board attached to the record, old photos, and evidence of stagnated careers. Most were in-the-primary-zone candidates, meeting the board at the proper time commensurate with their date of rank, and most of them had a polished, professional, well-managed look.

Most all of the flyers' OERs were "firewalled," and Norman scrutinized those even more closely for telltale signs of deficiency. The nonflying line officer OERs always seemed more honest, forthright evaluations. The flying community was indeed a closed fraternity, and Norman took this opportunity to take some chips out of their great steel wall every chance he could. If a flyer's OER wasn't firewalled, Norman mentally tossed it aside, taking big dings out of the score.

The chips he was breaking off flyers' OERs quickly became chunks, but Norman didn't care. If a flyer was really great, he would get a good rating. But just being a flyer wasn't a plus in Norman's book. Everyone had to earn their score, but the flyers would have to really shine to pass Norman's muster.

The British Indian Ocean Territories, or BIOT, was a chain of fifty-six islands covering twenty-two thousand square miles of the Indian Ocean south of India. The total land area of the BIOT was only thirty-six square miles, about half the size of the District of Columbia. Located only four hundred miles south of the equator, the weather was hot and humid year-round. The islands were far enough south of the Indian subcontinent, and the waters were colder and deeper, so typhoons and hard tropical storms were rare, and the islands only received about one hundred inches of rain per year. If there had been any appreciable landmass or infrastructure in the BIOT, it might be considered an idyllic tropical paradise. The tiny bits of dry land and coconut groves on the islands had saved many hungry, storm-tossed sailors over the centuries since the islands were discovered by Western explorers in the late seventeenth century, although the reefs had also claimed their share of wayward sailors as well.

The largest and southernmost island in the BIOT was Diego Garcia, a V-shaped stretch of sand, reefs, and atolls about thirty-four miles long, with a thirteen-mile-long, six-mile-wide lagoon inside the V. The British Navy claimed Diego Garcia and other islands of the Chagos Archipelago in the late eighteenth century and established copra, coconut, and lumber plantations there. The island was an isolated and seldom-used stopover and resupply point for the British Navy until after the independence of India, when it began to languish. Native fishermen from the African nation of Mauritius claimed Diego Garcia, citing historical and cultural precedents, and it appeared as if the British might hand over the island to them.

The United States stepped into the fray in December of 1966. Eager for a listening post to monitor Soviet Navy activity in the Indian Ocean during the height of the Cold War, the United States signed a bilateral agreement to improve and jointly administer the BIOT for defensive purposes. The native Il-iots on the islands were relocated back to Mauritius with a promise that if the islands were no longer needed for defense, they would be returned to them. The U.S. Navy immediately landed a Seabee battalion on Diego Garcia and began work.

Seven years later, the U.S. Navy commissioned a "naval communications facility"—an electronic and undersea surveillance post—on Diego Garcia, along with limited naval-vessel support facilities and an airstrip. Five years later, the facility was expanded, making it a full-fledged—albeit still remote—Navy Support Facility. The few dozen sailors assigned there—donkeys, left over from copra and coconut-harvesting operations, far outnumbered humans—lived in primitive hootches and lived only for the next supply ship to take them off the beautiful but lonely desert island.

But the facility took on a more important role when the Soviet Navy began a rapid buildup of forces in the region in the late 1970s, during the oil crisis, and during the Iranian Revolution of the early 1980s. With Western influence in the Middle East waning, Diego Garcia suddenly became the only safe, secure, and reliable port and air facility in southwest Asia. Diego Garcia became a major forward predeployment and prepositioning base for the U.S. Central Command's operations in the Middle East. The facilities were greatly expanded in the early 1980s to make it "the tip of the spear" for American rapid-deployment forces in the region. The U.S. Navy began flying P-3 Orion antisubmarine patrols from Diego Garcia, and several cargo ships loaded with fuel, spare parts, weapons, and ammunition were permanently prepositioned in the little harbor to support future conflicts in the southwest Asia theater.

There was only one highway on the island, the nine-mile-long main paved road leading from the Naval Supply Facility base on Garcia Point to the airfield. Until just a few years ago, both the road and the runway were little more than crushed coral and compacted sand. But as the importance of the little island grew, so did the airfield. What was once just a lonely pink runway and a few rickety shacks, euphemistically called Chagos International Airport, was now one of the finest airfields in the entire Indian Ocean region.

With the advent of Operation Desert Shield, the rapid buildup of forces in the Middle East to counter the threat of an Iraqi invasion of the Arabian Peninsula, Diego Garcia's strategic importance increased a hundredfold. Although the tiny island was almost three thousand miles away from Iraq, it was the perfect place to deploy long-range B-52 Stratofortress bombers, which have an unrefueled range in excess of eight thousand miles. As many as twenty B-52G and-H model bombers and support aircraft deployed there. When the shooting started, the "BUFFs"—Big Ugly Fat Fuckers—began 'round-the-clock bombing missions against Iraqi forces, first using conventionally armed cruise missiles and then, once the Coalition forces had firm control of the skies over the region, pressing the attack with conventional gravity bombs. One-half of all the ordnance used in Operation Desert Storm was dropped by B-52 bombers, and many of them launched from Diego Garcia.

The lone runway on Diego Garcia was eleven thousand feet long and one hundred and fifty feet wide, only four feet above sea level, on the western side of the island. At the height of the air war against Iraq, the aircraft parking ramps were choked with bombers, tankers, transports, and patrol planes; now, only days after the Coalition cease-fire, only a token force of six B-52G and -H bombers, one KC-10 Extender aerial-refueling tanker/cargo plane, and three KC-135 Stratotanker aerial-refueling tankers remained, along with the usual and variable number of cargo planes at the Military Airlift Command ramp and the four P-3 Orion patrol planes on the Navy ramp. Things had definitely quieted down on Diego Garcia, and the little atoll's peaceful, gentle life was beginning to return to normal after months of frenetic activity.

Before the war there was only one aircraft hangar on the island for maintenance on the Navy's P-3 Orion subchasers—the weather was perfect, never lower than seventy-two degrees, never warmer than ninety degrees, with an average of only two inches of rain per week, so why work indoors?—but as the conflict kicked off the U.S. Air Force hastily built one large hangar at the southernmost part of the airfield complex, as far away from curious observers in the harbor as possible. Many folks speculated on what was in the hangar: Was it the still-unnamed B-1B supersonic intercontinental heavy bomber, getting ready to make its combat debut? Or was it the rumored supersecrect stealth bomber, a larger version of the F-117 Goblin stealth fighter? Some even speculated it was the mysterious Aurora spy/attack plane, the hypersonic aircraft capable of flying from the United States to Japan in just a couple of hours.

In reality, the hangar had mostly been used as a temporary overflow barracks during the Persian Gulf War, or used to store VIP aircraft out of the hot sun to keep it cool until just before departure. Since the cease-fire, it had been used to store dozens of pallets of personal gear for returning troops before loading on transport planes. Now, it held two aircraft—two very special aircraft, tightly squeezed in nose to tail.

The two EB-52 Megafortress bombers had arrived separately—Brad Elliott's plane was returning from its patrol near Iran, while the second bomber had been en route to replace the first when it had been diverted to Diego Garcia—but they had arrived within minutes of one another. The airfield had been closed down and blacked out, and all transient ships in the harbor had been moved north toward the mouth of the harbor, until both aircraft touched down and were parked inside the Air Force hangar. A third Megafortress bomber involved in the 'round-the-clock aerial patrols near Iran remained back at its home base in Nevada, with crews standing by ready to rotate out to Diego Garcia if a conflict developed. Roving guards were stationed inside and outside the hangar, but the lure of the island's secluded, serene tropical beauty and every warrior's desire to escape the stress and strains of warfighting combined to keep all curious onlookers away. No one much cared what was inside that hangar, as long as it didn't mean they had to go back to twenty-four-hour shifts to surge combat aircraft for bombing raids.

Patrick McLanahan had spent all night buttoning up the Megafortress, downloading electronic data from the ship's computers, and preparing a detailed intelligence brief for the Air Force on the strange aircraft they had encountered near the Strait of Hormuz. Now it was time to summarize their findings and prepare a report to send to the Pentagon.

"We need to come up with a best guess at what we encountered last night," Brad Elliott said. "Wendy? Start us off."

"Weird," Wendy said. "He had a big, powerful multimode X-band surface-search radar, which meant it was a big plane, maybe bomber-class, like a Bear, Badger, Backfire, Nimrod, or Buccaneer attack plane. But it also had an S-band air-search radar, like a Soviet Peel Cone system or like an AWACS. He was fast, faster than six hundred knots, which definitely eliminates the Bear and AWACS and probably eliminates a Badger, Nimrod, or Buccaneer attack plane. That leaves a Backfire bomber."

"Or a Blackjack bomber," Patrick offered, "or some other class of aircraft we haven't seen yet." The Backfire and Blackjack bombers were Russia's most advanced warplanes. Both were large intercontinental supersonic bombers, still in production. The Backfire bomber, similar to the American B-1 bomber, was known to have been exported to Iran as a naval attack plane, carrying long-range supersonic cruise missiles. Little was known about the Blackjack bomber except it was larger, faster, more high-tech, and carried many more weapons than any other aircraft in the Communist world—and probably in the *entire* world.

"But with air-to-air missiles?" John Ormack remarked. "Could we have missed other planes with him, maybe a fighter escort?"

"Possible," Wendy said. "But normally we'd spot fighter intercept radars at much longer distances, as far as a hundred miles. We didn't see him until he was right on top of us—less than forty miles away. In fact, we probably wouldn't have detected him at all except he turned on his own radar first and we detected it. He was well within our own air-search radar range, but we never saw him."

"A *stealth bomber*?" Patrick surmised. "A stealthy Backfire or Blackjack bomber?"

"There's nothing stealthy about a Backfire," Wendy said, "but a Blackjack bomber—interesting notion. Armed with air-to-air missiles?"

"It's the equivalent of a Megafortress flying battleship, except built on a supersonic airframe," Patrick said. "Three years after we first flew the EB-52 Megafortress, someone—probably the Russians—builds their own copy and sells it to the Iranians. Remember we thought we heard a Russian voice on the radio before we heard the Iranian pilot respond in

English? *The Russians built a Megafortress flying battleship and sold it to the Iranians.*"

"Hol-ee shit," Brad Elliott murmured. "It would sure keep the Russians in the Iranians' good graces to sell them a hot jet like a Megafortress. That would be worth a billion dollars in hard currency, something I'm sure the Russians need badly. It would be the ultimate weapon in the Middle East."

"We know how capable our system is—we *know* we can sneak up on any ship in the U.S. Navy and launch missiles and drop bombs before they know we're there," John Ormack said. "If the Iranians have a similar capability . . ."

"The entire fleet in the Persian Gulf could be in danger," Brad Elliott said ominously. "With Iraq all but neutralized and the Coalition forces going home, this could be Iran's best chance to take over the Persian Gulf. I want an abbreviated after-action and intelligence summary ready to transmit in thirty minutes, and then I want a detailed report prepared and ready to send out to Washington on the next liaison flight. Let's get busy."

The crew had the report done in twenty minutes, and they were hard at work on the after-action report when a communications officer brought in a message from the command post. Brad read it, his face darkened, and he crumpled it up into a ball and stormed out of the room, muttering curses.

John picked up the message form and read it. "We've been ordered to stand down," he said. "Apparently the Iranians filed a protest with the State Department, claiming an American warplane tried to violate Iranian airspace and attack a patrol. Almost every Gulf country is demanding an explanation, and the President doesn't have one . . ."

"Because he didn't know what we were doing," Patrick said. "The President must be ready to bust a gut."

"We've been ordered to bring the Megafortresses back to Groom Lake immediately." He gulped, then read, "And Brad's been relieved of duty." Patrick shook his head and made an exasperated sigh, then closed his classified notebook, collected his papers, and secured them in a catalog case to turn back in to the command post. "Where are you going, Patrick?"

"Out. Away from here. I'm on a beautiful tropical island—I want to enjoy a little of it before I get tossed into prison."

"Brad wanted us to stay in the hangar . . ."

"Brad's no longer in charge," Patrick said. He looked at John Ormack with a mixture of anger and weariness. "Are you going to order me to stay, John?" Ormack said nothing, so Patrick stormed out of the room without another word.

After turning in his classified materials, Patrick went to his locker in the hangar, stripped off his smelly survival gear and flying boots, found a beach mat and a bottle of water, took a portable walkie-talkie and his ID card, grabbed a ride from the shuttle bus to one of the beautiful white-sand beaches just a few yards from the Visiting Officers' Quarters, found an inviting coconut tree, stripped off his flight suit and undergarments to the waist, and stretched out on the sand. He heard the walkie-talkie squawk once—someone asking him to return to answer a few more questions—so Patrick finally turned the radio off. But he immediately felt bad for doing that, so he set his "internal alarm clock" for one hour and closed his eyes.

He was exhausted, bone-tired, but the weariness would not leave his body—in fact, he was energized, ready to go again. There was so much excitement and potential in their group—and it seemed it was wasted because Brad Elliott couldn't control himself. He was too eager simply to charge off and do whatever he felt was right or necessary. Patrick didn't always disagree with him, but he wished he could channel his energy, drive, determination, and patriotism in a more productive direction.

It seemed as if only a few minutes passed, but when Patrick awoke a quick glance at his watch told him fifty minutes had gone by. The sun was high in the sky, seemingly overhead—they were close enough to the equator for that to happen—but there was enough of a breeze blowing in off the Indian Ocean to keep him cool and comfortable. There were a few sailors or airmen on the beach a few dozen yards away to the east, throwing a Frisbee or relaxing under an umbrella.

"Helluva way to fight a war, isn't it?"

Patrick looked behind him and saw Wendy Tork sitting cross-legged beside him. She had a contented, pleased, relaxed look on her face. Patrick felt that same thrill of excitement and anticipation he had felt on the Megafortress. "I'll say," Patrick commented. "How long have you been sitting there?"

"A few minutes." Wendy was wearing nothing but her athletic bra and a pair of dark blue cotton panties; her flying boots and flight suit were in a pile beside her. Patrick gulped in surprise when he saw her so scantily clad, which made her smile. She motioned toward the Visiting Officers' Quarters down the beach. "Brad decided to let us get rooms in the Qs rather than sleep in the hangar."

Patrick snorted. "How magnanimous of him."

"What were *you* going to do—sleep on the beach?"

"Damn right I was," Patrick said. He shook his

head disgustedly. "We were cooped up in that plane for over seventeen hours."

"And it was all unauthorized," Wendy said bitterly. "I can't believe he'd do that—and then have the *nerve* to chew you out for what you did."

"You mean, you can't believe he'd do that *again,*" Patrick said. "That's Brad Elliott's MO, Wendy—do whatever it takes to get the job done."

"Flying the Kavaznya sortie—yes, I agree," she said. The first flight of the experimental EB-52 Megafortress bomber three years earlier, against a Soviet long-range killer laser system in Siberia, was also unauthorized—but it had probably saved the world from a nuclear exchange. "But with half the planet involved in a shooting war in the Middle East, why he would commit three Megafortresses to the theater without proper authorization and risk getting us all killed like that? Hell, it boggles my mind."

"No one said Brad was the clearheaded all-knowing expert in everything military," Patrick pointed out. "If he was, he'd probably build Megafortresses for just one person. He has a crew behind him." He turned toward her. "Rank disappears when we step into that bird, Wendy. It's our job, our responsibility, to point out problems or discrepancies or errors."

"Aren't you obligated to follow his orders?"

"Yes, unless I feel his orders are illogical or illegal or violate a directive," Patrick replied. "Brad wanting to engage that unidentified aircraft—that was wrong, even if we were on an authorized mission. We can't just go around shooting down aircraft over international airspace. We did what we were supposed to do—disengage, identify ourselves, turn, run, and get out. We prevented a dogfight and came home safely." He paused, then smiled.

"Why are you smiling?"

"You know, I was a little miffed at Brad ordering us up on this mission at first," Patrick admitted. "But you know, I probably . . . . no, I *definitely* wanted to go. I *knew* we had no tasking or execution order. If I wanted, I could have asked the question, demanded he get authorization, and stopped this sortie from ever leaving the ground. The fact is, I wanted to do it." His expression grew a bit more somber as he added, "In fact, I probably betrayed you, maybe even betrayed myself for *not* saying anything. I had a responsibility to speak up, and I didn't. And if things went completely to shit and some of us were killed or captured or hurt, I know that Brad would be the one responsible. I accused Brad of being irresponsible, of wanting to get into the fighting before it was over—and at the same time, I was thinking and doing the exact same thing. What a hypocrite."

"You are not a hypocrite," Wendy said, putting a hand on his shoulder as his eyes wandered out across the beach toward the open ocean. "Listen, Patrick, there's a war on. There might be a cease-fire now, but the entire region is still ready to explode. You know this, Brad knows this, I know this—and soon some smart desk jockeys in Washington will know this. They really did want our team warmed up and ready to go in case we were needed. Brad just advanced the timetable a little . . ."

"No, a *lot*," Patrick said.

"You played along because you recognized the need and our unit's capabilities. You did the right thing." She paused and took a deep breath, letting her fingers slide along his broad, naked shoulders. Patrick suppressed a pleased, satified moan, and Wendy responded by beginning to massage his shoulders. "I just wish Brad was a little more . . . user-friendly," she went on absently. "Commanders need to make decisions, but Brad seems a little too eager to pull the trigger and fight his way in or out of a scrape." She paused for a few long moments, then added, "Why can't *you* be our commander?"

"Me?" He hoped his surprised reaction sounded a lot less phony than it sounded to himself. In fact, ever since joining the High Technology Aerospace Weapons Center, Patrick thought about being its commander—now, for the first time, someone else had verbalized it. "I don't think I'm leadership material, Wendy," Patrick said after a short chuckle.

His little laugh barely succeeded in hiding the rising volts of pleasure he felt as her fingers aimlessly caressed his shoulder. "Sure you are," she said. "I think you'd be a great commanding officer."

"I don't think so," Patrick said. "They made me a major after the Kavaznya mission only because we survived it, not because I'm better than all the other captains in the Air Force . . ."

"They made you a major because you deserve to get promoted."

Patrick ignored her remark. "I think I might be meeting a lieutenant-colonel promotion board sometime this month—a two-year below-the-primary-zone board—but I have no desire to become a commander," he went on. "All I want to do is fly and be the best at whatever mission or weapon system they give me. But they don't promote flyboys to O-5 if they want to just stay flyboys."

"They don't?"

"Why should they? If a captain or a major can do the job, why do they need a lieutenant colonel doing it? L-Cs are supposed to be leaders, commanding squadrons. I don't want a squadron." Wendy looked at the sand for a long moment, then drummed her fingers on his shoulder. He glanced at her and smiled when she looked up at him with a mischievous smile. "What?"

"I think that's bull, Major-soon-to-be-Lieutenant-Colonel McLanahan." Wendy laughed. "I think you'd make an ideal commanding officer. You're the best at what you do, Patrick—it's perfectly understandable that you wouldn't want to spoil things by moving on to something else. But I see the qualities in you that other high-ranking guys lack. John Ormack is a great guy and a fine engineer, but he doesn't have what it takes to lead. Brad Elliott is a determined, gutsy leader, but he doesn't have the long-range vision and the interpersonal skills that a good commander needs.

"So stop selling yourself short. Those of us who know you can see it's total bull. The Strategic Air Command has got you so brainwashed into believing the mission comes first and the person comes last that you're starting to believe it yourself." She lay on the warm sand, facing him. "Let's talk about something else—like why you were watching me last night."

Her frankness and playfulness, combined with the warm sand, idyllic tropical scenery, fresh ocean breezes—not to mention her semiundressed attire—finally combined to make Patrick relax, even smile. He lay down on the sand, facing her, intentionally shifting himself closer to her. "I was fantasizing about you," he said finally. "I was thinking about the night at the Bomb Comp symposium at Barksdale that we spent together, how you looked, how you felt."

"Mmm. Very nice. I knew you were thinking that. I thought it was cute, you trying to stammer your way out of it. I've been thinking about you too."

"Oh yeah?"

Her eyes grew cloudy, tumultuous. "I had been thinking for the longest time if we'd ever get back together again," Wendy said. "After the Kavaznya mission, we were so compartmentalized, isolated—I thought I'd never touch you ever again. Then you joined Brad in the Border Security Force assignment, and that went bust, and it seemed like they drove you even deeper underground. And then the Philippines conflict . . . we lost so many planes out there, I was sure you weren't coming back. I knew you'd be leading the force, and I thought you'd be the first to die, even in the B-2 stealth bomber."

Wendy rolled over on her back and stared up into the sky. The clouds were thickening—it looked like a storm coming in, more than just the usual daily late-afternoon five-minute downpour. "But then Brad brought us back to refit the new planes to the Megafortress standard, and you were back at work like nothing ever happened. We started working together, side by side, sometimes on the same workstation or jammed into the same dinky compartment, sometimes so close I could feel the heat from your temples. But it seemed as if we had never been together—it was as if we had always been working together, but that night in Barksdale never happened. You were working away like crazy and I was just another one of your subcontractors."

"I didn't mean to hurt you, Wendy . . ."

"But it did hurt," she interjected. "The way you looked at me at Barksdale, the way you treated me at Dreamland, the way you touched me on the Megafortress just before we landed in Anadyr . . . I felt something between us, much more than just a one-night stand in Shreveport. That felt like an eternity ago. I felt as if I waited for you, and you were never coming back. Then I caught you looking at me, and all I could think of to do was come up with subtle ways to hurt you. Now, I don't know what I feel. I don't know whether I should punch your damned lights out or . . ."

He moved pretty quick for a big guy. His lips were on hers before she knew it, but she welcomed his kiss like a pearl diver welcomes that first deep, sweet breath of air after a long time underwater.

The beach was beautiful, soothing and relaxing, but they did not spend much time there. They knew that the world was going to come crashing down on them very, very soon, and they didn't have much time to get reacquainted. The Visiting Officers' Quarters were only a short walk away. . . .

"Damn shit-hot group we got, that's what I think," Colonel Harry Ponce exclaimed. He was "holding court" in the Randolph Officers Club after breakfast, sitting at the head of a long table filled with fellow promotion board members and a few senior officers from the base. Ponce jabbed at the sky with his unlit cigar. "It's going to be damn hard to choose."

Heads nodded in agreement—all but Norman Weir's. Ponce jabbed the cigar in his direction. "What's the matter, Norm? Got a burr up your butt about somethin'?"

Norman shrugged. "No, Colonel, not necessarily," he said. Most of the others turned to Norman with surprised expressions, as if they were amazed that someone would dare contradict the supercolonel. "Overall, they're fine candidates. I wish I'd seen a few more sharper guys, especially the in-the-primary-zone guys. The above-the-primary-zone candidates looked to me like they'd already thrown in the towel."

"Hell, Norman, ease up a little," Ponce said. "You

look at a guy that's the ops officer of his squadron, he's got umpteen million additional duties, he flies six sorties a week or volunteers for deployment or TDYs—who the hell cares if he's got a loose thread on his blues? I want to know if the guy's been busting his hump for his unit."

"Well, Colonel, if he can't put his Class A's together according to the regs or he can't be bothered getting a proper haircut, I wonder what else he can't do properly? And if he can't do the routine stuff, how is he supposed to motivate young officers and enlisted troops to do the same?"

"Norm, I'm talkin' about the *real* Air Force," Ponce said. "It's all fine and dandy that the headquarters staff and support agencies cross all the damned t's and dot the i's. But what I'm looking for is the Joe that cranks out one hundred and twenty percent each and every damned day. He's not puttin' on a show for the promotion board—he's helping his unit be the best. Who the hell cares what he looks like, as long as he flies and fights like a bitch bulldog in heat?"

That kind of language was typical in the supercolonel's verbal repertoire, and he used it to great effect to shock and humor anyone he confronted. It just made Norman more defensive. Anyone who resorted to using vulgarity as a normal part of polite conversation needed an education in how to think and speak, and Ponce was long overdue for a lesson. "Colonel, a guy that does *both*—does a good job in *every* aspect of the job, presenting a proper, professional, by-the-book appearance as well as performing his primary job—is a better choice for promotion than just the guy who flies well but has no desire or understanding of all the other aspects of being a professional airman. A guy that presents a poor appearance may be a good person and a good operator, but obviously isn't a complete, well-balanced, professional officer."

"Norm, buddy, have you been lost in your spreadsheets for the past nine months? Look around you—we're at war here!" Ponce responded, practically shouting. Norman had to clench his jaw to keep from admonishing Ponce to stop calling him by the disgusting nickname "Norm." "The force is at war, a real war, for the first time since Vietnam—I'm not talkin' about Libya or Grenada, those were just finger-wrestling matches compared to the Sandbox—and we're kicking *ass*! I see my guys taxiing out ready to launch, and I see them practically jumpin' out of their cockpits, they're so anxious to beat the crap outta Saddam. Their crew chiefs are so excited they're pissin' their pants. I see those guys as heroes, and now I have a chance to promote them, and by God I'm gonna do it!

"The best part is, none of our officers are over there in the 'Sandbox' ordering someone to paint the rocks or having six-course meals while their men are dying all around them. We're going over there, kicking ass and taking names, and we're coming home alive and victorious. Our troops are being treated like professionals, not conscripts or snot-nosed kids or druggies or pretty-boy marionettes. Our officers are applying what they've learned over the years and are taking the fight to Saddam and shovin' Mavericks right down his damned throat. I want guys leading the Air force that want to train hard, fight hard, and come home."

"But what about . . . ?"

"Yeah, yeah, I hear all the noise about the 'whole person' and the 'total package' crapola," Ponce interjected, waving the cigar dismissively. "But what I want are *warriors*. If you're a pilot, I want to see you fly your ass off, every chance you can get and then some, and then I want to see you pitch in to get the paperwork and nitpicky ground bullshit cleaned up so everyone can go fly some more. If you're an environmental weenie or—what are you in, Norm, accounting and finance? Okay. If you're a damned accountant, I want to see you working overtime if necessary to make your section hum. If your squadron needs you, you slap on your flying boots, fuck the wife good-bye, and report in on the double. Guys who do that are aces in my book."

Norman realized there was no point in arguing with Ponce—he was just getting more and more flagrant and bigoted by the second. Soon he would be bad-mouthing and trash-talking lawyers, or doctors, or the President himself—everyone except those wearing wings. It was getting very tiresome. Norman fell silent and made an almost imperceptible nod, and Ponce nodded triumphantly and turned to lecture someone else, acting as if he had just won the great evolution vs. creation debate. Norman made certain he was not the next one to leave, so it wouldn't appear as if he was retreating or running away, but as soon as the first guy at the table got up, Norman muttered something about having to make a call and got away from Ponce and his sycophants.

Well, Norman thought as he walked toward the Military Personnel Center, attitudes like Ponce's just cemented his thoughts and feelings about flyers—they were opinionated, headstrong, bigoted, loudmouthed Neanderthals. Ponce wasn't out to promote good officers—he was out to promote meat-eating jet-jockeys like himself.

It was guys like Ponce, Norman thought as he entered the building and took the stairs to the Selection and Promotion Branch floor, who were screwing up the Air Force for the rest of us.

"Excuse me, Colonel Weir?" Norman was striding down the hallway, heading back to his panel deliberation room. He stopped and turned. Major General Ingemanson was standing in the doorway to his office, smiling his ever-present friendly, disarming smile. "Got a minute?"

"Of course, sir," Norman said.

"Good. Grab a cup of coffee and c'mon in." Norman bypassed the coffee stand in the outer office and walked into Ingemanson's simple, unadorned office. He stood at attention in front of Ingemanson's desk, eyes straight ahead. "Relax and sit down, Colonel. Sure you don't want some coffee?"

"I'm fine, sir, thank you."

"Congratulations on finishing up the first week and doing such a good job."

"Thank you, sir."

"You can call me 'Swede'—everybody does," Ingemanson said. Norman didn't say anything in reply, but Ingemanson could immediately tell Weir wasn't comfortable calling him anything but "General" or "sir"—and of course Ingemanson noticed that Weir didn't invite him to call him by his first name, either. "You're a rare species on this board, Colonel—the first to come to a promotion board from the Budget Analysis Agency. Brand-new agency and all. Enjoying it there?"

"Yes, sir. Very much."

"Like the Pentagon? Wish you were back in a wing, running a shop?"

"I enjoy my current position very much, sir."

"I had one Pentagon tour a couple years ago—hated it. Air Division is okay, but boy, I miss the flying, the flight line, the cockpit, the pilots' lounge after a good sortie," Ingemanson said wistfully. "I try to keep current in the F-16 but it's hard when you're pulling a staff. I haven't released a real-live weapon in years."

"Yes, sir. Sorry, sir." He was sorry he didn't get to drop bombs and get shot at anymore? Norman definitely didn't understand flyers.

"Anyway, all the panel members have been instructed to call on you to explain any technical terminology or references in the personnel files relating to the accounting and finance field," Ingemanson went on. "A few line officer candidates had AFO-type schools, and some of the rated types on the panels might not know what they are. Hope you don't mind, but you might be called out to speak before another panel anytime. Those requests have to come through me. We'll try to keep that to a minimum."

"Not at all. I understand, sir," Norman said. "But in fact, no one has yet come to me to ask about the accounting or finance field. That could be a serious oversight."

"Oh?"

"If the flyers didn't know what a particular AFO school was, how could they properly evaluate a candidate's file? I see many flyers' files, and I have to ask about a particular school or course all the time."

"Well, hopefully the panel members either already know what the school or course is, or had the sense to ask a knowledgeable person," Ingemanson offered. "I'll put out a memo reminding them."

"I don't suppose too many AFOs will rate very highly with this board," Norman said. "With the war such a success and the aircrews acquitting themselves so well, I imagine they'll get the lion's share of the attention here."

"Well, I've only seen MPC's printout on the general profile of the candidates," Ingemanson responded, "but I think they did a pretty good job spreading the opportunities out between all the specialties. Of course, there'll be a lot of flyers meeting any Air Force promotion board, but I think you'll find it's pretty evenly distributed between the rated and nonrated specialties."

"If you listen to the news, you'd think there was a pilot being awarded the Medal of Honor every day."

"Don't believe everything you hear in the press, Colonel—our side practices good propaganda techniques too, sometimes better than the Iraqis," Ingemanson said with a smile. "The brass didn't want to give kill counts to the press, but the press eats that up. Helps keep morale up. The talking heads then start speculating on which fictional hero will get what medal. Stupid stuff. Not related to the real world at all." He noticed Weir's hooded, reserved expression, then added, "Remember, Colonel—there was Operation Desert Shield before there was Operation Desert Storm, and that's where the support troops shone, not just the aircrew members. None of the heroics being accomplished right now would be even remotely possible without the Herculean efforts of the support folks. Even the AFOs." Weir politely smiled at the gentle jab.

"I haven't seen any of the personnel jackets, but I expect to see plenty of glowing reports on extraordinary jobs done by combat support and nonrated specialties," Ingemanson went on. "I'm not telling you how I want you to mark your ballots, Colonel, but keep that in mind. Every man or woman, whether they're in the Sandbox or staying back in the States, needs to do their job to perfection, and then some, before we can completely claim victory."

"I understand, sir. Thank you for the reminder."

"Don't mention it. And call me 'Swede.' Everyone does. We're going to be working closely together for another week—let's ease up on some of the formalities." Norman again didn't say a word, only nodded uncomfortably. Ingemanson gave Weir a half-humorous, half-exasperated glare. "The reason I called you in here, Colonel," Ingemanson went on, "is I've received the printout on the scoring so far. I'm a little concerned."

"Why?"

"Because you seem to be rating the candidates lower than any other rater," the general said. "The board's average rating so far is 7.92. Your average line officer rating is 7.39—and your average rating of pilots, navigators, and missile-launch officers is 7.21, far below the board average."

Norman felt a brief flush of panic rise up to his temples, but indignation shoved it away. "Is there a problem, sir?"

"I don't know, Colonel. I asked you here to ask that very same question of you."

Norman shrugged. "I suppose someone has to be the lowest rater."

"Can't argue with that," Ingemanson said noncommittally. "But I just want to make sure that there are no . . . hidden agendas involved with your ratings decisions."

"Hidden agendas?"

"As in, you have something against rated personnel, and you want your scores to reflect your bias against them."

"That's nonsense, sir. I have nothing against flyers. I don't know many, and I have little interaction with them, so how can I have a bias against them?"

"My job as board president is to make sure there

is no adverse bias or favoritism being exercised by the panel members," Ingemanson reminded him. "I look at the rater's individual average scores. Generally, everyone comes within ten or fifteen percent of the average. If it doesn't, I ask the rater to come in for a chat. I just wanted to make sure everything is okay."

"Everything is fine, sir. I assure you, I'm not biasing my scores in any way. I'm calling them like I see them."

"A flyer didn't run over your cat or run off with your wife . . . er, pardon me, Colonel. I forgot—you're divorced. My apologies."

"No offense taken, sir."

"I'm once divorced too, and I joke about it constantly—way too much, I'm afraid."

"I understand, sir," Norman said, without really understanding. "I'm just doing my job the way I see it needs to be done."

Ingemanson's eyes narrowed slightly at that last remark, but instead of pursuing it further, he smiled, rubbed his hands energetically, and said, "That's good enough for me, then. Thanks for your time."

"You aren't going to ask me to change any of my scores? You're not going to ask me how I score a candidate?"

"I'm not allowed to ask, and even if I was, I don't really care," the two-star general said, smiling. "Your responsibility as a member of this board is to apply the secretary's MOI to the best of your professional knowledge, beliefs, and abilities. I certify to the Secretary of the Air Force that all board members understand and are complying with the Memorandum of Instruction, and I have to certify this again when I turn in the board's results. My job when I find any possible discrepancies is to interview the board member. If I find any evidence of noncompliance with the MOI, I'll take some action to restore fairness and accuracy. If it's a blatant disregard of the MOI, I might ask you to rescore some of the candidates, but the system is supposed to accommodate wild swings in scoring.

"I'm satisfied that you understand your responsibilities and are carrying them out. I cannot change any ratings, try to instruct you in how to rate the candidates, or try to influence you in any way about how to carry out your responsibilities, as long as you're following the MOI. End of discussion. Have a nice day, Colonel."

Norman got to his feet, and he shook hands with General Ingemanson when he offered it. But before he left, Norman turned. "I have a question, sir."

"Fire away."

"Did you have this same discussion with anyone else . . . say, Colonel Ponce?"

General Ingemanson smiled knowingly. Well well, he thought, maybe he's not as stuck in the world between his ears as he thought. "As a matter of fact, Colonel, I did. We spoke last Saturday evening at the O Club over a few drinks."

"You spoke with Colonel Ponce about the board, at the Officers' Club?"

Ingemanson chuckled, but more out of exasperation than humor. "Colonel, this is not a sequestered criminal jury," he said. "We're allowed to speak to one another outside the Selection Board Secretariat. We're even allowed to discuss promotion boards and the promotion process in general—just not any specifics on any one candidate or anything about specific scores, or attempt to influence any other board members. You probably haven't noticed, but Slammer spends just about every waking minute that he's not sitting the panel at the Club. That seemed to me the best place to corral him."

" 'Slammer'?"

"Colonel Ponce. That's his call sign. I thought you two knew each other?"

"We were assigned to the same wing, once."

"I see." Ingemanson filed that tidbit of information away, then said with a grin, "If I'd run into you at the Club, Norman, I would've spoken to you there too. You seem to spend most of your time in your VOQ or out jogging. Neither is conducive to a heart-to-heart chat."

"Yes, sir."

"Harry and I have crossed paths many times—I guess if you've been around as long as we have in the go-fast community, that's bound to happen. I've got seven years on the guy, but he'll probably pin on his first star soon. He might have been one of the Provisional Wing commanders out in Saudi Arabia or Turkey if he wasn't such a hot-shit test pilot. He designed two weapons that were developed in record time and used in the war. Pretty amazing work." Norman could tell Ingemanson was mentally reliving some of the times they'd had together, and it irritated Norman to think that he could just completely drift off like that—take a stroll down Memory Lane while talking to another officer standing right in front of him.

"Anyway," Ingemanson went on, shaking himself out of his reverie with a satisfied smile, "we spoke about his scores. They're a little skewed, like yours."

"All in favor of the flyers, I suppose."

"Actually, he's too *hard* on flyers," Ingemanson admitted. "I guess it's hard to measure up with what that man's done over his career, but that's no excuse. I told him he's got to measure the candidates against each other, not against his own image of what the perfect lieutenant colonel-selectee is."

"Which is himself," Norman added.

"Probably so," Ingemanson said, with a touch of humor in his eyes. He looked at Norman, and the humor disappeared. "The difference is, Slammer is measuring the candidates against a rigid yardstick—himself, or at least his own image of himself. On the other hand, you—in my humble nonvoting opinion—are not measuring the candidates at all. You're chipping away at them, finding and removing every flaw in every candidate until you come up with a chopped-up thing at the end. You're not creating anything here, Colonel—you're destroying."

Norman was a little stunned by Ingemanson's words. He was right on, of course—that was exactly Norman's plan of attack on this board: Start with a perfect candidate, a perfect "10," then whittle away at their perfection until reaching the bottom-line man or woman. When Ingemanson put it the way he did, it did sound somewhat defeatist, destructive—but so what? There were no guidelines. What right did he have to say all this?

"Pardon me, sir," Norman said, "but I'm not quite clear on this. You don't approve of the way I'm rating the candidates?"

"That's not what I'm saying at all, Colonel," Ingemanson said. "And I didn't try to correct Slammer either—not that I could even if I tried. I'm making an unofficial, off-the-record but learned opinion, on a little of the psychology behind the scoring if you will. I have no authority for any of this except for my experience on promotion boards and the fact that I'm a two-star general and you have to sit and listen to me." He smiled, trying to punctuate his attempt at humor, but Weir wasn't biting. "I'm just pointing out to you what I see."

"You think I'm destroying these candidates?"

"I'm saying that perhaps your attitude toward most of the candidates, and toward the flyers in particular, shows that maybe you're gunning them down instead of measuring them," Ingemanson said. "But as you said, there's no specific procedure for scoring the candidates. Do it any way as you see fit."

"Permission to speak openly, sir?"

"For Pete's sake, Colonel . . . yes, yes, *please* speak openly."

"This is a little odd, General," Norman said woodenly. "One moment you criticize my approach to scoring the candidates, and the next moment you're telling me to go ahead and do it any way I want."

"As I said in my opening remarks, Colonel Weir—this is *your* Air Force, and it's your turn to shape its future," Ingemanson said sincerely. "We chose you for the board: you, with your background and history and experience and attitudes and all that other emotional and personal baggage. The Secretary of the Air Force gave you mostly nonspecific guidelines for how to proceed. The rest is up to you. We get characters like you and we get characters like Slammer Ponce working side by side, deciding the future."

"One tight-ass, one hard-ass—is that what you're saying?"

"Two completely different perspectives," Ingemanson said, not daring to get dragged into that most elegant, truthful observation. "My job is to make sure you are being fair, equitable, and open-minded. As long as you are, you're in charge—I'm only the referee, the old man what's in charge. I give you the shape of one man's opinion, like Eric Sevareid used to say. End of discussion." Ingemanson glanced at his watch, a silent way of telling Norman to get the hell out of his office before the headache brewing between his eyes grew any worse. "Have a nice day, Colonel."

Norman got to his feet, stood at attention until Ingemanson—with an exasperated roll of his eyes—formally dismissed him, and walked out. He thought he had just been chewed out, but Ingemanson did it so gently, so smoothly, so affably, that Norman was simply left wondering, replaying the general's words over and over in his head until he reached the panel deliberation room.

The other panel members were already seated, with Ponce at his usual place, his unlit cigar clenched in his teeth. "Gawd, Norm, you're late, and you look a little tight," Ponce observed loudly. "Had a wild weekend, Norm?"

"I finished my taxes and ran a ten-K run in less than forty minutes. How was your weekend?"

"I creamed the general's ass in three rounds of golf, won a hundred bucks, met a cute señorita, and spent most of yesterday learning how to cook Mexican food buck naked," Ponce replied. The rest of the room exploded in laughter and applause. "But shit, I don't have my taxes done. What kind of loser am I?" They got to work amidst a lot of chatter and broad smiles—everyone but Norman.

The day was spent on what was called "resolving the gray area." In the course of deliberations, many candidates had a score that permitted them to be promoted, but there weren't enough slots to promote them all. So every candidate with a potentially promotable score had to be rescored until there were no more tie scores remaining. Naturally, when the candidates were rescored, there were candidates with tie scores again. Those had to be rescored, then the promotable candidates lumped together again and rescored yet again until enough candidates were chosen to fill the slots available.

In deliberating the final phase of rescoring the "gray area," panel members were allowed to discuss the rationale behind their scores with each other. It was the phase that Norman most dreaded, and at the same time most anticipated—a possible head-to-head, peer-to-peer confrontation with Harry Ponce.

It was time, Norman thought, for the Slammer to get slammed.

"Norm, what in blue blazes are you thinking?" Ponce exploded as the final short stack of personnel jackets were passed around the table. "You torpedoed Waller again. Your rating pushes him out of the box. Mind tellin' me why?"

"Every other candidate in that stack has Air Command and Staff College done in residence or by correspondence, except him," Norman replied. He didn't have to scan the jacket—he knew exactly which candidate it was, knew that Ponce would want to go to war over him. "His PME printout says he ordered the course a second time after failing to finish it within a year. Now why do you think he deserves to get a promotion when all the others completed that course?"

"Because Waller has been assigned to a fighter wing in Europe for the past three years."

"So?"

"Jesus, Norm, open your eyes," Ponce retorted. "The Soviet Union is doin' a free fall. The Berlin Wall came down and Russia's number one ally, East Germany, virtually disappears off the map overnight. A Soviet premier kicks the bucket every goddamned year, the Baltic states want to become nonaligned nations, and the Soviet economy is in meltdown.

Everyone expects the Russkies to either implode or break out and fight any day now."

"I still don't get it."

"Fighter pilots stationed in Europe are practically sleeping in their cockpits because they have so many alert scrambles and restricted alert postures," Ponce explained, "and Waller leads the league in sorties. He volunteers for every mission, every deployment, every training mission, every shadow tasking. He's his wing's go-to guy. He's practically taken over his squadron already. His last OER went all the way up to USAFE headquarters. He flew one-fifth of all his squadron's sorties in the Sandbox, and still served as ops officer and as acting squadron commander when his boss got grounded after an accident. He deserves to get a promotion."

"But if he gets a promotion, he'll be unavailable for a command position because he hasn't completed ACSC—hasn't even officially started it, in fact," Norman pointed out. "And he's been in his present assignment for almost four years—that means he's ready for reassignment. If he gets reassigned he'll have to wait at least a year, maybe two years, for an ACSC residence slot. He'll get passed up by officers junior to him even if he maintains a spotless record. A promotion now will only hurt him."

"What the hell kind of screwed-up logic is that, Weir?" Ponce shouted. But Norman felt good, because he could see that the little lightbulb over Ponce's head came on. He was getting through to the supercolonel.

"You know why, Colonel," Norman said confidently. "If he doesn't get promoted, he'll have a better chance of staying in his present assignment—in fact, I'd put money on it, if he's the acting squadron commander. He's a kick-ass major now—no one can touch him. He's certainly top of the list in his wing for ACSC. As soon as he gets back from Saudi Arabia, he'll go. When he graduates from ACSC in residence, he'll have all the squares filled and then some. He'll be a shoo-in for promotion next year."

"But he'll miss his primary zone," Ponce said dejectedly. He knew Norman was right, but he still wanted to do everything he could to reward this outstanding candidate. "His next board will be an above-the-primary-zone board, and he'll be lumped in with the has-beens. Here's a guy who works his butt off for his unit. Who deserves it more than him?"

"The officers who took a little extra time in professional career development and got their education requirements filled," Norman replied. "I'm not saying Waller's not a top guy. But he obviously knew what he had to do to be competitive—after all, he's taken the course twice, and he still didn't do it: That's not a well-rounded candidate in my book. The other candidates have pulled for their units too, but they also took time to get the theoretical and educational training in. Four other guys in that stack finished ACSC, and two of *them* have been selected to go in residence already. They're the ones that deserve a promotion."

"Well of course they had time to do ACSC—they're ground-pounders," Ponce shot back.

The remark hit a nerve in Norman's head that sent a thrill of anger through his body. "*Excuse* me?"

"They're ground-pounders—support personnel," Ponce said, completely ignorant of Norman's shocked, quickly darkening expression. "They go home every night at seventeen hundred hours and they don't come to work until oh-seven-thirty. If they work on weekends, it's because there's a deployment or they want face time. They don't have to pull 'round-the-clock strip alert or fly four scrambles a day or emergency dispersals."

"Hey, Colonel, I've done plenty of all those things," Norman retorted angrily. "I've manned mobility lines seventy-two hours straight, processing the airmen at the end of the line who've been up working all night because all the flyers insisted on going first. I've worked lots of weekends in-processing new wing commanders who don't want to be bothered with paperwork or who want to get their TDY money as soon as they hit the base or their precious teak furniture from Thailand got a scratch on it during the move and they want to sue the movers. Just because you're a flyer doesn't mean you got the corner on dedication to duty."

Ponce glared at Norman, muttered something under his breath, and chomped on his cigar. Norman steeled himself for round two, but it didn't happen. "Fine, fine," Ponce said finally, turning away from Norman. "Vote the way you damned want."

Resolving the "gray area" candidates took an entire workday and a little bit of the evening, but they finished. The next morning seemed to come much too quickly. But it started a little differently—because General Ingemanson himself rolled a small file cabinet into the room. He carried a platter of breakfast burritos and other hot sandwiches from the dining hall atop the file cabinet.

"Good morning, good morning, folks," he said gaily. "I know you all worked real hard yesterday, and I didn't see most of you in the Club this morning, so I figured you probably skipped breakfast, so I brought it for you. Take a couple, grab some coffee, and get ready for the next evolution." Hungry full birds fairly leaped for the food.

When everyone was seated a few moments later, General Ingemanson stepped up to the head of the room, and said, "Okay, gang, let's begin. Since you worked hard yesterday to finish up your gray area candidates, you're a little ahead of the game, so I have a treat for you today.

"As you may or may not know, once a promotion board is seated, the Military Personnel Center and the Pentagon can pretty much use and abuse you any way they choose, which means they can use you for any other personnel or promotion tasks they wish. One such task is below-the-zone promotions. We're going to take two hundred majors who are two years below their primary promotion zone, score them, then combine them with the other selected candidates, resolve the gray areas, and pass their names along for promotion along with the others. This panel gets one hundred jackets."

"Shit-hot," Harry Ponce exclaimed. "We get our hands on the best of the best of the best."

"I don't fully understand, sir," Norman said, raising a hand almost as if he were in grade school. "What's the purpose of such a drastic promotion? Why do those officers get chosen so far ahead of their peers? It doesn't make sense to me. What did they do to deserve such attention?"

"As in all promotion boards, Colonel," Ingemanson replied, "the needs of the Air Force determine how and why officers get promoted. In this case, the powers that be determined that there should be a handful of individuals that represent the absolute best and most dedicated of the breed."

"But I still don't . . ."

"Generally, below-the-zone promotions are incentives for motivated officers to do even better," Ingemanson interrupted. "If you know that the Air Force will pick a handful above the rest, for those who care about things like that, it's their chance to work a little harder to make their jacket stand out. It's been my experience that generally the BTZ guys become the leaders in every organization."

"That's to be expected, I suppose," Norman said. "You give one person a gold star when everyone else gets silver stars, and the one with the gold star will start behaving like a standout, whether he really is or not. Classic group psychology. Is this what we want to do? Is this the message we want to send young officers in the Air Force?"

Ponce and some of the others rolled their eyes at that comment. Ingemanson smiled patiently and responded, "It sounds like a never-ending 'chicken-or-the-egg' argument, Colonel, which we won't get into here. I prefer to think of this as an opportunity to reward an officer whose qualities, leadership, and professionalism rise above the others. That's your task.

"Now, I must inform you that some of these jackets are marked 'classified,' " General Ingemanson went on. "There is nothing in these files more classified than 'NOFORN' and 'CONFIDENTIAL,' but be aware that these files do carry a security classification over and above a normal everyday personnel file. The files may contain pointers to other, more sensitive documents.

"Bottom line is, that factoid is none of your concern. You evaluate each candidate by the physical content of the file that you hold in your hands. You won't be given access to any other documents or records. You should not try to speculate on anything in the file that is not on a standard promotion board evaluation checklist. In other words, just because a candidate has annotations and pointers regarding classified records doesn't mean his file should be weighed any heavier than someone else, or because a candidate doesn't have any such annotations shouldn't count against him. Base your decisions on the content of the files alone. Got it?" Everyone nodded, even Norman, although he appeared as perplexed as before.

"Now, to save time, we do below-the-primary-zone selections a little differently," Ingemanson went on. "Everyone goes through the pile and gives a yes or no opinion of the candidate. The candidate needs four of seven 'yes' votes to go on to round two. This helps thin out the lineup so you can concentrate on the best possible candidates in a shorter period of time. Round two is precisely like a normal scoring routine—minimum six, maximum ten points, in half-point increments. Once we go through and score everyone, we'll resolve the gray areas, then put those candidates in with the other candidates, then rescore and resolve until we have our selectees. We should be finished by tomorrow. We present the entire list to the board on Thursday, get final approval, and sign the list Friday morning and send it off to the Pentagon. We're on the home stretch, boys. Any questions?"

"So what you're saying, sir," Norman observed, "is that these below-the-zone selectees could displace selectees that we've already chosen? That doesn't seem fair."

"That's a statement, not a question, Colonel," Ingemanson said. There was a slight ripple of laughter, but most of the panel members just wanted Norman to shut up. "You're right, of course, Colonel. The BTZ selectees will be so identified, and when their OSRs are compared with the other selectees, you panel members will be instructed that a BTZ selectee must really have an outstanding record in order to bump an in-the-primary-zone or above-the-primary-zone selectee. As you may or may not know, BTZ selectees usually represent less than three percent of all selectees, and it is not unusual for a board to select *no* BTZ candidates for promotion. But again, that's up to you. No more questions? Comments? Jokes?" Ingemanson did not give anyone a chance to reply. "Good. Have fun, get to work."

The Officer Selection Reports began their circulation around the table, each member receiving a stack of about fifteen. Norman was irked by having to do this chore, but he was intrigued as well. These guys must be really good, he thought, to be chosen for promotion so far ahead of their peers.

But upon opening his first folder, he was disappointed again. The photograph he saw was of a chunky guy with narrow, tense-looking blue eyes, a crooked nose, irregular cheeks and forehead, thin blond hair cut too short, uneven helmet-battered ears, a thick neck underneath a shirt that appeared too small for him, and a square but meaty jaw. He wore senior navigator's wings atop two and a half rows of ribbons—one of the smallest numbers of ribbons Norman had seen in six days of scrutinizing personnel files. The uniform devices appeared to be on straight, but the Class A uniform blouse looked as if it had a little white hanger rash on the shoulders, as if it had hung in the closet too long and had just been taken out for the photograph.

He was ready to vote "no" on this guy right away, but he didn't want to pass the folder too early, so he glanced at the Officer Effectiveness Reports. What in hell were they thinking—this guy wasn't anywhere ready to be promoted *two years* ahead of his peers! He had only been to *two* assignments in eight years, not including training schools. Up until recently, he was a line navigator—an instructor, yes, but still basically a line officer, virtually the same as a second lieutenant fresh out of tech school. Sure, he had won a bunch of trophies at the Strategic Air Command Giant Voice Bombing and Navigation Competition, and several raters had called him "the best bombardier in the nation, maybe the world."

But one rater, a year before he left his first PCS assignment, had only rated him "Above Average," not "Outstanding." He didn't have a "firewalled" OER. One of his last raters at his first assignment had said "A few improvements will result in one of the Air Force's finest aviators." Translation: He had problems that he apparently wasn't even trying to fix. He wasn't officer material, let alone a candidate for early promotion! He wasn't even promotable, let alone leadership material! How in the world did he even get promoted to major?

What else? A master's degree, yes, but only Squadron Officer School done, by correspondence—no advanced leadership schools. What in hell was he doing with his time? One temporary assignment with the U.S. Border Security Force—which went bust before the end of its third year, disgraced and discredited. His OERs at his second PCS assignment in Las Vegas were very good. His last OER had one three-star and two four-star raters—the four-star raters were the chief of staff of the Air Force and the chairman of the Joint Chiefs of Staff, a very impressive achievement. But there were very few details of exactly what he did there to deserve such high-powered raters. He had some of the shortest rater's comments Norman had ever seen—lots of "Outstanding officer," "Promote immediately," and "A real asset to the Air Force and the nation" type comments, but no specifics at all. His flying time seemed almost frozen—obviously he wasn't doing much flying. No flying, but no professional military schools? One temporary assignment, totally unrelated to his primary field? This guy was a joke.

And he didn't have a runner's chin. Norman could tell immediately if a guy took care of himself, if he cared about his personal health and appearance, by looking at the chin. Most runners had firm, sleek chins. Nonexercisers, especially nonrunners, had slack chins. Slack chins, slack attitudes, slack officers.

Norman marked Patrick S. McLanahan's BTZ score sheet with a big fat "No," and he couldn't imagine any other panel member, even Harry Ponce, voting to consider this guy for a BTZ promotion. Then, he had a better idea.

For the first time as a promotion board member, Norman withdrew an Air Force Form 772—"Recommendation for Dismissal Based on Substandard OSR," and he filled it out. A rated officer who didn't fly, who was obviously contently hiding out at some obscure research position in Las Vegas twiddling his thumbs, was not working in the best interest of the Air Force. This guy had almost nine years in service, but it was obvious that it would take him many, many years to be prepared to compete for promotion to lieutenant colonel. The Air Force had an "up or out" policy, meaning that you could be passed over for promotion to lieutenant colonel twice. After that, you had to be dismissed. The Air Force shouldn't wait for this guy to shape up. He was a waste of space.

A little dedication to yourself and dedication to the Air Force might help, Norman silently told the guy as he signed the AFF772, recommending that McLanahan be stripped of his regular commission and either sent back to the Reserves or, better, dismissed from service altogether. Try getting off your ass and do some running, for a start. Try to act like you give a damn . . .

Mother Nature picked that night to decide to dump an entire week's worth of rain on Diego Garcia—it was one of the worst tropical downpours anyone had seen on the little island in a long time. The British civilian contracted shuttle bus wasn't authorized to go on the southeast side of the runway, and Patrick wasn't going to wait for someone to pick him up, so he ran down the service road toward the Air Force hangar. He had already called ahead to the security police and control tower, telling them what he was going to do, but in the torrential storm, it was unlikely anyone in the tower could see him. Patrick made it to the outer perimeter fence to the Air Force hangar just as one of the security units was coming out in a Humvee to pick him up.

Patrick dashed through security in record time, then ran to the hangar to his locker for a dry flight suit. Inside he saw maintenance techs preparing both Megafortress flying battleships for fueling and weapons preloading. Patrick decided to grab his thermal underwear and socks too—it looked as if he might be going flying very soon.

"What happened?" Patrick asked as he trotted into the mission planning room.

"An American guided-missile cruiser, the USS *Percheron,* was transiting the Strait of Hormuz on its way into the Persian Gulf when it was attacked by several large missiles," Colonel John Ormack said. "Two of them missed, two were shot down, two were near misses, but two hit. The ship is still under way, but it's heavily damaged. Over a hundred casualties."

"Do they know who launched the missiles?"

"No idea," Ormack replied. "Debris suggests they were Iraqi. The missiles were fired from the south, across the Musandam Peninsula over Oman. The warhead size was huge—well over five hundred pounds each. AS-9 or AS-14 class."

"The *Percheron* couldn't tag the missiles?"

"They didn't see them until it was too late," Ormack reported. "They were diving right on top of the cruiser from straight overhead. They were already supersonic when they hit. No time to respond. The *Percheron* is a *California*-class cruiser, an older class of guided-missile cruiser—even though it was fitted with some of the latest radars, it wasn't exactly a spring chicken."

"I thought every ship going into the Gulf had to be updated with the best self-defense gear?"

"That's the Navy for you—they thought they had cleaned up the Gulf and could just waltz in with any old piece of shit they chose," Lieutenant General Brad Elliott interjected as he strode into the room. He glared at Patrick's wet hair and heavy breathing, and added, "You don't look very rested to me, Major. Where's Tork?"

"On her way, sir," Patrick replied. "I didn't wait for the SPs to come get me."

"I guess it's not a very good night for a romantic stroll on the beach anyway," Elliott muttered sarcastically. "I could've used both of you an hour ago."

"Sorry, sir." He wasn't really that sorry, but he tried to understand what kind of hell Brad had to be going through—stripped of the command that meant so much to him—and he felt sorry for Brad, not sorry that he wasn't there to help out.

"The Navy's officially started an investigation and is not speculating on what caused the explosions,"

Elliott went on. "Defense has leaked some speculation to the media that some older Standard SM-2 air-to-air missiles might have accidentally exploded in their magazines. Hard to come up with an excuse for an above-deck explosion in two different sections of the ship. No one is yet claiming responsibility for the attack.

"Unofficially, the Navy is befuddled. They had no warning of the attack until seconds before the missiles hit. No missile-launch detection from shore, no unidentified aircraft within a hundred miles of the cruiser, and no evidence of sub activity in the area. They were well outside the range of all known or suspected coast defense sites capable of launching a missile of that size. Guesses, anyone?"

"How about a stealth bomber, like the one we ran into?" Patrick replied.

"My thoughts exactly," Brad said. "The Defense Intelligence Agency has no information at all about Iran buying Blackjack bombers from Russia, or anything about Russia developing a bomber capable of launching air-to-air missiles. They got our report, but I think they'll disregard it."

"I wonder how much DIA knows about us and *our* capabilities?" Wendy asked.

"I think we've got to assume that Iran is flying that thing, and it's got to be neutralized before it does any more damage," Patrick said. "One more attack—especially on an aircraft carrier or other major warship—could spark a massive Middle East shooting war, bigger and meaner than the war with Iraq." He turned to Brad Elliott and said, "You've got to get us back in the fight, Brad. We're the only ones that can secretly take on that Blackjack battleship."

Elliott looked at Patrick with a mixture of surprise, humor, and anger. "Major, are you suggesting that we—dare I even say it?—launch *without* proper authorization?" he asked.

"I'm suggesting that perhaps we should follow orders and return the Megafortresses to Dreamland," Patrick said. "But I don't recall any specific instructions about a specific route of flight we should take."

"You think it makes any sense for us to fly from Diego Garcia all the way to the Strait of Hormuz and tell the Pentagon we were on the way back to Nevada?" Brad asked, a twinkle of humor in his eyes.

"We always file a 'due regard' point in our flight plans, which means we disappear from official view until we're ready to reenter American airspace," Patrick said. Classified military flights, such as spy plane or nuclear-weapon ferry flights, never filed a detailed point-by-point route flight plan—they always had a "due regard" point, a place where the flight plan was suspended, the rest of the flight secret. In effect, the flight "disappears" from official or public purview. The flight simply checks in with authorities at a specific place and time to reactivate the flight plan, with no official query about where it was or what it did. "Even the Pentagon doesn't know where we go. And our tankers belong to us, so we don't have to coordinate with any outside agencies for refueling support. If we, for example, fly off to Nevada and, say, develop an in-flight emergency six hours in the mission and decide to head on back to Diego Garcia, I don't think the Air Force or the Pentagon can blame us for that, can they?"

"I don't see how they can," John Ormack said, smiling mischievously. "And we very well can't fly a Megafortress into Honolulu, can we?"

"And in five hours, we can be back on patrol over the Strait of Hormuz," Wendy Tork said. "We know what that Blackjack looks like on our sensors. We keep an eye on him and jump him if he tries to make another move." Everyone on the crew was getting into it now.

"In the meantime, we get full authorization to conduct a search-and-destroy mission over the Strait of Hormuz for the mysterious Soviet-Iranian attack plane," Patrick said. "If we don't get it, we land back here at Diego, get 'fixed,' and return to Dreamland. We've done all we can do."

"Sounds like a plan to me," Brad Elliott said, beaming proudly and clasping Patrick on the shoulder. "Let's work up a weapons list, get our guys busy loading gas and missiles, and let's get this show on the road!" As they all got busy, Brad stepped over to Patrick, and said in a low voice, "Nice to be working together with you again, Muck."

"Same here, Brad," Patrick said. Finally, thankfully, the old connection between them was back. It was more than reestablishing crew connectivity—they were back to trusting and believing in one another again.

"Any idea how we're going to find this mystery Iranian Megafortress?" Brad asked. "We've only got one chance, and we have no idea where this guy's based, what his next target is, or even if he really exists."

"He exists, all right," Patrick said. He studied the intelligence reports Elliott had brought into the mission-planning room for a moment. "We must have a couple dozen ships down there protecting the *Percheron.*"

"I think the Navy's going to move a carrier battle group to escort the cruiser back to Bahrain."

"A carrier, huh?" Patrick remarked. "A cruiser is a good target, but a carrier would be a great target. Iraq made no secret of the fact they wanted to tag a carrier in the Gulf. Maybe Iran would like to claim that trophy."

"Maybe—especially if they could pin the blame on Iraq," Brad said. "But that still doesn't solve our problem: How do we find this mystery attack plane? The chances of him and us being in the same sky at the same time is next to impossible."

"I see only one way to flush him out," Patrick said. "It'll still be a one-in-a-thousand chance, but if he's up flying, I think we can make him come to us."

At over three hundred tons gross weight and with a wingspan longer than the Wright Brothers' first flight, the Tupolev-160 long-range supersonic bomber, code-named "Blackjack" by the West, was the largest attack plane in the world. It carried more than its own empty weight in fuel and almost its own weight in weapons, and it was capable of delivering any weapon in the Soviet arsenal, from dumb bombs to multimegaton gravity weapons and cruise missiles, with pinpoint precision. It could fly faster than the speed of sound up to sixty thousand feet, or at tree-top level over any terrain, in any weather, day or night. Although only forty Blackjack bombers had been built, they represented the number one air-breathing military threat to the West.

But as deadly as the Tu-160 Blackjack was, there was one plane even deadlier: the Tupolev-160E. The stock Blackjack's large steel and titanium vertical stabilizer had been replaced by a low, slender V-tail made of composite materials, stronger but more lightweight and radar-absorbing than steel. Much of the skin not exposed to high levels of heat in supersonic flight was composed of radar-absorbent material, and the huge engine air inlets for the four Kuznetsov NK-32 afterburning engines had been redesigned so the engines' compressor blades wouldn't reflect radar energy. Even the jet's steeply raked cockpit windscreens had been specially shaped and coated to misdirect and absorb radar energy. All this helped to reduce the radar cross section of this giant bird to one-fourth of the stock aircraft's size.

The only thing that spoiled the Blackjack-E's sleek, stealthy needlelike appearance was a triangular fairing mounted under the forward bomb bay and a smaller fairing atop the fuselage that carried the aircraft's phase-array air and surface search radars. The multimode radar electronically scanned both the sky and the sea for aircraft and ships, and passed the information both to allied ground, surface, and airborne units, as well as automatically programming its attack and defensive weapons.

The Blackjack-E and its weaponry were the latest in Soviet military technology—but that meant little to a starving, nearly bankrupt nation on the verge of total collapse. The weapon system was far more useful to the Soviet Union as a commodity—and they found a willing buyer in the Islamic Republic of Iran. Still oil-rich—and, with the rise in oil prices because of the war, growing richer by the day—but with a badly shaved-back military following the devastating nine-year Iran-Iraq War, Iran needed to rebuild its arsenal quickly and effectively. Money was no object. The faster they could build an arsenal that could project power throughout the entire Middle East, the faster they could claim the title of the most powerful military force in the region, a force that had to be reckoned with in any dealings involving trade, commerce, land, religion, or legal rights in the Persian Gulf.

The Blackjack-E was the answer. The bomber was capable against air, ground, and surface targets; it was fast, it had the range to strike targets as far away as England without aerial refueling, and it carried a huge attack payload. After watching the Americans destroy nearly half of the vaunted Iraqi army with precision-guided weapons, the Iranians were positive they had spent their money wisely—any warplane they invested in had to be stealthy, had to be fast, had to have all-weather capability, and had to have precision-guided attack capability, or it was virtually useless over today's high-tech battlefield. The Russians were selling—not just the planes, but the weapons, the support equipment, and Russian instructors and technicians—and the Iranians were eagerly buying.

The USS *Percheron* was the first operational test of the new attack platform. A large American warship, transiting the shallow, congested, narrow waters of the Strait of Hormuz alone, was an inviting target. The *Percheron* was a good test case because its long-range sensors and defensive armament were highly capable, some of the best in the world against all kinds of air, surface, and subsurface threats. If the Blackjack-E could penetrate the *Percheron*'s defenses, it was indeed a formidable weapon.

The test was a rousing success. The Blackjack-E's crew—an Iranian pilot as aircraft commander, a Russian instructor pilot in the copilot's seat, two Iranian officers as bombardier and defensive-systems officer, and one Russian systems instructor in a jump seat between the Iranian systems officers—launched their entire warload of six Kh-29 external missiles—painted and modified with Iraqi Air Force markings—from maximum range and medium altitude. The missiles dived to sea-skimming altitude, then popped up to five hundred meters when only five kilometers from their targets and then dived straight down at their target. Two of the missiles missed the cruiser by less than a half a kilometer; two made direct hits. The explosions could be seen and heard by observers twenty kilometers away. Although the *Percheron* was still able to get under way, it was certainly out of action.

This time, however, the Blackjack-E would have a full weapons load. This would be the ultimate test. On this flight, the Blackjack-E was loaded for a multirole hunter-killer mission. In the aft bomb bay, it carried a rotary launcher with twelve Kh-15 solid-rocket attack missiles. Each missile had a top speed of Mach 5—five times the speed of sound—a range of almost ninety miles when launched from high altitude, and a three-hundred-and-fifty-pound high-explosive warhead. The missiles, covered with a rubbery skin that burned off while in flight, were targeted by the Blackjack's navigator by radar, or they would automatically attack large ships using its onboard radar, or home in on preprogrammed enemy radar emissions. Designed to destroy target defenses and attack targets well beyond surface-to-air missile range, the Kh-15s were unjammable, almost invisible to radar, and almost impossible to intercept or shoot down.

Externally, the Blackjack-E carried eight R-40 long-range air-to-air missiles, four under the attach point of each swiveling wing; two of the missiles on each wing were radar-guided missiles and two were heat-seeking missiles. It was the first Soviet heavy bomber to carry air-to-air missiles. Also under each wing were two Kh-29 multirole attack missiles, which had a range of sixteen miles, a top speed of just over Mach 2, and a massive six-hundred-pound high-explosive warhead. The Kh-29 was steered to its target by a TV datalink, giving it a precision-guided capability day or night or in poor weather, or it would home in on enemy radar emissions. Once locked on to its target, the Kh-29 would automatically fly an evasive sea-skimming or ballistic trajectory, depending on the target, followed by a steep dive into its target. The Kh-29 was designed to deliver a killing blow to almost any size target, even a large surface vessel, underground command post, bridges, and large industrial buildings and factories.

As predicted, the Americans erected an air umbrella around the stricken USS *Percheron* to protect it against sneak attacks. Because it was the closest, they moved CV-41, the venerable USS *Midway*, and its eight-ship escort group south to cover the *Percheron*'s crippled retreat. The *Midway*, the oldest carrier in active service in the U.S. fleet and the only carrier homeported on foreign soil, was overdue for decommissioning and reserve duty when Operation Desert Shield began. It was sent to the Persian Gulf and played mostly a short-range land-attack role with its three squadrons of F/A-18 Hornet fighter-bombers and one squadron of A-6 Intruder bombers.

If there was more time, or the need to get the crippled ship out of harm's way not so pressing, the Navy would have chosen another ship to protect the *Percheron*. The *Midway* was the lightest armed ship for self-defense, with only two Sea Sparrow surface-to-air missile launchers, two Phalanx close-in Gatling gun systems, and no F-14 Tomcat fighters for long-range defense—it relied heavily on its escorts for protection. It had little up-to-date radars and electronic-countermeasure equipment, since it was on its way to reserve status before the start of the war. The second carrier battle group stationed in the Persian Gulf, the USS *America*, maintained its patrol in the northern half of the Gulf, about two hundred and fifty miles away—too far from *Midway* to be of any help in case some disaster took place.

The Blackjack-E, call sign Lechtvar ("Teacher"), launched from its secret base near Mashhad, about six hundred kilometers east of Tehran, using an Iran Air, the official Iranian government airline, flight number. It followed the commercial air-traffic route, overflying the Persian Gulf and central Saudi Arabia on its way to Jiddah, Saudi Arabia. In late February, with air superiority established over the entire region and no threat from Iraq's air force, the Coalition forces agreed to reopen commercial air routes from Iran and other Islamic countries to the east into Jiddah to accommodate pilgrims visiting the Muslim holy cities of Mecca and Medina. As long as a flight plan was on file and the flight followed a strict navigation corridor, overflying Saudi Arabia was permitted during the conflict.

The flight was handed off from Riyadh Air Traffic Control Center to Jiddah Approach, just before coming within range of American naval radar systems operating in the Red Sea. As it descended over the Hijaz Mountains south of Jiddah, the Blackjack-E bomber crew activated their terrain-following radar system, deactivated its transponder radar tracking system, and descended below radar coverage in less than two minutes. The crew allowed a few seconds of a "7700" transponder signal—the international code for Emergency—before shutting off all radios and external lights completely and descending into the mountains. Within moments, the flight had completely disappeared from radar screens.

Saudi and Coalition rescue teams, both civilian and military, immediately started fanning out from Jiddah south to the suspected crash site. But by the time the rescuers launched, the Blackjack-E was already far to the east, speeding across the deserts of the central Arabian Peninsula.

As the Blackjack-E sped across the sands and desolate high plains of eastern Saudi Arabia, air-defense radar sites began popping up all across their intended route of flight. It seemed as if there was a surface-to-air missile site stationed every forty of fifty miles apart along the Persian Gulf from Al-Khasab on the tip of Cape Shuraytah in Oman all the way to Kuwait City, with more sprinkles of air-defense radars on warships on or over the Persian Gulf itself. But the sites that were the most dangerous threat to the Blackjack-E—the various Coalition Patriot, Rapier, and Hawk antiaircraft batteries—were all fixed sites, and their precise locations had been known for weeks—they would make easy targets. In addition, although all of them were capable of attacking targets in any direction, they were set up and oriented to attack targets flying in from the Persian Gulf or Strait of Hormuz, not from the Arabian Peninsula. There were a few scattered mobile antiaircraft artillery emplacements, and the shipborne Aegis, Standard, and Sea Wolf antiaircraft missile systems represented a significant threat, but those would not be able to engage a fast-moving low-flying stealthy target in time.

Just before starting its attack, the Blackjack-E accelerated to just under supersonic speed—it was now traveling more than a mile every ten seconds. From fifty miles away, the Blackjack-E crew launched inertially guided Kh-15 missiles against the known antiaircraft emplacements in the United Arab Emirates. As the plane sped closer, it polished off any remaining antiaircraft radar sites with radar-homing Kh-15 missiles. As the bomber neared the United Arab Emirates coastline heading east, many radar sites saw the big bomber coming, but before they could direct their missile units to fire, the Kh-15 missiles were blowing the radars and communications nets off the air. Coalition air-defense fighters based all up and down the Persian Gulf, from half a dozen bases, launched in hot pursuit. The aircraft carrier *Midway* had ten F/A-18 Hornet fighter-bombers in air-defense configuration airborne in combat air patrols all around the carrier group, and it quickly launched another pair and prepared more launches, even though no one had a definite fix on the unknown aircraft.

The biggest threat to the Blackjack-E crew, however, was the French-made Mirage 5 and Mirage 2000 air-defense fighters based in Dubai. One Mirage 2000 acquired the Blackjack shortly after liftoff along with his wingman, but it was blown out of the sky by a radar-guided R-40 missile before the Mirage could even complete its first vector to the bandit. The second Mirage disengaged when he saw his leader explode in a ball of fire, and by the time he was ready to pursue and engage again, the Blackjack-E was almost out of radar range and on its missile attack run against the USS *Midway*.

The gauntlet was squeezing tighter and tighter on the Blackjack-E, but it was still heading for its target. The crew accelerated to supersonic speed, staying less than one hundred feet above the dark, shallow waters of the Persian Gulf as the bomber closed in on its quarry. The Blackjack climbed higher only to launch Kh-15 radar-homing missiles on the greatest threats in front of them, the *Perry*-class guided-missile frigate guarding the *Midway*'s western flank. It took five Kh-15 missiles fired at the frigate to finally shut its missile-search-and-guidance radars down. The *Midway*'s Hornets' APG-65 attack radar was not a true look-down, shoot-down-capable system; although F/A-18 Hornets had the Navy's first two aerial kills of the Gulf War, the fighter was designed primarily as a medium bomber and attack plane, not as a low-altitude interceptor. Three Hornets took beyond-visual-range shots at the Blackjack with AIM-7 radar-guided Sparrow missiles, and all missed.

Strange, the Blackjack crew remarked to themselves—the Americans were all around them, taking long-range shots but not pressing the attack. It was a stiff defense, but not nearly as severe as they expected. Why . . . ?

But it didn't matter—now there was nothing to stop the Blackjack-E. At three minutes to launch point, the Blackjack's attack radar had locked on to the *Midway* and fed inertial guidance information to the four Kh-29 attack missiles. The final launch countdown was under way . . .

The UHF GUARD radio channel had been alive for several min- utes with warnings from American and Gulf Cooperative Council air-defense networks in English, French, Arabic, and Farsi, demanding that the unidentified aircraft leave the area. The Blackjack crew ignored it . . .

. . . until new warning messages in English on both UHF and VHF emergency radio channels began: "Unidentified intruder, unidentified intruder, this is the Islamic Republic of Iran Army Air Defense Network command center, you are in violation of sovereign Iranian airspace. You are directed to leave the area immediately or you will be attacked without warning. Repeat, reverse course and leave the area immediately!"

The Iranian pilot in command of the Blackjack-E bomber looked at the Russian copilot in surprise.

"What is happening?" he asked in English, their common language.

"Ignore it!" the Russian shouted. "We are on the attack run, and we still have many American warships to contend with. Stay . . ."

"Attention, attention, all air-defense units, this is Abbass Control," they heard in Farsi, "implement full air-defense configuration protocols, repeat, full air-defense protocols, all stations acknowledge." The message was repeated; then, in Farsi, Arabic, and English, they heard, "Warning, warning, warning, to all aircraft on this frequency, this is the Islamic Republic of Iran Army Air Defense Network, full air-defense emergency restrictions are in effect for the Tehran and Bandar Abbass Flight Information Regions, repeat, full air-defense emergency restrictions are now in effect. All aircraft, establish positive radio contact and identification with your controller immediately. All unidentified aircraft in the Tehran and Bandar Abbass Flight Information Regions may be fired upon without warning!"

"What should we do?" the Iranian bombardier asked. "Should we ask . . . ?"

"We maintain radio silence!" the Russian shouted. "The Americans can home in on the briefest radio transmission! Stay on the attack run!"

"Our Mode Two—should we transmit?" the defensive-systems officer asked. The Mode Two was an encrypted identification signal. Although it could only be decoded by Iranian air-defense sites, transmitting any radio signals was dangerous over enemy territory, so they had it deactivated.

"*No!*" the Russian responded. "Pay attention to the attack run! Ignore what is happening . . ."

Just then, they saw a bright flash of light far off on the horizon. The weather was ideal, cloudy and cool, with no thunderstorms predicted. That wasn't lightning.

"Did you get the transfer-alignment maneuver yet, bombardier?" the Russian systems officer instructor asked.

"I . . . no, I have not," the Iranian bombardier replied, still distracted by what was happening over his own country. The transfer-alignment maneuver was a required gyroscopic routine that removed the last bit of inertial drift from their missiles' guidance system.

"Then get busy! Program it in and inform the crew. You had better hurry before . . ."

"Birjand Four-Oh-Four flight, cancel takeoff clearance!" the Blackjack crew heard on the emergency channel in Farsi. "Maliz Three, hold your position, emergency vehicles en route, passing on your right side. Attention all aircraft, emergency evacuation procedure in effect, report to your shelter assignments immediately."

"Shelter assignments?" the defensive systems officer shouted. "It sounds like one of our bases is under air attack!"

"I don't understand what you're saying!" the Russian copilot shouted. "But ignore any radio messages you are hearing. They could be fake messages. Stay on the attack run!"

But the defensive-systems officer couldn't ignore it. He switched his radio over to the tactical command frequency: "Abbass Control, Abbass Control, this is Lechtvar, we copy your emergency reports, requesting vectors to last-known position of enemy aircraft. We are able to respond. Over." No response, just more emergency messages. "Abbass Control, this is Lechtvar, we are en route to your location, sixty miles southwest, request you pass vectors to enemy aircraft, we can respond! Over! Respond!"

"Damn your eyes, I said stay off the radios!" the Russian pilot shouted. "Don't you understand, the Americans can track your transmissions! Now get back on the attack run! That's an order!"

But just then they heard in English on their own tactical command frequency: "Attention, Iranian Blackjack bomber, this is your old friend from the Strait from last week. Do you recognize my voice?"

The Iranian pilot of the Blackjack-E was stunned. It was the same voice that had contacted them, the unidentified American military flight!

"Calling Abbass Control," they heard an Iranian voice say in English, "this is an official military frequency. Do not use this frequency. It is a violation of international law. Vacate this frequency immediately."

"Abbass Control, this is Lechtvar," the Iranian Blackjack pilot called. "We copied your emergency evacuation messages. Give us vectors to the enemy aircraft and we will respond immediately."

"Lechtvar, this is Abbass Control, negative!" the confused controller replied after a few moments. "We detected some unidentified aircraft, and then a flare was set off over the Strait. But there are no Iranian installations under attack and no one has implemented any evacuation procedures. Clear this channel immediately!"

The Blackjack crew finally realized they had been tricked. The crew was stunned into embarrassed silence. The Russian crew members cursed loud enough in Russian to be heard without the interphones—they realized that their chances of surviving this mission suddenly went from very good to very poor. The bombardier directed the transfer-alignment maneuver, a forty-five-degree left turn followed by two more turns back to course—all missiles were fully functional and . . .

"Hey, Blackjack. We know you're up here listening to us. We'll have you on our radar any second now. You'll never finish your attack. Why not forget about the carrier and come get us? We're waiting for you."

It was impossible! The mystery plane was back—and they knew all about their mission! How was that possible? How could they . . . ?

Suddenly, the radar-warning indicators blared a warning—an enemy airborne radar had swept across them. Seconds later, with sixty seconds to launch, the radar-warning receiver indicated a radar lock. They had been found! The Blackjack's radar jammers were functioning perfectly, but they were unable to keep the enemy tracking radar from completely breaking lock—it changed frequencies too fast and changed in such a broad range that the Blackjack's trackbreakers could not quite keep up.

"Got ya, Blackjack," the American said. "You're not as stealthy tonight as last time. You must be carrying some heavy iron tonight. Got some more air-to-air missiles loaded up tonight? Maybe a few big antiship missiles? Why don't you just jettison all that deadweight and come on up here and let's you and me finish this thing, once and for all?"

"We must break off the attack," the Iranian defensive-systems officer shouted. "If they have us on radar, they can vector in the other fighters. We'll be surrounded in seconds."

"Process the launch!" the Russian mission commander shouted. "Ignore this American bastard! He did not attack us before—perhaps he cannot stop us."

As if they could hear their interphone conversation, the American said, "Hey, Blackjack, you better bug out now. I just relayed your position to my little buddies, the F/A-18 Hornets from the *Midway*. They're not very happy that you've come to try to blow up their ship. In about two minutes you'll have an entire squadron of Hornets on your ass."

The Iranian pilot could no longer contain his anger. He opened the channel to the GUARD frequency and mashed his mike button: "You cowardly pig-bastard! If you want us, come and get us!"

"Hey, there you are, Blackjack," the American said happily. "Nice to talk to you again."

"You know who I am—who are you?"

"I'm the pig-bastard at your two o'clock position and closing fast," the American replied. "I'll bet my interceptor missiles are faster and have longer range than your attack missiles—I'll reach my firing point in about ten seconds. You don't want to die flying straight and level, do you? C'mon up here and let's get it on."

"You will never stop us!" the Iranian shouted.

"Oops—I think I overestimated our firing point. Here they come." And just then, the radar-warning receiver blared a shrill MISSILE LAUNCH warning—the Americans had fired radar-guided missiles!

The Russian pilot reacted instinctively. He immediately started a shallow climb and a steep right bank into the oncoming missiles. "Chaff! Chaff!" he shouted; then: "Launch the Kh-29s! *Now!*"

"We are not in range!" the bombardier shouted.

"Launch anyway!" the Russian ordered. "We will not get another chance! Launch!" The bombardier immediately commanded the Kh-29 missiles to launch. The missiles all had solid lock-ons, and with the slightly greater altitude, the Kh-29s had a little greater range . . . it might be enough to score a hit.

* * *

"They launched missiles!" Patrick shouted. The Megafortress's attack radar, a derivative of the APG-71 radar from the F-15E Eagle, immediately detected the big Kh-29 missiles speeding toward the *Midway.* "I got four big missiles, very low altitude, going supersonic. Wendy . . . ?"

"I got 'em," Wendy Tork reported. The APG-71 weapon system had immediately passed targeting information to Wendy's defensive system, and all Wendy had to do was launch-commit her AIM-120 Scorpion missiles. "We're at extreme range—I'm going to have to ripple off all our Scorpions. Give me forty right and full military power."

As Brad Elliott followed Wendy's orders, the fire-control computers went to work. Within twenty seconds, eight Scorpions fired off into space. At first they used the Megafortress's attack radar for guidance, but soon they activated their own active radars and tracked the Russian missiles with ease. All four Kh-29 missiles were shot down long before they reached the *Midway.*

"Splash four missiles," Wendy reported. "But we're in trouble now—we used up all our defensive missiles." And, as if the Blackjack crew heard them, Wendy saw that the Iranian attack plane was turning very, very quickly—heading right for them. "We got a big, big bandit at fifteen miles, low. He . . ." Just then, the EB-52C's threat-warning receiver issued a RADAR WARNING, a MISSILE WARNING, and a MISSILE LAUNCH warning in rapid succession. *"Break right!"* Wendy shouted. "Stingers coming online! Chaff!"

The Soviet-made R-40 missiles were well within their maximum range, and the Blackjack's big fire-control radar had a solid lock-on. The Megafortress's rear-defense fire-control radar locked on to the incoming missiles and started firing Stinger airmine rockets, but this time they couldn't score a hit. One R-40 missile was decoyed enough for a near miss, but a second R-40 scored a hit, blowing off the left V-tail stabilator on the Megafortress and shelling out two engines on the left side.

The force of the explosion and the sudden loss of the two left engines threw the Megafortress into a jaw-snapping left swerve so violent that the big bomber almost succeeded in swapping nose for tail. Only Brad Elliott's and John Ormack's superior airmanship and familiarity with the EB-52C Megafortress saved the crew. They knew enough not to automatically jam on full power on all the operating engines, which would have certainly sent them into a violent, unrecoverable flat Frisbee-like spin—instead, they had to *pull* power on the right side back to match the left, trade precious altitude so they could gain some even more precious flying airspeed, recover control, and only then start feeding in power slowly and carefully. The automatic fire-suppression systems on the Megafortress shut down the engines and cut off fuel, preventing a fatal fire and explosion. They lost two hundred knots and five thousand feet of altitude before the bomber was actually flying in some semblance of coordinated flight and was not on the verge of spiraling into the Persian Gulf.

But the Megafortress was a sitting duck for the speedy Blackjack bomber. "His airspeed has dropped off to less than five hundred kilometers per hour," the defensive-systems officer reported as he studied his fire-control radar display. "He has dropped to one thousand meters, twelve o'clock, ten miles. He is straight and level—not maneuvering. I think he's hit!"

"Then finish him off," the Iranian pilot shouted happily. "Finish him, and let's get out of here!"

"Stand by for missile launch!" the defensive-systems officer said. "Two missiles locked on . . . ready . . . ready . . . *launch*! Missiles . . ."

He never got to finish that sentence. A fraction of a second before the two R-40 missiles left their rails, three pairs of AIM-9 Sidewinder heat-seeking missiles from three pursuing F/A-18 Hornet fighters from the USS *Midway* plowed into the Blackjack-E bomber, fired from less than five miles away. They had used guidance information from the as-yet-unknown but friendly aircraft, so were able to conduct the intercept and lock on to the enemy attack plane without having to use their telltale airborne radars. The Sidewinders turned the Blackjack's four huge turbofan engines into four massive clouds of fire that completely engulfed, then devoured the big jet. The pieces of Blackjack bomber not incinerated in the blast were scattered across over thirty square miles of the Persian Gulf and disappeared from sight forever.

"Hey, buddy, this is Dragon Four-Zero-Zero," the lead F/A-18 Hornet pilot radioed on the UHF GUARD channel. "You still up?"

"Roger," Brad Elliott replied. "We saw that bandit coming in to finish us off. I take it we're still alive because you nailed his ass."

"That's affirmative," the Hornet pilot replied happily. "We saw the hit you took. You need an escort back to King Khalid Military City?"

"Negative," Brad replied. "That's not our destination. We've got a tanker en route that'll take us home."

"You sure, buddy? If you're not going to KKMC,

it's a long and dangerous drive to anywhere else."

"Thanks, but we'll limp on outta here by ourselves," Brad replied. "Thank for clearing our six."

"Thank you for protecting our home plate, buddy," the Hornet pilot responded. "We owe you big-time, whoever you are. Dragon flight, out."

Brad Elliott scanned his instruments for the umpteenth time that minute. Everything had stabilized. They were in a slow climb, less than three hundred feet a minute, nursing every bit of power from the remaining engines. "Well, folks," he announced on interphone, "we're still flying, our refueling system is operable, and we've still got most essential systems. I want everyone in exposure suits. If we have to ditch, it's going to be a very, very long time before anyone picks us up. Might as well get up and stretch a bit—at this airspeed, it's going to be a real long flight back to Diego Garcia."

"The good news is," John Ormack interjected, "the weather report looks pretty good. I can't think of a nicer place to be stuck at fixing our bird."

"Amen," Brad Elliott agreed. He waited a few moments; then, not hearing any other comments, added, "You agree, Muck, Wendy? Can you use a few weeks on Diego while our guys fix us up? Patrick? Wendy? You copy?"

Patrick let his lips slowly part from Wendy's. He returned once more for another quick kiss, then drank in Wendy's dancing eyes and heavenly smile as he moved his oxygen mask to his face, and replied, "That sounds great to me, sir. Absolutely great."

"Ladies and gentlemen, thank you for your time, energy, dedication, and professionalism," Major General Larry Dean Ingemanson said. He stood before the last assembly of the entire promotion board in the Selection Board Secretariat's main auditorium. "The final selection list has been checked and verified by the Selection Board Secretariat staff—it just awaits my final signature before I transmit the list to the Secretary of the Air Force. But I know some of you have planes to catch and golf games to catch up on, so I wanted to say 'thank you' once again. I hope we meet again. The board is hereby adjourned." There was a relieved round of applause from the board members, but most were up and out of their seats in a flash, anxious to get out of that building and away from OSRs and official photographs and sitting in judgment of men and women they did not know, deciding their futures.

Norman Weir felt proud of himself and his performance as a member of the board. He was afraid he'd be intimidated by the personalities he'd encountered, afraid he wouldn't match up to their experience and knowledge and backgrounds. Instead, he discovered that he was just as knowledgeable and authoritative as any other "war hero" in the place, even guys like Harry Ponce. When it came to rational, objective decision-making, Norman felt he had an edge over all of them, and that made him feel pretty damned special.

As he walked toward the exits, he heard someone call his name. It was General Ingemanson. They had not spoken to one another since Ingemanson accepted the Form 772 on McLanahan, recommending he be dismissed from the active-duty Air Force. Ingemanson had requested additional information, a few more details on Norman's observations. Norman had plenty of reasons, more than enough to justify his decision. General Ingemanson accepted his additional remarks with a serious expression and promised he'd upchannel the information immediately.

He did warn Norman that a Form 772 would probably push the candidate completely out of the running for promotion, not just for this board but for any other promotion board he might meet. Norman stuck to his guns, and Ingemanson had no choice but to continue the process. McLanahan's jacket disappeared from the panel's deliberation, and Norman did not see his name on the final list.

Mission accomplished. Not only strike back at the pompous prima donnas that wore wings, but rid the Air Force of a true example of a lazy, selfish, good-for-nothing officer.

"Hey, Colonel, just wanted to say good-bye and thank you again for your service," General Ingemanson said, shaking Norman's hand warmly. "I had a great time working with you."

"It was my pleasure, sir. I enjoyed working with you too."

"Thank you," Ingemanson said. "And call me 'Swede'—everybody does." Norman said nothing. "Do you have a minute? I'm about ready to countersign your Form 772 to include in the transmission to the Secretary of the Air Force, and I wanted to give you an opportunity to look over my report that goes along with your 772."

"Is that necessary, sir?" Norman asked. "I've already put everything on the 772. McLanahan is a disgrace to the uniform and should be discharged. The Reserves don't even deserve an officer like that. I think I've made it clear."

"You have," Ingemanson said. "But I do want you to look at my evaluation. You can append any rebuttal comments to it if you wish. It'll only take a minute." With a confused and slightly irritated sigh,

Norman nodded and followed the general to his office.

If Norman saw the man in a plain dark suit sitting in the outer office behind the door talking into his jacket sleeve, he didn't pay any attention to him. General Ingemanson led the way into his office, motioned Norman inside, and then closed the door behind him. This time, Norman did notice the second plain-clothed man with the tiny silver badge on his lapel and the earpiece stuck in his right ear, standing beside Ingemanson's desk.

"What's going on, General?" Norman asked. "Who is this?"

"This is Special Agent Norris, United States Secret Service, Presidential Protection Detail," General Ingemanson replied. "He and his colleagues are here because that man sitting in my chair is the President of the United States." Norman nearly fell over backwards in surprise as he saw the President of the United States himself swivel around and rise up from the general's chair.

"Smooth introduction, Swede," the President said. "Very smooth."

"I try my best, Mr. President."

The President stepped from behind Ingemanson's desk, walked up to the still-dumbfounded Norman Weir, and extended a hand. "Colonel Weir, nice to meet you." Norman didn't quite remember shaking hands. "I was on my way to Travis Air Force Base in California to meet with some of the returning Desert Storm troops, and I thought it was a good idea to make a quick, unofficial stopover here at Randolph to talk with you."

Norman's eyes grew as wide as saucers. "Talk to . . . *me*?"

"Sit down, Colonel," the President said. He leaned

against Ingemanson's desk as Norman somehow found a chair. "I was told that you wish to file a recommendation that a Major Patrick McLanahan should be discharged from the Air Force on the basis of a grossly substandard and unacceptable Officer Selection Record. Is that right?"

This was the grilling he'd expected from Harry Ponce or General Ingemanson—Norman never believed he'd get it from *the President of the United States*! "Yes . . . yes, sir," Norman replied.

"Still feel pretty strongly about that? A little time to think about it hasn't changed your opinion at all?"

Even though Norman was still shocked by the encounter, now a bunch of his resolve and backbone started to return. "I still feel very strongly that the Air Force should discharge Major McLanahan. His background and experience suggests an officer that just wants to coast through his career, without one slight suggestion that he has or wants to do anything worth contributing to the Air Force or his country."

"I see," the President said. He paused for a moment, looked Norman right in the eye, and said, "Colonel, I want you to tear up that form."

"*Excuse* me?"

"I want you to drop your indictment."

"If you drop your affidavit, Colonel," Ingemanson interjected, "McLanahan will be promoted to lieutenant colonel two years below the primary zone."

"What?" Norman retorted. "You can't . . . I mean, you shouldn't do that! McLanahan has the worst effectiveness report I've seen! He shouldn't even be a major, let alone a lieutenant colonel!"

"Colonel, I can't reveal too much about this," the President said, "but I can tell you that Patrick McLanahan has a record that goes way beyond his official record. I can tell you that not only does he deserve to be a lieutenant colonel, he probably deserves to be a four-star general with a ticker-tape parade down the Canyon of Heroes. Unfortunately, he'll never get that opportunity, because the things he's involved in . . . well, we prefer no one find out about them. We can't even decorate him, because the citations that accompany the awards would reveal too much. The best we can do for him in an official manner is to promote him at every possible opportunity. That's what I'm asking you to do, as a favor to me."

"A . . . favor?" Norman stammered. "Why do you need me to agree to anything? You're the commander in chief—why don't you just use your authority and give him a promotion?"

"Because I'd prefer not to disrupt the normal officer selection board process as much as possible," the President replied.

"The President knows that only a board member can change his rating of a candidate," Ingemanson added. "Not even the President has the legal authority to change a score. McLanahan received a high enough score to earn a below-the-zone promotion—only the 772 stands in his way. The President is asking you to remove that last obstacle."

"But how? How can McLanahan possibly earn a high enough rating?"

"Because the other board members recognized something that exists in Patrick McLanahan that you apparently didn't, Colonel," the President replied. "Great officers exhibit leadership potential in many other ways than just attending service schools, dress, and appearance, and how many different assignments they've had. I look for officers who perform. True, Patrick hasn't filled the squares that other candidates have, but if you read the personnel file a little closer, a little differently, you'll see an officer that exhibits his leadership potential by doing his job and leading the way for others."

The President took the Form 772 from Ingemanson and extended it to Norman. "Trust me, Colonel," he said. "He's a keeper. Someday I'll explain some of the things this young man has done for our nation. But his future is in your hands—I won't exercise whatever authority I have over you. It's your decision."

Norman thought about it for a few long moments, then reached out, took the Form 772, and ripped it in two.

The President shook his hand warmly. "Thank you, Colonel," he said. "That meant a lot to me. I promise you, you won't regret your decision."

"I hope not, sir."

The President shook hands and thanked General Ingemanson, then stepped toward the door. Just before the Secret Service agent opened it for him, he turned back toward Norman, and said, "You know, Colonel, I'm impressed."

"Sir?"

"Impressed with you," the President said. "You could've asked for just about any favor you could think of—a choice assignment, a promotion of your own, even an appointment to a high-level post. You probably knew that I would've agreed to just about anything you would have asked for. But you didn't ask. You agreed to my request without asking for a thing in return. That tells me a lot, and I'm pleased and proud to learn that about you. That's the kind of thing you'll never read in a personnel file—but it tells me more about the man than any folder full of papers."

The President nodded in thanks and left the office, leaving a still-stunned, confused—and very proud—Norman Weir to wonder what in hell just happened.

GLOSSARY

ACSC—Air Command and Staff College, an Air Force military school for junior field grade officers that prepares them for more leadership and command positions.

AFO—Accounting and Finance Officer—handles pay and leave matters

ASAP—"as soon as possible"

AWACS—Airborne Warning and Control System, an aircraft with a large radar on board that can detect and track aircraft for many miles in all directions

Backfire—a supersonic Russian long-range bomber

Badger—a subsonic Russian long-range bomber

Bear—a subsonic turboprop Russian long-range bomber and reconnaissance plane

BIOT—British Indian Ocean Trust, a chain of small islands in the Indian Ocean administer by the United Kingdom

Blackjack—an advanced supersonic Russian long-range bomber

Buccaneer—a British long-range bomber

Candid—a Russian cargo plane

Chagos—the Iliot native name for the islands administered by the British Indian Ocean Trust

Class A's—the business-suit-like uniform of the U.S. Air Force

DIA—Defense Intelligence Agency, the U.S. military's intelligence-gathering service

Diego Garcia—the largest island of the Chagos Archipelago in the Indian Ocean, part of the British Indian Ocean Trust

Dreamland—the unclassified nickname for a secret military research facility in south central Nevada

Extender—a combination aerial-refueling tanker and cargo plane operated by the U.S. Air Force

firewalled—on an Officer Effectiveness Report, when all raters rate the officer with the highest possible marks

Goblin—nickname for the U.S. Air Force F-117 stealth fighter

GUARD—the universal radio emergency frequency, 121.5 KHz or 243.0 MHz

HAWC (fictional)—the High Technology Aerospace Weapons Center, one of the top-secret Air Force research units at Dreamland

Iliots—the natives of Diego Garcia in the British Indian OceanTrust

IRSTS—Infrared Search and Track System, a Russian heat-seeking aircraft attack system where the pilot can detect and feed targeting information to his attack systems without being detected

Mainstay—a Russian airborne radar aircraft

Megafortress (fictional)—an experimental, highly modified B-52H bomber used for secret military weapons and technology tests

MiG—Mikoyan-Gureyvich, a Soviet military aircraft design bureau

MOI—Memorandum of Instruction, the directives issued by the Secretary of the Air Force to a promotion board on how to conduct candidate evaluations and scoring

MPC—Military Personnel Center, the U.S. Air Force's manpower and personnel agency

Nimrod—a British reconnaissance and attack plane

NOFORN—"No Foreign Nationals," a security subclassification that directs that no foreign nationals can view the material

O-5—in the U.S Air Force, a lieutenant-colonel

OER—Officer Effectiveness Report, an officer's annual report on his job performance and his or her commander's remarks on his suitability for promotion

Orion—a U.S. Navy antisubmarine warfare aircraft

OSR—Officer Selection Report, the file members of a promotion board receive to evaluate and score a candidate for promotion

PCS—Permanent Change of Station, a long-term job change

Peel Cone—a nickname for a type of Soviet airborne radar

PME—Professional Military Education, a series of military schools that teach theory and practice to help develop knowledge and skills in preparation for higher levels of command

PRF—Pulse Repetition Frequency, the speed at which a radar is swept across a target: a higher PRF is used for more precise tracking and aiming; when detected, it is usually a warning of an impending missile launch

SATCOM—Satellite Communications, a way aircraft can communicate with headquarters or other aircraft quickly over very long distances by sending messages to orbiting satellites

Scorpions (fictional)—the AIM-120, a radar-guided medium-range U.S. Air Force antiaircraft missile

SP—Security Police

Strait of Hormuz—the narrow, shallow, winding waterway connecting the Persian Gulf with the Gulf of Oman, considered a strategic chokepoint for oil flowing out of the Gulf nations

Stratotanker—the U.S. Air Force's KC-135 aerial-refueling tanker aircraft

USAFE—U.S. Air Forces in Europe, the major Air Force command that governs all air operations in Europe

warning order—a document notifying a combat unit to prepare for possible combat operations

DALE BROWN is a former U.S. Air Force captain and the superstar author of eleven consecutive *New York Times* best-selling military-action-aviation adventure novels, including *Flight of the Old Dog, Silver Tower, Day of the Cheetah, Hammerheads, Sky Masters, Night of the Hawk, Chains of Command, Storming Heaven, Shadows of Steel, Fatal Terrain,* and *The Tin Man.* He graduated from Penn State University with a degree in Western European history and received his Air Force commission in 1978, serving as a navigator-bombardier on the B-52G Stratofortress heavy bomber and the FB-111A supersonic medium bomber. During his military career he received several awards, including the Air Force Commendation Medal with oak leaf cluster and the Combat Crew Award. He is a member of the Writers' Guild and a Life Member of the Air Force Association and the U.S. Naval Institute. A multiengine and instrument-rated private pilot, he can be found in the skies all across the United States, piloting his own plane. He also enjoys tennis, skiing, scuba diving, and hockey. He lives with his wife, Diane, and son, Hunter, near the shores of Lake Tahoe, Nevada.

BREAKING POINT

BY DAVID HAGBERG

Spring
Xiamen, Fujian Province
People's Republic of China

Their black rubber raft threaded silently through the densely packed fishing fleet at anchor for the night, the waves, even in the protected harbor, nearly one meter high. The four men were Taiwanese Secret Intelligence Service Commandos, and their chances for success tonight were less than one in ten. Of course all of Taiwan faced about the same dismal odds when it came to remaining free, squad leader Captain Joseph Jiying thought. But the heavy winds, sometimes gusting as high as thirty-five knots, did not help their chances much. They had been in constant danger of flipping over ever since they had left their twelve-man submarine twenty klicks out into the Taiwan Strait just off the entry between Quemoy Island and the Sehnu Peninsula. Now they faced the danger of discovery by patrol boats that darted around the harbor twenty-four hours per day, or by the underwater sound sensors laid on the floor of the bay, or by the infrared detectors installed on the shore batteries, and by the thousands of pairs of eyes always on the lookout. It was estimated that every fifth person in the PRC was a government informer. It meant that at least one hundred fishing boats at anchor tonight held spies.

Xiamen was a city of a half million people and home to an East Sea Fleet base that along with headquarters at Ningbo seven hundred kilometers to the north, and twelve others, was the dominating presence on the East China Sea and more specifically on the Taiwan Strait. Commanded by Vice Admiral Weng Shi Pei, the base was homeport to thirty-seven ships, among them one fleet submarine, three patrol submarines, including a Kilo-class, two frigates, one destroyer, and a variety of smaller boats, among them fast-attack missile, gun, torpedo, and patrol craft. The bulk of the fleet was berthed in a narrow bay to the southwest of the city, while a small naval air squadron was based at the municipal airport on the northeast side of the sprawling city. The sky was overcast, the night pitch-black, the water foul with stinking garbage, oil slicks, and a brown stain that clung to the carbon composite oars they had used since entering the harbor. It was too dangerous this close in to use the highly muffled outboard motor, but no one minded the extra work. It kept them warm.

They rounded the eastern terminus of the commercial port and entered the brightly lit fleet base harbor, the rubber raft passing well over the submarine nets. Keeping to the deeper shadows alongside the frigates and patrol craft, they made it to Dry Dock A, which an earlier recon mission reported was empty. Its massive steel doors were in the open position, and the box was flooded.

Their bowman, Xu Peng Tei, grabbed the metal

ladder at the head of the dry dock, tied them off, and scrambled to the top. He cautiously peered over the steel lip three meters above them, then gave the sign for all clear and disappeared over the edge. At twenty-seven he was the oldest man in the group, and although he was not the squad commander, everyone called him Uncle.

Joseph and his other two commandos stripped the protective sheaths from their silenced 9mm Sterling submachine guns, checked the magazines and safeties, then climbed silently to the top of the dry dock and over the edge.

They dropped immediately into a low crouch, invisible in the darkness because of their night-fighter camos and black balaclavas. Joseph checked his watch. It was three minutes until 0100. They were on schedule.

Xu appeared suddenly out of the darkness and crouched beside them. He had also unsheathed his weapon, and the hot diffuser tube around the barrel ticked softly as it cooled. "It's clear for the moment."

"How many guards, Uncle?" Joseph asked.

"Two, as we expected. One outside, one in the guard post. They're down."

The mid-phase mission clock started at that point. "Ten minutes," Joseph said, and they headed directly across to a low, windowless, concrete building a hundred meters away. Surrounded by a four-meter-tall electrified razor-wire fence, the only way in or out was through a gate operated from the guard shack. The outside patrols were on a fourteen-minute schedule, so ten minutes was cutting it close.

The building was the base brig, and for the moment it contained only one prisoner. The PRC was trying to be very low-key about him, which was the only reason tonight's action had the slightest chance of success.

No one wanted to make waves, Joseph thought. Not the PRC, and especially not the United States.

Well, after tonight, waves were exactly what they were going to get. And he expected that when the U.S. was finally pushed to the breaking point they would come through. Either that or there wouldn't be anything left of Taiwan except for smoldering cinders and radioactive waste.

But he was betting his life tonight that the U.S. would save them one more time. If his four years at Harvard had taught him nothing else about Americans, he learned that they loved the underdog, and they loved their heroes coming to the rescue. Superman. It was the one serious indulgence he'd picked up in the States. He had copies of Superman comics numbers five through ten, twelve, fifteen, sixteen, and eighteen, from the thirties, plus a hundred others, all original and all in cherry condition. Truth, justice, and the American way . . . now the Taiwanese way, because he'd rather be dead than under main-land rule.

One guard, a neat bullet hole in the middle of his forehead, lay in the darkness beside the fence, and the other was crumpled in the doorway of the guard post just inside the compound.

The lights were very bright there, but no alarms had been sounded, no troops were coming on the run. But the clock was counting down.

Zhou Yousheng dropped down in front of the fence and quickly clamped four cable shunts across a five-foot section. Next he cut the wire between the shunts with insulated cutters and carefully peeled them back. Although the fence now had a wide hole in it, the electrical current had never been interrupted, so no alarm would show up at Security Headquarters across the base.

Zhou gingerly crawled through the opening and as Chiang Kunren clamped the wires back together and removed the shunts, he darted inside the guard post where he released the electric gate lock.

They slipped inside, dragged the dead guards out of sight, and relocked the gate. Joseph led two of his men up the path to the blockhouse. Zhou remained at the guard post. They all wore comms units with earpieces and mikes. One click meant trouble was coming their way.

Chiang, their explosives expert, molded a small block of slow-fire Semtex into the lock on the steel door. He cracked a thirty-second pencil fuse, jammed it into the plastique, then quickly taped a two-inch-thick pad of nonflammable foam over the explosive to deaden the sound.

He'd barely taken his hands away from the foam when the Semtex went off with a muffled bang.

"One of these days you're going to lose a finger," Joseph observed, and Chiang shot him a quick smile.

"Then I'll have to ask for help every time I need to unzip my fly. Female help."

A long, wide corridor led from the front of the building to the back, five cells on each side. There were no adornments, not even numbers over the cell doors. Only a few dim lightbulbs hung from the low concrete ceiling.

Shi Shizong, who was known in Taiwan and in the west as Peter Shizong, was in the last cell on the left. He rose from his cot when Joseph appeared at the tiny window. He was very slight of build and young-looking, even for a mainlander, to be the PRC's most reviled villain. He preached democracy, and for some reason unknown even to him, his message and his presence touched a deep chord among half of China's vast population. Farmers and doctors, factory workers and engineers, fishermen and even some politicians were buying into his message. In the three years he'd been preaching and somehow managing to stay ahead of the authorities, massive waves of discontent had swept across the country, thousands of innocent demonstrators had been killed, their homes and assets confiscated by the state, martial law had been declared in two dozen cities, and even the West had finally begun to sit up and take notice.

Three days ago Shizong's odyssey had finally ended in a small apartment in Xiamen, with his arrest. The next day he was to be moved to a small, undisclosed city somewhere inland, where he would stand trial for treason. There would be no media, no witnesses, no publicity. He would be found guilty, of course, and would be executed within twenty-four hours of his trial.

His name and philosophy would soon be forgotten. It was something that China needed if its present government were to survive. And it was exactly what Taiwan wanted to prevent, at all costs. Reunification with the PRC was suicide, but reunification with a democratic China was not only desirable, in Joseph's estimation, it was worth giving his life for.

"Here," he called softly, and he waved Shizong away from the door.

Chiang rushed over, molded a small block of Semtex on the lock, cracked a ten-second fuse, shoved it into the plastique and stepped aside. This time he didn't bother with the foam; the building itself would muffle the sounds.

The plastique blew with an impressive bang. Joseph hauled the door open and stepped inside the cell. "We're from Taiwan Intelligence, Mr. Shizong. We're here to rescue you."

Shizong hesitated for just a moment, weighing the possibilities. This could be some sort of PRC trick. "Where are you taking me?"

"Taipei."

Understanding dawned on his face, and he smiled and nodded. "I see," he said, warmly. Joseph was instantly under his spell. Shizong had intelligence and kindness; he and he alone knew the answers for China.

Shizong was dressed in dark trousers, but his open-collared shirt was white. Joseph pulled a black blouse out of his pack and handed it to the man.

"We don't have much time. Put this on over your shirt, please."

Xu was at the front door when they came out of Shizong's cell. He motioned for them to hurry.

Chiang closed the cell door, knocked out the lightbulb above it, and joined them outside as Shizong finished pulling the blouse over his head. The night was still except for the occasional boat whistle outside the harbor somewhere. So far there were no alarms, but the next patrol would be at the gate in under four minutes.

Joseph and Xu hustled Shizong down the walk. Chiang closed the steel door and wedged it shut. The lock was gone, but from a distance in the dark the damage might not be noticeable. At least they hoped it wouldn't be.

Zhou powered the gate open, and as soon as the other four were safely through he hit the button to close and relock it, came out of the guardhouse on the run and just managed to slip through the narrowing opening before the gate clicked home.

The lone sentry came around the corner fifty meters away. Joseph and the others raced across the road and dived for cover in the ditch. The son of a bitch was two minutes early, Joseph thought bitterly.

He laid his submachinegun aside and pulled out a stiletto. If need be he was going to have to take the guard out. But silently. The others understood, and got ready to cover him.

It seemed to take an eternity before the guard reached the gate. He said something that they couldn't quite make out, then peered inside. After several moments he shook his head and continued along the fence past the section that had been cut and reconnected just minutes before.

Joseph released the pent-up breath he'd been holding, sheathed his stiletto, and picked up his gun.

The only thing that they had not been able to find out was how often the gate guard was supposed to check in with base security. Whatever that schedule might be they were racing against it now.

When the sentry finally turned the far corner, they jumped up and raced the rest of the way down to the dry dock, keeping as low as they could. Xu and Chiang went down the ladder first, followed by Shizong and Joseph and finally Zhou.

Fifteen minutes later they crossed over the submarine net, and made their way past the commercial docks and through the fishing fleet. The weather had begun to calm down, but it wasn't until they were well outside the harbor and could start the outboard, that Joseph allowed himself to relax.

"It seems that you've actually done it," Shizong said. He smiled. "Congratulations, gentlemen. But now, as the Americans would say, the fat is in the fire."

Joseph laughed. "Indeed it is," he said. "I didn't know that you lived in the United States."

"It's been a secret. But I spent three years in the Silicon Valley as a spy for Chinese Intelligence."

Joseph decided that nothing would ever surprise him again. "Tell me, do you know anything about Superman comics?"

Two Months Later
The White House

Kirk Cullough McGarvey, Deputy Director of Operations for the Central Intelligence Agency, showed his credentials at the door three stories beneath the ground floor even though the civilian guard recognized him.

"Good morning, Mr. McGarvey, how's it out there?" the Secret Service officer asked.

"Hot and muggy, Brian, same as yesterday, same as tomorrow."

"Worst place in the world to build a capital city."

"Amen," McGarvey agreed. He entered the basement situation room and took his place next to Tom Roswell, director of the National Security Agency. At fifty, McGarvey certainly wasn't the youngest man ever to hold the third-highest job in American intelligence, but he was the most fit and had more field experience than all his predecessors put together. He'd worked for the Company in one capacity or another for the past twenty-five years: sometimes on the payroll, at other times freelance. But in the parlance of the go-go of days of the sixties and seventies at the height of the Cold War, he'd been a shooter. An assassin. A killer. The ultimate arbiter. Now he was the spy finally come in from the cold.

There wasn't a man or woman on either side of the Atlantic or Pacific who'd ever looked into his startlingly green, sometimes gray, eyes who'd ever come away unchanged. At a little over six feet, with a broad, honest, at times even friendly, face, he still maintained the physique of an athlete because he swam or ran nearly every day, and he worked out at least twice a week with the CIA's fencing team. His enemies feared him, and his friends and allies revered him. An old nemesis had once said that although Mac was an anachronism in this high-tech day and age, he was still a force to be reckoned with. "Never, ever underestimate the man. If you do, he's likely to hand you your balls on a platter."

The long conference table was filled with the President's civilian and military advisors this morning. Among them were all four of the Joint Chiefs, the Secretaries of State and Defense; representatives from all the law-enforcement and intelligence services, including the FBI, Secret Service, and Defense Intelligence Agency, along with the National Reconnaissance Office, which was responsible for all the photographic data received from our KeyHole and Jupiter satellite systems as well as a host of others. His National Security Advisor, Dennis Berndt, and his Chief of Staff, Anthony Lang, were also present. *All the big dogs,* McGarvey thought. But he wasn't surprised.

Roswell had been talking to the FBI's Associate Director, Bob Armstrong. He turned to McGarvey. "You giving the briefing this morning, Mac?"

"Gene will start us off."

Eugene Carpenter was the Secretary of State. Nearing eighty, he was the oldest man in government, but everyone respected his intellectually astute, though usually practical, views. He was sitting slumped in his chair lost in his own thoughts.

"If we don't watch our step, this business over Taiwan is going to jump up and bite us on the ass, because the Chinese sure as hell aren't going to forget the *Nanchong*."

"Just like the *Maine*, is that what you're saying?" McGarvey asked.

"Worked for us," Roswell said.

The *FF502 Nanchong* was a PRC frigate that had been destroyed overnight fifty miles off the southwest coast of Taiwan in international waters. The Chinese claimed that it was attacked by a Taiwanese gunboat or perhaps a submarine, while Taiwan denied any involvement. The PRC's state-controlled media were already clamoring for retribution, and the Chinese military had been brought to the highest state of readiness they'd been in since the Vietnam War.

The President walked in, and everyone stood until he had taken his seat. He looked tired, as if he hadn't been getting enough sleep. It was the same affliction that every president since FDR had suffered; the job was a tough one, and it took its toll. He gave McGarvey a nod.

"People, let's get started, I have some tough calls to make and I'm going to need your help this morning." He turned to the Secretary of State. "Gene?"

Carpenter looked up as if out of a daze, and he sat up with a visible effort. He looked pale and drawn, in even greater need of rest than the President.

"Thank you, Mr. President. Ladies and gentlemen, we're here this morning because of an incident last night in the East China Sea in which a People's Republic Of China warship was blown up and sunk with all hands lost. I'm going to leave the actual briefing to Mr. McGarvey, who warned us two months ago that something like this was bound to happen. But there's something that you all need to know before he gets started. Ever since the most recent round of trouble between mainland China and Taiwan started two months ago, we've been trying to find a way to keep the situation out there stable."

Carpenter passed a hand across his eyes. "It's no secret that we've not done a very good job of it. Eight weeks ago, in response to a PRC naval exercise in the area, we moved our Seventh Fleet out of Yokosuka: the *George Washington* and her battle group north of Taiwan and the *Eisenhower* and her support group to the south. Our committment, of course, was and still is to honor our pledge to keep the East China sea-lanes open.

"China's response in turn was to augment her East Sea Fleet presence in the region with elements of her North and South Sea Fleets, greatly outnumbering us."

Carpenter shuffled some papers in front of him.

"Four weeks ago our two Third Fleet carrier battle groups—the *Nimitz* and *John F. Kennedy*—arrived from Honolulu to cover Taiwan's north and east coasts, which prompted China to completely strip her North and South Sea Fleets, concentrating every ship that they could commission in an area barely three hundred miles long and half that wide. In addition, the entire PRC Air Force has been moved east. Along with their army and Missile Service, the entire military might of China was placed this morning on DEFCON One."

"My God, what the hell do they want, war?" Attorney General Dorothy Kress demanded angrily. "Over one man?"

"They've done this before," Admiral Richard Halvorson, the Chairman of the Joint Chiefs, said. "The last time they rattled their sabres was during Taiwan's elections. So long as we stand our ground they back down." He turned to the President. "Hell, Mr. President, Shizong isn't worth that much to them."

"How much is Taiwan worth to us, Admiral?" McGarvey asked across the table. All of them were in for a rude awakening that morning. They would be faced with recommending one of the toughest decisions any president could ever be faced with.

Halvorson shrugged. "That's a civilian policy decision, one thank God that I don't have to make," he said. "Ask me if we can defend Taiwan against a PRC invasion, I'll give you the numbers. And frankly, at this moment they do not look good. We're spread too thinly."

"But that's exactly the decision we're going to have to work out here this morning," McGarvey pressed. He didn't know why he was angry, except that we had worked very hard and long to get ourselves into this position. Getting ourselves back out wasn't going to be easy. Nor would it be safe.

The President motioned for McGarvey to back off for the moment. It was the same game we'd been playing out there ever since Nixon had opened the door and stuck his foot into it, McGarvey wanted to tell them. But they knew it; hell, everybody knew it. China was getting Most Favored Nation trading status because she was a vast market. It had to do with money and almost nothing else. The fact was we couldn't ignore a country whose population was one-fourth that of the entire world's. But we couldn't give in to them either; abandon our friends and allies just as the British had abandoned Hong Kong. When the solution to a little problem was distasteful Americans lately seemed to put it off until the problem got much bigger and the solution became even tougher. Sooner or later, as Roswell suggested, the situation over Taiwan was going to bite us in the ass.

Like now.

"Okay, Gene, everything we've tried so far has failed," the President said. "Tell them the rest."

"I've just returned from a three-day shuttle-diplomacy mission between Beijing and Taipei. I was trying to talk some sense into them; find an opening, even the slightest hint of an opening, so that we could resume a meaningful dialogue." Carpenter pursed his lips. "I was afraid that I was coming back with the worst possible news: that there was going to be no simple way out of the morass except to continue the Mexican standoff between our navy and theirs. I thought that the best we could hope for would be, as Admiral Halvorson suggested, that the Chinese would sooner or later tire of the exercise and go home.

"But then the *Nanchong* incident occurred last night while I was over the Pacific on my way home. Now all bets are off."

"What do they want?" Secretary of Defense Arthur

Turnquist asked. His was one cabinet appointment that McGarvey never understood. The man was an asshole; he spent almost as much time saving his own reputation as he did on any real work. But he was well connected on the Hill.

"The mainland Chinese want the immediate return of Peter Shizong, dead or alive. And the Taiwanese want nothing less than their independence unless mainland China is willing to open itself to free elections and a totally free market economy. Neither side is willing to discuss the issue beyond that."

"That's hardly likely anytime soon," the President's advisor on national security affairs, Dennis Berndt, pointed out unnecessarily.

"It comes down to the simple question: Do we abandon Taiwan? Do we turn tail and run? Or do we stay and risk a shooting war?" Carpenter said. "The sinking of the *Nanchong* may well be the catalyst. We have to consider where our breaking point is." He sat back, the effort of bringing the discussion this far completely draining him.

"What's the military situation out there at the moment?" the President asked.

"It's a mess, Mr. President," Admiral Halvorson answered. "We've offered to help with the search-and-rescue mission, but the Chinese have refused, as we expected they would. The actual effect of the sinking was to move the bulk of the PRC's naval assets about twenty-five miles closer to Taiwan."

"What about the Taiwanese military?"

"Fortunately their naval units in the near vicinity have all moved back an appropriate distance, but they, along with their Air and Ground Defense units, are at DEFCON One. In the meantime we're keeping four Orions and five A3 AWACS aircraft in the air around the clock to make sure that this doesn't spin out of control and blindside us. All of our carrier fighter squadrons are at a high state of readiness, as are our Air Force fighter wings in Japan and on Okinawa." The admiral looked around the table at the others to make sure that they all would catch his exact meaning. "If someone starts an all-out shooting war over there, we'll be the first to know about it. The PRC knows that we know, and so does Taiwan."

"If we have the region so well covered, how'd the *Nanchong* get hit without warning?" SecDef Turnquist asked peevishly.

"I can't answer that one, Mr. Turnquist," Admiral Halvorson admitted. "Al Ryland's people are the best, and he told me this morning that he was damned if he knew what happened." Vice Admiral Ryland was the Seventh Fleet CINC. His flag was on the *George Washington.*

"If it happened once, it can happen again."

"No, sir, that's not a possibility you need consider," the admiral said in such a way that it was clear he would not be pushed. "Mr. President, I would sincerely hope that we can come to some sort of an agreement with Tiawan over Shizong. I'm not saying that we turn him over to the Chinese, but Taipei could certainly be made to stop his radio and television broadcasts. Christ, it's driving them nuts." He looked around the table at the others to emphasize his point. "The longer our military forces are in such close proximity to the Chinese the more likely it'll become that there'll be a serious accident. We're going to start killing people over there—our own kids. And on top of that my commanders have their hands tied."

"They are authorized to use whatever force necessary to defend themselves, Admiral," the President said. It was clear that he wasn't going to be pushed either. Unlike his predecessor, he had spent time in the military.

"That's the point. Mr. President. They might need more authority than that, and they might need it so fast that there'd be no time to phone home. Al Ryland would like full discretion—" Ryland was in overall command of the combined fleet.

"No," the President said even before Admiral Halvorson finished the sentence. He sat forward for emphasis in his tall, bulletproof leather chair. "This *will not* spin out of control into an all-out shooting war between China and the United States."

"Then, Mr. President, let's pack our bags and get the hell out of there," McGarvey said from across the table.

The President shot him an angry, irritated look, as if he hadn't expected a comment like that from the CIA, and especially not from McGarvey, for whom he had a great deal of respect. "The CIA does not set policy."

"No, sir, nor will the CIA tell this administration what it *wants* to hear."

"When have you played it any differently?"

McGarvey had to smile, and there were a few chuckles around the table though the mood was anything but light. Friend and enemy alike all agreed that McGarvey never bullshitted the troops. Never.

"Okay, let's hear the CIA's version of the situation, because I sure as hell need the unvarnished truth before I can come to a decision that makes any sense."

McGarvey hesitated for just a moment. He'd been in this kind of a position many times before. It never got any easier. What he wanted to do had one-hundred-to-one odds against it. But the alternatives were either losing Taiwan or going to war with mainland China. In either case tens of thousands, maybe hundreds of thousands of lives would be lost. Needlessly.

"There may be no acceptable solution, Mr. President. At least not in the ordinary sense of the word, because the Chinese themselves engineered this situation."

The Secretary of Defense started to object, but the President held him off with a sharp gesture. "Go on."

"First of all the *Nanchong* was ready for the scrap heap. We believe that she was headed for the cutting yard when she was diverted at the last minute and sent out on this mission. She was a *Riga*-class frigate, built in 1955 in the Soviet Union and transferred to Bulgaria in 1958. Her name at that time was the *Kobchik*, which made her a KGB boat. Navy ships have numbers but no names.

"The *Kobchik* was extensively retrofitted in '80 and '81, and then sold to the PRC in 1987, when she was renamed the *Nanchong*. By that time she was already an outdated piece of junk."

"Like most of the Chinese navy," SecDef Turnquist said. He was going to make a run for the presidency next election, and the rumors were already flying that he was taking Chinese soft money. But McGarvey wasn't going to go there right now.

"The *Nanchong*'s skipper, a man by the name of Shi Kiyang, was convicted of treason eighteen months ago and sentenced to life in prison without parole at East Sea Fleet headquarters in Ningbo. His mother, his wife, and his two children were sent into exile to Yulin, in the far north, and all of his assets, car, bicycles, bank account, Beijing apartment, and furniture were confiscated by the state.

"But he made an amazing comeback. Six weeks ago he was released from prison and sent to Xiamen on the coast. His family was brought back to Beijing, where their old lives were reinstated.

"The *Nanchong* left port three days ago on her one and only mission with a skeleton crew of officers and men who had all been convicted of a variety of crimes from treason to theft of state property."

"Goddammit, we were set up," Admiral Halvorson

said angrily. "But why? What did the bastards expect to accomplish?"

"Get our attention."

"Are you telling us that the Chinese sank their own ship?" the President asked.

"Yes, sir."

"They got our attention. What do they want?"

"They want exactly what they told Gene they wanted. Peter Shizong. Dead or alive."

"They're using the *Nanchong* as an excuse to punish Taiwan. I can understand that. But they want us to back off this time, and they're willing to fight."

"That's the conclusion we're drawing, Mr. President," McGarvey said. "They're not merely rattling their sabers this time, they've pulled them. The ball is in our court."

"We have the *Carl Vinson* and her battle group still in Yokosuka. We could park them just offshore from Taipei. Any invasion force would have to get through us first," Admiral Halvorson said. He was mad. "Might make them stop and think before they pulled the trigger."

"They would only be fighting a delaying action," Turnquist objected.

"That's if we stuck to conventional weapons," Halvorson countered. "We have six submarines patrolling the strait, three of them strategic missile boats. Their combined nuclear throw weight is five times that of the entire Chinese missile force."

"Most of the Chinese missiles are ICBMs, are they not?" the President's National Security Advisor, Berndt, asked. He was clearly alarmed. "Capable of reaching the United States a half hour from launch?"

"Our first targets would be their launch sites," Admiral Halvorson shot back.

The President gestured for them to stop talking. "How reliable is your information, Mac?"

"We have a high confidence."

"What do we do about it?"

"Whatever we do, Mr. President, will involve a risk—either of losing Taiwan or of getting into a nuclear exchange with China."

"If it's about getting into a nuclear war, Taiwan's independence isn't worth the price," Berndt said. It was obvious that most of the others around the table agreed with him.

"It's about our word," McGarvey interjected softly.

"That's what was said about Vietnam," Berndt pressed. He was an academic. He'd never been out in the real world.

"Taiwan is an ally."

"So was South Vietnam."

"Maybe we could have won that war," McGarvey said patiently. After twenty-five years working for the CIA, he didn't think he'd heard a new argument in the past twenty years.

"I'll repeat my question, Mac, what does the CIA suggest we do?"

"Play the PRC at their own game, Mr. President," McGarvey said.

"Okay, how do we do that?"

"You're going to lend me a *Seawolf* attack submarine and I'm going to sink it with all hands lost."

Three Days Later
CVN George Washington

Even at a distance from the air the *George Washington* was an impressive sight. At over a thousand feet in length, she displaced more than ninety thousand tons, carried a crew of three thousand men, women, and officers, plus another three thousand in the air wing. The carrier had ninety planes and an arsenal of Phalanx cannons, Sams and Sea Sparrow missiles, and yet her two pressurized water-cooled nuclear reactors, which needed refueling only every thirteen years, could push the largest warship afloat to speeds well in excess of thirty knots. McGarvey peered out the window of the Marine Sea King CH-46G troop-carrying helicopter that brought him and his escort, Navy SEAL Lieutenant Hank Hanrahan, down from Okinawa.

It was early morning, the sun just coming up over the eastern horizon, and the day promised to be glorious. The north coast of Taiwan was a very faint smudge on the horizon to the southeast, and arrayed for as far as the eye could see in all directions were war ships: the *George Washington*'s battle group of Aegis cruisers, guided-missile destroyers, and ASW frigates directly below; Taiwanese gunboats, destroyers, and guided-missile frigates to the east; and the PRC fleet along a three-hundred-mile line to the west. The *George Washington*'s air wing maintained a screen one hundred miles out, which of necessity brought them into very close proximity with the Chinese. And below the surface were six U.S. submarines, four Taiwanese boats and eleven Chinese submarines, three of which were nuclear-powered Han-class boats, old but deadly.

"There're almost enough assets out there to leapfrog from Taiwan to the Chinese mainland without getting your feet wet," Admiral Halvorson had told McGarvey after the President's briefing. What he meant was that once the shooting started it would be impossible to control the battle or stop it until there was a clear victory. In the meantime a lot of good people would be dead for no reason.

"Ever been on a carrier before, Mr. M?" Lieutenant Hanrahan asked, breaking into McGarvey's thoughts. He was twenty-six, with a freshly scrubbed wide-eyed innocent look of a kid from some small town in the Midwest. But he was a service brat, his dad was a retired navy captain, and he was as calm and as hard as nails as any man in the SEALs. You only had to look into his eyes to see it. He'd been there done that, and when called upon he was ready, willing, and very able to go there again and do it again.

"A couple of times, but you forget how big they are."

"About the size of a small city. Only problem is you can't find a decent saloon anywhere aboard."

McGarvey had to smile. He was being tested. "A decent *legal* saloon, you mean." Hanrahan gave him a sharp look. "I wasn't always a DDO. And grunts tend to hear a hell of a lot more than their superiors. Don't shit an old shitter."

Hanrahan grinned happily. "I read you, Mr. M."

A red shirt guided them to touch down just forward of the island. The Grumman E-2C Hawkeye AWACS aircraft normally parked there was airborne, and for the moment the elevator to the hangar deck was in the up position and clear. Fully one-third of the Seventh and Third Fleet's assets were in the air at any one time, making this one of the busiest pieces of air real estate in the world, even busier than Chicago's O'Hare.

The seas were fairly calm and as soon as the helicopter came to a complete stop, McGarvey and Hanrahan unbuckled and grabbed their bags. There was no sense whatsoever that they were aboard a ship at sea. The deck was as rock solid as a parking lot in a big city, but noisier.

"Thanks for the ride," McGarvey shouted up to the crew forward.

"Yes, sir. Hope you enjoyed the meal service and in-flight movie," the pilot quipped.

"Just great," McGarvey said. A cheese sandwich and a ginger ale while looking out a small window were not usually his first choices for breakfast and entertainment, but he'd had worse.

The red shirt motioned them to the island structure as the chopper was already being prepped to be moved below and refueled for the 350-nautical mile return trip. Just inside the hatch a Marine sergeant in battle fatigues, a Colt Commando slung over his shoulder, saluted.

"Gentlemen, please follow me to flag quarters."

He led them down a maze of passageways, the machinery noises not as bad as McGarvey remembered from the *Independence*, but the corridors just as narrow and covered in stenciled alphanumeric legends. Pipes and cable runs were everywhere, and seemingly around every corner there were firefighting stations built into the Navy gray bulkheads. The ship was very busy, evident by all the activity they saw through the hatches in the bulkheads, decks, and overheads, and the constant PA announcements.

Men all good and true, busy at the work of war, the line came back to McGarvey from somewhere. Only these days it was men *and women* all busy at the work of war.

Another armed Marine sergeant in battle fatigues was stationed at the admiral's door. He stiffened to attention. Their escort knocked once, then opened the door and stepped aside.

"Gentlemen, the admiral is expecting you."

Flag quarters was actually a well-furnished suite, sitting room, bedroom, and bathroom, that equaled anything that a luxury ocean liner could offer—thick carpeting, rich paneling, nice artwork, expensive furniture, except there were no sliding glass doors or balconies.

"Good morning," Vice Admiral Albert Ryland said. He put down his coffee cup and he and the other two men with him got to their feet.

"Good morning, Admiral," McGarvey said, shaking hands.

Ryland, who was from Birmingham, Alabama, looked and sounded like a tall, lean Southern gentleman from the old school. He was one of the most respected officers in the Navy; it was Halvorson's opinion that he would probably end up Chairman of the Joint Chiefs within five years. "Don't try to hold anything back on him, or he'll cut you off at the knees," Halvorson warned.

"This is the *George*'s captain, Pete Townsend, and my Operations Officer, Tom Byrne."

They shook hands. The captain looked like a banker or the chairman of some board of directors. He wore wire-rimmed glasses, his hair was thin and gray, and his face was round and undistinguished. Byrne, however, was a very large black man who looked like he could play with the Green Bay Packers. His grip was as strong as bar steel.

"Sir, I'm Lieutenant Hank Hanrahan. I have orders to assist Mr. McGarvey."

"You Mike Hanrahan's son?"

"Yes, sir."

"How's your old man doing these days?"

"He misses the Navy, sir."

Ryland chuckled. "This would be just the kind of brouhaha he'd like to be in." He turned back to McGarvey. "Well, the Chinese know that you're here. They're watching every move we make. Satellites and OTH radar."

"Hopefully they don't know who I am," McGarvey said. "And we're going to keep it that way because Hank and I are not going to be aboard very long. Just until nightfall."

"I thought your helicopter was heading back right away," Townsend said.

"We're not leaving that way."

"Unless they're sending another bird for you, I don't have anything to spare."

"We're not flying."

"Are you going to swim?" Townsend demanded angrily.

"As a matter of fact that's exactly what we're going to do, Captain," McGarvey said. "Tonight."

He couldn't blame Ryland or his officers for being in a bad temper. They were in the middle of a likely very hot situation with their hands practically tied behind their backs. This was a fight between China and Taiwan. The U.S. was Taiwan's ally and was supposed to back them up if they were attacked, but the Navy was here only to show the flag. The President's orders remained very specific: Ryland was not to shoot unless the Chinese shot at his people first. In effect if the PRC navy simply wanted to sail right through the middle of the Seventh and Third Fleets, engage every Taiwanese warship they encountered, and then send troops ashore, there was nothing Ryland could do about it.

Ryland shook his head. "Dick Halvorson said that you were inventive."

McGarvey smiled faintly. "I don't think that was exactly the word he used."

"No."

Byrne poured them coffee. "Admiral Halvorson said that we were to give you whatever you wanted." He looked at Hanrahan, who did not avert his gaze. "That's a pretty tall order."

McGarvey took a plain white envelope out of his pocket and handed it to Ryland. He figured that if the flag officers were unhappy before, they would be even less happy after reading the letter.

When Ryland was done he handed it to Townsend, and looked at McGarvey. "Okay, the Chairman of the Joint Chiefs calls to tell me than the CIA's Deputy Director of Operations is flying out, and I'm supposed to give him all the help I can. I'm thinking that perhaps you're bringing a magic bullet to get us out of the mess we're in. And now this."

Townsend had finished the letter, and he handed it to Byrne. He was clearly upset.

"No magic bullets this time, Admiral. But I think we might have a chance of coming out of this situation with our asses more or less intact," McGarvey replied. He had decided long ago never to try to argue with a man who has just been blindsided. If you wanted to get through to him, you waited until he calmed down a little.

"That's a comfort," Ryland said acerbically. "I'm told to defend Taiwan, but I can't fire a shot to do it." He glanced at Byrne, who had also finished the letter. "Now the President tells me that I can't even ask any questions. Christ on the cross, if we lose here, we lose everywhere!"

"If we start a shooting war, it could escalate. Go nuclear."

"McGarvey, there's a real chance that every time we untie one of our carriers from the dock and send her to sea we'll get ourselves into a nuclear war. Are you telling me that Taiwan isn't worth the risk?"

"That's the current feeling in Washington."

Ryland glanced again at his officers. "A dose of refreshing honesty for a change. It's a wonder that you've kept your job for so long. What are we doing here then?" he asked angrily. "Sooner or later there'll be another accident. Then another, and another until all hell breaks loose! That's the way it works, you know."

"The *Nanchong* was no accident, Admiral. The Chinese sank her. That's why the President sent me out here, to work out a solution that'll keep everybody happy—Taipei and Beijing."

"If that's true, it explains a couple of things that we were wondering about," Byrne said. He and Ryland exchanged a look.

"How many men were aboard her?" Ryland asked.

"We're not sure, but probably no more than a dozen. Just enough to take her to sea, but not enough to fight her."

"Gives the PRC a supposedly legitimate reason to be here," Byrne observed.

"And us, too," Ryland agreed. "What do we do about it?"

"We're going to sink one of our own."

Ryland sat forward so fast that he practically levitated from his chair. But he hesitated for just a moment before he spoke. McGarvey could almost hear him counting to ten. "I don't think that you're saying what I just heard. The Chinese may be willing to kill their people, not us."

"Thirty-six hours from now there'll be an underwater explosion a hundred miles from here. Five minutes later one of our submarines, the *Seawolf,* will send up a slot buoy to report that they have engaged an unknown enemy, were damaged, and are in immediate danger of sinking. Before the message is completed the communications buoy will break loose from the submarine, there'll be another intense underwater explosion, and then nothing."

Byrne got a chart of the area, and McGarvey pinpointed the approximate location for them. The *George Washington*'s captain saw the plan immediately.

"That's sandwiched between us and the *Kennedy.* No Chinese assets that we're aware of within a hundred fifty miles." Townsend looked up. "That gives the *Seawolf* a clear path into the open Pacific. Is that what you have in mind?"

McGarvey nodded. "There'll be an extensive search, of course, and some wreckage will be found. Twenty-four hours later we'll announce that the *Swordfish* was lost with all hands, and was probably torpedoed."

"The *Swordfish*? She was pulled from duty six months ago," Byrne said. "She's back at Groton."

"That's right. And when this is over with, she'll be taken in secret and sunk just off our continental shelf."

"If we blame the Chinese, they'll have to figure that we've pulled the same stunt on them that they pulled on the Taiwanese," Byrne said.

"It won't matter," McGarvey told them. "Everybody will back off to let the situation cool down and allow the politicians to hash it out."

"That'll only buy us a few days, maybe a week, and then we'll be right back in the same situation we're in right now," Ryland opined. "What will we have gained?"

"After seven days the PRC Navy will return to their home bases and so will we."

Ryland glanced at the President's letter on the coffee table. "That's the part I'm not supposed to ask any questions about."

"You wouldn't want to know, Admiral. As soon as it gets dark we'll be out of your hair."

Ryland turned to Hanrahan. "You're in on this, Lieutenant?"

Hanrahan stiffened. "Yes, sir."

Ryland waved him off. "Relax, I'm not going to order you to tell me. Except how in the hell do you think you're going to get off this ship without the Chinese knowing something is going on? If you're not flying, you'll have to be transferred to one of our frigates or destroyers, and they'll see that, too."

"Sir, we're exiting the ship from the port hangar deck just forward of the Sea Sparrow launcher."

"What the hell—" Townsend exploded.

"Relax, Pete, I think I know at least part of what they're up to," Ryland said. "The *Seawolf* is coming to pick you up." He shook his head. "That's a dicey maneuver no matter how you slice it." He turned to the captain again. "We'll have to warn sonar."

"That won't be necessary, Admiral. Your people haven't detected her yet, have they?" McGarvey asked.

"No," Townsend said, tight-lipped. "Where is she?"

McGarvey glanced at his watch. It was a few minutes after seven in the morning. "Actually we're passing over her about right now. She's been lying beneath a thermocline nine hundred feet down since yesterday morning."

"We're on a twelve-hour pattern," Townsend said. "We'll be right back here around seven this evening."

"That's about when we go overboard," McGarvey said. "When you're clear, she'll come up to about fifty feet, we'll dive down to her and lock aboard."

"Does Tom Harding know what's going on?" Ryland asked. Harding was the *Seawolf*'s skipper, and a very good if somewhat conservative sub driver.

"No."

"Well, I can think of at least a hundred things that could go wrong. But considering the alternatives we'll do whatever it takes to get you down to her in one piece."

"In secret," McGarvey said. "As few people outside this room as possible are to know that we've gone overboard."

"I'll arrange that," Townsend said, and he shook his head. "I think you're nuts."

McGarvey nodded. "You're probably right, Captain."

1920 Local
SSN 405 *Hekou*

Lying just off the floor of the ocean one thousand feet beneath the surface, the PRC Han-class nuclear submarine *Hekou* was leaking at the seams, the air was going stale, and the radiation levels inside the hull continued to rise, the last fact of which was being withheld from the crew. Her home base was at East Sea Fleet Headquarters in Ningbo, and she had been among the first to sail when the trouble begin. By luck she had been lying on the bottom eight days ago hiding from the American ASW aircraft above while the engineers were frantically correcting a steering problem when sonar picked up the *George Washington* passing almost directly overhead. When the steering problem had been fixed, and the aircraft carrier was well past, the *Hekou*'s skipper sent up a communications buoy to get instructions. He was told to stay where he was, maintain complete silence, and wait for the moment to strike.

The message unfortunately was not clear on when that moment might be. In the meantime Captain Yuan Heishui was having problems keeping his boat alive, and there was the American submarine five hundred meters off its starboard bow, also hovering just off the bottom mush.

Twenty-four hours ago sonar had detected the American *Seawolf*-class submarine approaching their position very deep and very slowly. The approach had been so slow and so stealthy that the Americans had been on top of them before they knew what was happening. Even before Heishui could order his torpedo tubes loaded and prepared to fire, the *Seawolf* went quiet and settled silently in place, apparently completely unaware that they were not alone.

Since that time Captain Heishui had ordered all nonessential machinery and movements aboard his boat to stop.

He picked the growler phone from its bracket, careful not to scrape metal against metal. "Engineering, conn," he said softly.

Their chief engineer, Lieutenant He Daping, answered immediately. "*Shi de*," yes. He sounded harried and in the background the captain could hear the sounds of running water.

"This is the captain. How is it going back there?"

"Without the pumps we're eventually going to take on so much water that we won't have the power to rise to the surface."

"We must not run the pumps. How long do we have?"

"Six hours, Captain, maybe less," Daping answered. Captain Heishui knew the man well and respected him. He came from a very good family, and his service record was totally clean, an accomplishment in itself.

"Seal off the engineering spaces, then introduce some high-pressure air in there. That should slow the leaks."

"I was just about to do that," Daping said. If they could not get out of the fix they were in now and get moving soon, sealing the aft section of the boat would doom the crewmen back there. If the flooding got too bad, there would be no way of opening the hatches.

"I'll do what I can," the captain promised. "But we might have to fight. *Hăo yùngi*," good luck.

"Yes, you too, Captain."

"Conn, sonar."

Heishui glanced up at the mission clock, then switched circuits. "This is the captain. Is Sierra Seven back early?" They had designated the American Aircraft carrier as Sierra Seven and had timed her movements. She was on a zigzag course that brought her back to the same point approximately every twelve hours. It was 1120 GMT, the standard time kept aboard all submarines, which put it at 1920 on the surface. If it was the *George Washington*, he was slightly early.

"She's fifteen thousand yards out, Captain, but it's Sierra Eighteen," Chief Sonarman, Ensign Shi Zenzhong, reported excitedly. "He's moving. He's on the way up, very slowly, on an intercept bearing with Seven." Sierra Eighteen was the American submarine, and the captain could not imagine what he was up to.

"Have they sent up a slot buoy?"

"No, sir. And they're running silent. No one on the surface will hear them." Zenzhong's voice was cracking, and the captain considered pulling him off duty immediately. But the man was the best.

"Have we been detected?"

"I don't think so, sir," the sonarman replied. The captain's calm demeanor was helping him and everyone in the control room.

"Stand by," the captain said. He motioned his XO, Lieutenant Commander Kang Lagao, over. "Get down to sonar and give Ensign Zenzhong some help. Sierra Eighteen is on the way up."

"Maybe they're rendezvousing with the *George Washington*," Lagao suggested. He was the oldest man aboard the submarine, even older at forty-six than the captain. And he was wise even beyond his years. Exactly the steady hand they all need. The American command structure could take a lesson.

"That's what I think, but something is strange about it," Heishui said. "See what's happening and then start a TMA."

Lagao was startled. "You're not going to shoot, are you?" A TMA, or Target Motion Analysis, was a targeting procedure used to guide torpedoes in which the enemy vessel's speed and position were continually tracked and plotted against the relative speed and position of the tracking boat.

"Not yet. But I want to be prepared. There's no telling what they're up to, or when we might have to shoot."

"Very well."

When Lagao was gone, Heishui picked up the growler phone. "Forward torpedo room, this is the captain."

"Yes, sir."

"I want all six tubes loaded, but not flooded, with 65-Es." Heishui glanced over at his weapons control officer and chief of boat, whose jobs he was doing. They were studiously watching their panels. The captain did not want to bring any shame to them, but he wanted to make absolutely sure that no mistakes were made. Their lives depended on it. "I want this done with no noise. Do you understand?"

"Yes, sir."

"I'll send the presets momentarily, but if there is any noise whatsoever, whoever was responsible will be court-martialed and shot as a traitor—if we survive to make it home. Do you understand that as well?"

"Yes, sir. Very well."

"Carry on," Heishui said. He replaced the phone, confused about many things though not about why he was here. Taiwan needed to come home, as Hong Kong had, or else be punished as a naughty child.

1930 local
SSN 21 *Seawolf*

Hearing anything with precision from beneath the sharp thermocline was difficult except for a ship the size of the *George Washington.* Named for her class, the *Seawolf* was the state of the art in nuclear-powered attack submarines. No other navy in the world had a boat that could match her stealth, her nuclear and conventional weapons, her speed, and her electronics. Especially not her BQQ-8 passive sonar suite, which, according to the sonarmen who used it, could hear a gnat's fart at fifty thousand yards. Her mission had been to patrol an area well north of the Seventh and Third Fleets in case the PRC tried an end run on them. The long ELF message they had received forty-eight hours ago irritated the *Seawolf*'s captain because it put his boat at risk without an explanation why. He was ordered to rendezvous with the *George Washington* without allowing the carrier or any other ship to detect her. And less than an hour from now he was to pick up two passengers. The only reason he hadn't "missed" the damn fool message was the last line: *McGarvey Sends.*

"Skipper, we're at seven hundred twenty feet," the Chief of Boat Lieutenant Karl Trela reported.

"Okay, hold us here," Commander Thomas Harding told him. The bottom edge of the thermocline where the water got sharply colder was just twenty feet above the top of their sail. They were at the edge of the safety zone where they were all but invisible to surface sonars. He picked up the phone. "Sonar, conn."

"Sonar, aye."

"Where's the *George*?"

"Four thousand yards and closing, skipper. He's on his predicted course and speed."

"What else is up there, Mel?" Commander Harding asked in a calm voice. The trademark of his boat was a relaxed vigilance. A few of the crewmen called him Captain Serenity, though not to his face.

"There's some action southeast. I think it might be the *Marvin Shields*. And there're faint noises southwest, maybe thirty thousand yards. My guess would be the *Arleigh Burke*, but I'm not real sure, sir." The *Shields* was a Knox-class frigate, and the *Burke* was a guided-missile destroyer. Both were a part of the *George Washington*'s battle group.

"Any subsurface contacts?"

"Negative, sir."

"Very well. Keep your ears open. I want to know as soon as the *George* has passed us and gets ten thousand yards out. We'll be heading up."

"Aye, aye, skipper."

Commander Harding got his coffee and leaned nonchalantly against the periscope platform rail, a man without a care in the world. Whoever McGarvey was sending down in secret would be bringing the explanation with them. *And it better be damned good,* he thought, *or there will be hell to pay*. But then he'd had dealings with the man before. And McGarvey was, if nothing else, a man of consummate *cojones*. The mission would be, at the very least, an interesting one.

1940 Local
George Washington

Nobody said a thing on the way across the hangar deck. Their Marine escort, Sergeant Carlos Ablanedo, stopped them for a moment behind an A-6E Intruder, its wings in the up position, its nose cover open exposing the electronics inside. There was some activity forward, but it was far enough away, and the cavernous deck was lit only with dim red battle lights so there was no chance that they would be spotted.

Word had been sent down to the various section chiefs to make themselves and their crews scarce from about midships aft between 1930 and 2000 hours. It was done in such a way that no questions were asked. A personal favor for the old man.

The military services were not usually particularly friendly toward the CIA; too many mistakes had been made in the past, not the least of which was the Bay of Pigs fiasco. But McGarvey had to admit that this time they were treating him with kid gloves. They were looking for a solution that would require no shooting, and they were willing to go along with just about anything to get it.

The night was pitch-black, the sky overcast, so that there was no line to mark the horizon. The seas were fairly flat, so the huge wake trailing behind the massive warship was not as confused and dangerous as it could have been. Nonetheless, Hanrahan warned him that once they hit the water they were to swim at right angles from the ship to put as much distance between themselves and the tremendous suction of the gigantic propellers as possible. To help them the captain would order a sharp turn to port at 1950, which would take the stern away from them.

There was no rail on the open elevator bay, and it was a long way down to the water, maybe thirty or forty feet, McGarvey estimated. He and Hanrahan were dressed in black wet suits with hoods, small scuba tanks attached to their chests, buoyancy control vests and swim fins strapped to their backs. Hanrahan also carried a GPS/Inertial Navigator about the size of a paperback book. On the surface it established its location from satellites. Underwater it "remembered" its last satellite fix, and then kept track of every movement: up, down, left, and right, along with the speed to continuously update its position. It was a new toy that the SEALs had been given just two months ago. In trials it had worked like a charm. But this would be its first real-world test. McGarvey carried a bag with his things.

They flipped a pair of lines over the side, attached their hooks to the six-inch lip at the edge of the deck, then threaded the lines through their rappelling carabiners.

"Okay, Sarge, we were never here," Hanrahan said.

"Yes, sir. I'll take care of your ropes, but you guys stay cool."

McGarvey looked over the side at the black water rushing by. "I don't think we're going to have much of a choice in about two minutes."

The sergeant grinned. "At least this ain't the North Atlantic."

"Some guys have all the luck," Hanrahan said.

The carrier began its ponderous turn to port. They could actually feel the list, which McGarvey figured had to be at least five degrees, maybe more. The white wake curled away from them, and Hanrahan gave him the thumbs-up sign.

They went over the side together, rappelling in long but cautious jumps down the ship's flank, until they were just a few feet above water that moved as fast as a mountain stream.

Hanrahan unclipped his line and held it away from his body. McGarvey did the same, and on a signal from the SEAL they pushed off, hitting the water almost as hard as if they had jumped off a garage roof and landed on their backs on a concrete driveway.

McGarvey tumbled end over end and then he was swept deep beneath the surface. It seemed to go on for an eternity, until gradually the turbulence began to subside. When he surfaced, the ship was already ahead of him, and a ten-foot wall of water from the wake was curling around, heading right for him.

He yanked his swim fins free, struggled to put them on, and headed directly away from where he figured he had gone into the water and at right angles to the wake.

After five minutes he stopped and looked over his shoulder, involuntarily catching his breath. The ocean was empty. There was no sign that the *George Washington* had ever been there. No wake, no lights on the horizon, nothing. There were no other ships in sight, nor were there any aircraft lights in the sky. No sounds, no smells. He could not remember ever having such an overwhelming feeling of being alone. Facing a human enemy, one bent on killing you, was one thing. But facing the sea, which was a supremely indifferent enemy, was another matter altogether.

He saw a flash of light out of the corner of his eye to the left. He turned toward it, raised the tiny strobe light attached to his left arm and fired a brief burst in return.

A couple of minutes later Hanrahan materialized out of the darkness. "Are you okay?"

"I'm wet," McGarvey said. "How close are we to the rendezvous point?"

"Just about on top of it."

They donned their masks and mouthpieces, and on Hanrahan's lead they let the excess air out of their BC vests and started down at an angle toward the northeast. Almost immediately the massive hulk of the *Seawolf*'s sail appeared directly beneath them. The submarine had risen so that the top of her sail-mounted sensors were twenty feet beneath the surface.

McGarvey followed Hanrahan down the trailing edge of the sail to the submarine's deck, where the forward escape trunk hatch was open. The trunk was like a flooded coffin: the fleeting thought crossed McGarvey's mind as Hanrahan reached up and pulled the hatch closed. This was definitely not a job for someone with claustrophobia.

2015 Local
SSN 405 *Hekou*

Captain Heishui studied the chart, which showed the present positions of his submarine and the American boat, as well as the track of the *George Washington* and her battle group. He was trying to reconcile what he was seeing with his own two eyes and what his XO was telling him.

"She's on her way back down," Lagao said. "There's no doubt about it. It's my guess that she rendezvoused with the American carrier long enough to exchange messages, perhaps more."

Heishui looked up. "More?"

Lagao was a little uneasy, but he held it well. Heishui was an exacting captain. He did not suffer mistakes very well. "It's possible that the *Seawolf* took on supplies or passengers. He didn't surface, at least Zenzhong doesn't think so. But we may have picked up machinery noises. Possibly the pump for an escape trunk."

"All that information from beneath the thermocline?"

"There have been fluctuations in the temperature and salinity. But it's just a guess, Captain."

Heishui nodded. "I think that you may have something," he conceded. "Let's see what he does now."

"What if he tries to run?"

"Then we will follow in his baffles so that he will not detect us." Heishui studied the chart for a moment, trying to read something from it, some clue. "He can outrun us, of course, but not if he wants to remain stealthy." He looked up again. "That in itself would tell us something."

"We will have to keep a very close ear on him," Lagao warned.

"I want a slot buoy prepared. If he does head away we'll send up the buoy on a one-hour delay to inform Ningbo what we're attempting to do. The delay will give us plenty of time to get clear."

"I'll see to it now," Lagao said.

Heishui called sonar. "What is he doing?"

"Still on his way down, Captain."

"I think he means to get under way as soon as he reaches the thermocline. Keep a close watch."

"Yes, sir."

"Prepare to get under way," he told his Chief of Boat. "We're done waiting."

2020 Local
SSN 21 *Seawolf*

By the time McGarvey and Hanrahan changed clothes and were led down one deck and forward to the officers' wardroom directly beneath the attack center, the *Seawolf* had already started down. The XO, Lieutenant Commander Rod Paradise, who had been waiting for them when they emerged from the escape trunk, shook his head and grinned. "It's getting to be a habit, picking you up," he told McGarvey. "This is one time I think the captain is finally going to be surprised."

On a mission last year the *Seawolf* had rescued him from the Japanese Space Center on the island of Tanegashima. While aboard he'd gotten to know the captain and some of the crew. He had developed a great deal of respect for them. It was one of the reasons he wanted this sub for the mission. Harding was unflappable.

"I'd take five dollars of that," McGarvey said.

Paradise started to say something, but then shook his head. "I don't think I'd care to bet against you after all."

The angle on the bow was sharp. Harding was wasting no time getting back to the protection of the thermocline. But it made walking difficult, especially down ladders.

"Here we are," Paradise said, shoving back the curtain.

Harding was just pouring a cup of coffee. He turned around and smiled pleasantly. "Ah, McGarvey. It's nice to see you again." After the Tanegashima mission they had gotten together with their wives for drinks and dinner in Washington. The women had gotten along very well, and McGarvey and Harding had talked over dinner and then at the bar afterward until midnight. There didn't seem to be a subject that they disagreed on.

"Hello, Tom. Thanks for the lift."

"Getting off the *George* must have been interesting."

"Next time I'll leave it to the kids," McGarvey said. "This is Lieutenant Hank Hanrahan. He's along for the ride."

The captain noticed the SEAL insignia. "I suspect that you're going to have an interesting time of it."

"Yes, sir," Hanrahan agreed happily.

They sat down at the compact table, and Paradise poured them coffee. If anything, it was better than the coffee on the *George*, which was going some because the carrier was the flag vessel for both fleets during this operation.

"Okay, Mac, you're aboard safe and sound, and a lot of people went through a whole lot of trouble to get you here, so what's the program?" Harding asked. He was not a man to beat around the bush; not with his questions, nor with his orders. When you dealt with Harding you were dealing with a straight shooter. It was one of the qualities McGarvey liked about the man.

McGarvey handed him the carte blanche letter from the President. Harding quickly read it and handed it back. He was not overly impressed.

McGarvey handed him another envelope, this one sealed. "Once you've taken a look at that you're committed, Tom."

A flinty look came into the captain's eyes. "I wouldn't have picked you up if I wasn't already committed."

"No one outside of this room can know what the real mission is."

Harding considered it for a moment. He looked at Hanrahan. "Do you know what this contains, Lieutenant?"

"Yes, sir."

Harding opened the envelope, quickly scanned the three pages it contained, then read them again before handing them to his XO. This time he was impressed.

"You'll have to maintain radio silence," McGarvey

said. "We're on our own now until we get back to Pearl, no matter what happens."

"All this because the old men in Beijing are frightened," Harding said, amazed. "But this isn't all of it. There's more."

"Frightened men are capable of just about anything."

"The question becomes how far are we willing to go to protect an ally," Harding mused. "We're talking about the potential for a nuclear exchange here. So I suppose just about anything should be considered. Even a stunt as harebrained as this one."

McGarvey didn't have a chance to answer before Harding cut him off.

"I think it's worth a try, Mac," he said. He glanced at Hanrahan. "When I said interesting, that was one hell of an understatement."

Paradise finished reading the mission statement, then reached behind him and took out a chart of northern Taiwan and the waters around it. They moved the coffee cups so that he could spread it out on the table.

"Keelung will be your best bet," Harding said. "It's a big enough city so you might not be noticed. And if we make our approach from the southeast, we'll have deep water to within just a few miles of the coast."

"That's what we thought," McGarvey agreed. "We can get transportation there, and Taipei is only fifteen miles away."

"We can supply you with an inflatable and a muffled outboard, but you'll have to find someplace secure to hide it. I expect that the Taiwanese are a little jumpy about now. They'll have plenty of shore patrols out and about."

"We're going in as just about who we really are," McGarvey explained. "We're American military advisors, so it'll be up to the Taiwanese to keep quiet about us. It's something they'll understand."

"Okay, so that gets you to Taipei, then what?" Paradise asked. "It's a big city, maybe two million people."

"That's why they pay me the big bucks, Rod, to figure out things like that," McGarvey said. There was no reason for him or Harding to know what that part of the plan was. In fact no one knew, not even Hanrahan. Nor would they ever.

"How about a time line, then?" Harding asked.

"If we're not back in twenty-four hours, get the hell out, someplace where you can phone home and let them know that we're overdue. The mission name is MAGIC LANTERN."

"What's the earliest we can expect you?"

"That depends on when you get us to Keelung."

"We could have them ashore by midnight," Paradise said, looking up from the chart. "Even if we take it slow and easy."

"In that case with any luck we'll be back before sunrise," McGarvey said. "But the bad news is you'll have to surface."

"We can mask just about any surface radar, but if a surveillance aircraft or fighter/interceptor gets close enough, the game will be up."

"We'll have to take the chance."

"You're bringing something or someone aboard?"

"Something like that."

Harding looked at the mission outline again. "We have one thing going for us. This side of the island is fairly secure. If the PRC makes a move, they'll come from the west. The bulk of Taiwan's ASW assets are directed that way." He looked up. "Getting in and out will be the least of our problems, I think. Your mission ashore will be the tough nut to crack."

"Like I said, Tom, that's why they pay me the big bucks," McGarvey replied.

2050 Local
SSN 405 *Hekou*

"Conn, sonar."

Heishui grabbed the phone. "This is the captain."

"Sir, Sierra Eighteen is on the move. She just turned southeast, relative bearing two-zero-eight, and she's making turns for ten knots."

Heishui turned to his Officer of the Deck. "Turn right to two-zero-eight, and make your speed ten knots."

"Aye, sir. Make my course two-zero-eight, my speed one-zero knots."

Heishui turned back to the phone. "If he starts to make a clearing turn, or you even *think* that he might be about to do it, let me know immediately."

"Yes, sir."

Heishui replaced the phone. "Prepare to commence all stop and emergency silent operations on my command," he told his COB.

"Yes, sir."

Heishui went to the chart table, where he laid out the American submarine's present position, course, and speed. Projecting her line of advance brought her to the north coast of Taiwan about midnight. *A mystery within a mystery,* he thought glumly.

United Nations Security Council

Chou en Ping, the Chinese ambassador to the United Nations, got slowly to his feet, an all-but-unreadable expression on his flattened oriental face. Until his appointment three years ago he had been head of the Mathematics Department at Beijing University. Very few people in the entire UN were smarter than he was. Sometimes talking to him seemed like an exercise in futility.

"We have come to an impasse," he said in English. He directed his remark to Margaret Woolsey, the U.S. ambassador. "I have been directed by my government to ask that the voice of reason prevail. We call on the provincial government of Taiwan to immediately hand over the criminal Shi Shizong. We are sending a military delegation to Taipei to arrest him within twelve hours."

Margaret Woolsey looked around the chamber at the others, trying to gauge their moods this morning. It was a few minutes after 8:00 A.M., and the session had been going with only a couple of short breaks since nine o'clock the previous evening. They were all tired, their thinking somewhat dulled. It was exactly what Ping wanted. She offered a faint smile. "There will forever be an impasse when it involves the issue of individual freedom," she said. It was the harshest condemnation of mainland China's current actions, and some of the other delegates looked up in interest.

"Do you wish to debate the human rights issue again, Madame Ambassador?" Ping asked, pleasantly. "Shall we begin with Harlem, Detroit, or Watts?"

"Let us start with political asylum."

"That would first presuppose the criminal seeking such protection were to seek it of a legitimate nation. Illinois can no more offer political asylum to a federal fugitive than can Taiwan from China."

Margaret Woolsey felt a cautious thrill of triumph. Ping was apparently as tired as the rest of them.

"That's exactly what I'm talking about, Mr. Ambassador."

Ping seemed momentarily confused.

"The issue is Taiwan, not Peter Shizong." She held up a hand before Ping, realizing his stupid blunder, could interrupt. "But I agree that Mr. Shizong's case is a special one of great concern to your government, as well as to mine. It is an issue that should be considered by an impartial panel of judges. I propose that Mr. Shizong be handed over at once to the World Court in The Hague, where he should stand trial to show cause why he should not be returned to the People's Republic of China to face charges of treason."

Ping nodded. "Shall we prepare a list of U.S. criminals who should be handed over to the World Court for the same consideration?"

"If you wish, Mr. Ambassador," Margaret Woolsey said. "Though I would sincerely hope that a connection will be made between them and the current problem between Taiwan and China."

Ping was holding a fountain pen in his hand. He put it in his coat pocket. "Twelve hours, Madame Ambassador. And I do hope that reason will prevail when our delegation arrives in Taipei." His gaze swept around the chamber, then he turned and walked out.

0405 Local
SSN 21 *Seawolf*

McGarvey climbed up into the escape trunk. They were about three miles off Taiwan's coast, just west of Keelung. He was worried that they were running out of time. It would be light on the surface soon.

Unless they got off shortly, they would have to withdraw and lie on the bottom until nightfall. As it was they were running way behind schedule. Every hour that the standoff between the PRC and Taiwan, with the U.S. in the middle, continued, the chances that shooting would begin and someone would get hurt increased exponentially.

The problem was the patrol boats. They were unexpectedly swarming all over the place topside. Along with the increased commercial traffic, this part of the ocean was practically as busy as New York's Times Square on New Year's Eve. No one had considered that since the entire west coast of Taiwan was all but cut off from outside traffic, the major ports on the island's east side, among them Keelung, would have to take up the slack. They had been waiting for an opening since before midnight.

The phone outside the trunk buzzed, and Paradise answered it. "This is the XO." He nodded, then looked up and gave them the thumbs-up sign. "I'll tell them." He hung up. "Okay, it's clear for now. The captain says that we'll wait on the bottom here until you get back. Sonar will pick up your outboard, and we'll surface if it looks okay."

There were Chinese spies everywhere. If the *Seawolf* was spotted on the surface, the game would be all but up. "If it's not clear, come to fifty feet and we'll get aboard the same way we did last night," McGarvey said. He did not want to get stuck in the middle of a war zone.

Hanarahan looked startled. "But we were told that he can't swim."

"He'll have to learn," McGarvey shot back.

Paradise picked up on the exchange, but he shook his head. "I don't even want to know what you guys are talking about. We'll be here, okay? Just watch your asses."

"If we're not back by midnight, pull the pin, Rod, and call home."

"I'll tell the captain," Paradise said. He swung the escape-trunk hatch shut. Hanrahan dogged it tight, then hit the flood button, and immediately the cold water began to rise.

"What do you figure our chances are, Mr. M?" Hanrahan asked.

"Name's Mac, and I'd guess about fifty-fifty."

Hanrahan grinned from ear to ear. "Good deal. When we started they were only a hundred to one."

0410 Local
SSN 405 *Hekou*

"Sir, that is definitely their escape trunk," Zenzhong reported excitedly. "The hatch is opening now." The chief sonarman pressed his earphones tighter. "Wait."

"Stand by," Lagao told the captain waiting on the phone.

"They've released something into the water."

"A life raft?" Lagao suggested.

Zenzhong looked up and nodded. "Yes, sir. I can hear the inflation noises now."

"Any idea how many people are leaving the submarine?"

"No, sir. But the hatch remains open, so no one else is leaving the boat."

"Keep a close ear, Ensign," Lagao said. He hung up the phone and walked back to the control room, where he and the captain hunched over the chart table.

The *Hekou* was like a puppy dog lying behind its mother. The *Seawolf* had cleared her baffles three times on the way in, but each time Heishui was just a little faster shutting down because he anticipated the maneuver, whereas the American captain had no reason to believe that his boat was being followed.

"They put someone on the surface with an inflatable, but they left the door open, so it means they're coming back," Lagao said. He had a wild idea what the Americans might be up to, but he didn't dare voice his opinion to the captain. Not yet. It was just too crazy.

Heishui studied the chart. "They went through a great deal of trouble to rendezvous in secret with their carrier and then take someone aboard. That was a very risky maneuver. And now, presumably whoever transferred from the *George Washington* is going ashore. Interesting."

"Yes, sir."

"Navy SEALs?"

"They're trained for such maneuvers," Lagao said. The PRC Navy didn't have a unit quite like the American SEALs. To the average Chinese sailor an American SEAL was ten feet tall, could run the hundred-yard dash in four seconds, and ate raw concrete for breakfast.

"But why go ashore in secret?" Heishui asked. "The U.S. and the criminal government of Taiwan are allies. Why didn't they simply fly in? Unless they didn't want us to know about it."

"That's a reasonable assumption, Captain."

Heishui looked up at his executive officer. "What is it? What are you thinking?"

Lagao was uncomfortable. He had served with many officers in his career but never with one who so hated speculation as Heishui. Yet his captain had asked him a direct question, and one of the primary functions of an executive officer was to make suggestions.

"I was thinking that the reason we're here is to resolve the issue of Shi Shizong. Taipei has gone too far this time. They need to come home."

Heishui looked at his XO thoughtfully. "Go on."

"If Shizong were suddenly to disappear from Taiwan, and show up someplace else, our position would not be quite as tenable." Lagao chose his words with extreme care. He was walking a fine line between reason and treason.

"We have spies at every international airport on the island: He would be spotted if he tried to fly out," Heishui said. "And there are probably others who are very close to him, watching his every move. How else would we know as much about him as we do?" Heishui dismissed the suggestion. "The Taiwanese are not interested in giving him up in any event. They want him as badly as we want him." He shook his head. "And you're forgetting the *Nanchong*."

"What if the Americans mean to kidnap him?" Lagao pressed.

A startled expression crossed Heishui's face. "Take him away aboard the American submarine?"

"However improbable, Captain, it is a possibility that we should consider."

"What would they do with him?"

"It doesn't matter," Lagao said. "The point is he would no longer be on the island. Other than the *Nanchong*, there'd no longer be any current reason for us to be here."

"Unless we could prove that he was aboard the *Seawolf*, and report it to Ningbo," Heishui answered. He picked up the growler phone. "Sonar, this is the captain."

"Sonar, aye."

"What's Sierra Eighteen doing now?"

"He's heading to the bottom, sir."

"What about the inflatable they sent up?"

"It's heading ashore, sir."

"How do you know that?"

"I can hear the small outboard motor."

That's exactly what Heishui thought. "The moment it returns I want to know. It may be hours, even days, but I want to know."

"Yes, sir."

Heishui hung up. "When they come back the *Seawolf* will lift off the bottom. They'll make noise. In the confusion we'll send a man up with night-vision glasses to see with his own eyes who is aboard the inflatable."

0445 Local
Taiwan

"Cut the motor," McGarvey ordered urgently. Hanrahan complied instantly. They were about fifty yards off a commercial wharf. There were no boats tied up, nor were there any lights except for one pinprick of a yellow beam. Hanrahan spotted it.

"A patrol?"

"Looks like it." The flashlight moved slowly to the left, stopping every few feet. At one point the narrow beam of light flashed across the water. It was far too weak to reach out to them, but they ducked nevertheless.

On their chart the dock belonged to a fisheries company. Either the fleet was out tending nets, which McGarvey found hard to believe in the middle of a war situation, or all fishing had been suspended and the boats had been commandeered for patrols. They had expected to find minimal activity there tonight, but this was even better than they'd hoped for.

The city of Keelung, just a few kilometers to the

southeast, was mostly in darkness, blacked out because of the threat of invasion. But behind them, for as far as they could see in every direction were the dim red-and-green lights of the commercial fleet and the numerous military patrol boats the *Seawolf*'s sonar had picked out. Coming in had been like playing dodgeball.

After ten minutes the point of light disappeared around the corner of the warehouse and processing center. They waited another full five minutes to make sure that the guard wasn't coming back, then paddled the rest of the way in.

The old wooden docks were up on pilings. They worked their way beneath them, the water black, oily, and fetid with rotting fish and other garbage, then pulled themselves back to the seawall and to the west side, where they found a ladder. The only way anyone would spot the inflatable in what amounted to an open sewer would be to get into the water to make a specific search for it.

They had changed into civilian clothes on the way in: light sweaters, khaki trousers, soft boots, and jackets. After they secured the boat they scrambled up the ladder and stepped ashore with the credentials of U.S. Navy advisors to the Republic of China's Maritime Self-Defense Force.

"Welcome to Taiwan, Lieutenant," McGarvey said, and keeping low they headed across the net yard in the dank humidity of the nearly silent early morning.

0520 Local
SSN 21 *Seawolf*

Harding hadn't slept in more than thirty-six hours. Once they were settled on the bottom, and he had made sure that his boat was secure, he drifted back to his cabin, where he kicked off his shoes and lay down on his bunk. McGarvey was one tough character, and Harding held a grudging admiration for the man that was beginning to grow into a friendship. But in Harding's estimation McGarvey was also one lucky son of a bitch. By all laws of reason he and Hanrahan should have been spotted on their way ashore. Four different patrol boats had come to within spitting distance of their inflatable and yet had passed right by. And they were still going to have to get back tonight after dark if they were successful ashore. There was another worry, too. Paradise had reported the conversation between McGarvey and Hanrahan in the escape trunk. They were apparently bringing someone back with them, and there was only one person on all of Taiwan he could think of who'd be worth the risks they were taking.

The phone over his bunk buzzed. He switched on the light and answered it. "This is the captain."

"Hate to bother you, skipper, but we've got company," Paradise said.

Harding sat up. "What are you talking about?"

"Sonar's picked up some stationary noises. Maybe pumps, nuclear-plant noises. It looks as if we've got a PRC Han-class submarine parked on our back porch."

"I'm on my way."

Taiwan
in Country

Hanrahan was in the front seat of the ancient cloth-goods delivery truck speaking Mandarin with the driver. They'd hitched a ride on the main highway into Keelung just as the rain began in earnest. The drab old city was known unofficially as the rainiest seaport in the world, and although it was dawn by the time they reached the train station, visibility was limited to less than one hundred feet in the heavy traffic.

"Syeh syeh ni," Hanrahan told the old man.

"Boo syeh," you're welcome, the driver said, an odd expression on his wizened old face.

Everything that came to Keelung by sea had to leave either by rail or by highway, so the train station was busy twenty-four hours per day. Passengers and small parcels were loaded from the street side through the terminal, while trucks and a special spur line running up from the docks used a commercial loading yard across the tracks.

"Your Mandarin sounded pretty good," McGarvey said as they hurried across the street.

"Thanks, but I only had two years of it at Fort Benning."

"It's gotten us this far."

"Yeah, but I think the old man'll probably never trust an American again. I think I might have told him that I'd love to screw his mother, his sister, and his goat."

McGarvey had to laugh. "Would you?"

Hanrahan shrugged. "Well, maybe not his mother."

The train station was a madhouse, filled mostly with merchants and tradespeople bringing goods and services from Keelung to the rest of the country. Taiwan had only one rail line, which circled almost the entire island along the coast, with only a couple of branch lines. The trains were always overcrowded with people and animals, and loaded beyond belief with everything from candle wax and strawberries to cod-liver oil and machine screws.

Hanrahan headed for the lines at the ticket windows, but McGarvey steered him directly down to trackside, where he produced a pair of first-class tickets to Taipei. The police guards demanded to see their passports before they were allowed to board the train. When they were settled near the rear of the car Hanrahan leaned nearer.

"Good thinking about the tickets, but we're not going to be able to get back this way, not with . . . him."

McGarvey watched the policeman at the gate. He'd not made a move to use the telephone beside him. A couple of Americans boarding a train in Keelung were evidently not unusual enough for him to report to his superior. It was another break for them. But he didn't think that their luck would last forever. It never did.

He turned back to Hanrahan. "We're coming back by car, so keep your eyes peeled on the highway for roadblocks or military patrols. We might have to make a detour."

Hanrahan nodded. "Now that we're here, are you going to let me in on the rest of it, or am I going to have to guess?" He looked out the window at the police. "These people have their backs to the wall. If something starts to go down that they don't understand, they're likely to start shooting first and ask questions later."

"I brought you along to get us on and off the sub, and because you speak Chinese. The rest of it you're going to have to leave up to me."

Hanrahan started to object, but McGarvey held him off.

"We're probably going to run into some major shit in Taipei. And if it does hit the fan, if it looks like some of the good guys might get hurt, you're going to turn around and walk away from it. And that's an order, Lieutenant. At that point it becomes strictly a Company operation, and you're not going to be the one holding the dirty laundry."

The train was completely full now. The conductor came in, shouted something over the din, and moments later they lurched out of the station for the fifteen miles to the capital city.

Hanrahan's jaw tightened. It was clear that he was anything but happy. "Just one thing, Mr. M," he said, his voice low but with a hard edge to it. "I know how to follow orders—"

"Nobody is questioning you. But if something goes down, no matter whose fault it is, who do you suppose they're going to blame? It won't be me. It'll be a grunt lieutenant."

"The SEALs have never left one of their own behind, never," Hanrahan said. "I don't give a shit what's going down, 'cause that's a fact."

East Fleet Headquarters
Ningbo

"Captain Heishui is a reliable officer," Sun Kung Kee, the fleet's political commissar, told the CINC, Vice Admiral Pei. "I know his father. He will do as he is ordered."

"I expect nothing less from all of my officers." Admiral Pei reread the slot buoy message that had been sent last night from the *Hekou.*

"Presumably he followed the American submarine to the coast near Keelung. If he is right, the Americans meant to put someone ashore in secret. Since there have been no incidents reported, we must assume that Captain Heishui is still there and has not been detected."

"Nothing from our satellites?" the admiral asked.

"The weather is too bad for visual images, and nothing has shown up on infrared, Admiral," Commander Sze Lau, his Operations Officer replied.

"What about our spies on the ground in Keelung and Taipei, if that's where the Americans are heading? Have there been any reports?"

"Nothing yet," Commissar Kee told him. "But we must ask ourselves why the Americans chose to put somebody ashore in such a secret manner. The operation was not without its very considerable risks, which means that the Americans must be expecting a very considerable reward."

Admiral Pei put the slot buoy message down and sat back. "Yes?"

"Shi Shizong," the political commissar said, and both officers were startled though it was immediately clear that they understood the logic. "I think they mean to kidnap him."

"Do we know where he is being held?" Commander Lau asked. "We could intercept the Americans and take Shizong ourselves."

"His location is a secret. Apparently they move him every few days. Beijing, however, thinks that the Americans will almost certainly make contact with someone from their illegal consulate, who might know where the criminal is being hidden. If we were to wait there, our agents might be able to follow them to the traitor."

"Beijing was consulted?" Admiral Pei asked, his voice as soft as a summer's breeze but as bitter as a Tibetan winter's gale.

"Naturally I wanted to provide you with all the support you might need without the necessity of asking for it if and when the need should arise," Commissar Kee answered smoothly.

"Go on."

"If Shizong cannot be returned home to stand trial, he must never be allowed to leave Taiwan alive."

"That is a job for your agents on the ground," the admiral said.

"But if they fail, it will be up to Captain Heishui and his submarine."

"It would be a suicide mission."

"An acceptable loss providing Shizong does not escape," Commissar Kee pressed. "Word must somehow be gotten to him."

"It will be difficult without revealing his position, if indeed he is hiding just off the coast from Keelung, but not impossible," Commander Lau said, and Admiral Pei nodded his approval for the mission. The nation was willing to go to war over this issue; what was the possible loss of one submarine and crew by comparison?

Taipei

McGarvey watched from the train window as they entered Taiepi from the northeast. The capital was a city ready for invasion. The government was taking the Chinese threat seriously. Street corner antiaircraft batteries were protected behind sandbag barriers. Rooftops bristled with machine-gun emplacements. He counted six Patriot missile launchers set up in parking lots and empty fields, something the PRC had to be really unhappy about.

"This is going to be on my lead," he told Hanrahan. "You don't do a thing unless I tell you to do it."

"This place is crawling with PRC spies."

"That's right," McGarvey said. "The problem is

that you can't tell them from the good guys. And if they get wind that we're here on a mission we're screwed. *Capisce?*"

Hanrahan nodded. Jumping off aircraft carriers, diving down to submarines, and even storming ashore prepared to fight an army of trained commandos was one thing. In-your-face daylight covert operations where you were outnumbered a few billion to one was another ball game.

The press of people on the train platform all the way up to the street-level terminal was constant. They had to bull their way forward in order to get outside to the cab rank, and practically had to knock over three businessmen to get a cab. McGarvey gave Hanrahan an address on Hoping Road a few blocks from the university to give to the cabbie, and they headed away.

The streets were as crazy as the train station. Traffic was all but stalled at many intersections, and their driver had to backtrack and make several detours around the downtown area. Especially around the government buildings. The military presence was everywhere, yet there seemed to be a look of inevitability, of resigned indifference, on the faces of the people here and aboard the train. War was coming, and there wasn't much that anyone could do about it.

"How the hell do they expect to get anything done like this?" Hanrahan asked, watching out the windows. The cab was not air-conditioned, and already the heat and humidity had plastered their clothes to their bodies.

"You oughta see New Delhi at rush hour in midsummer," McGarvey said absently, watching for any signs that an organized resistance movement had been formed.

The Taiwanese were great soapbox orators. They took their politics more seriously than just about any other country on earth. Their representatives regularly got into fistfights on the floor of the legislature. And just like the South Koreans, who were also faced with a constant threat of annihilation, there were staunch Taiwanese supporters for every side of just about every issue that was raised. There was a sizable minority of Taiwanese who wanted a return to the mainland. If they wanted to start something, now would be a perfect time for it. If Taiwan were suddenly to find itself in the middle of a bloody civil war, it would give the PRC one more reason to come in and take over by force: to save human lives.

Taiwan was like a powder keg with a short fuse in the middle of an armory packed with dynamite. Lit matches were being held out from every direction. It was only a matter of time before one of them caught.

The driver left them off in front of the Bank of South Africa building, in an area of offices and apartment high-rises. They had just passed the sandbagged entrance to Taiwan University, where a mob of a thousand or more students wearing headbands and carrying banners was parading up and down in front of a Patriot missile emplacement on the grass. Soldiers had cordoned off the area, keeping the students from spilling out onto the busy street and further disrupting traffic. It was the only evidence of any sort of dissension that McGarvey had seen so far.

The Parisian Lights was a sidewalk café set under a red-and-white-striped awning across Hoping Road from the university demonstration. The place was crowded, but they got a table in the corner. Their waiter spoke French with a Chinese accent. McGarvey ordered coffee and beignets, and when the waiter was gone he used his cell phone to call the American Institute three blocks away on Hsinyi Street.

"Peyton Graves," he told the operator.

"He's not in," she answered.

"Yes, he is," McGarvey insisted. "I'll hold." Graves was the CIA's Chief of Taiwan Station and a very capable old China hand. He was in the hot seat right now, so he wasn't going to be in to most people. It was SOP. McGarvey had met the man only once, and although Graves had struck him as a bit officious and bureaucratic, he was doing a good job for them out here.

"This is Peyton Graves, what can I do for you?"

"Is this a secure line?" McGarvey asked.

"Jesus," Graves said softly. He'd recognized McGarvey's voice. "It can be."

"Switching now," McGarvey said. He pressed star-four-one-one, and his cell phone's encryption circuits kicked in. "How's this?"

"Clear," Graves said. "You're in-country, but nobody said anything to me, Mr. McGarvey."

"I want to keep it that way, Peyton, you probably have a PRC leak in the embassy."

"This place is like a sieve. Where are you?"

McGarvey told him. "We're going to need a windowless van and a driver who knows the city, and someplace to lie low just until tonight."

"I'll have somebody pick you up within ten minutes. It'll be a gray Chevy delivery van, Han Chi Bakeries, Ltd. on the side. Driver's name is Tom Preston. Tall, dark hair, mustache."

"Good enough. No one else is to know that we're here, and I mean no one, not even the ambassador."

"I understand," Graves said. "I'm not even going to ask how you got here without flags going up. The city is crawling with PRC supporters. But if you've come here to do what I think you came here to do, tonight will be cutting it a tad close."

"What are you talking about?"

"Apparently you haven't heard. The PRC are sending a military delegation of some sort over here early this evening to arrest Shizong. Nobody knows how it's going to play, but the word is out that the delegation will at least be allowed to land. From that point it's anybody's guess."

"Does the PRC know where Shizong is being kept?"

"It's possible, but I don't think so. The Taiwanese CIA have been handling it, and they've done a good job so far. But the politicians might take it out of their hands. Taiwan wants to keep him here, but they're afraid that if the PRC pushes it, we'll just sit on our hands and watch."

"They're right," McGarvey said. "Do you know where he's being kept?"

"They switch him around every few days. But for now he's up on Grass Mountain at Joseph Lee's old place." Lee was a Taiwanese multibillionaire whom McGarvey had run up against a couple of years ago in a Japanese operation to put nuclear weapons in low-earth orbit. Lee was dead and the Taiwanese government had confiscated most of his properties, including the Grass Mountain house.

"Who'll be with him tonight?"

"I don't know for sure, but considering what might be going down I'd guess the same team that snatched him from Xiamen."

"I know them. They're all good men."

"Tough bastards," Graves said. "They're not going to take kindly to anyone barging in up there, friend or foe. Especially friend. If the PRC is allowed to arrest him and take him back to the mainland, Taipei will be able to make a very large international stink over it. They'll win *beaucoup* points in the UN. But if you mean to grab him and bury him someplace deep and out of sight, nobody will win. They're not going to want that."

"You're wrong about one thing, Peyton. If we do pull this off, *everybody* will end up on top in the long run."

"Do you want some help then?"

"Just Tom Preston, the van, and someplace to crash until tonight," McGarvey said.

"If anything breaks this afternoon, I'll get it to you," Graves said.

"Thanks. But then forget that we were ever here."

"You'd better take Tom with you. After tonight he'll be useless here."

"Will do," McGarvey said, and he broke the connection.

YAK 38 Forger A
Tail Number 13/13

Captain Xia Langshan was flying right wing escort for the Boeing 727 bringing the arresting officers to Taipei. Lieutenant Qaixo was flying left wing. Their transponders were all squawking 11313, which was the code for a peaceful-mission incursion into Taiwanese airspace. The same code was used when Taiwanese weather-spotting airplanes flew into PRC airspace. They just cleared the beach on their long approach.

"Green One, this is Eagle thirteen/thirteen, feet dry," Langshan radioed his AWACS controller circling at thirty-five thousand feet, thirty klicks to the west.

"Thirteen/thirteen, this is Green One. You are clear to proceed, out."

Langshan switched to the civilian frequency in time to hear the Boeing whose ID was Justice Wind Four receiving its landing instructions from Chiang Kai-shek International Airport at Taoyuan. He could hear the tension in the controller's voice.

"PRC Flight Four, your escort aircraft will not be allowed to land. Acknowledge."

"Taoyuan Airport tower, this is Justice Wind Four on final to one-seven with delta. We acknowledge your last transmission."

"We want your escorts to leave our airspace the moment you land."

"Negative, tower. They have been ordered to remain on station until their fuel has been exhausted, at which time they will be relieved."

"Permission is denied, PRC Flight Four."

"We didn't ask for permission, Taoyuan tower," the pilot, Colonel Hezheng, replied in polite but measured tones. "We will view any hostile response as an act of war, acknowledge."

The radio was silent for several long seconds, and Langshan could almost imagine the scene in the tower as the controllers talked to their superiors by telephone.

"Acknowledge," Colonel Hezheng repeated calmly.

The airport was visible now about twenty kilometers to the west. Langshan's threat-assessment radar was clear, although he was being painted by at least a half-dozen ground-radar sets. None of them, however, were missile-facility radars. Those signatures were different. The Taiwanese military well understood that if they illuminated a target it was tantamount to aiming a loaded gun. It was universally recognized as an act of aggression. In that case Langhsan had permission to shoot, though it was not his primary mission.

"We acknowledge your last transmission," the tower finally responded. "Your escorts will maintain flight level one-zero and remain within ten kilometers of the airport."

"My escorts have been ordered to establish and maintain twenty-five-kilometer patrol zones centered on Taipei."

"Negative, negative, negative!" the tower controller practically screamed.

Colonel Hezheng overrode the transmission, his voice still maddeningly calm. "The provincial government of Taiwan has not adequately informed the people about the real issue of the criminal Shi Shizong. We will drop leaflets guaranteeing the truth of our peaceful mission, and let the people decide for themselves who are the warmongers."

Langshan grinned behind his face mask.

"PRC Four, we will shoot your escort aircraft out of the sky if they stray outside of the airport containment zone."

The 727 was losing altitude for its final approach to landing. Langshan looked over at Qaixo and rocked his wings left-right-left. Qaixo responded.

"If our aircraft are fired upon, they will shoot back, tower. And we will request immediate backup. In force."

The radio was silent again. Civilian traffic to Taiwan had been sharply curtailed since the troubles had escalated in the past ten days. And all traffic for the duration of this mission had been diverted to the airport at Kaoshiung in the far south.

Qaixo peeled off to the north to start the outer leg of his patrol zone. When he got over the city of

Taoyuan itself he would begin to drop his leaflets.

Langshan watched for a few moments as the 727 continued gracefully down for landing, then hauled his throttles back and shot northeast directly for the heart of Taipei, maintaining an altitude of ten thousand feet while his mach indicator climbed past .7, the hard bucket seat pressing into his back.

In less than two minutes he was directly over the city, Grass Mountain rising off to his north, Green Lake spread out to his south, and the city of Keelung on the coast lost under a thick blanket of low-lying clouds directly ahead.

His threat-radar screen remained blank, and the moment he crossed the Tamsui River he released the first of his canisters programmed to fall like a bomb to one thousand feet before opening and spreading the leaflets on the wind. At the very least, he thought, the bastards would have a big cleanup job tomorrow. In his underwing pods he carried one million messages on long, thin strips of rice paper, like giant fortune cookie fortunes.

He dropped a second canister near the stadium and a third on the densely populated shantytown in the western suburbs before he continued to Keelung and the coast twenty-five kilometers to the west-northwest. Within a half minute he was enveloped in a dense cloud, rain smashing into the canopy like machine-gun bullets. His forward-looking radar was clear of any air traffic, and his look-down-shoot-down radar showed him exactly what was happening on the ground.

In two minutes he was over the city of Keelung, where he dropped two more of his canisters and then made a long, sweeping turn out over the harbor.

At the last minute, about three miles off the coast,

Langshan dialed up a special canister on his port wing rack, checked his position, hit the release button, and then headed back for his second run over Taipei.

1920 Local
SSN 21 *Seawolf*

"Conn, sonar."

"This is the captain speaking. What do you have, Fisher?"

"Skipper, something just hit the water eighteen hundred yards out, bearing one-eight-seven. It's not very big, but from the angle it made I'd say that it was dropped from something moving real fast. Maybe a jet, but definitely not a boat."

"Any idea what it is?"

"I think it's a comms buoy, sir . . . stand by."

Paradise came in from the officer's wardroom with a couple of cups of coffee. He handed one to Harding. It had been a very long day since McGarvey and Hanrahan had locked to the surface. They'd all existed on coffee.

"Okay, skipper, that's definitely a comms buoy. She's started to transmit acoustically."

"Good work," Harding said. He switched to the radio room. "Comms, this is the captain. Somebody just dropped an acoustical communications buoy to our south and it's starting to transmit. It's probably in Chinese and in code, but see what you can do with it."

"Aye, aye, skipper," the radio officer said with even less enthusiasm, for a job he was not equipped to handle, than he felt.

"A message from home for our friend?" Paradise asked.

"So it would seem. Question is, what kind of a message is it?"

"It could be about us," Paradise said. "But you have to wonder what makes them think that they haven't told the entire world where their boat is hiding."

1945 Local
SSN 405 Hekou

Z112530ZJUL
TOP SECRET
FR: CINCEASTSEAFLEET
TO: 405 HEKOU
A. ACKNOWLEDGE UR Z145229ZJUL
1. DETERMINE AT ALL COSTS IF SHI SHIZONG IS TRANSPORTED TO SEAWOLF UR REPORT.
2. THIS IS A MOST URGENT OPERATIONS FLASH MESSAGE. COMPLIANCE IS MANDATORY.
3. SHIZONG MUST NOT BE ALLOWED TO LEAVE TAIWAN. ALL OTHER CONSIDERATIONS ARE SECONDARY. GOOD LUCK SZE LAU SENDS BT BT BT

Captain Heishui handed the decoded message across the table to Lagao. They were alone in the officers' wardroom. His XO read the message, then read it again before he looked up, a grave expression on his face.

"If they manage to get him aboard the American boat, we will be obligated to attack," he said.

Heishui nodded. "But we would have two advantages," he said. "In the first place, they don't know that we're back here. But even if they do find out, they'll never believe that we would open fire. You have to shoot at an American six times before he will start to respond."

"Yes, Captain. But when he does it's usually fatal."

Chiang Kai-Shek International Airport

Peyton Graves powered down his window and pointed a tiny parabolic receiver at the PRC Air Force 727 as the boarding stairs were brought up and the forward hatch swung open.

A lot of cars and military vehicles surrounded the jet, which was parked in front of the old Pan Am hangar. Everyone seemed restrained. No one wanted this situation to accelerate out of control. There were no media.

Lieutenant Colonel Thomas Daping, chief of the Counterespionage Division for the Taiwan Police, went up the stairs, followed by a lieutenant in uniform whom Graves did not recognize.

They stood at the head of the stairs for a few moments until a full bird colonel in the uniform of a civilian police officer, blue tabs on his shoulder boards, appeared in the doorway. A much taller man in a captain's uniform showed up right behind him.

"Good evening, I am Colonel Lian Shiquan, Beijing Police. I am here with a warrant for the arrest of the criminal Shi Shizong."

Graves turned up the gain on his receiver. Even so it was hard to pick up the Taiwanese officer's reply because his back was turned to the receiver. When it came, however, it was a complete surprise to Graves. The government had caved in even faster and more completely than he thought it would.

"Yes, sir," Colonel Daping replied. "He is being

held not too far from here, at a home on Grass Mountain. We have transportation standing by to take you there immediately."

It was too far for Graves to see the expression on the Chinese colonel's face, but he heard the surprise and the smug satisfaction in his voice. "I should think so. There are eight of us, plus myself and my adjutant, Captain Qying. Let's proceed."

Graves tossed the receiver on the passenger seat and headed past the hangars toward the back gate. He used his cell phone to call the safe house where McGarvey was staying.

"Switch," he said as soon as McGarvey answered.

"Right."

Graves hit star-four-one-one. "You've run out of time. I'm just leaving the airport. The Taiwanese are handing him over without an argument. They're taking the PRC delegation up to Grass Mountain right now, so you're going to have to hustle."

"How many of them?"

"Ten PRC and I don't know how many Taiwanese cops. But if you get caught in the middle of them, you'll get yourself shot."

"Thanks for your help, Peyton. We'll take it from here," McGarvey said. "Get back to the embassy and keep your head down, there's no telling what might happen in the next twenty-four hours."

"Good luck."

Taipei

It was after 8:00 P.M., but still light by the time they cleared the city and headed east on the Keelung Highway. Grass Mountain, off to their left, was tinged in brilliant pinks and salmons at the higher levels, but the sky toward the coast was dark and threatening. The highway was choked with traffic of all descriptions, from eighteen-wheelers to hand-drawn carts. There seemed to be tiny scraps of paper blowing everywhere.

"I think we've got a tail," Tom Preston said from the front.

McGarvey crawled forward to the passenger seat, opened the window, and adjusted the door mirror. Preston switched lanes to get around an old canvas-covered flatbed, and a yellow Fiat followed.

"It was outside the apartment this afternoon," McGarvey said. In the middle of an operation he had a photographic memory for people and things. Patterns and anomalies. The ability had saved his life on more than one occasion.

"Sorry, I missed it." Preston had struck McGarvey as easygoing but very capable. He and Hanrahan, who were football fans, had argued heatedly, but good-naturedly, about the Pack versus the Vikes all afternoon. But he was apologetic now.

"I only saw him the one time," McGarvey said, studying the image in the mirror. "Same driver, but he's picked up a passenger." He missed the look Preston gave him.

"They're not our people," Preston said. "I'm sure of at least that much."

"Taiwanese police?"

"No. I know all of their tag series. That's not one of them. Civilians. PRC supporters. Maybe spies. Either they knew about the safe house and were watching it, or someone from inside the consulate tipped them off. Whatever it is, we're going to have to deal with it pretty soon because our turnoff is coming up."

"What do you want to do, Mac?" Hanrahan asked from the back. "We've got the PRC delegation from the airport breathing down our necks, so we don't have a hell of a lot of time."

McGarvey took out his Walther PPK and checked the load. "No matter what happens, we're not going to hurt any Taiwan national if we can help it. That means cops and soldiers as well as civilians." He checked the mirror. The yellow Fiat was still behind them. He holstered his pistol and checked the two spare magazines.

"Here's the turn," Preston said.

"Head up toward the house: I'll tell you where to pull over," McGarvey said. It was an early evening like this when he'd come up here nine months ago. Visiting the spoils of war, he'd told his chief of staff in Washington. In reality he was picking up the pieces of a mission that had nearly cost him his life. After all was said and done he wanted to see the house where Lee had lived in order to get some measure of the man who'd almost brought the world to a nuclear showdown. Not terribly unlike the situation they were in again.

Lee's eighteen-room house was perched on the side of the mountain a couple of hundred feet above its nearest neighbor. A maze of narrow roads led in all directions into narrow valleys and defiles, in which other mansions were built. But Lee's compound was at the head of a very steep switchback that had been cut through the living rock. Except for the helicopter pad, there was only one way in or out. Had the Taiwanese police decided to bring the PRC delegation up by chopper, the mission would have been over before it had begun.

Within a few blocks of the highway the Grass Mountain road rose up sharply from the floor of the valley. The traffic, except for an occasional Mercedes or Jaguar, ended, and a thin fog began to envelop the twisting side streets and houses set back in the trees in an air of gloom and mystery. This was the Orient, and yet a lot of people with money built Western-style homes up here. It was a curious mixture, just like Taipei itself.

"Okay, Lee's driveway is coming up around the next curve," Preston said.

McGarvey had spent only a half hour up there, looking around the house and down across the valley toward the city from the balconies. The view had been nothing short of spectacular. But he tried to recall how steep the slope was just below the house on the side of the compound away from the road. Maybe negotiable, but he wasn't sure. He'd not been on a life-or-death mission that time.

"As soon as we're around the curve and out of sight of the Fiat, you're going to slow down and let me off," McGarvey said. "Then drive past Lee's road, pull into the next driveway, turn around, and wait there."

"What about the guys in the Fiat?" Preston asked.

"I'm going to try an end run. If they miss me, they'll come past you, probably turn around, and wait to see what you're going to do next." McGarvey screwed the silencer on the end of the Walther's barrel.

"You'll need some help. I'm coming with you," Hanrahan said, taking out his Beretta.

"I know one of the guys up at the house. If I show up alone, they might listen before they start shooting."

"Goddammit, Mac, that's not why I signed on—."

"You signed on to take orders, Lieutenant," McGarvey said harshly. "If I can grab Shizong and get him out of there, I'll be moving fast. I'll need someone to watch the back door. I don't want to get caught between the PRC delegation coming up from the airport and the goons in the car behind us. Do you understand?"

Hanrahan wanted to argue, but he held himself in check. "Yes, sir."

McGarvey softened. "If we do this right, nobody will get hurt."

"Here we go, guys," Preston said. They came around the sharp curve, passed Lee's driveway, and Preston jammed on the brakes.

"If the group from the airport makes it up here, give me ten minutes and then get the hell out," McGarvey said. He popped open the door, jumped out on the run, then ducked into the trees and brush beside the road as the van disappeared and the Fiat came charging around the curve.

He got the impression of two men, both of them intent on catching up with the van. He was sure that they had not seen him.

As soon as they were gone he jumped up, hurried across the road, and raced up the driveway, conscious that the mission clock was counting down in earnest now.

The road was steep and switched back several times. In a couple of minutes he reached the top, the road splitting left and right around a fountain in front of the low, rambling, steel-and-glass house. The fountain was operating, and there were lights on inside the house. Anyone watching from the outside would have to assume that nothing suspicious was going on up here. No one was trying to hide anything. Life as normal.

Holding his hands in plain sight out away from his sides, McGarvey headed to the right around the fountain. The hairs at the nape of his neck prickled. He couldn't see anyone at the windows, but he got the distinct impression that he was being watched, and that guns were pointed at him.

A wooden footbridge arched gracefully over a winding pond that contained large golden carp. When McGarvey got to the other side the front door opened and Joseph Jiying stepped out. He wore jeans and an open-collar shirt. He was unarmed.

"Good evening, Mr. McGarvey. I've gotta say that you being up here is one big surprise." Jiying had spent eight months working in Langley on an exchange program. McGarvey had gotten to know him and some of the others; all of them dedicated, and most of them pretty good intelligence officers.

"I've come for Peter Shizong."

Jiying looked beyond McGarvey toward the empty driveway. "Did you come alone, on foot?"

"I have a van waiting on the road below. But we don't have much time. There's a PRC delegation along with a Taiwanese police escort on its way up here from the airport to arrest him."

Jiying's expression didn't change except that his eyes narrowed slightly. "That's news to me."

"They didn't want you to do something stupid, like try to take off or barricade yourselves up here."

"My people would have warned me by now."

"Maybe not if they were ordered by someone high enough to stay out of it." McGarvey could see that Jiying didn't want to believe what he was being told, and yet he could see the truth to it. "If I can get him out of here in time, the PRC won't be able to take him."

"They'd turn Taiwan upside down."

"They probably would. And if you knew where he was, you'd be made to tell them. You know that."

Jiying shook his head, more in anger and frustration than in denial. "There's too much at stake, dammit. We're winning. We're finally starting to make points. We're the good guys here—"

One of his men appeared at his elbow, looked

pointedly at McGarvey, then told something to his boss. McGarvey did not understand the Chinese, but he caught the urgency. The expression on Jiying's face changed to one of anger and resignation.

"There was no reason for you to come all this way in secret to lie to me, was there," he said. "There are seven Taipei Special Services Police Humvees on the Keelung Highway." He said something to his man that clearly upset him. He tried to argue, but Jiying barked a command at him, and he left.

"How close?"

"They just turned onto Grass Mountain Road. I hope the van is well hidden."

"It's just past the driveway. Is there another way down from here for me?"

"There's a path on the other side of the house. It's steep, but you should be able to make it."

"There's room in the van for all of us."

Jiying shook his head again. "You'll need time to make it down the hill and then get the hell out. We can delay the bastards all night if need be."

McGarvey understood that it was the only way. "All we need is a couple of hours, Captain. After that give it up. Don't get yourselves killed."

A faint smile curled his lips. "Believe me I'll do my best to make sure I die an old man in my own bed."

The commando returned with a bemused Peter Shizong. Jiying said something to him in rapid-fire Mandarin. Shizong looked at McGarvey, asked Jiying a question, and when he was given the answer he nodded.

"It seems as if I am to go with you, sir," he said.

"I have a warrant for your arrest on a charge of spying on the United States for the People's Republic of China."

"You've come all this way," Shizong said with a hint

of amusement. "Will you read me my Miranda rights?"

McGarvey had to smile. "If you wish, and if I can remember them from watching *NYPD Blue*."

"Beijing has sent someone to arrest you," Jiying said seriously. "And my government has agreed to hand you over. Tonight."

Shizong suddenly understood the gravity of the situation. "I see."

"You need to go right now, Peter," Jiying said. He brought his heels together, placed his hands at his sides, and bowed formally.

Shizong did the same. When he rose he said something in Mandarin to Jiying, and then turned to McGarvey. "I have no idea how you mean to get me out of here in one piece, but then some really extraordinary things have happened to me in the last couple of months."

Jiying hustled them to a broad veranda on the west side of the house, where the rock-strewn hill plunged steeply a couple hundred feet to a line of trees.

"The road is just below the trees," Jiying told them.

It was finally starting to get dark. The city of Taipei was coming alive with a million pinpricks of light. What sounded like a fighter jet passed overhead to the south.

One of the commandos called something from inside the house. It sounded urgent.

"We're out of time. Take it easy going down and good luck," Jiying said.

McGarvey started down the hill first, and once they were out from under the veranda it was a little easier to pick out the path. At first he went slowly for Shizong's sake, but within thirty feet he realized that the much younger man was in very good shape and as surefooted as a mountain climber, so he picked up the pace.

They reached the bottom in five minutes and made their way through the dense stand of trees. They came out about twenty yards beyond where the Fiat was parked at the side of the road, facing downhill. McGarvey could not see the van, but he suspected that Preston had pulled into the driveway another thirty or forty yards farther down the hill. The road up to Lee's house was just beyond it.

"Is that our transportation?" Shizong whispered.

"No, they followed us up from Taipei. There's two of them."

"PRC supporters?"

"Yes, but I don't want to kill them unless I have no other choice."

"They wouldn't return the favor, believe me," Shizong said. "What are we going to do?"

"Wait until the delegation from the airport arrives. These guys might follow them up the hill."

"They might not—" Shizong said when they spotted lights coming up the road around the curve. They could hear the Humvees' exhausts hammering off the side of the hill, and after they had all turned up Lee's driveway the night got relatively quiet again. But the Fiat did not move.

"Shit," McGarvey said, half under his breath. He took out his pistol. "Wait here," he told Shizong, and he stepped out on the road. Keeping his eye on the car for any sign of movement, and his pistol hidden behind his leg, he walked down to the Fiat. As he got closer he could see the two men inside, but they were not moving, and it wasn't until he was on top of them that he saw why.

They were both alive and frantic with rage. Hanrahan and Preston had gotten the drop on them and had duct-taped them to their seats. They were covered head to toe except for their noses and eyes.

McGarvey motioned for Shizong to come ahead when Hanrahan stepped out of the darkness below and waved them on. Shizong stopped in his tracks, suddenly not sure what was happening.

"Get the van," McGarvey called down to Hanrahan, keeping his voice as low as possible. He hurried back to where Shizong was about ready to bolt.

"I don't know—"

"It's okay, Mr. Shizong," McGarvey said. The man was only in his twenties, and despite his intelligence, training and charisma he was still just a young man faced with a very uncertain and potentially deadly situation. "There's a submarine waiting for us off Keelung. If we can get you aboard, we'll take you to Honolulu. It's either that or Beijing. But you can't stay here any longer."

The van, its headlights off, nosed out from the driveway.

Shizong looked at the van and then back at McGarvey. "Do you think that I can find some old Superman comics in a shop there?"

McGarvey spread his hands, at a loss. "I imagine you can."

"It's a present for someone," Shizong said, and he motioned toward the van. "I believe that our ride is waiting for us."

Hanrahan was holding the side door open for them. Just as they reached the van they heard gunshots from above, and again Shizong was stopped in his tracks. He turned back, and McGarvey grabbed his arm.

"We have to go now," McGarvey said urgently.

"Those are my friends up there." Shizong tried to pull away.

"And they're also Taiwanese intelligence officers who risked their lives to pull you out of Xiamen. They're buying us some time."

"They might be killed."

"Yes, they might be," McGarvey said harshly. "So might we."

Shizong gave him a look of genuine anguish, and McGarvey wanted to tell him: Welcome to the club. You now have blood on your hands like the rest of us. But he didn't say it because it was too cruel, too without feeling or compassion. It was this business; it made people into its own terrible mold, not the other way around. Shizong still had his idealism. McGarvey hoped that it would last at least a little longer.

They clambered into the van and even before Hanrahan had the door shut, Preston took off down the hill like a rocket, the sounds of gunfire up at Lee's mansion intensifying.

2120 Local
SSN 21 *Seawolf*

Harding was in the control room studying the chart. The water didn't get deep for another five miles offshore, and the Han-class submarine blocked the way. There was no real contest if it came to a battle. But he didn't think that the Chinese skipper wanted to start a shooting war any more than the rest of them did.

He glanced at the boat's master clock. McGarvey had given himself until midnight local before he should be considered overdue. There was no way to tell what was happening ashore. Technically that wasn't his responsibility. His boat and his crew were.

He grabbed the growler phone. "Sonar, this is the captain," he said.

"Sonar, aye."

"What's our friend doing?"

"He's still back there, skipper. Trying to be real quiet. But he's got a noisy motor somewhere. Probably in his air-circulation system."

"Any sign of the outboard?"

"Nothing yet."

"How's traffic topside?"

"That's some good news, Captain. It's thinned out."

"Keep me posted, Fisher," Harding said. He hung up the phone. He had to think it out for only a moment, then he looked up. "Come to battle stations, torpedo," he said calmly.

"Aye, sir, battle stations, torpedo," a startled Chief of Boat responded, and he began issuing orders.

"Load tubes one, two, three, and four, but do not open the outer doors."

"Do we have a target, sir?" the weapons control officer asked.

"Start a TMA on Sierra Twenty-one. I want a continuous solution on the target, and I don't want to lose it no matter what happens."

"Yes, sir," the officer said, impressed. It was the first time he'd ever heard the captain speak that sharply. But God help the poor sorry Chinese son of a bitch if he so much as twitched a whisker.

Keelung

McGarvey watched the road from where he sat in the rear of the van. Traffic had slowed to a crawl outside Keelung because of a military roadblock. Some people tried crossing the fields in the steady rain to reach the railroad tracks, but soon got stuck because of the deep mud. Soldiers went on foot to arrest them.

"There were no roadblocks this morning," Hanrahan said.

It had taken them more than an hour to drive the twelve miles from the Grass Mountain road. Time enough, McGarvey wondered, for the battle at Lee's house to be finished, the house searched, and the PRC spies duct-taped inside of their car to be released and give them the description of the van? If that was the case, they would somehow have to bluff their way through because there was no turning back, the highway was impossibly clogged; and he wasn't going to get into a shooting battle with Taiwanese soldiers doing their legitimate duties.

"What do you want to do?" Preston asked. "In the mood these guys are in it won't take much to set them off."

"We're going to talk our way past them," McGarvey said, an idea turning over in his mind.

"If they're looking for us specifically, it's going to be all over but the shouting once we get up there," Hanrahan pointed out unnecessarily. They all knew it.

McGarvey turned and looked at Shizong who was hunched down in the darkness in the back. Their eyes met, and Shizong nodded and smiled. McGarvey turned back. "I'll do the talking," he told Preston and Hanrahan. "No matter what happens, there'll be no gunplay. Understood?"

They both nodded.

It was another twenty minutes before their turn came. The highway was blocked in both directions, and there was just as big a traffic jam trying to get out of the city as there was trying to get in. Most of it was trucks trying to pick up or deliver goods.

A pair of APCs were parked beside the highway, their fifty-caliber machine guns covering both directions. There were at least five Humvees and a couple of dozen soldiers in battle fatigues, all of them armed with M16s and very serious-looking. There were two lanes of traffic in each direction, each lane with its own cadre of soldiers.

A sergeant and PFC came to the driver's window. McGarvey reached over Preston's shoulder and handed the sergeant his military ID, "I need to talk to your CO."

The sergeant looked at the ID and then looked up at McGarvey. "Get out of the van, all of you," he ordered.

"You're going to be in a world of shit, Sergeant, if you don't get your CO over here on the double. We have something here he's got to see."

"Get out of the vehicle—"

"Call him," McGarvey ordered. "Now!"

The sergeant, a little less certain, checked McGarvey's ID again, which identified him as a captain in the U.S. Navy. He stepped back and said something into his lapel mike. A minute later a young lieutenant wearing camos charged over, said something to the sergeant, and then came over to the van.

"Get out now," he shouted.

"As you wish," McGarvey said. "But there's a friend of yours in back who wants to tell you something." He pulled back and slid open the side door. His eye caught Shizong's. The young man nodded. He knew exactly what he was supposed to do.

McGarvey and Hanrahan climbed out of the van as the lieutenant came around from the driver's side where Preston had dismounted.

There were soldiers all over the place, sensing that something was going on, their weapons at the ready.

"Step away from the vehicle—" the lieutenant said, as Shizong appeared at the open door. Recognition dawned on the lieutenant's face instantly. He was visibly shaken. Shizong had been on Taiwan television for more than six weeks. He'd become a celebrity.

"Lieutenant, come here for a moment, please, I would like to ask you something," Shizong said. Then he switched to Mandarin.

The lieutenant, who had taken out his pistol, lowered it and walked over to the open door. He and Shizong shook hands, and Shizong began to speak, softly, slowly, his voice calm, reasonable, and sympathetic.

Some of the soldiers drifted closer so that they could hear. All of them recognized Shizong. Civilians from the trucks and cars came up, and soon there were at least one hundred people gathered in the chill rain to listen to Shizong, who never once raised his voice. It was, as Hanrahan would later recall, as if he was whispering in your ear; as if he was talking to you personally. It was clear that he affected everybody that way. It was the reason that the old men of Beijing were so frightened of him that they were willing to risk nuclear war to silence him.

At one point the lieutenant looked sheepishly at the pistol still in his hand. He holstered it, then bowed stiffly in front of Shizong. Without looking at McGarvey or the others, he turned and walked away, taking his soldiers with him.

"We may go now," Shizong said. "There will be no further roadblocks."

As McGarvey and the others were climbing back into the van, the APCs were already pulling back, and the soldiers were breaking off from their duties and hustling to the Humvees.

Preston started out, slowly at first but gaining speed as the traffic began to spread out. The rain and overcast deepened the night so that coming into a city that was under military blackout orders was like coming into some medieval settlement before electric lights had been invented.

McGarvey directed Preston past the railroad station to the vicinity of the fisheries warehouse and dock where they had come ashore. They parked the van in a dark narrow side alley and walked back to the still-unattended gate into the net yard.

As before there was no activity there, and this time they didn't even see the guard. Fifteen minutes after leaving the van, they'd made their way down the ladder and scrambled aboard the inflatable, which was tied exactly where they'd left it. They pulled themselves out from under the long dock and began rowing directly out to sea, the rain flattening even the small ripples and hiding everything farther out than twenty yards behind a fine dark veil.

A half mile offshore Hanrahan shipped the oars, lowered the outboard, and started the highly muffled engine; the only question left was how four men were going to get aboard the submerged submarine with only three sets of closed circuit diving equipment.

2305 Local
SSN 21 *Seawolf*

"Conn, sonar, I've got the outboard," Fisher reported excitedly. "Bearing zero-one-zero, range four thousand four hundred yards and closing."

"Okay, prepare to surface," Harding told the diving officer. Paradise looked up from the chart he was studying and came over.

"We're going to make a lot of noise," he said. "The PRC captain will know that something is going on."

"That's right, Rod. But he won't know what," Harding replied. He wasn't in the mood to explain what he was doing, not even to his XO. He had a good idea what McGarvey was facing and what he was trying to accomplish, and he was going to give the man all the help he could.

The diving officer relayed the captain's orders, and the boat was made ready to come to periscope depth for a look-see before they actually surfaced. It was SOP.

"Keep a sharp watch on the target," Harding told sonar.

"Aye, skipper."

"Flood tubes one through four and open the outer doors as soon as we start up."

"Aye, skipper," the weapons-control officer responded.

"Bring the boat to sixty feet."

"Bring the boat to six-zero feet, sir," the diving officer said crisply, and they began noisily venting high-pressure air into the ballast tanks. *Seawolf* started up.

He had everybody's attention now, and they were working as an efficient unit, exactly as they had been trained to do. The real test, however, Harding expected, was yet to come.

"Take Scotty and two other men and stand by the main stores hatch," he told Paradise. "I won't surface until they're on top of us. But as soon as they're aboard we're getting out of here."

"Are you expecting trouble?" Paradise asked. Dick Scott was their sergeant at arms.

"It's possible, Rod," Harding said. "Have Scotty break out the sidearms."

2310 Local
SSN 405 *Hekou*

Heishui was in his cabin looking at a photograph of his wife and daughter, when his XO called him.

"Captain, the American submarine is on the way up!"

"What are the conditions on the surface?" Heishui asked, putting the photograph down. Now was the moment of truth for his boat and crew; and for himself.

"We're picking up the same small outboard engine as before, about four thousand meters out, and traffic is down to almost nothing. We show two targets, both of them outside ten thousand meters and both seaward." Their new Trout Creek sonar suite rivaled that of just about any submarine anywhere. Heishui had a high degree of confidence in it.

"Send up the fire squad. But tell them to make certain they have the right target. If we're lucky, we can end this right now and never have to engage the American submarine."

"Yes, sir," Lagao said.

Heishui took a long last look at the photograph of his family, then buttoned the top button of his uniform and went forward and up one level to the attack center.

"Flood all tubes and open all outer doors," he ordered.

"Aye, sir." The weapons officer repeated the orders.

"Prepare to get under way," the captain told his chief of boat, an icy calm coming over him. It was just as good as a day as any to win or lose, he told himself. Live or die.

2320 Local
On The Surface

"We're on station," Hanrahan said, checking his GPS navigator. The night was completely still except for the hiss of the rain on the water and the soft buzz of the idling outboard.

"They know that we're here," McGarvey said. He did a 360 and so far as he could tell they were completely alone on the ocean. "You'll have to dive down, lock aboard, and bring up some more equipment—"

"But I cannot swim," Shizong interrupted.

"You won't have to do a thing, we'll do it all for you," McGarvey said. "Trust me."

"Periscope," Hanrahan said excitedly.

They all turned in the direction that he was looking in time to see the light at the top of the *Seawolf's* periscope mast about eight feet out of the water, blinking in Morse code.

Hanrahan held up a hand. "Retreat one hundred yards. We will surface. Repeat. Retreat one hundred yards. We will surface."

Shizong turned to say something, when a narrow pinpoint of red light appeared in the middle of his forehead. It was a weapons guidance laser and it seemed to come from somewhere to the right of the *Seawolf,* very low to the water. McGarvey drove forward, his shoulder catching Shizong in the chest and shoving him back.

"Get down," he shouted.

Preston cried out in pain, blood erupting from a very large hole in his chest. He was flung to the side like a rag doll, out of the raft and into the water.

Hanrahan rolled out right behind him as they continued to take rounds from somewhere in the darkness. He grabbed a handful of Shizong's shirt as he went. McGarvey, holding on to Shizong's arm, followed him, the raft and the water all around them erupting in a hail of bullets fired from at least two silenced machine guns.

"Take Peter and get out of here," he ordered urgently.

Hanrahan grabbed the floundering Shizong. "What about Tom?"

"He's dead. Go!"

Hanrahan wanted to stay, but he started away from the deflated raft with Shizong in tow.

The gunfire stopped. McGarvey found Preston a few yards away, facedown in the water. He turned him over, but the man was dead as expected. Preston had taken a round in the middle of the back, which had mushroomed through his body, tearing a hole six inches wide in his chest. The bastards were using dumdums or explosive bullets.

He cocked an ear to listen. He could hear what sounded like a small outboard motor coming toward him. Off to his left a broad section of water for as far as he could see was boiling, as if someone had put it on the heat. It was the *Seawolf* on the way up.

Hanrahan and Shizong were gone in the darkness, and the motor was very close now. They were PRC, and they had been waiting out here for Shizong. How that could possibly happen didn't matter now. They had probably scoped the raft with night-vision equipment, identified Shizong out of the four men, and had targeted him specifically. They were coming in to make sure he was dead.

McGarvey passed his hand over Preston's chest wound, smeared the blood and gore over his face, and floated loosely on his back, his arms spread, his eyes open and fixed as if he were dead.

The motor was practically on top of him, and he had to let himself sink under the water for a second or two without blinking, without closing his mouth.

A black-rubber inflatable, almost the twin of the one they had brought up from the *Seawolf*, appeared out of the mist and came directly over to where Preston's body had drifted. They slowed and circled, shining a narrow beam of light on his face. They said something that McGarvey couldn't make out, then came over to where he was floating. They shined the light in his face, and he had to fight not to blink or move a muscle.

There were three of them, dressed in black night fighters' uniform, their faces blackened. It came to him all of a sudden that they had gotten there the same way that he and Hanrahan had. They were off a submarine. Possibly a PRC boat that had been lying in wait just off shore for the Chinese attack on Taiwan to begin. The *Seawolf* coming in had missed it.

Something very large and black rose up out of the water to McGarvey's left. One of the Chinese sailors said something urgently, and he gunned the outboard motor. As the inflatable started to pass him, McGarvey reached up, grabbed the gunwale line with his left hand, pulled himself half out of the water, and grabbed a handful of the tunic of the sailor running the outboard motor and yanked him overboard.

The inflatable immediately veered sharply to the left. McGarvey had taken a deep breath at the last moment. He dragged the surprised sailor underwater, the man taking a very large reflexive breath as his head submerged.

The sailor got very still within seconds and as McGarvey surfaced with the body the outboard was circling back.

He took the weapon, which he recognized by feel as a Sterling, from the dead man's hands, reared up out of the water to keep the holes in the silencer casing free, and unloaded the weapon point-blank at the inflatable as it was practically on top of him.

The raft swerved widly to the right, flipping over

as it collapsed from the explosive release of air from its chambers. McGarvey dropped the empty weapon and backpedaled, trying to put as much distance between himself and whoever was left alive as possible. But it wasn't necessary. Except for the roiled water behind him, the night was utterly silent.

"Hank," he called.

"Here," Hanrahan replied from somewhere to the left.

"Do you have Peter?"

"Here," Shizong called back, his voice surprisingly steady for a man who could not swim and found himself in the middle of the ocean.

A few seconds later a beam of light from the deck of the *Seawolf* caught McGarvey, and he turned and swam toward it as fast as he could manage. They still weren't out of the woods. Not with a PRC submarine lurking around somewhere nearby.

2329 Local
SSN 405 *Hekou*

"Sierra Eighteen is on the surface," Zenzhong told the captain nervously.

"Open doors one and two," Heishui ordered "Prepare to fire."

"Captain, what about our men on the surface?" Lagao asked at his side.

Heishui turned and gave him a bland look. "It's a moot point, Commander. Either their mission is already a success or they have failed. They can't fight the crew of an entire submarine."

"At least give them five minutes," Lagao pleaded. "Some sign that they are alive and trying to make it back aboard."

The *Hekou* had risen to thirty meters in order to lock them out, and then had settled back to one hundred meters behind and below the American submarine. There was no way that even an experienced diver could make that depth, nor was he going to put his boat and crew at risk by heading back up to rescue them. They knew what they were facing when they had volunteered.

"Three minutes," Heishui said. "It will take us that long to get ready to fire." He turned away.

2332 Local
SSN 21 *Seawolf*

"We have three people aboard, and the hatch is sealed," Paradise called to the captain.

"Get up here on the double, Rod, we have work to do," Harding said. He switched channels. "Sonar, this is the captain. What's the target doing?"

"He's about two thousand yards out, skipper, just lying there. Bearing one-seven-five, and below us at three hundred feet," Fisher reported. "I think he might have opened at least two of his outer doors when we were on the way up."

"If there's any change, let me know on the double," Harding said. He hung up the phone. "Get us out of here," he told the Chief of the Boat.

"Aye, sir."

"Emergency dive to three hundred feet, come right to new course zero-six-zero, and give me turns for forty knots as soon as possible." The submarine had to be at least one hundred feet beneath the surface before she could begin to develop her top speed submerged.

Trela relayed the orders and within seconds the *Seawolf* surged forward, her decks canted sharply downward and to the right.

"Don't lose the solution," Harding warned the weapons-control officer.

"No, sir."

2335 Local
SSN 404 *Hekou*

"He's on the move, Captain," Zenzhong shouted. "Sierra Eighteen is diving, and his aspect is definitely changing left to right."

"He's leaving in a big hurry; do you think that he knows we're back here?" Lagao asked Heishui.

"Perhaps," the captain replied. A million conflicting thoughts were running through his head with the speed of light, his family among them. But his blood was up. Serving on a Han-class submarine for any length of time meant certain death in any event from leukemia or some other form of cancer because the reactors leaked. Only the officers understood that for a fact, but most of the crews knew it, too. Love of country and the special privileges for their families were the incentives to serve. "No word from our crew on the surface?"

"No, sir."

Heishuo gave his XO a look of sympathy, then turned to his fire-control officer. "Do we have a positive solution on the enemy?"

"Yes, sir."

"Fire one, fire two."

2336 Local
SSN 21 *Seawolf*

"Torpedoes in the water!" Fisher called out. "Two of them, bearing one-nine-five, and definitely gaining."

"Turn left, come to flank speed," Harding said calmly.

"Aye, sir, turning left full rudder, ordering flank speed," Lieutenant Trela repeated.

"Time to impact?" Harding asked the sonarman.

"Ninety seconds, skipper."

"Release the noisemakers as soon as we pass three-six-zero degrees," Harding ordered. "Prepare to fire tubes one and two."

"Don't do it, Captain," McGarvey shouted, coming into the control room directly on Paradise's heels.

Harding's head snapped around. McGarvey stood dripping next to the plotting tables, blood covering his face, a wild look in his eyes. "Get out of here, Mac. Now!"

"Listen to me, Tom. We have to make the PRC skipper think that he's destroyed us."

"He very well might do just that."

"Sixty-five seconds to impact," Fisher reported.

"Tubes one and two ready to fire, Captain," the fire-control officer said.

"If it can be done without risking our own destruction, we have to try it," McGarvey argued. "That's the entire point of the mission. Getting Shizong out of here in secret, or making the Chinese believe that he's dead." McGarvey shook his head. "They were waiting for us up there. They knew we were bringing him. And I lost one of my people."

"Captain?" the Chief of Boat prompted.

"Release the noisemakers now," Harding said. "All stop, rudder amidships."

"All stop, rudder amidships, sir," Trela responded crisply after only a moment's hesitation. He hoped the old man knew what he was doing this time.

"Fifty seconds to impact."

Harding looked at McGarvey and Paradise. "I'm

sorry that you took a casualty," he said. "Stand by to fire tube one, *only* tube one."

"Stand by one, aye," the weapons-control officer said.

"Sonar, this is the captain. I want you to pull up the BRD program that we were given in Pearl. Feed it to the main sonar dome." BRD was Battle Response Decoy system. The *Seawolf* was supposed to have tested it on the initial part of this cruise, but not under actual battle conditions.

"Aye, skipper, I understand. Forty seconds to impact."

"I'll tell you when to transmit. Just be ready."

"Yes, sir."

Harding motioned for Paradise to man the ballast control panel. "On my mark I want all aft tanks explosively vented." This would fill them with water all at once, making the boat stern-heavy. She would sink to the bottom tail first.

"Thirty seconds to impact," Fisher reported.

"Fire tube one," Harding said.

"Fire one, aye," the weapons-control officer said. "Torpedo one is away."

"Sonar, conn. Stand by, Fisher."

"Aye, sir."

"Send autodestruct," Harding told the weapons-control officer.

The man looked up. "Sir—?"

"Twenty seconds to impact."

"Autodestruct now!" Harding ordered.

The weapons-control officer uncaged the button and pushed it. Their wire-guided HE torpedo, which had not had enough time to began searching for a target, exploded less than eight hundred feet from the *Seawolf,* and directly in the path of the oncoming Chinese torpedoes.

"Brace yourselves," Harding shouted as the first tremendous shock wave hammered the hull.

Both Chinese torpedoes fired almost simultaneously, slamming the *Seawolf*'s hull as if they had been hit by a pair of runaway cement trucks.

"Transmit now," Harding told sonar. An instant later the water all around them reverberated with the transmitted noises of a submarine breaking up; internal explosions, water rushing, bulkheads collapsing, even men screaming, machinery spinning wildly out of control and breaking through decks as the boat was torn apart.

Paradise was waiting at the ballast control panel, and Harding gave him the nod.

"Take us down."

Paradise twisted the controls, air was vented out of the aft tanks, and immediately they began a rapid descent to the bottom. Harding reached up to a handhold on the overhead and braced himself. Everyone else did the same.

2340 Local
SSN 405 *Hekou*

Heishui held the earphones close. He was hearing the noises of a dying submarine. It excited him and saddened him at the same time. More than one hundred officers and men were dead or dying beneath him.

He focused on Zenzhong and the other sonar operators who had done such brilliant jobs. He felt a great deal of respect and affection for them. For all of his crew. They had gone up against one of the best ships in all the U.S. Navy and had been victorious.

"Good job," he said, smiling warmly as he took off the earphones and handed them to one of the sonarmen. "Our mission was a complete success, and now it is time for us to go home."

Zenzhong was busy with his equipment. At least six distinct white horizontal lines were painted on his sonar display scopes. "We have many targets incoming," he said. He marked them on the screen with a grease pencil as quickly as he identified them.

"Then we'll thread the needle," Heishui said. "And you will lead us to safety."

Zenzhong looked up, his eyes wide, but then he started to work out the relative bearings of the incomings.

Heishui went back to the control room. His crew all looked respectfully at him. He smiled and bowed to them all. "Thank you. We have succeeded in fulfilling our orders. We will go home now."

"What is our course and speed, Captain?" his Chief of Boat asked.

Heishui went to the plotting table and took the bearings of the incoming warships as Zenzhong gave them. They were almost boxed in, but not quite. One lane leading out to sea was somehow still open to them.

"Make our course three-five-zero, speed two-five knots," he told the Chief of Boat, who immediately relayed his orders. At that speed they would be very noisy.

Lagao came over and studied the plots. "They have left us a way out," he said.

"Either it's a mistake for it's a political decision on their part," Heishui said, looking up. He felt at peace, but it was clear that his XO was troubled.

"Or it may be a trap."

Heishui nodded. "Prepare a message for Admiral

Pei. Tell him that we have succeeded and are en route to Ningbo."

"When shall I send it?"

"Immediately," Heishui said, and he turned back to the chart as his boat accelerated. There was no possibility that they would make it home this time. But their mission was a success. The traitor Shi Shizong was dead, and a war with Taiwan had been avoided. At least for the moment.

Two Weeks Later
United Nations General Assembly

On the way up to New York from Langley, McGarvey had a lot to think about. There was a new, troubling situation heating up in the Balkans, more unrest in Greece, rumors that someone at the highest levels inside the Mexican government was in bed with the leading drug cartels, and Castro's successor was courting Pakistan for nuclear technology.

The funeral for Tom Preston had been a quiet affair at Arlington, with only a handful of friends and relatives. He hadn't been married, and there weren't any children. There'd been some confusion about who he was, but the Taiwanese Coast Guard had finally gotten it figured out, and his body had been flown home.

The Chinese Navy and Air Force had finished their extensive exercise, packed up their toys, and gone home all of a sudden with no explanation about Peter Shizong, or about the apparent destruction of two submarines, an American boat somewhere off Taiwan's north coast and a PRC boat a couple of hours later and fifty miles north. There were no survivors.

The media never got the last story, and at the diplomatic level China and the U.S. politely avoided mentioning the issue at all. It was, as far as both sides were concerned, a completely fair and equitable exchange.

That was a position that the Chinese would regret having taken, McGarvey thought with pleasure as he got off the elevator on the third floor. He crossed the hall and after he showed his credentials was allowed inside the sky boxes, where the translators worked looking down on the General Assembly.

Captain Joseph Jiying, in civilian clothes, jumped up from where he was watching the proceedings, a big grin on his face. "Good to see you, Mr. McGarvey," he said. They shook hands.

"My friends call me Mac, and it's *really* good to see you in one piece."

"It was a little hairy there for a couple of hours, but we finally realized the error of our patriotic zeal, and we gave up. No casualties."

U.S. Ambassador Margaret Woolsey had just come to the podium amid some polite applause.

"You might want to check out Chou en Ping. He's the PRC's ambassador to the UN," Jiying said. He was enjoying himself to the max. "The poor bastard doesn't know what's about to hit him."

"It's not going to be so easy," McGarvey said.

"You're right, of course," Jiying said, suddenly very serious. "Maybe it'll take another hundred years for the mainland to recognize who and what Taiwan has become. Look how long it took before Hong Kong went back." He smiled and nodded as a very large round of applause swept across the General Assembly. "But ain't it great to win once in a while? You know, truth, justice, and the American way?"

Down on the floor Peter Shizong was slowly making his way to the podium, shaking hands as he and his UN-supplied bodyguards were completely mobbed by well-wishers.

McGarvey took a pair of binoculars from Jiying and tried to spot Chou en Ping and the Chinese delegation at their seats, but they had already gotten up and were marching up a side aisle for the exits.

He handed the binoculars back. "Gotta go."

"What's your rush, it's just getting good," Jiying said.

"I'm meeting a friend for drinks. And then our wives are coming up to join us."

"Anyone I should know?"

McGarvey shook his head. "Just an old friend. A submarine driver. Good man to have around in a pinch."

DAVID HAGBERG is an ex-Air Force cryptographer who has spoken at CIA functions and traveled extensively in Europe, the Arctic, and the Caribbean. He also writes fiction under the pseudonym Sean Flannery, and has published more than two dozen novels of suspense, including *White House, High Flight, Eagles Fly, Assassin,* and *Joshua's Hammer.* His writing has been nominated for numerous honors, including the American Book Award, three times for the Edgar Allan Poe award, and three times for the American Mystery award. He lives in Florida, and has been continuously published for the past twenty-five years.

AL-JIHAD

BY STEPHEN COONTS

Five

Blowing up the fort was an impractical idea and always had been. When Julie Giraud first mentioned destroying the fort with the bad guys inside, back in Van Nuys, I had let her talk. I didn't think she had any idea how much explosives would be necessary to demolish a large stone structure, and she didn't. When I finally asked her how much C-4 she thought it would take, she looked at me blankly.

We had brought a hundred pounds of the stuff, all we could transport efficiently.

I used the binoculars to follow the third plane through the sky until it disappeared behind the ridge. It was some kind of small, twin-engined bizjet.

"How come these folks are early?" I asked her.

"I don't know."

"Your CIA friend didn't tip you off about the time switch?"

"No."

The fact these people were arriving a day early bothered me and I considered it from every angle.

Life is full of glitches and unexpected twists—who ever has a day that goes as planned? To succeed at anything you must be adaptable and flexible, and smart enough to know when backing off is the right thing to do.

I wondered just how smart I was. Should we back off?

I drove the Humvee toward the cliff where we had the Osprey parked. The land rolled, with here and there gulleys cut by the runoff from rare desert storms. These gulleys had steep sides, loose sand bottoms, and were choked with desert plants. Low places had brush and cacti, but mainly the terrain was dirt with occasional rock outcroppings. One got the impression that at some time in the geologic past the dirt had blown in, covering a stark, highly eroded landscape. I tried to keep off the exposed places as much as possible and drove very slowly to keep from raising dust.

Every so often I stopped the vehicle, got out and listened for airplanes. Two more jets went over that I heard. That meant there were at least five jets at that desert strip, maybe more.

Julie sat silently, saying nothing as we drove along. When I killed the engine and got out to listen, she stayed in her seat.

I stopped the Humvee in a brushy draw about a mile from the Osprey, reached for the Model 70, then snagged a canteen and hung it over my shoulder.

"May I come with you?" she asked.

"Sure."

We stopped when we got to a low rise where we

could see the V-22 and the area around it. I looked everything over with binoculars, then settled down at the base of a green bush that resembled greasewood, trying to get what shade there was. The temperature must have been ninety by that time.

"Aren't we going down to the plane?"

"It's safer here."

Julie picked another bush and crawled under.

I was silently complimenting her on her ability to accept direction without question or explanation when she said, "You don't take many chances, do you?"

"I try not to."

"So you're just going to kill these people, then get on with the rest of your life?"

I took a good look at her face. "If you're going to chicken out," I said, "do it now, so I don't have to lie here sweating the program for the whole damned day."

"I'm not going to chicken out. I just wondered if you were."

"You said these people were terrorists, had blown up airliners. That still true?"

"Absolutely."

"Then I won't lose any sleep over them." I shifted around, got comfortable, kept the rifle just under my hands.

She met my eyes, and apparently decided this point needed a little more exploring. "I'm killing them because they killed my parents. You're killing them for money."

I sighed, tossed her the binoculars.

"Every few minutes, glass the area around the plane, then up on the ridge," I told her. "Take your time, look at everything in your field of view, look for movement. Any kind of movement. And don't let the sun glint off the binoculars."

"How are we going to do it?" she asked as she stared through the glasses.

"Blowing the fort was a pipe dream, as you well know."

She didn't reply, just scanned with the binoculars.

"The best way to do it is to blow up the planes with the people on them."

A grin crossed her face, then disappeared.

I rolled over, arranged the rifle just so, and settled down for a nap. I was so tired.

The sun had moved a good bit by the time I awakened. The air was stifling, with no detectable breeze. Julie was stretched out asleep, the binoculars in front of her. I used the barrel of the rifle to hook the strap and lift them, bring them over to me without making noise.

The land was empty, dead. Not a single creature stirred, not even a bird. The magnified images I could see through the binoculars shimmered in the heat.

Finally I put the thing down, sipped at the water in my canteen.

South Africa. Soon. Maybe I'd become a diamond prospector.

There was a whole lot of interesting real estate in South Africa, or so I'd heard, and I intended to see it. Get a jeep and some camping gear and head out.

Julie's crack about killing for money rankled, of course. The fact was that these people were terrorists, predators who preyed on the weak and defenseless. They had blown up an airliner. Take money for killing them? Yep. And glad to get it, too.

* * *

Julie had awakened and moved off into the brush out of sight to relieve herself when I spotted a man on top of the cliff, a few hundred yards to the right of the Osprey. I picked him up as I swept the top of the cliff with the binoculars.

I turned the focus wheel, tried to sharpen the dancing image. Too much heat.

It was a man, all right. Standing there with a rifle on a sling over his shoulder, surveying the desert with binoculars. Instinctively I backed up a trifle, ensured the binoculars were in shade so there would be no sun reflections off the glass or frame. And I glanced at the airplane.

It should be out of sight of the man due to the way the cliff outcropped between his position and the plane. I hoped. In any event he wasn't looking at it.

I gritted my teeth, studied his image, tried by sheer strength of will to make it steadier in the glass. The distance between us was about six hundred yards, I estimated.

I put down the binoculars and slowly brought up the Model 70. I had a variable power scope on it which I habitually kept cranked to maximum magnification. The figure of the man leaped at me through the glass.

I put the crosshairs on his chest, studied him. Even through the shimmering air I could see the cloth he wore on his head and the headband that held it in place. He was wearing light-colored trousers and a shirt. And he was holding binoculars pointed precisely at me.

I heard a rustle behind me.

"Freeze, Julie," I said, loud enough that she would plainly hear me.

She stopped.

I kept the scope on him, flicked off the safety. I had automatically assumed a shooting position when I raised the rifle. Now I wiggled my left elbow into the hard earth, settled the rifle in tighter against my shoulder.

He just stood there, looking right at us.

I only saw him because he was silhouetted on the skyline. In the shade under this brush we should be invisible to him. Should be.

Now he was scanning the horizon again. Since I had been watching he had not once looked down at the foot of the cliff upon which he was standing.

He was probably a city soldier, I decided. Hadn't been trained to look close first, before he scanned terrain farther away.

After another long moment he turned away, began walking slowly along the top of the cliff to my right, away from the Osprey. I kept the crosshairs of the scope on him until he was completely out of sight. Only then did I put the safety back on and lower the rifle.

"You can come in now," I said.

She crawled back under her bush.

"Did you see him?" I asked.

"Yes. Did he see the airplane?"

"I'm certain he didn't."

"How did he miss it?"

"It was just a little out of sight, I think. Even if he could have seen it, he never really looked in the right direction."

"We were lucky," she said.

I grunted. It was too hot to discuss philosophy. I lay there under my bush wondering just how crazy ol' Julie Giraud really was.

"If he had seen the plane, Charlie Dean, would you have shot him?"

What a question!

"You're damned right," I muttered, more than a little disgusted. "If he had seen the plane, I would have shot him and piled you into the cockpit and made you get us the hell out of here before all the Indians in the world showed up to help with the pleasant chore of lifting our hair. These guys are playing for keeps, lady. You and me had better be on the same sheet of music or we will be well and truly fucked."

Every muscle in her face tensed. "We're not leaving," she snarled, "until those sons of bitches are dead. All of them. Every last one."

She was over the edge.

A wave of cold fear swept over me. It was bad enough being on the edge of a shooting situation; now my backup was around the bend. If she went down or freaked out, how in the hell was I going to get off this rock pile?

"I've been trying to decide," she continued, "if you really have the balls for this, Charlie Dean, or if you're going to turn tail on me when crunch time comes and run like a rabbit. You're old: You look old, you sound old. Maybe you had the balls years ago, maybe you don't anymore."

From the leg pocket of her flight suit she pulled a small automatic, a .380 from the looks of it. She held it where I could see it, pointed it more or less in my direction. "Grow yourself another set of balls, Charlie Dean. Nobody is running out."

I tossed her the binoculars. "Call me if they come back," I said. I put the rifle beside me and lay down.

Sure, I thought about what a dumb ass I was. Three million bucks!—I was going to have to earn every damned dollar.

Hoo boy.

Okay, I'll admit it: I knew she was crazy that first day in Van Nuys.

I made a conscious effort to relax. The earth was warm, the air was hot, and I was exhausted. I was asleep in nothing flat.

The sun was about to set when I awoke. My binoculars were on the sand beside me and Julie Giraud was nowhere in sight. I used the scope on the rifle to examine the Osprey and the cliff behind it.

I spotted her in seconds, moving around under the plane. No one else visible.

While we had a little light, I went back for the Humvee. I crawled up on it, taking my time, ensuring that no one was there waiting for me.

When we left it that morning we had piled some dead brush on the hood and top of the vehicle, so I pulled that off before I climbed in.

Taking it slow so I wouldn't raise dust, I drove the mile or so to the Osprey. I got there just as the last rays of the sun vanished.

I backed up to the trailer and we attached it to the Humvee.

"Want to tell me your plan, Charlie Dean?" she asked. "Or do you have one?"

As I repacked the contents of the trailer I told her how I wanted to do it. Amazingly, she agreed readily.

She was certainly hard to figure. One minute I thought she was a real person, complete with a conscience and the intellectual realization that even the enemy were human beings, then the next second she was a female Rambo, ready to gut them all, one by one.

She helped me make up C-4 bombs, rig the detonators and radio controls. I did the first one, she watched intently, then she did one on her own. I checked it, and she got everything right.

"Don't take any unnecessary chances tonight," I said. "I want you alive and well when this is over so you can fly me out of here."

She merely nodded. It was impossible to guess what she might have been thinking.

I wasn't about to tell her that I had flown helicopters in Vietnam. I was never a rated pilot, but I was young and curious, so the pilots often let me practice under their supervision. I had watched her with the Osprey and thought that I could probably fly it if absolutely necessary. The key would be to use the checklist and take plenty of time. If I could get it started, I thought I could fly it out. There were parachutes in the thing, so I would not need to land it.

I didn't say any of this to her, of course.

We had a packet of radio receivers and detonators—I counted them—enough for six bombs. If I set them all on the same frequency I could blow up six planes with one push of the button. If I could get the bombs aboard six planes without being discovered.

What if there were more than six planes? Well, I had some pyrotechnic fuses, which seemed impractical to use on an airplane, and some chemical fuses. In the cargo bay of the Osprey I examined the chemical fuses by flashlight. Eight hours seemed to be the maximum setting. The problem was that I didn't know when the bad guys planned to leave.

As I was meditating on fuses and bombs, I went outside and walked around the Osprey. There was a turreted three-barreled fifty-caliber machine gun in the nose of the thing. Air Force Ospreys didn't carry stingers like this, but this one belonged to the Marine Corps, or did until twenty-four hours ago.

I opened the service bay. Gleaming brass in the

feed trays reflected the dim evening light.

Julie was standing right behind me. "I stole this one because it had the gun," she remarked. "Less range than the Air Force birds, but the gun sold me."

"Maximum firepower is always a good choice."

"What are you thinking?" she asked.

We discussed contingencies as we wired up the transfer pump in the bladder fuel tank we had chained down in the cargo bay. We used the aircraft's battery to power the pump, so all we had to do was watch as three thousand pounds of jet fuel was transferred into the aircraft's tanks.

My plan had bombs, bullets, and a small river of blood—we hoped—just the kind of tale that appealed to Julie Giraud. She even allowed herself a tight smile.

Me? I had a cold knot in the pit of my stomach and I was sweating.